**Carla Cassidy** is an award-bestselling author who has written over 170 books, including 150 for Mills & Boon. She has won the Centennial Award from Romance Writers of America. Most recently she won the 2019 Write Touch Readers' Award for her Mills & Boon Heroes title *Desperate Strangers*. Carla believes the only thing better than curling up with a good book is sitting down at the computer with a good story to write.

**Cindi Myers** is the author of more than 75 novels. When she's not plotting new romance storylines, she enjoys skiing, gardening, cooking, crafting and daydreaming. A lover of small-town life, she lives with her husband and two spoiled dogs in the Colorado mountains.

### Also by Carla Cassidy

**Marsh Mysteries**
*Stalked Through the Mist*

**The Scarecrow Murders**
*Killer in the Heartland*
*Guarding a Forbidden Love*
*The Cowboy Next Door*
*Stalker in the Storm*

**Cowboys of Holiday Ranch**
*The Cowboy's Targeted Bride*
*The Last Cowboy Standing*

### Also by Cindi Myers

**Eagle Mountain: Criminal History**
*Mile High Mystery*
*Colorado Kidnapping*
*Twin Jeopardy*
*Mountain Captive*

**Eagle Mountain: Critical Response**
*Deception at Dixon Pass*
*Pursuit at Panther Point*
*Killer on Kestrel Trail*
*Secrets of Silverpeak Mine*

Discover more at millsandboon.co.uk

# SWAMP SHADOWS

## CARLA CASSIDY

# CANYON KILLER

## CINDI MYERS

MILLS & BOON

All rights reserved including the right of reproduction in whole or in part in any form. This edition is published by arrangement with Harlequin Enterprises ULC.

This is a work of fiction. Names, characters, places, locations and incidents are purely fictional and bear no relationship to any real life individuals, living or dead, or to any actual places, business establishments, locations, events or incidents. Any resemblance is entirely coincidental.

This book is sold subject to the condition that it shall not, by way of trade or otherwise, be lent, resold, hired out or otherwise circulated without the prior consent of the publisher in any form of binding or cover other than that in which it is published and without a similar condition including this condition being imposed on the subsequent purchaser.

® and ™ are trademarks owned and used by the trademark owner and/or its licensee. Trademarks marked with ® are registered with the United Kingdom Patent Office and/or the Office for Harmonisation in the Internal Market and in other countries.

First Published in Great Britain 2025
by Mills & Boon, an imprint of HarperCollins*Publishers* Ltd
1 London Bridge Street, London, SE1 9GF

www.harpercollins.co.uk

HarperCollins*Publishers*
Macken House, 39/40 Mayor Street Upper,
Dublin 1, D01 C9W8, Ireland

*Swamp Shadows* © 2025 Carla Bracale
*Canyon Killer* © 2025 Cynthia Myers

ISBN: 978-0-263-39710-9

0525

This book contains FSC™ certified paper and other controlled sources to ensure responsible forest management.

For more information visit: www.harpercollins.co.uk/green

Printed and Bound in the UK using 100% Renewable Electricity at CPI Group (UK) Ltd, Croydon, CR0 4YY

# SWAMP SHADOWS

## CARLA CASSIDY

## Chapter One

Heather LaCrae crawled through the darkness of sleep, seeking the light of full consciousness. She felt as if she'd been asleep for days...weeks even, so deep had her dreamless slumber been.

The first thing she noticed before she even opened her eyes was the strange smell of antiseptic and disinfectant. She frowned. Her shanty didn't smell like this, rather it was fragrant with the scents of all kinds of herbs and flowering plants.

She finally opened her eyes and stared around her. She was in a hospital bed. Had she somehow hurt herself? The last thing she remembered was sitting on a stool at the bar in the Voodoo Lounge. Had she fallen off the high chair and somehow hit her head?

That was the only thing that could explain her lack of memory from the night before. She moved her legs, and they seemed to be okay. She then moved her arms and froze. Her right wrist was handcuffed to the bed's railing.

Panic seared through her as she stared at the metal ring encircling her wrist. She was handcuffed! What on earth was going on? She jerked up to a sitting position and then saw the uniformed officer seated in a chair in the doorway to her hospital room.

"Hello? Uh... Officer?"

The young man got to his feet. "My name is Officer Joel Smith." He offered her no smile.

"Uh... Officer Smith, can you tell me what's going on here?" She tried to tamp down the anxiety that threatened to close off the back of her throat. She didn't know why she appeared to be arrested, but this all had to be some sort of a huge mistake.

"I'll just go get the doctor and the chief. They'll be able to explain everything to you," he said. He stepped out into the hallway, where she heard him put in a call to Chief of Police Etienne Savoie. All Smith said was "She's awake," and then he ended the call.

He then called to somebody down the hall and asked for the doctor. It was obvious he wasn't leaving her alone. What did he think she was going to do? Gnaw through the handcuff and then throw herself out of the nearby window?

"Somebody will be in here to explain things to you soon," he said and then returned to his chair in the doorway.

She felt as if she were in a bad dream, one that she couldn't awaken from. She was no criminal. She'd never been in trouble in her entire life. So, what could she have done that warranted the handcuff and an armed guard at her door? And why...oh why couldn't she remember the events of the night before? Whatever it was that had happened that found her here?

She raised the head of her bed and glanced toward the window. The sun was setting in the sky. How was that possible? Where had the day gone? Confusion twisted and turned in her mind, adding to the vague headache that had been present since she had first opened her eyes.

About fifteen minutes later, the chief of police of the small town of Crystal Cove, Louisiana, came into her room along with Dr. Dwight Maison. She knew the doctor because he had treated her less than a month ago when she'd fallen ill with a sinus infection. A round of strong antibiotics had fixed her right up, but she had a feeling there was no prescription that was going to fix this situation easily.

She focused on Chief Etienne Savoie. She'd seen him around town before and knew he was considered one of the town's most eligible bachelors. His gray eyes gazed at her soberly. "Ms. LaCrae," he began with a curt nod of his head.

"Please...make it Heather," she replied, her nerves burning so hot inside her she feared she might internally combust. "Can you please tell me what's going on here?"

"Heather LaCrae, you are under arrest for the murder of Wesley Simone."

"What?" She stared at him in utter shock. "Wh-what are you talking about? I didn't murder anyone. I... I could never murder anyone."

"Late last night, you were found in the alley behind the Voodoo Lounge. Wesley was next to you, dead by several stab wounds. You had the knife in your hand, and you were covered in his blood. There was also a confession in your phone messages."

Heather stared at the dark-haired official in horror. "Is this some kind of a bad joke? This is all a huge mistake," she protested, her voice growing in volume and intensity. "I don't care how I was found, I couldn't kill anyone."

"I need to inform you of your rights," Etienne said, and as he went into the whole spiel, she continued to stare at him in disbelief. She'd had a murder weapon in her hand? A knife? And she'd been covered in Wesley's blood? No way...there was no way in hell she believed she'd stabbed a man—any man—to death.

"What happens now?" she asked once Etienne was finished with the Miranda rights.

"Dr. Maison will check you out and make sure there are no lingering complications from whatever you took to commit suicide last night."

Heather hadn't believed she could be any more stunned, but she'd been wrong. This news finally brought tears of frustration to her eyes. "I would never commit suicide, and I would never, ever stab a man to death."

"Then you want to talk to me about what happened last night at the Voodoo Lounge?" Etienne asked.

How could she tell him what had happened when she didn't know what happened. Her last memory was sitting in the Voodoo Lounge next to Wesley at the bar. She remembered small-talking with the man, and that was it.

"I... I think I'd like a lawyer," she said, realizing the severity of the situation. The tears came faster and faster, chasing each other down her cheeks, one right after another.

She silently cried as Dr. Maison took her blood pressure and then listened to her heart. She continued to weep as he removed the IV line and then pronounced her good to go.

At that point Etienne handed her a brown paper bag that she hadn't even noticed he'd held. "I took the liberty of speaking to Lucy Dupree this afternoon. Somebody told me you are close friends. Anyway, she gathered up some clothes for you to wear out of here since the clothing you had on last night has been taken as evidence. You can go ahead and change now." He unlocked the handcuff that had chained her to the railing.

She slid out of the bed, and on shaky legs she headed to the bathroom. Once there, she managed to get her emotions under control, although she was still in a daze of disbelief. Lucy had apparently gone to her shanty to get the clothes. The two were good enough friends that Lucy had a key to her place and Heather had a key to Lucy's.

She tossed the blue-flowered hospital gown to the floor and then dressed in the panties and bra Lucy had provided. She pulled on the pair of gray jogging pants and the pink T-shirt. There was also a hairbrush, which she was grateful for.

For several minutes, she stood in front of the small mirror over the sink and brushed out her long, dark hair. After that, she remained in front of the mirror, staring at her reflection.

She didn't care how much evidence they had against her, there was no way she had killed a man who had only been a casual acquaintance to her. But it worried her that she couldn't remember what had happened. How had she gotten into the alley, covered in blood and next to a dead man?

Something evil was at play here. She couldn't help but believe somebody had set her up. She had to have been drugged, and once her body was placed next to Wesley's body, whoever it was had typed a confession into her phone.

It was the only scenario that made a kind of sick sense. But who? Who could have done this to her?

A knock on the door pulled her from her troubling thoughts. "Heather, it's time for us to go," Etienne called through the door.

With a deep breath for strength, Heather opened the door and stepped out of the bathroom. "I'm sorry, but I have to follow protocol," Etienne said as he turned her around and then placed her in handcuffs.

The cold bite of the metal around her wrists made everything even more real. Once again, she was in a daze as Etienne and Officer Smith escorted her out of the room and down the long hallway to the exit.

Darkness had begun to fall outside as they led her to a patrol car and helped her into the back seat. The two men spoke for a minute or two, and then Officer Smith took off walking, and Etienne got into the driver seat of the car she was in.

Once again Heather was in a frightened haze as he started the car and they left the hospital parking lot. Chief Savoie didn't speak to her, and she didn't talk to him. She had nothing to say at this point and was afraid to say anything without a lawyer present.

It didn't take them long to reach the police station. The Crystal Cove Police Department was housed in a large, one-story building painted an attractive turquoise.

Etienne drove around to the back of the building and parked. He helped her out of the back seat and then led her through the back door.

"You are going to be arraigned tomorrow afternoon, so you might want to line up a lawyer before then," he said as they walked down a long hallway. "I'll be glad to provide you with a list of names of public defenders."

They walked into a large room where three jail cells were side-by-side. There were no prisoners at the moment, but the sight of the bars and the bunk beds and open toilets shot a new wave of fear through her. This was serious. Oh God, she was in deep trouble, and she wasn't sure she trusted a public defender to represent her in a murder case.

"Actually, I'd like to call Nick Monroe," she replied. She had never met the man before, didn't even know what he looked like, but she had heard he had represented several people from the swamp in a variety of matters. "Could you get me his number?"

"Absolutely. In fact, I'll take you to a conference room right now so you can have some privacy while you make the call." Instead of putting her into one of the cells, he took her back down the hallway to a small room with a table and four chairs.

"I'll be right back," he said. He was gone only minutes, and then he returned with a cell phone and a phone number written down on a piece of paper. "One call, Heather, and when you are finished just knock on the door." With that, he left and closed the door behind him.

Gingerly, she picked up the phone and turned it on. She went to the phone icon and pulled up the keypad. Her fingers trembled as she punched in Nick Monroe's number.

It rang three times, and then a deep voice answered. "Monroe Law. This is Nick Monroe."

"Mr. Monroe, my name is Heather LaCrae, and I'm in terrible trouble." To her horror, once again she began to cry.

IT TOOK NICK over fifteen minutes to calm the crying woman on the other end of the phone. Finally, she told him why she had called and that she was to be arraigned the next afternoon. He agreed to meet with her the next morning, and from there he would decide if he was going to represent her.

The first thing he did after speaking to her was call Etienne to get the rundown of the case and the evidence found at the scene. It was all definitely damning. He had no idea if Heather LaCrae was guilty or not. He would know more after meeting with her in the morning.

If he did decide to represent her, it would be one of the most serious cases he'd ever worked. He not only represented people from the town of Crystal Cove, but also those who lived in the swamp that half surrounded the small town.

He charged a good fee to the people he knew could afford it, and he made other arrangements for the people from the swamp who he knew couldn't.

That was his way of giving back. Having been raised in an affluent family and blessed with a large trust fund, Nick had never had to worry about money. However, he knew there were others who didn't have what he had, and those were the ones he tried to help.

He didn't know Heather LaCrae, but Etienne had told Nick that Heather was from the swamp and made a living by selling fresh herbs to the café and the restaurant in town. She also had a little store in town where she sold her herbs, spices, flowers and plants.

Even though she appeared to have a strong work ethic, he suspected there was no way she could ever pay him for his services. So, if he represented her, it would probably be a pro bono case. Still, he was definitely intrigued by the elements of the crime.

The next morning at ten o'clock, he arrived at the jail to meet with his potential client. Etienne met him in the police station lobby. Despite their opposing professions, the two had been good friends for years.

"Good morning, Chief Savoie," he greeted his friend.

"Good morning to you. I'm assuming you're here to meet with your client. I've got to tell you, Nick, if you decide to take this one on, it's definitely going to be an uphill battle for you," Etienne said.

Nick grinned at him. "You know I've always liked a good challenge."

"I don't know, Nick. All I can tell you is the physical evidence is definitely stacked against her," Etienne replied. "I'll take you to the conference room so you can talk to her."

Etienne led him to the small conference room where Nick had met many clients in the past. The chief of police left him to go get Heather, and while Nick cooled his heels, he opened the notebook he'd brought with him and pulled a pen from his shirt pocket.

He was definitely intrigued to see what the woman accused of such a heinous crime looked like. He already knew the physical evidence was damning and she would be facing a murder charge.

He sat up straighter as he heard Etienne approaching the room again. A rivulet of surprise raced through him as Heather LaCrae came into the room.

The first thing that surprised him was her beauty. Her hair fell around her shoulders in a curtain of rich darkness, and her dark eyes were long-lashed. High cheekbones and lush-looking lips added to her overall loveliness.

The second thing that surprised him was the fact that she was a petite, slender woman who, at the moment, looked frail and frightened. She wore a pair of jogging pants and a pink T-shirt that showed off her slim but shapely body.

He immediately got to his feet. "Hi, I'm Nick Monroe, and you must be Heather LaCrae. Please, have a seat." He gestured to the chair across the table from him.

"It's nice to meet you," she said, and once she was seated, Nick sat back down. "I... I seem to be in need of a defense attorney." Tears suddenly appeared in her eyes and clung to her long lashes.

"Well, as luck would have it, I am a defense attorney," he replied lightly, hoping to halt her tears.

"I didn't do this," she said fervently and leaned forward in the chair. "I could never kill anyone. I definitely couldn't stab a man to death. I'm innocent, Mr. Monroe. I would have no reason to kill Wesley."

"Please, make it Nick. Why don't we start by you telling me what happened on Saturday night. Start with when you first got to the Voodoo Lounge. Why did you go there?"

"I'd had my store open late and just decided to go have a drink or two before heading home. Occasionally on Saturday nights, I do that."

At least her tears had stopped. "What happened when you got there?" Nick asked.

She frowned, the gesture doing nothing to detract from her beauty. "It was fairly crowded, but I spied a stool at the bar, and so that's where I sat. From that vantage point, if I turned on the stool, I could see the dance floor, and I always enjoyed watching people dance."

"And who was next to you at the bar?"

"Wesley was on one side of me, and Beau Bardot was on the other side. I ordered a strawberry daiquiri. I visited with Beau for a little while, and then Wesley and I chatted."

"What did you two talk about?" Nick asked as he began writing down notes.

"Nothing in particular...the weather and things going on in town."

"Were you interested in him romantically?"

Her eyes widened. "Heavens no, besides Wesley is... was married."

"Do you have a significant other?" Nick asked. It might be helpful to the defense if she had a steady boyfriend.

"No, there's nobody in my life right now," she replied.

"And you weren't having a secret affair with Wesley?"

She looked at him in horror. "No, I would never have an affair with a married man. Wesley was only a casual acquaintance to me, nothing more. I don't know who killed him. I don't even know how I got into that alley. The last thing I remember is sitting at the bar and sipping on my second drink."

Tears once again shone in her eyes. "I don't know what happened that night. It's all a blank, but I know I didn't do this. I had absolutely no reason to hurt Wesley, and in any case I could never kill anyone."

She swiped the tears from her eyes. "Please, Mr. Monroe... Nick, will you help me? I have some money tucked back, and I'll pledge my future earnings to you. Whatever it takes, I want... I need you to represent me."

"We can talk about payment later," Nick replied. "You're being arraigned this afternoon, and I'll represent you in that process."

"Thank you," she replied in obvious relief. "So, what happens there?"

"The main thing for you to remember is I do most of the talking. You will stand or sit next to me, and you don't need to say a word unless the judge asks you a direct question. Even then, you will consult with me before giving a response."

"Okay, I can do that," she replied tremulously.

Nick got to his feet. "I think we're done here for now. I'll meet you at the courthouse this afternoon right before the arraignment."

She stood as well. "Thank you so much for your help."

"If I do decide to represent you in this case, you have to understand that I'm no miracle worker. You're facing some serious charges, and the evidence against you is very damning. The prosecutor's case is that you were having an affair with Wesley, and when he refused to leave his wife, you killed him."

She looked at him in horror. "All I can tell you is I'm innocent," she replied with a lift of her chin. "There was no affair, and I didn't kill anyone."

"We'll talk more once the arraignment is over."

Nick walked over to the door and knocked to let the officer outside know they were finished. Once she was escorted out of the room, Nick sat back down at the table.

Everyone always proclaimed their innocence when they were arrested, but in this case, Nick leaned toward believing her. First of all, physically, it was difficult for him to believe that a woman of her small stature had managed to stab a man to death. Wesley was a tall, big man, making it even more difficult for Nick to believe in her guilt.

There had just been something about her that made him believe she was innocent. If he was right about her, then the last thing he wanted to see was an innocent woman railroaded for a crime she didn't commit.

That meant somewhere out there in the small town of Crystal Cove, Louisiana, was a cunning killer who had not only gotten away with a cold-blooded murder, but had also managed to thoroughly frame an innocent woman.

## Chapter Two

"Ms. LaCrae has no passport and no financial resources to flee. In fact, she's an innocent woman who is eager to stand and fight these charges against her. Therefore, I request that she be released on her own recognizance," Nick said to Judge Henry Cooke.

"Your honor, this is absolutely outrageous," Prosecutor Tommy Radcliffe exclaimed loudly. "This woman is charged with a monstrous murder. Beneath her pretty face is a calculating, cunning person who had an affair with the victim. When he wouldn't leave his wife for her, she took a knife and stabbed him not once, not twice, but three times to murder him." Tommy hit his desk three times for emphasis. "I want her remanded until she stands trial."

Nick felt Heather's outrage as she stood stiffly beside him, but thankfully she didn't say anything to protest what Tommy had said.

She had met with him just minutes before these proceedings. She was still clad in her sweat pants and pink T-shirt. She looked exhausted and stressed. She'd been given her hairbrush and had quickly run it through her long, dark, rich-looking tresses. Then they'd been called into the courtroom.

"Mr. Radcliffe, save your histrionics for the trial," Judge Cooke replied dryly.

"Your Honor, Ms. LaCrae owns a small business here in town and is a solid member of the community. However, posting any kind of bail would be a hardship for her. She is no danger to society."

Judge Cooke pulled on his white beard and frowned. He looked at Tommy and then back at Nick and Heather. "Okay, I hope I don't regret this. I hereby order that Heather LaCrae be released on her own recognizance. Trial date is set for one month from today, and we are done here." He banged down his gavel.

Nick remained standing with Heather by his side as the portly Radcliffe closed his briefcase and then approached them. "You won this round today, slick Nick, but don't expect a success at trial."

"We'll see, Tommy. We'll see," Nick replied easily. He and Tommy had butted heads many times in trial, and Nick wasn't worried about doing it once again.

"So, what happens now?" Heather asked once it was just the two of them left in the courtroom. "Do I have to go back to jail?"

"No, it means you don't have to go back to jail," Nick replied. "You're free to go home right now."

To his stunned surprise, she threw her arms around his neck and gave him a big hug. "Thank you, thank you," she whispered against his neck and then stepped away from him.

"You're welcome," he replied. He had to admit, to his surprise, her hug felt good. It had been a very long time since Nick had been hugged by anyone. "Do you have a ride home?"

"If I could use your cell phone, I can call my friend Lucy,

and she will come to get me when she can. The police kept my phone for evidence. I guess I'll have to see about getting another one."

"You will definitely need one so you and I can keep in touch. In the meantime, I've got nothing going on right now. I can take you home," Nick replied.

"You've already done so much for me. I hate to bother you anymore," she protested.

"Nonsense, it's not a bother. Besides, on the drive, we can talk a little more about the case."

"Does this mean you're going to represent me through the whole case?" Her lovely eyes gazed up at him with obvious hope.

"It does. Now, let's get you home." They left the courtroom and then walked out into the heat and humidity of the day. He led her to his car and opened the passenger door to usher her in. He then walked around the car and got in behind the steering wheel.

"Okay, what directions do I need?" he asked as he pulled away from the curb.

"Do you know where the big parking lot is, next to the swamp's largest entrance?"

"I do," he replied.

"If you can drop me there then I can walk in to my place."

"Got it," he replied. They rode for a few minutes in silence. He cast her several surreptitious gazes, drawn to her beauty.

*Beneath her pretty face is a calculating, cunning person.* Tommy's words replayed in his mind. Nick glanced over at her once again. She certainly didn't appear to be that woman right now. She looked small and fragile. He'd noticed earlier that while she had lovely hands, two of her fingernails appeared chewed to the quick. Did calculating killers bite their fingernails?

"Do you have a car?" he asked curiously as he approached the parking area in front of the looming swamp.

"I do," she replied.

"Could you meet me at my office tomorrow morning around ten? We need to get the paperwork taken care of for me to officially represent you, among other things."

"I'll be there," she replied.

"Do you know where my office is?"

She flashed him a quick smile. It was the first real smile he'd seen from her, and it shot an unexpected rivulet of warmth through him. "No, but trust me, I'll find it."

He returned her smile. "My office is at 221 Main Street. I'm right next to Bella's Ice Cream Parlor."

"I definitely know where that is," she replied. "My friend Lucy and I indulge in ice cream way too often." As he parked the car, she took off her seat belt and turned to look at him. "Thank you, Nick."

"Don't thank me yet. We have a big challenge ahead of us."

Her smile instantly vanished. "I'm aware of that. At least I don't have to spend another night in jail. Well, thank you for bringing me home, and I'll see you tomorrow morning."

"Okay, see you then." She got out of the car, and he watched as she walked toward the jungle-like marsh and quickly vanished from his view, swallowed up by the swamp she lived in.

He turned his car around, his thoughts still on the woman he'd just left. The women he'd encountered who lived in the swamp fascinated him. The few he had defended on misdemeanor charges had been incredibly strong women who had to work hard to survive.

He'd never been to any of the shanties where they lived, but he imagined they were quite primitive. No matter how she lived, he hoped Heather had a strong support system in the swamp. Etienne had told him that her parents had passed, and she had no siblings.

Still, from what he had heard, the people who lived in the swamp had become a closer-knit community in the past few months. They all had a common enemy to fear. Someplace in the swamp, there was a man the newspaper had dubbed the Swamp Soul Stealer. So far, he had kidnapped two men and three women, and nobody knew whether the people he had taken were dead or still alive.

There was more hope they were alive since one of the women had turned up. Colette Broussard had been found half dead at the edge of the swamp. She'd been badly beaten and apparently had been starved. She had also been dangerously dehydrated and now remained in a medically induced coma. She had been gone for three months when she'd been found.

The hope was that when she was a little better, she would be able to tell Etienne who had taken her, where she had been held and the condition of the other captives.

However, he couldn't think about that right now. He had to find a defense for a woman charged with murder and facing years in prison and possibly the death penalty. He had to find a way to defend a woman who didn't know how she got soaked in the victim's blood, holding the murder weapon in her hand, with a confession typed into her phone.

He thought about that confession now. It had been fairly

simple. *I killed Wesley. I loved him but he refused to leave his wife, so I stabbed him to death and I can't live with myself.* If not her, then who had left that damning message in her phone?

All he knew for sure was that her defense that she was innocent and she didn't remember anything that had happened certainly wasn't enough to keep her out of prison.

HEATHER RACED TOWARD the tangled growth she called home. The swamp seemed to embrace her as she ran down first one trail and then another to get to her shanty.

She wanted to hug the cypress trees she passed with their knobby knees poking out of the dark pools of water. She drew in deep lungfuls of the air that smelled of myriad plants and mysterious flowers and the ever-present faint scent of decay.

She needed to embrace all that was the swamp in case there came a time when she couldn't be here. Her heart squeezed tight at the very thought of spending years in a prison and away from this place that fed her soul.

Her shanty came into view, and she raced across the bridge that would take her to her front door. Once inside, she collapsed on the sofa. She was exhausted, first from the sleepless night in the jail cell and then from the stress of her time before the judge.

Despite her exhaustion, she was too wired to rest. She sat for only a moment and then got up and went into her kitchen, part of which had been transformed into an herb garden.

In here, the scents of basil and parsley, of mint and thyme, were redolent in the air, along with half a dozen other fragrant herbs.

She went out the back door and started her generator, then went inside and turned on the lights that helped the growing plants flourish. She could only run the lights for about two hours a day, but it, along with the natural sunlight that shone through the windows, was enough to keep them healthy and thriving.

When the fledgling plants got big enough, she would take them into her little store off Main Street. It took her fifteen minutes or so to water them all, and she had just finished when a knock fell on her door.

She opened the door to her best friend, Lucy Dupree. The short-haired, slightly plump woman immediately wrapped her arms around Heather and held her tight. "Are you okay?" She finally released Heather, but grabbed her hand and pulled her down on the sofa next to her. Her brown eyes gazed at Heather worriedly.

"I'm fine for now," Heather replied.

"What the hell, Heather?" Lucy squeezed her hand and then released it. "It's going all around town that you stabbed Wesley Simone in a fit of passion and then took drugs to commit suicide. How on earth did this happen? I know you didn't... I mean I know you couldn't stab anyone. And I definitely know you weren't romantically involved with Wesley Simone unless you've been keeping some major secrets from me."

"Trust me, I certainly have no secrets like that. I would never get involved with a married man, and in any case, Wesley definitely wasn't my type. I don't know how this all happened. I have no memory of that night. My first conscious moment was waking up handcuffed to a hospital bed.

I was drugged, Lucy. Somebody drugged me and set me up to take the fall for Wesley's murder."

"Who would do that?" Lucy frowned.

"I wish I knew."

"At least you're home today," Lucy replied. "And that means you must have a good lawyer."

"Nick Monroe, and time will tell just how good he is. So far, I'm impressed with him," Heather replied. "Do you know him?"

"I don't think so, although I might have waited on him at the café at one time or another. What does he look like?"

"Very nice looking...with dark hair and blue eyes." Among the many things that had happened to her, Nick had been yet another surprise. She wasn't sure what she'd expected of the defense attorney, but the very hot man with dark hair and piercing blue eyes had not been what she'd anticipated.

Nick Monroe was definitely a hunk. His attractive facial features were boldly sculpted, and when he smiled, twin dimples had danced in his cheeks.

He'd worn a black suit to court, and she could tell his shoulders were broad and his hips were slim. But it didn't matter how hot he was. What she needed from him was his legal mind. She was depending on him to get her out of this horrid mess she found herself in.

"Hmm, I don't know, that could describe lots of men who come into the café," Lucy replied. "As long as he can get you out of these charges against you, that's all that really matters."

"I agree," Heather replied. For the next hour, the two talked about the charges against Heather. "We really haven't talked much yet about my defense, but the only way I see that I can get off is if we find the real killer," Heather said. "Somehow I need to remember things that happened that night in the bar."

"And how do you intend to find the real killer?" Lucy asked.

"I don't know. All I do know is I don't want to spend a minute in prison for a crime I didn't commit," Heather replied fervently. "One night in that awful jail was more than enough for me."

It was soon after that when Lucy left. For dinner, Heather fried up some fish, and then she turned off the generator. By eight o'clock, her exhaustion finally overwhelmed her, and she got into bed.

The croak of bullfrogs sounded, along with the gentle lapping of water against the stilts that held her shanty up out of the swamp waters. It was the soothing rhythms of home, but on this night, it pulled tears to her eyes. Would she really go to prison for a crime she didn't commit? After her trial, would she never again hear the sounds of the sweet lullabies of home?

## Chapter Three

Heather found a parking space on Main just down the street from Nick's office. She shut off her car but remained seated. She was a little early for her appointment with him, but at least she'd already accomplished getting a new cell phone. What she hadn't accomplished was remembering anything that might help her case.

She sat for several long moments, and then realizing it was almost time to go in, she smoothed down the peasant-style white blouse she wore. She'd paired it with a red-and-white long flowy skirt and a pair of white sandals. She'd dressed with the intention of opening her store after this meeting.

Anxiety filled her as she thought about going to the store to work. By now most people in town would know that she'd been arrested and charged with Wesley's murder. They might believe she'd been having an affair with him and had killed him. She had no idea how people would react to her now.

She gazed up the block. Crystal Cove was a charming little town with the buildings along Main Street painted in pinks, yellows and turquoises. People walked along the sidewalk, laughing and seemingly without a worry in the world. Her heart clenched. That was the way she had been before she was charged with murder.

She got out of the car and walked toward Nick's office, her stomach muscles tight with anxiety. Monroe Law was on the front window in neat, silver letters. She opened the door and went inside, where a woman with short, curly reddish-brown hair and brown eyes sat behind a desk.

"Hello, I'm Heather LaCrae and I'm here to see Mr. Monroe," Heather said.

"Hi, Heather, I'm Sharon Benoit, the coffee-fetching, brainstorming, paralegal receptionist." She smiled at Heather. "Now I'll just go back and see if they're ready for you." She got up and disappeared through a doorway just to the right of her desk.

They? Did Nick have a partner? Partners? As far as Heather was concerned, the more the merrier when it came to her defense. She waited only a minute or two, and then Sharon returned. "Just go through the door, and they're in Nick's office...the first doorway on the left."

"Thank you," Heather replied. A new wave of anxiety swept over her as she pushed through the door that led into the interior of the building. She knew she had no real defense. She could only hope that her lawyer came up with something to keep her out of prison.

She came to the first door on the left and knocked. Nick opened the door and smiled at her. "Ah, good, you're right on time. I like a client who is punctual."

He opened the door wider to allow her entry. He looked totally hot clad in a pair of black slacks and with the sleeves of his white dress shirt rolled up to his elbows. As she walked past him, she smelled the attractive, slightly spicy cologne that she'd noticed the day before.

A big, buff bald man stood from the chair he had been sitting in when she came into the room. He was clad in a pair of jeans and a black T-shirt that stretched taut across his massive chest and shoulders. He also wore a shoulder holster and a gun.

"Heather, this is Bruno Foret, private investigator extraordinaire and my right-hand man when I need him," Nick said.

"Hello, Mr. Foret," she replied to the big, intimidating man.

"Call me Bruno," he said in a deep, gravelly voice.

She nodded, then Nick gestured her toward a chair in front of his desk. She eased down into the chair, and then the two men sat.

"How are you feeling this morning?" Nick asked her.

"Nervous...anxious and worried," she replied honestly.

Nick nodded, as if unsurprised by her answer. "First of all, I have some paperwork for you to sign." He reached for several papers on the left of his desk and then stood to hand them and a pen to her. "Take your time reading through them, and if you have any questions, feel free to ask."

For the next few minutes, she read through the documents, the first granting Nick the right to represent her in all matters pertaining to the current charges against her, which she signed and handed back to him. She assumed it was for the court.

The second document was a contract between her and Nick. It also granted him the right to represent her. It stated that he was working the case pro bono. When she read this, she looked back up at him.

"I don't expect you to do this for free, Nick. I told you I have a little bit of money put away, and I can pledge you more from my future store earnings." She raised her chin slightly. "I don't want to be a charity case."

"You sell all kinds of herbs in your store, right?" he asked.

"Right," she replied.

"I like to cook, so why don't we agree that you will give me herbs in exchange for my services."

"Okay…deal, but you need to write that in here so it's legal." She handed him back the contract unsigned.

"I'll give it to Sharon and have her redo it, and you can sign it tomorrow," Nick replied. "Let's talk about what's going to happen now."

"Okay," she replied. She twisted her hands in her lap, anxious to hear how they were going to fight the murder charge. "But before we do that, I got a new phone this morning, and I should give you my number."

"Definitely." He picked up the cell phone on his desk, and it only took them a few moments to exchange numbers.

"Now," he continued. "The first thing we intend to do is conduct our own investigation of the crime. I believe there was a definite rush to justice in this case, and I intend to argue that in court, but in the meantime, Bruno will go to the Voodoo Lounge to question the bartenders and anyone else who might have been there that night. What I need from you is a list of all the people you remember being there, as we intend to talk to each and every one of them. Somebody had to have seen something that night that might help your defense. Can you take a few minutes to do that before you leave today?"

"Of course, I can do that," she replied.

Nick's blue eyes peered into hers intently. "I expect you to be an active participant in your own defense."

"I'll do whatever I can to help," she replied.

He grinned at her, his dimples flashing in a smile that warmed her from head to toe. "Good," he said.

Great, just what she needed...a mad crush on her lawyer. Surely a handsome, successful man like him had a wife or a significant other. She shoved the inappropriate thoughts away. She was facing a murder charge and thinking about romance. What on earth was wrong with her? Maybe she really had lost her mind.

"Do you have any enemies that you know of?" he asked, the question definitely pulling her back to the current topic.

"No, none," she replied firmly. "I get along with everyone, which is why I don't know why somebody would do this to me."

"You haven't had any disputes with anyone recently, no matter how big or small? Maybe a disgruntled customer at the store?"

She shook her head. "Really, I haven't had any problems with anyone."

Nick stood. "Okay, now I'll just take you to one of the conference rooms so you can write out that list for me." He grabbed a legal pad and pen and gestured for her to follow him.

"It was nice to meet you, Bruno," she said to the big man who had remained silent through the short meeting.

"Oh, I imagine you'll be seeing a lot of me from now on," he replied.

Heather followed Nick down a long hallway and into a small room with a table and four chairs. He handed her the notebook and pen. "Make yourself comfortable. Can I get you a cup of coffee or something else to drink?"

"No, thank you. I'm fine," she replied.

"Then I'll just leave you to get to it. When you're finished, just let Sharon know. I have an appointment with another client in fifteen minutes. It should be a relatively short meeting, and I'll see you after."

With that, he left the room and closed the door behind him. She stared down at the blank page in front of her, for a moment overwhelmed by the task before her.

God, she wished her parents were still alive. Her father had died eighteen months ago from lung cancer, and then six months ago her mother had suffered a massive heart attack and had passed away. Despite being twenty-nine years old, Heather had lived with them.

About the time she'd seriously considered finding her own place, her father had gotten ill. She had remained at home first to help nurse her father and then to support her grieving mother. Now, more than ever, she wished they were here to support and guide her.

She released a deep sigh and turned her thoughts to that night in the Voodoo Lounge. The first names she wrote down were the easy ones. She remembered the people who had been on the dance floor. They were regulars who were there on most Saturday nights. It became more difficult for her after that.

She searched her memory until the time when she had no memory left. Somebody had obviously drugged her drink in an effort to kill Wesley and frame her. Who had been close enough to her at the bar to do that?

There was one thing she did remember. She had done what no smart, single woman should ever do—she'd left her drink unattended when Jason Tremont had asked her to dance. That had to have been when the drink was tampered with. So, who had been around the bar when she had returned to her seat after her time on the dance floor? She needed to tell Nick this piece of information.

She wrote down all the names of the people she could remember and then sat for a few more minutes to see if any more came to her. One thing she did know was the bar had been packed that night, and there had been people there she didn't know by name.

When she finished, she had the names of about fifteen people written down. At least it would be a good place for Bruno to start, and hopefully she'd remember more people as time went on. Somebody had to have seen something that night that would help her.

She left the conference room and went back into the lobby, where Sharon smiled at her. "The meeting Nick is in is running longer than he expected. He said to tell you that he'll meet with you again tomorrow morning at nine."

"Okay, and here's the list he wanted from me." Heather handed over the legal pad and pen. "And I guess I'll just see you in the morning."

Heather left the office and returned to her car. Once inside, she released a deep sigh. Hopefully Nick and Bruno would be able to find somebody who could corroborate her story. She didn't even want to think about the consequences for her if they were unsuccessful.

"SO, WHAT DO you think of Ms. Heather LaCrae?" Nick asked Bruno. Nick had ended his meeting with Tony Bridges, who had been charged with trespassing and criminal mischief. By that time, Heather had left but Bruno hadn't, so he then had called Bruno back into his office. He and the big, muscled man had been good friends since they'd been kids, and Nick valued Bruno's opinion.

"I'm not sure what to think at this point. Could she be totally innocent? Sure. But could she be guilty as hell? Absolutely. She could definitely come off to a jury as a femme fatale. She's drop-dead gorgeous and could have easily seduced Wesley, who is…was a very wealthy man and was married to the crankiest woman in town. Heather could have gotten Wesley drunk enough to follow her into the alley, where she demanded he leave his wife for her, and when he ultimately refused, she stabbed him to death."

"I don't know—I believe she was set up and is totally innocent in all this," Nick replied.

Bruno raised one of his thick, dark eyebrows. "It's awfully early in the game for you to have that opinion." He cast Nick a sly smile. "It doesn't have anything to do with the fact that her big brown eyes gazed at you with unbridled hero worship, does it?"

Nick laughed. "I didn't even notice that."

Bruno shot him a look of disbelief and then stood. "On that note, I'll get out of here and see what I can dig up at the Voodoo Lounge."

"Thanks, Bruno. I'll just talk to you later," Nick replied. The minute Bruno left his office, Nick reared back in his chair thoughtfully.

Was he jumping too quickly to conclusions because he wanted Heather to be innocent? Because she looked small and helpless and had, indeed, looked at him as if he was her hero?

He'd made that mistake before. Her name was Delia Hunter, and she'd been charged with aggravated assault on another woman. According to the prosecution, Delia had broken into Laura Dillon's home in the middle of the night and had beaten her so badly that Laura had suffered numerous serious injuries. The beef between the two women apparently had started when Laura dinged Delia's car in a parking lot.

Delia had been a slender, attractive blond who had insisted she hadn't done the crime. She'd been passionate about her innocence, and immediately Nick had believed her.

As he worked on her case, the two developed an intimate relationship, and Nick had believed himself in love with her. He'd also believed that she was deeply in love with him.

He was ecstatic when he won her defense case, but once that happened, she dropped him like a hot potato and left town with another man. Two years later, he'd heard she'd been arrested for the same kind of crime, and he realized she had probably been guilty when he'd defended her.

Delia had been three years ago, and he certainly didn't intend to make that same kind of mistake with Heather. Bruno was right, it was far too early in the game for him to make sweeping judgments about Heather's innocence.

However, as her defense attorney, it really wasn't his place to determine whether she was guilty or innocent. His job was to defend her to the best of his ability. And in order to do that, he wanted to know more about her. He wanted to know her life inside and out.

With this thought in mind, he got up from his desk, strapped on his gun, pulled on his suit jacket and then grabbed his car keys. Heather's best friend, Lucy, worked as a waitress at the café, and he was in the mood for an early lunch and a little conversation with her. Hopefully, she was working that day.

Even though it was a bit early for the lunch crowd, the Crystal Cove Café was busy. He found a parking space in the lot behind the building and then headed around to the front door.

As he stepped inside the establishment, he was greeted by a number of delicious scents. The smell of frying hamburgers and onions wafted in the air, along with the aroma of seafood and cooking vegetables. There was also the fragrance of freshly baked bread and pastries.

Hopefully Lucy was working, but since he had no idea what she looked like, he grabbed a table for two and sat. He was in luck, the slightly plump waitress who came to his table had short dark hair, a friendly smile and a name tag that read Lucy.

"Ah, just the woman I wanted to see," he said.

"Are you hungry?" she asked as she placed a glass of water and a menu on the table.

"Yes, both for food and some information. I'm Nick Monroe, and I am the lawyer representing Heather," he explained.

"Oh, Mr. Monroe, it's so nice to meet you. Heather told me all about you. She's totally innocent, you know. I've known her since we were kids, and she isn't capable of hurting anyone. It's simply not in her. She's a wonderfully kind and gentle woman," she said in a quick explosion of words.

"Before I order, I was wondering if there was some place we could go where I could have a short chat with you. Would you be able to take a ten-minute break?"

She frowned and looked around. "We're pretty busy right now. I could take a break after the lunch rush, but I really can't right now. But I want to do whatever I can to help Heather."

Nick nodded, realizing it had been stupid of him to come in for an interview around lunchtime and expect a waitress to stop working. "Why don't I come back around one thirty, and hopefully then you can take a break and talk to me."

"That sounds perfect," she replied. "Now would you like to order something anyway while you're here?"

He ordered a burger and fries, and as he ate, he listened to the gossip that swirled around the room along with the clink of silverware and laughter.

There was no question that the majority of the conversations he could overhear were about the murder and Heather's involvement. The general consensus was that she had to be guilty.

"I guess this just goes to show that you never know what's really going on in somebody's life," a woman at the next table said.

"Poor Millie, she must be reeling. Not only is her husband dead, but she also found out that he was apparently cheating on her with a much younger woman," another woman at the same table replied.

"It doesn't really surprise me at all. After all, she's one of those swamp people who have no morals at all." This was said by Brett Mayfield, a large man who worked as a handyman and building contractor and came from a wealthy family.

It was disheartening that, before the trial even began, apparently most of the people in town had already judged Heather guilty. And it was particularly disheartening that there were still people who were blatantly prejudiced against anyone who came from the swamp. He finished his burger and then lingered over a cup of coffee.

He finally left the café and headed to the police station. He wanted to have another quick chat with Etienne. When he arrived, the chief of police was in his office, and he welcomed Nick in.

"I'm assuming you're here about the murder case," Etienne said.

"I just thought I'd give you a heads-up that as part of the defense I intend to argue that there was a rush to judgment," Nick said.

Etienne released a small, dry laugh. "Good luck with that. She was caught covered in blood and with the murder weapon in her hand, and let's not forget the confession in her phone."

"She didn't do it, Etienne. Somebody drugged her and then framed her for the murder. Somebody wanted Wesley dead, but it wasn't Heather. I know you have a lot on your plate with the Swamp Soul Stealer, but I would suggest you investigate what was going on in Wesley's life. Bruno and I will be investigating all aspects of this crime."

Etienne released a deep sigh. "It would have been poor police work not to arrest and charge Heather for the crime given all the physical evidence at the scene. It's highly unusual to do an investigation after somebody has already been charged, but I'll tell you what I'll do. I'll try to get a couple of men to look into Wesley's life and see if there's any motive there for somebody else to kill him."

"And if you find out anything, you'll share that information with me?"

"Of course."

"Anything new with Colette?" Nick asked.

Etienne frowned. "She's still in a coma. We're just waiting for her to come out of it. Medically, there's no reason for the coma. The doctors suspect it's trauma that's keeping her from waking up."

"I know you hope she can give you some answers in the Soul Stealer case."

The lawman nodded. "Definitely."

Nick stood. "I'll just get out of here and let you get back to work."

"Thanks, Nick. I'll talk to you later."

Nick left the police station and returned to the café, where he had his chat with Lucy. She told him Heather didn't have a boyfriend, that for much of her adult life she'd been caring first for her sick father and then for her mother.

She painted a picture of a kind and thoughtful woman who had never had problems with anyone. Lucy obviously adored her friend and would make a good character witness for her. Of course, the prosecutor would try to make a case that Lucy would lie for her best friend.

It was just after two when he decided to check out Heather's store. The little shop was housed in a pink building with a sign out front proclaiming the business as Heather's Herbs and Plants.

A bell tinkled to announce his entrance. It was like walking into an enchanted garden with plants hanging overhead and rows of spices and other plants displayed on shelves. Myriad pleasant scents filled the air and Heather greeted him from behind a counter with an old-fashioned register on top of it.

"Nick...what a surprise," she said as she stepped out into the aisle and walked toward him. She smiled, the beautiful gesture surprisingly once again warming him from head to toe.

"I figured I'd stop by and see your shop for myself. Nice place. How's business?"

Her smile instantly fell. "Today, not so good. Nobody has

been in, although several people have walked by, stopped and stared inside the front window. I guess I should get used to people staring at me now."

"I'm sorry that's happening to you," he replied sympathetically. She stood close enough to him that he could now smell her scent. It was one of wildflowers with a hint of vanilla, and it was very attractive.

"I'm just hoping that as time goes by, I'll be less of a sensational figure for people to stare at."

Talking about sensational figures, she definitely had one. Her breasts were full and her waist was small. Her hips were slender, but the whole package was definitely sensational.

He frowned inwardly. These were the last kind of thoughts he needed to be having about his client. "Why don't you show me around the place," he said.

For the next twenty minutes or so, he walked with her up and down the two aisles, and as she explained the plants to him it was obvious she loved what she did. Her entire face lit up and her eyes sparkled brightly as she told him about the various herbs. She also looked good in the white blouse and the skirt that swirled around her long legs. He'd noticed that when she had first walked into his office that morning.

"What made you go into this business?" he asked curiously.

"My mother always had a little herb garden, and I saw how people would come to her to get the fresh herbs they wanted to cook with. So, I just decided to expand on what she was doing. I figured there might be a lot of people here in town wanting herbs and plants, and so here I am."

"It's all quite impressive," he replied.

"Why don't I send you home with some of the herbs. All they really need to stay healthy is some sunshine and water."

As she spoke, she grabbed a box and began to place some of the plants inside it. "You mentioned you like to cook. It will be nice for you to be able to have on hand some fresh parsley and oregano."

"Whoa, that's enough for today," he said when she had four plants in the box.

"Are you sure?"

"I'm positive," he replied. He took the box from her. "I have a perfect windowsill in my kitchen for these."

"Good," she said with another beautiful smile.

"And now I'll just get out of here. I need to check in with Bruno and see what he's found out." He was instantly sorry that his words stole the smile from her face. "In the meantime, I'll see you in my office in the morning."

She walked toward the door with him, and when they reached it, they both stepped outside into the bright sunshine. "Thanks for stopping by," she said.

"I was intrigued to see what you did here," he replied. "And thanks for the herbs."

He'd barely gotten the words out of his mouth when there was a loud pop and a bullet slammed into the building just to the left of where Heather stood.

## Chapter Four

Nick quickly shoved Heather behind him. He dropped the tray of plants to the ground and immediately surprised her by pulling a gun from beneath his sport jacket. Deep gasps of fear escaped her as her brain tried to process the fact that somebody had just shot at them...at her.

Nick's body shielded hers and radiated tension as he remained unmoving, his gun at the ready. They remained that way for several long minutes.

"Get inside," he finally said to her. "Get back into your store and call Etienne. I'll stay right here until he arrives. And if you have a back door, make sure it's locked up." The words fired out of him, and he moved away from her just enough so she could open the shop door.

She escaped inside and went over by the register. Her cell phone was on the counter. Her fingers shook as she punched in the emergency number.

"Crystal Creek Police Department. Officer Smith speaking. How can I help you?" the voice said on the other end of the line.

"This is Heather LaCrae. I... I'm at my shop w-with Nick Monroe and s-somebody just s-shot at us. We need Chief

Savoie here right away." Her voice shook uncontrollably as sheer terror fully gripped her.

"We'll be right there," Officer Smith replied.

Heather hung up and rushed to her back door to make sure it was secured. She returned to the store floor and stood staring at Nick's back just outside. Tears welled up in her eyes as shivers of fear raced up and down her back.

Who had shot at her? There was little question in her mind that the bullet had been meant for her. Had it been one of Wesley's relatives looking for revenge? That night in the Voodoo Lounge, he had bragged on his two grown sons.

Or maybe the bullet had been meant for Nick. Somebody wanted him dead because he dared to defend her. She really had no idea what to believe. All she knew for sure was that chills of fear overtook her. The tears that had burned hot in her eyes now fell down her cheeks.

At that moment, Nick came back into the shop. "Whoever it was, he or she is probably gone by now." He strode toward her and obviously saw her tears.

"Hey...hey, don't cry," he said softly, and then he drew her into his arms and held her. "We're safe and everything is going to be all right. I've got you."

His strong arms embraced her, and his scent filled her head. For just that moment, she felt protected and cared for. He held her for several long moments, his heartbeat strong and steady against her frantic one. The sound of a siren blared from outside, and he finally released his hold on her.

She swiped the tears from her cheeks as the siren stopped, letting them know that the police had arrived. Etienne was the first one in, while an officer Heather didn't know stood outside in front of the door.

"You both okay?" he asked, looking first at Nick and then at Heather.

"We're okay," Nick replied. "Thank God I decided to wear my gun today."

"So, talk to me, Nick," Etienne said tersely. "Tell me exactly what happened."

Nick explained about them walking out of the door and the bullet that slammed into the building far too close to them. "Did you see anyone?" Etienne asked.

"No, in fact I can't even tell you what direction it came from. It was so dammed unexpected," Nick said. Frustration was rife in his tone.

"You two stay in here, and we'll see what we can find outside," Etienne instructed. "I'll be back in to talk to you in a little while."

He left the shop, and Heather went into the little break room at the back and grabbed a folding chair for Nick to use while they waited for Etienne's return. She had a stool behind the register to sit on.

At least some of the abject terror that had tightened the back of her throat and brought on her tears had passed. While she was still scared and unsettled by what had happened, she felt better in control of her emotions.

"Thanks," Nick said as he took the folding chair from her. They both sat, and she finally drew her first real breath since the whole ordeal had occurred. "Are you doing okay?" His blue eyes held a wealth of concern as he gazed at her.

"I'm doing better than I was, but I'm not going to lie. I'm still a bit scared. It's not every day that I get shot at." She released a deep sigh. "I just wish I knew who it was."

"Yeah, me, too," he replied.

"I know Wesley has a couple of grown sons. Maybe one

of them wants revenge on me for supposedly killing their father," she speculated.

"Hopefully Etienne will find something that will point to the guilty party. He should be able to retrieve the bullet, and sometimes that can hold some answers. And I'm sure he'll interview Wesley's family to find out where they all were when this happened."

"Excuse me if Etienne isn't my favorite person right now. He's responsible for charging me with a murder I didn't commit," she replied indignantly.

"You can't fault him for doing his job, Heather. Besides, he didn't charge you, the prosecutor did," he replied.

"And now I feel like everyone in town hates me and wants me dead," she said miserably.

"Heather, you know that isn't true. Just because some nut fired a gun at us, that doesn't mean that everyone in town wants you dead." His eyes gazed at her softly. Oh, she could easily fall into those beautiful blue depths. "Etienne will figure this out, just give him a chance."

She sighed and nodded. Her world had been turned upside down, and she had no clue who was responsible. She was frightened not just by the bullet that had come far too close to her head, but also by what her future might hold.

"I forgot to tell you something about last Saturday night when I was in the bar," she said, suddenly remembering she needed to tell him about leaving her drink unattended.

"It was a stupid thing to do," she said once she'd finished telling him. "I guess I just never dreamed that anyone would want to drug me for any reason."

"And you still don't remember anyone being at the bar and around your drink when you returned from the dance floor?"

"No. I'm still trying to remember anything I can about that night."

"Anything you do remember might help your case."

They fell silent for several long minutes. She stared out the shop's front window, where she could see several police officers walking around the cars parked along the street. She could only be so lucky that they would find something that identified the shooter.

It was about an hour later when Etienne came back into the shop to speak to them. "We got the bullet out, and it's in perfect shape to check the striations and see if the gun it came from has been used in another crime. We also found several gum wrappers lying on the ground around where we believe the shooter might have parked. Somebody who chewed spearmint gum was in that parking space for some time."

"And it could have been the shooter just waiting for Heather to step outside. At least that's something to go on," Nick said as he stood.

"We're done here," Etienne said and then looked at Heather. "However, we'll be conducting interviews, especially with Wesley's family members." The lawman frowned. "We're going to do our very best to find this person. I don't like vigilantes, and I suspect that's what this might be. In the meantime, Heather, you need to be observant and watch your surroundings."

"Trust me, I will," she replied. A new shiver raced up her back. "I think I'll close up shop for the rest of the day."

"I'll walk you to your car," Etienne offered.

"And I'll follow you back to the swamp," Nick added.

"Thank you both," she replied as the threat of tears once again pressed heavy against her eyelids. Right now, all she wanted was to be home in her shanty, where she felt safe and secure.

Minutes later, she was in her car and headed toward home. It was a comfort to glance in her rearview mirror and see Nick's car following closely behind hers.

Hopefully Etienne would be able to identify and arrest the guilty party quickly, and there was nobody else in town who might want her dead.

She hoped the wheels of justice moved quickly and fairly, and when this was all over, she would be both alive and free.

DAMMIT, THE BULLET had missed her. He drove away from the flower shop and then turned on Main to head home. She was supposed to have died in that alley with Wesley's bloody body next to her. But he obviously hadn't drugged her enough, and now she was a loose end he couldn't afford.

She had been the perfect patsy, and when she'd walked out on the dance floor, leaving her drink behind on the bar, he knew it was fate. He saw the perfect opportunity to make an example out of Wesley and set the woman up for the murder.

But she'd survived, and now he worried about what she might remember from that night. She apparently hadn't remembered him yet because if she had, he would be in jail already facing charges. But that didn't mean she wouldn't still remember some detail that could eventually see him in jail.

He'd been stupid to take a shot at her while the man had been with her, but he'd been parked for over two hours waiting for her. When they had finally stepped outside, he hadn't been able to help himself. He'd fired one shot, hoping it would hit the mark, but unfortunately it hadn't.

There would be another opportunity with her. He would

make sure of it. He couldn't allow her to live, and the sooner he took care of her, the better.

NICK FOLLOWED HER to the area where most of the people who lived in the swamp parked their cars. He suspected one of Wesley's sons had fired that shot at her, and he hoped like hell Etienne managed to get the guilty party into jail for attempted murder. The last thing Heather needed was a grief-crazed vigilante after her.

He now pulled up behind her car and shut off his engine. He got out of his vehicle while she exited hers. He approached her and tried not to think about how wonderful she'd felt in his arms for the brief moments when he'd held her.

Even though he'd been trying to comfort her, he'd still noticed the press of her full breasts against his chest and the way she'd fit perfectly in his arms. It had been a very long time since a woman had stirred him the way she had when he'd embraced her.

She now gazed at him with slightly haunted eyes. "Are you okay?" he asked even though he knew she wasn't. How was she supposed to be all right when somebody had just shot at her?

"I will be," she replied and lifted her chin. "I'm just going to have to watch my back from now on."

"Do you own a gun?" he asked. He now stood close enough that he could smell the evocative scent of her.

"I don't, but my father did, and it's still at my house," she said.

"Do you know how to use it?" he asked.

Her big, doe-like eyes narrowed slightly. "I do."

"You might want to start carrying it with you. I can get

you off a charge of possessing and firing a gun that doesn't belong to you better than I can resurrect you from the dead."

A corner of her lush lips turned slightly upward. "Are you telling me you don't have godlike powers?"

He laughed. "Afraid not, although if I did have that kind of power, the first thing I would do is drop the charges against you."

"But what about world peace?"

"That would be the second thing on my agenda," he replied with a small laugh.

She cast him a full smile that ignited a flicker of heat deep inside him. "You're a nice man, Mr. Monroe."

"You won't think that when you see me at trial. I can be a real mean son of a bitch when I'm cross-examining witnesses. Don't mistake me for a nice man, Heather."

"Duly noted," she replied. "And on that note, I'll just see you in your office tomorrow morning." She turned and raced onto the trail that took her into the swamp and quickly out of his sight.

He released a deep sigh and then turned and headed back to his car. He couldn't believe he'd just basically told her he was a jerk, but he found himself incredibly attracted to her and had needed to put up a wall so things would go no further.

He'd been burned once before by a client with winsome eyes and a beautiful smile, and he wasn't about to allow it to happen again. He would defend Heather to the best of his ability, and then they would go their own ways.

Damn, he was overthinking all of this. Just because he'd enjoyed holding her in his arms for a minute didn't mean anything at all other than he was a normal, healthy man. His reaction to her had simply surprised him. And besides, she hadn't given him any indication that she might be interested in him on a personal level.

"Hey, boss," Sharon greeted him as he came back into his office. "I have a little gossip to share with you."

"Come on back," he said.

Moments later he was at his desk, and Sharon sat in a chair before him. "What's up?"

"While you've been gone, I've been trying to find out what I can about Wesley Simone. Word on the street is he wasn't a very popular guy. According to several sources, he was a real pompous ass. He owns a bunch of rental houses, and he was never reluctant to toss out a family for a late rental payment."

"Sounds like he was a real gem," Nick said with a thoughtful frown. "Tomorrow, see if you can find out the names of people he dislocated recently. Each one of them could be the potential killer."

"Will do," Sharon replied.

"Now you'd better get out of here. It's late and although I thank you for staying, I don't want to give you a reason to tell everyone what an ogre of a boss I am."

She laughed and got up from the chair. "Oh, I've already done that."

He grinned at her. "Get out of here, and I'll see you tomorrow."

Hiring Sharon had been one of the best things he'd ever done for himself. Four years ago, when he'd decided he needed a receptionist, he advertised for one. Several women had applied, but Sharon had been a clear winner. She was a paralegal who knew the law. She was very bright and had a good sense of humor, and she'd definitely been a big asset to him since he'd hired her.

With Sharon gone and the place closed up for the night, Nick got on his phone and called Bruno. Bruno told him he'd come by the office in a half an hour or so.

While waiting for his friend, Nick opened up one of his desk drawers and pulled out a half-empty bottle of brandy and a glass. He should just go home and meet Bruno there, but lately he'd been reluctant to spend the long hours of the evening all alone in his big house.

Before Delia, he had thrown himself into the dating game. He had dated a lot of women but hadn't found that special one who would fill his life with the kind of love he yearned for. Still, he wanted a wife and a family and was determined to find that particular woman. He thought he'd found her with Delia.

After Delia's betrayal, he'd finally given up and had quit dating altogether. He no longer thought about marriage or a family. At the age of thirty-four, he'd pretty much resigned himself to the fact that he'd probably be alone for the rest of his life, and he'd made peace with that.

He now leaned back in his chair and took a sip of the brandy. The liquor slid down his throat in a smooth burst of warmth. He hoped Bruno was bringing him some information that would help in Heather's defense. He also hoped that Etienne had arrested the person who had shot at her today.

Heather. He took another sip of the brandy as thoughts of his client filled his head. There was no question that he was physically attracted to her, but he certainly didn't intend to act on it. It was a fool's game to mix business with pleasure, and he was no fool.

He sat up straighter as he heard the whoosh of the front door opening. He assumed it was Bruno, who had a key to the office.

A moment later, the big man entered the office. "I'll take one of those," he said and gestured to the bottle of brandy.

"Coming right up," Nick replied. He reached into his drawer and withdrew another glass and then half filled it with the brandy.

"Thanks," Bruno said as he took the drink and then sank down in the chair facing Nick. "So, what's new?"

"We had a little incident at Heather's shop today," Nick said, and then he proceeded to tell Bruno about the bullet that had been fired at Heather.

"What did Etienne have to say about it?"

"He thinks it's a good guess that it was one of Wesley's sons," Nick replied. "I intend to follow up with him tomorrow to see what he found out. So, what's new with you?"

"I talked to Greyson Labone, who is one of the bartenders at the Voodoo Lounge. He was working on Saturday night and remembers seeing Heather that night, but she was at the other end of the bar and was being served by Jeffrey Cooke. I tried to catch up with Cooke all afternoon but had no luck. I'll try again tomorrow." He took a sip of his drink.

"Anything else you discovered?" Nick asked.

"I talked to several people who were on the list that Heather gave you, and while some of them saw Heather at the bar, none of them noticed when she left."

Nick frowned. "Damn, all we need is one person who saw Heather leaving the bar and who was with her."

"I have a lot more people to talk to tomorrow, and in the meantime, I do have a tidbit of rumor information that might tickle your hide."

Nick leaned forward. "And what's that?"

"Word out on the street is that not only was Wesley a real jerk, but he also had recently begun dabbling in drugs."

"Drugs? What are we talking?" Nick asked as a burst of adrenaline sparked through his veins.

"Snow," Bruno replied, using one of the street names for cocaine.

"Wow, I would have never guessed he was a drug user," Nick said.

"Not only a user, but a seller as well," Bruno added.

Nick's brain worked to process this new information. "How sure are you of your sources?"

"At this point, it's just a whisper of gossip, but I think it's something we need to follow up on," Bruno replied.

"Hell, yes, we need to follow up on this. If this information is true, then we need to find out just how deep he was in this and who he might have owed money to. This definitely could be an alternative theory of the crime."

"I'll dig deeper into all this tomorrow. In the meantime, I intend to hang out at the Voodoo Lounge later tonight and see what else I can find out about our client and her movements that night."

"I don't know what I'd do without you, Bruno," Nick said.

The big man laughed. "I love you, too, bro," he replied. "And on that note, I'm going to get out of here, and I'll see you in the morning." He stood and downed the last of the brandy and then handed Nick the empty glass.

"Don't have too much fun tonight without me, and I'll see you tomorrow," Nick replied.

Minutes later Bruno was gone, and Nick put the bottle of brandy back in the drawer and then carried the two glasses into a small breakroom in the back where there was a table, a coffee machine, a microwave and a sink. He quickly washed the glasses and then dried them and carried them back to his desk drawer to be used again.

It was after eight when he finally headed home. As he drove toward his large four-bedroom house, he thought about everything Bruno had told him.

If it was true that Wesley was using and selling cocaine, then they somehow needed to prove it. He could definitely argue to a jury that Wesley's drug involvement might have been what caused somebody in that same dark world to kill him.

But he needed more than just idle gossip about it. Hell, if he believed all the gossip he'd heard about people in Crystal Cove, then the women who served him in the café were all part of a prostitution ring, and the eighty-year-old city clerk was embezzling millions of dollars a year from city funds.

Gossip was cheap in the small town, and what he needed was facts. It sounded like their investigation was going to go to dark places, and he was definitely willing to go there to save Heather.

*Chapter Five*

Heather raced toward home, eager to get inside the one place in the world where she felt safe and secure. She still couldn't believe that somebody had shot at her, that a bullet had flown precariously close to her head.

She hoped Etienne now had the guilty party behind bars and nothing like that would ever happen to her again. Still, it had been nice when Nick had pulled her into his arms. In fact, it had been far better than just nice. She had liked being in his arms far too much.

She was almost at the bridge to cross to her front door when a man stepped out of the tangled foliage next to her. "Hey, girl," he said, his unexpected presence making her jump.

"Dammit, Jackson Renee Dupris, you scared the hell out of me," she exclaimed.

The old man's face wrinkled up like a prune as he grinned at her, exposing a missing front tooth. "What did you think? That I was the Swamp Soul Stealer come to get you?"

Nobody knew exactly how old Jackson was, although if she were to guess, she'd say the man was in his late seventies or early eighties. He told people he was as old as the cypress trees in the swamp, and his knees were just as knobby. He made a living by fishing and selling the fish to other locals, and everyone in the swamp knew he had an illegal still and also sold a lot of moonshine.

"I've had a rough morning, Jackson," she said wearily.

"From what I hear, you've had a rough couple of days," he replied. "Anyone who thinks you could kill a man sure don't know you very well."

"Thank you, Jackson."

"You know you have plenty of friends here, *mon petit*. All your neighbors adore you. We can't help you in the courtroom, but we'll do whatever is necessary to keep you safe around here."

She smiled at the old man. "Thanks, Jackson, and now I just want to get inside and relax."

"I'll be keeping my eyes on you and my ear to the ground. I'll let you know if I hear anything that might help you out." He spit a string of tobacco out of the side of his mouth. "Prove to everyone that the no-good Tommy Radcliffe isn't as smart as he thinks he is. That man has been on my ass for years, wanting to get me locked up for selling a little hooch."

"Believe me, there's nothing I want more than for my attorney to make mincemeat out of Mr. Radcliffe," she replied fervently.

Jackson slapped his thigh and grinned at her once again. "Now that's what I like to hear. Okay, get inside and relax, and I'll quit jawing at you."

She smiled. "You can jaw at me anytime, Jackson."

Minutes later she was inside her shanty, where she sat back on her sofa and just breathed. It had definitely been a long, eventful day, and she had no idea what to expect going forward. Would somebody shoot at her again? Would somebody try to kill her again tomorrow?

She jumped up from the sofa, refusing to allow these kinds of negative thoughts to fill her head. Tomorrow she would carry her daddy's gun with her, and if necessary, she would use it to defend herself from anyone meaning her harm. In the meantime, she had plants to watch over and dinner to make.

The next morning at ten till nine, she walked into Nick's building, where Sharon greeted her brightly and told her to go on into Nick's office.

Nick and Bruno were in the room; Nick sat behind his large desk, and Bruno was in a chair in front of him. "Good morning," Nick said with a smile as he gestured to the empty chair next to Bruno's. Those flashing dimples stirred a spark deep in the pit of her stomach. He had such an amazing smile. "How are you feeling today?" he asked as she sat.

"So far, so good," she replied and set her oversize purse on the floor next to her. There was no man who wore a pair of tailored slacks better than Nick. Today he also wore a light blue dress shirt that did amazing things to his eyes. "At least nobody has shot at me so far today."

"Well, that's a good start to the day," Nick replied with a smile. "I spoke to Etienne early this morning, and he said he was still investigating the shooting from yesterday. He'd spoken to one of Wesley's sons but hadn't been able to make contact with the other one. He intends to chase him down today and question him, and hopefully he'll have some information for us by noon."

"I certainly hope so," she replied. "In the meantime, I've got something in my purse that I'll use for self-defense."

Bruno released a small, obviously skeptical laugh. "It's only good if you're willing to pull it out and use it."

She glared at him. "Believe me, if I need to protect myself, I'll definitely pull it out and use it." She held the big man's gaze challengingly for a long moment.

"Heather, I have the revised paperwork for you to sign. Read it over, and if you find it acceptable, then sign it and we'll get it out of the way," Nick said.

She got up and took the papers he held out to her. She sat back down and quickly read them over. It was the same as what he'd given her the day before, but under the terms of payment they'd added in that she would provide him with four plants a month for the next two years.

Even though it wouldn't begin to pay him for his services, at least she was now not a pro bono case, and so she was satisfied. She signed it and then handed it back to him.

"Now we can get down to the real business," Nick said. "Have you remembered anything more about that night at the bar?"

She wished she could tell him something…anything, but she couldn't. She shook her head. "I'm sorry, but I haven't remembered anything more."

"Just keep trying," he replied. "Bruno spent yesterday evening at the bar."

"I talked with several people who were there that night. Most of them remember seeing you there, but they didn't notice when you left and with whom," Bruno said. "If you were drugged up, then somebody had to escort or carry you out the back door and into that alley."

She got the distinct feeling that the big man didn't believe her story…that he believed she was guilty. What did Nick really believe? Did he think she was a liar and a murderer?

It was important to her that Nick believed her, not just because he was her defense lawyer, but also because he was a man she admired, and she wanted him to know what kind of a woman she really was.

"Bruno will keep talking to people. Somebody had to have seen you leave that night," Nick said. "It's just a matter of finding the right person."

"I know the bar was crowded that night. Usually when I went there, I only had one drink and I stayed for a couple of hours and then left," she said. "I don't know how long I stayed on that night. But I was there long enough to have two drinks."

"We'll try to piece together things with witnesses who were there that night. Bruno also heard a bit of nasty gossip about Wesley," Nick said.

"What's that?" she asked curiously.

"I heard that he was using and selling cocaine," Bruno said.

"Wesley? I find that really hard to believe," she said in surprise. "I thought he was a successful businessman. Why on earth would he get involved in something like that?"

"It's just a rumor, but it's one we need to check out. If he was a player in the drug world, then it's possible somebody from that world was the person who killed him," Nick said.

Suddenly a flash of memory shot off in her head. "He fought with somebody at the bar that night," she said. "I remember, now, him standing by the bathrooms and having loud words with another man. They were definitely having a heated argument."

Nick leaned forward. "Do you remember who he was arguing with?"

She closed her eyes and tried to capture more, but the fleeting memory was gone. She finally looked at Nick. "I'm sorry, but I don't know. It was just a flash of memory. Maybe more will eventually come to me."

"That's okay. Just keep trying. We've also learned that Wesley wasn't a popular figure around town. He owned some rental properties and was a tough landlord who often displaced families. We're going to try to find some of those people and see just how angry they might have been with him."

"So, the plan is that I will continue to interview people from the bar and follow up on the rumors about the drugs," Bruno said. "I'm also going to see if I can connect with the families who were displaced by Wesley." He stood. "I'll get started right now, and I'll check in later today."

"He thinks I'm guilty," Heather said the moment the big man left the room.

"Bruno is a skeptic by nature."

"But...but you believe me, right?" she asked and held his gaze worriedly. "Nick, do you believe me?"

"I believe you, Heather," he replied with a soft smile. "We're going to figure out what happened to you that night, and hopefully we'll see the guilty party behind bars. I've got you, Heather," he added with another smile. "Now have you had breakfast?"

She blinked at the swift change of subject. "Uh...no, I haven't."

"Neither have I. So why don't I take you to breakfast at the café."

"Would your wife have a problem with that?" she asked.

"She might, if I had one." He flashed her the big grin that made his dimples appear. "No wife...no girlfriend... nobody to get upset about me taking my client to breakfast this morning. So will you go with me?"

"Okay." Her heart warmed with a delicious heat. *He's my lawyer and nothing more*, she reminded herself as the two of them left the office together. Her brain got the memo, but there was no question that she was eager to get to know him better.

## Chapter Six

Nick had no idea why he'd invited her to breakfast, although it probably had something to do with how pretty she looked. She was clad in a pair of dark brown jeans that hugged her slender legs and shapely hips.

She'd paired them with a chocolate brown, long-sleeved button-up blouse that not only showcased her full breasts, but also her big, brown, long-lashed eyes. Her lengthy hair was clasped at the nape of her neck with a gold barrette, and gold hoop earrings completed her look.

She looked sexy as hell, and there was nothing more he'd like to do than unclasp her hair and run his fingers through the silky-looking strands. All he'd been able to think about this morning was how her full lips would taste.

The invitation to breakfast had fallen out of his mouth as if of its own volition. But as he escorted her to his car, he realized he was eager to learn more about her.

"I almost never eat out," she said once they were both in his car and they were headed toward the café.

"I eat out far too often," he replied with a laugh.

"But I thought you told me you love to cook," she replied.

"Oh, I do, but most nights I just don't bother with it.

What's the point of making a really good meal when you're the only one there to enjoy it?"

"I certainly understand that sentiment. I also love to cook, but most evenings I just fry up some fish for myself and call it good. I don't go to a lot of trouble just for me."

He pulled into the parking lot at the back of the café and found a space. "This place is always busy in the mornings."

They got out of the car, and he immediately threw his arm around her shoulders and pulled her close against him as he scrutinized the parking lot for any threat of danger.

She fit so neatly against him, and her wildflower and vanilla scent half dizzied his senses. He smiled down at her. "Now, if anyone takes a potshot at you, the odds are good I'll catch the bullet."

She smiled up at him. "And here I thought you'd pulled me close to you because you couldn't resist my charms."

"There's that, too."

They stepped into the café, and he immediately released his hold on her. "There's an empty booth down there." He pointed toward the back of the restaurant.

Heather headed for the booth, and as she walked down the aisle, he was acutely aware of people on either side of her watching her and whispering about her. She raised her chin and straightened her shoulders. When she reached the booth, she slid into the side facing the back of the big room.

Nick sat opposite her and grinned. "Good girl," he said. "You didn't look like a guilty woman walking in. You kept your head held high."

"And why shouldn't I?" she asked. "I am an innocent woman."

At that moment, Lucy appeared at the side of the booth. "Hey, fancy seeing you two here. Breakfast business meeting?" she asked as she placed a glass of ice water before each of them.

"A little business and a little pleasure," Nick replied and smiled at Heather once again.

"That's nice. Now, what can I get for you two?" Lucy asked.

They both ordered coffee, and he got the breakfast special of two eggs, hash browns, sausage and a side of biscuits and gravy. She ordered one egg, bacon and toast. Lucy served their coffee and then left to put their orders in.

"Tell me more about yourself," Nick said.

"What do you want to know?"

"I know you live in the swamp. Do you like it there?"

"Absolutely. It's in my blood…in my very soul. I love being someplace where it's so green, and I even find most of the animals there quite fascinating. The people there are all my family, and they are the kindest, most real people you ever want to meet."

"I'd like to meet some of your friends," he replied. He told himself it was strictly business, but the truth was he'd like to see her in her own element. The way her features had lit up just talking about it had only emphasized her beauty.

"I could arrange a little get-together if you're really interested in meeting them," she said.

"I would definitely be interested," he replied.

"Then how about the day after tomorrow you meet me at the parking lot at the swamp entrance around six thirty in the evening. I'll lead you in, and I'll get my friends to be there so you can meet them all."

He grinned at her. "Okay, it's a date."

Her cheeks pinkened slightly, and she quickly took a sip

of her coffee. "Now, tell me something about you. Are you close to your parents?"

The question surprised him, and he hesitated a moment before answering. "It's complicated," he finally replied truthfully. "I would love to be really close to them, but they have always been distant and very busy with their own lives. They travel a lot, and I was mostly raised by nannies."

Her gaze softened sympathetically. "Oh, I'm so sorry."

"Don't be. I survived. I heard from Etienne that you lost both your parents. I'm so sorry for your loss," he said.

"Thank you," she replied.

At that moment, Lucy reappeared with their breakfast orders. "Is there anything else I can get for you?" she asked once their plates were before them.

"I think we're good," Nick replied. "Thanks, Lucy."

"My pleasure," she replied. "Heather, we'll talk later," she added and then left their booth once again.

"I was very close with my parents," Heather said, picking up the conversation where they had left off. "I miss them a lot, especially now. I wish they were here to give me advice and support. But thank goodness I have my friends."

"Well, that's good."

"Do you have siblings?" she asked.

"No siblings," he replied. "And I know you don't have any, either. So, what do you like to do in your free time?" he asked.

She laughed. It was a musical, attractive sound. "To be honest, I don't even know how to answer that. I like to read and I love getting ice cream. Lucy and I hang out a lot, but most nights by the time I get home from the shop, I don't do much of anything. I have a lot of quiet nights by myself."

"We need to change that. You can't be all work and no play. Now, we'd better eat before this all gets cold."

As they ate, they small-talked about the hot and humid weather that late August always brought, what was going on in town and favorite kinds of music they enjoyed.

She was incredibly easy to talk to, and he found her more and more attractive as the breakfast continued. He told her his favorite dishes to cook, and she told him she thought her fried fish couldn't be beat.

"Ah, but you haven't tasted my chicken piccata yet," he replied with a challenging grin at her.

"And you haven't tasted my smothered skillet steak," she countered, her eyes glittering with what appeared to be suppressed laughter. "Besides, I'm at a distinct disadvantage here because I can only cook on an electric two-burner. I don't have the luxury of an oven or a microwave at my disposal, but I believe I could still beat you at making a tasty dish cooking without them."

He laughed, delighted by her challenging spirit. "We'll have to plan a cook-off in the near future."

"Just tell me when," she replied with another one of her charming laughs.

They lingered over coffee as if both of them were reluctant for the meal to end. He knew he was reluctant to leave as he was definitely enjoying the conversation.

They talked about favorite ice cream flavors and how much she enjoyed dancing. He told her about having two left feet on the dance floor and how much he liked to play chess.

"Bruno and I often play chess when we aren't working a case," he said.

"I've never learned how to play. Maybe you could teach me, and in return I'll teach you how to tear up the dance floor."

He laughed again. "I have a feeling I could teach you chess much quicker than you could teach me to dance."

"I don't know, you might find me a really good teacher, and before long you'll be dancing with the best of them," she replied.

His phone rang, and he pulled it out of his pocket and checked the identification. It was Etienne. "Excuse me," he said to Heather. "I really should take this call."

He'd almost forgotten that Heather was his client and not just a pretty, quick-witted woman he was having a breakfast date with. But seeing Etienne's name slammed him back to reality.

"What's up?" he answered. He listened to what the lawman had to say and then hung up and gazed at Heather solemnly. "Etienne just told me that both of Wesley's sons have solid alibis for the time of the shooting yesterday."

Her eyes appeared to darken as she held his gaze. "So who shot at me?" Her lower lip trembled.

God, he hated to see her so frightened, and he knew what he was about to tell her would only frighten her more. "I think it's very possible it's the person who killed Wesley. He intended for you to die in that alley, but you didn't. He's probably afraid of what you might remember about that night, that maybe you'll remember him being with you in that alley when Wesley was killed."

"But I don't remember him," she replied dismally.

"He doesn't know that, and so he sees you as a threat." He motioned to Lucy for their check. "It's vital that you keep trying to remember. Even the smallest detail might help us to identify him."

As Lucy arrived with their bill, Heather pulled her purse

into her lap. "Heather, this is on me. I invited you to breakfast, so I pay."

She hesitated and then nodded. "Okay, just this one time."

Nick paid and they exited the café. Once again, he placed his arm around her shoulders and hugged her close to him until she was safe in the passenger seat of his car.

"I don't want you working at your shop until this issue is resolved," he said as he headed back to his office. "Do you feel safe in your shanty?"

"I do," she replied. "My shanty is deep enough in that it would be hard to find for anyone."

"Then you need to sit tight there. If I need to speak to you, I'll come to you. I can meet you at the parking lot, and you can lead me in until I learn the way to your place."

"That's a lot of trouble for you," she said, obviously unhappy with the entire situation. "And I have people who come into the shop on a regular basis to get their fresh herbs. Nick, they depend on me for them."

He parked the car in front of his office. He unbuckled his seat belt and then turned to look at her. "Are those people worth your life? Heather, a man who cold-bloodedly stabbed another man and set you up to take the fall is now potentially after you. We can't know from what direction this danger might come. If you're sure you are safe in your shanty, then that's where you need to stay until Etienne gets this man arrested. People can do without their fresh herbs until we know you're safe."

"I'll stay at my shanty because I decide," she said a bit sharply.

Had he come off condescending or too domineering? That was the last thing he'd intended. He couldn't help himself. He reached out and caressed his fingers down the side of her face. "Heather, you're what matters here, not the people who frequent your shop or anyone else."

He pulled his hand back. God, what was wrong with him? Here they were talking about a killer after her, and what he really wanted to do in this moment was pull her into his arms and kiss her until all the danger had passed.

"Okay," she replied in capitulation. "I'll sit tight in my shanty until something changes."

"Good, and now I'll follow you to the parking lot at the swamp," he replied.

"My car is parked up there." She pointed up the street, and he saw her vehicle against the curb about three spaces up. He buckled up and then started his car again and pulled up next to hers.

She unbuckled and then grabbed her keys from her purse.

"Thank you for breakfast," she said as she opened his car door and prepared to leave.

"I enjoyed it. And in the meantime, I'll be in touch with you by phone with any updates in the case. I know it's ridiculous to say, but try not to worry."

She offered him a small smile. "Okay, and while I'm at it, I'll try not to breathe, either. Thank you for breakfast, Nick. I really enjoyed it."

"Me, too. I'll definitely see you the day after tomorrow."

She nodded and then got out of his car and into hers. He followed her out of town, his gaze shooting left and right looking for any sign of impending danger that might come her way.

He'd hoped the person who had shot at her the day before had been one of Wesley's sons, and Etienne would be able to immediately arrest the guilty party. Unfortunately, it hadn't been one of the sons, and it was a good bet it had been Wesley's murderer.

If he'd had any doubt about her innocence before, it was gone now. His worry now wasn't just keeping her out of prison, it was keeping her alive.

HEATHER WALKED THROUGH the shanty, checking to make sure everything was ready for an evening with her friends… an evening when Nick would be here.

Nick…even with everything that was going on in her life, she couldn't stop thinking about him and not just as her lawyer, but rather as a very handsome man she was definitely attracted to.

She'd enjoyed the breakfast she'd shared with him so much. She'd found him warm with a wonderful sense of humor. She'd been drawn to him so much, and when he'd caressed the side of her face, sparks of desire had shot off inside her. And she thought maybe he was drawn to her as well. She saw it in his eyes and had felt it in his touch.

She checked the time and then went into her bedroom, where there was a floor-length mirror on the back of her closet door. She was clad in a pair of jeans that fit her body to perfection, and a red, off-the-shoulder blouse that she knew looked good on her. She'd left her long hair loose, and her makeup was light and natural-looking.

The shanty was completely clean, and she had snacks ready to serve her guests, and it was almost six thirty, the time she and Nick had confirmed earlier in the day through a phone call. Everything was prepared, and she was ready for a nice little house party.

It would be nice to see people. The hours of the days all alone in her shanty had been lonely. However, during that time she'd deep-cleaned the shanty, had read two romance books and had spent a lot of time fishing off her back deck.

The time might have been lonely, but it was also peaceful and restful. She had a feeling she'd need plenty of energy going forward.

She left the shanty and headed down the narrow trails that would take her to the parking lot area. She couldn't help the edge of both excitement and nervousness that bubbled in her veins. She always enjoyed getting together with her neighbors and friends, but her excitement and nervous energy tonight was because Nick would be there.

What would he think about her shanty? More importantly, how would he and her friends interact? Only time would tell.

She moved confidently through the trails, having lived in the swamp all her life. It took her about ten minutes to reach the clearing. Nick was already there. He wore a wide smile as he got out of his car.

He looked hotter than she'd ever seen him. He was clad in a pair of jeans that fit him as if specifically made for him. He also wore a royal blue polo shirt that showed off his broad shoulders and matched his gorgeous blue eyes.

"Good evening, Heather," he greeted her, causing a wealth of warmth to suffuse her.

"Hi, yourself," she replied.

"It's good to see you alive and well," he said as he approached where she stood.

"So far, so good," she replied. "Are you ready to enter the jungle I call home?"

"Ready and willing," he said.

"Then just follow me." She turned and reentered the narrow paths that would take them back to her home. "Have you ever been in the swamp before?" she asked as they walked.

"No. I've represented a lot of clients from here, but they've always come to me in my office. This is a whole new experience for me."

"I hope you find it a pleasant one," she replied. He walked close enough to her that she could smell the heady scent of his cologne.

"So far, so good," he replied, making her laugh.

She continued to lead him, showing him where to jump to avoid dark pools of water and to duck under the lacy Spanish moss that hung low from some of the trees.

Finally, her shanty came into view. The four-room wooden structure stood on stilts and had trim painted in a dark green that made it meld into the greenery all around it. The early evening sunlight painted everything with a soft, golden glow, making it look like an enchanted cottage.

Together they went across the bridge to the porch that held a rocking chair. She often sat on the porch in the early evenings and watched as daytime animals went to bed and the nighttime animals came out to play.

In the mornings, she sometimes drank her first cup of coffee sitting in the rocking chair as the swamp all around her awakened for the day. It was so beautiful here in the mornings. She unlocked the front door and then opened it and ushered him inside.

"This is really nice," he said as he looked around. She followed his gaze and tried to see the place through his eyes. A tan sofa sat in place in front of the large window. Throw pillows in deep green, brown and rust decorated the sofa. A matching tan chair faced the sofa and a small pot-bellied stove and a bookshelf full of books completed the living room.

Beneath the furniture was a large, braided rug that she

and her mother had made together. It was also in the earth-toned colors she loved. To her, the room felt cozy and inviting, and she was pleased to see both a hint of surprise and approval in his eyes. "If you don't mind, can I see the rest of the place?" he asked.

"Of course." She took him to the kitchen area, where much of the space was dedicated to fledgling plants growing. She then showed him her bedroom, where the queen-size bed was covered with a green-flowered spread and the top of her dresser held a jewelry holder and her lotions and perfume. Next was the small bathroom that held only a stool and a sink.

"And I have a shower on the back deck," she explained.

"Then you have water service here?" he asked in surprise.

"I wish," she replied with a laugh. "Everything runs on complicated systems using filtration, rainwater and bottled water. Please, have a seat," she said as they returned to the living room. "The drink of the night is beer. Can I get you one?"

"That would be great," he replied and sat in one corner of the sofa.

"Anything new in the case?" she asked as she handed him a chilled bottle of beer from her cooler.

"No, but for tonight we aren't going to talk about any of it. Tonight, we only talk about pleasant things, deal?"

"Deal," she readily agreed.

He twisted the beer top to open it. "So, tell me who all I'll be meeting tonight," he asked and then took a drink of the beer.

She sank down in the chair facing him. "You already know Lucy, and she'll be here. Then there's my closest neighbors on the right side of me, Louis and Becca

Bergeron, and the neighbor on my left, Travon Guidry." Before she could say anything more, a knock fell on her door and Lucy came inside.

"I come bearing gifts," she said. She had a bag from the grocery store in her hands. "Seven-layer dip and a bag of chips." She handed the bag to Heather. "Good evening, Mr. Monroe," she said.

"Hi, Lucy, and please make it Nick," he replied.

"Have a seat, Lucy, and I'll grab you a beer," Heather said.

"That sounds great," Lucy replied and sat on the opposite side of the sofa from Nick.

Within minutes, her shanty was filled with her friends and neighbors. There was a total of nine people. She introduced each one of them to Nick, and then they sat on the floor and on the folding chairs she used in her kitchen. Most all of them had brought snacks or additional beer, so there was plenty to eat and drink.

"So, are you going to get our girl off these ridiculous charges against her?" Charles Landry asked. Charles was a big man who often brought Heather fish that he'd caught. He also caught gators for a living. "We all know she's innocent."

"Absolutely, I intend to get her off," Nick replied. "But Heather and I agreed earlier that we're not going to talk about any of that this evening. I'm just looking forward to getting to know you all better."

"Personally, my most favorite topic to talk about is me," Mollie LeBlanc quipped, making everyone laugh. "So, let me kick this off. I'm twenty-six years old and work as a clerk in the grocery store, but secretly I'm waiting for a rich man to sweep me off my feet and get me out of the swamp, preferably to Paris or London."

"Ah, don't listen to her," Becca replied. "What she really wants is to find a good swamp man like I did." She cast an adoring look at her husband, Louis.

"Are you married, Nick?" Brianna Ravines asked.

"No, and I don't have a significant other, either," he replied.

"Well, in that case." Mollie batted her eyes at him. "I've always been partial to lawyers."

Once again everyone laughed. The snacks were brought out to the coffee table, and the conversations continued to flow easily. Heather was pleased that her friends appeared to like Nick, who seemed to be enjoying himself. She felt his gaze lingering on her often, and each time a tiny thrill shot off inside her.

As the evening light began to fade, Heather got up and lit the various kerosene and battery-operated lamps around the room, giving it a soft glow as darkness fell outside.

Charles regaled them with his latest gator-catching adventures, and then Nick shared some stories from when he had been young and had worked as a private investigator for a brief time.

"A man hired me to spy on his girlfriend because he thought she was cheating on him. I watched her for several days, and then one night around midnight, I saw her going into her second-story apartment with a man who wasn't her boyfriend. I was well prepared. I had a ladder in my pickup, and I put it up against the side of the building and climbed up so I could see inside her apartment." Nick paused a moment to take a sip of his beer and then continued.

"I was only up there for about ten minutes when the boyfriend arrived on the scene. It was so dark he didn't recognize me. He thought I was your average peeping tom. He dragged me off the ladder and started beating the hell out of me until he finally realized I was the man he had hired to spy on her, but that was the end of my days as a private investigator. I decided it was too dangerous for me."

They all laughed. Heather found this side of Nick so appealing. He was vulnerable and open to everyone. He'd told her he could be a real jerk, but she found that hard to believe. He was so warm and kind to her friends.

It was after that when the conversation turned darker. "I heard through the grapevine this morning that Willie Trahan didn't come home from night fishing last night," Travon said.

"The Swamp Soul Stealer," Lucy whispered the words as if saying the name too loud might conjure up the monster.

"We don't know for sure the monster got him," Mollie protested. "Maybe he just got his nose in some of Jackson's sauce and is somewhere sleeping it off."

"Jackson must be in the same condition because I'm surprised he didn't show up here tonight," Heather said. "He almost always comes around when we all get together."

"I'll check on him before going home tonight. Since he lives alone, nobody would know if he was missing or in trouble," Louis said.

It was about a half an hour later when everyone began to leave. Heather stood at the door to tell her friends goodnight and to be safe on the way home. She always worried when they left her house after dark. Nighttime was when the monster came out to kidnap people.

Lucy was the last one to leave, and once she was gone, Heather and Nick were left alone. He got up from the sofa, bent over and began closing up chip bags that were left open on the coffee table.

"Nick, please leave all that," she protested. "I have all night to do cleanup."

He straightened and smiled at her, the smile that dizzied her senses and filled her with an amazing warmth that flowed through her. "Then I suppose I should get out of here, too," he said.

"I'll walk you out."

He frowned and took a step closer to her. "I don't like to think of you walking back here all alone in the dark."

"I can move through the swamp pretty silently, and if I were to be chased, I can either run really fast or find a good hiding place to wait until any danger passes." She smiled. "I'm used to being in the swamp in the daytime and in the night. Besides, I have a murderer trying to kill me, so the Swamp Soul Stealer doesn't bother me at all."

"That's not funny," he replied and took yet another step toward her. His eyes shone with a light she'd never seen before, a light that made her breath catch in the back of her throat and her mouth go dry.

He raised a hand and reached out and stroked it through her hair. "I've been wanting to do that all night long," he murmured softly. "Heather, I'm feeling very unprofessional at the moment."

"And exactly what does that mean?" she asked half breathlessly.

"It means I would really like to kiss you right now," he replied.

"That's nice because I would really like you to kiss me right now," she said.

He gathered her into his arms and took her mouth with his in a kiss that shot a delicious pleasure from her head to her toes. His lips were soft yet held a hunger and demand that was intoxicating.

She opened her mouth to him to allow the kiss to deepen, and his tongue slid in to dance with her own. He pulled her even closer, and she melded herself to him as the kiss intensified and continued.

Heather had never experienced the desire that flooded through her before. She had never felt this level of fire in her veins in the past.

It was him who ended the kiss and took a step back from her. His eyes still shone with what she believed was a hunger for her. He released a deep breath and slowly shook his head. "I'm so sorry, I... I don't know what came over me."

"It's okay," she replied and smiled up at him. "Whatever came over you, came over me as well."

"And now you'd better walk me out of here before it overcomes us again," he replied.

Minutes later, they were on the narrow paths back to the parking area. She had a small flashlight, mostly to light his way through the tangled marsh. A full moon helped as well, shining down a silvery illumination where it pierced through the tree leaves.

They didn't speak but rather moved quietly while the swamp filled with the night sounds of bullfrog croaks and night creatures rustling through the underbrush.

They finally broke through to the clearing. "I really enjoyed meeting your friends, Heather," he said softly when they reached his car. "You are right, they seem like a bunch of warm and real people."

"I think so. And you were a charming addition to the group," she replied.

"Thank you for inviting me into your world." He leaned

over and kissed her tenderly on her forehead. "Now you get home safely. In fact, why don't you call me so I know for sure you got home safe and sound."

"Okay, I can do that," she replied. "Good night, Nick."

He opened his car door. "Don't forget to call me."

"I won't."

She watched as he got into his car and pulled away from the parking lot. She couldn't remember the last time anyone had worried about her getting home safely. It felt good… really good.

She turned and headed back home. She moved as quietly as possible, always aware of the potential for danger from the monster who hunted at night.

When she arrived home, she grabbed her phone and made the call to Nick. It was a brief call; she just told him she was safely home, and then they hung up.

Once the call ended, she sank down on the sofa and thought about the night that had just passed. Nick had surprised her on so many levels. She hadn't expected him to be so open and warm to her friends. And she definitely hadn't expected that kiss.

Even thinking about it now shot rivulets of heat through her. She had only dated two men in the years before her father had fallen ill, and none of the kisses she had received from either of them had stirred her so deeply, even though she had given up her virginity to one of them.

Nick was from the upper crust of Crystal Cove. He was an intelligent, incredibly handsome man who could probably have any eligible woman in town, yet he had kissed her with an undeniable passion.

Was he just toying with the swamp woman as a novelty? Several of her girlfriends had shared the experience of being used by some man from town. There was even a legend of a young woman named Marianne who fell in love with a town man. She was only nineteen years old at the time, and she was all alone in the world after her parents had died in a car wreck.

Marianne had poured all her love into the man, and when she discovered herself pregnant, she couldn't wait to tell him. She had been sure he loved her, too. But when she told him the news, he confessed that he was just using her as a sidepiece while he courted a proper, respectable woman in town.

He told her he wanted nothing to do with her or the baby. Marianne had been devastated, and a week later her body was found hanging from a tree in the swamp. Marianne's story was a cautionary tale mothers in the swamp told their daughters.

Heather didn't want to believe Nick was that kind of man. She needed him to keep her out of prison, but she wouldn't mind if he cared a little about her in the process. No, she didn't believe Nick was the type of man to toy with a woman's affection, but ultimately only time would tell.

HE'D WATCHED THEM saying goodbye at the attorney's car in the clearing. He'd been in the parking lot for some time, staring at the swamp's tangled entrance.

The last thing he wanted to do was go into the swamp with its snakes and gators, but he needed to face his fear of the place to find out exactly where she lived.

He hadn't really expected to see her tonight, but when she'd walked out with Nick Monroe, his heartbeat accelerated and his blood began to boil. She needed to die. But he wasn't ready to take her down tonight.

She might get away from him and hide in the swamp, and the last thing he wanted to do was hunt for a woman in the dark in the swamp. Besides, he hadn't brought his mask with him. He would be vulnerable to someone seeing him and being able to identify him.

No, tonight was strictly a recognizance mission. When the attorney finally left, she turned and headed back into the swamp. He got out of his car and quickly followed her, keeping his distance so she wouldn't discover his presence behind her.

He followed her up one trail and then on another one, trying to remember the exact paths she took so he could repeat this trek when he was ready.

He tried not to freak out as rustling sounds came from the underbrush on either side of him and Spanish moss danced on his face like a thousand spider webs. How could anyone live in a place like this? A place where there were wild boars and all kinds of animals that could hurt or kill a person. Unfortunately, he couldn't depend on a gator eating her. He had to take care of her himself.

Finally, he watched her cross a bridge and go into a shanty. She was now home, and he now knew where she lived. As he turned to make his way back to where his car was parked, his heart beat with excitement.

Now that he knew where she lived, he and a couple of his buddies would pay her a little visit very soon. And when they left her shanty, she would be dead and no longer a loose end for him to worry about.

## *Chapter Seven*

Nick and Bruno sat down the street from a run-down house where rumor had it a lot of drug trafficking occurred. It was after midnight, and so far, there had been little happening.

The house was located in a relatively nice neighborhood. The suspected drug house's shoddy condition spoke of neglect and was definitely an eyesore amid the other well-kept homes on the block.

What Nick was trying to do was identify the drug players in town. It was quite possible one of them had murdered Wesley and set up Heather to either die or be arrested. At the very least, one of them could possibly confirm Wesley as a dope dealer. It wasn't Nick's job to solve the crime, but at this point, he believed solving it was the only way to keep Heather out of prison.

"We'll give it another hour or so and then call it a night," he said to the big man in the passenger seat.

"Whatever you decide. I'm just here to protect your ass in case you decide to do something stupid," Bruno replied.

Nick laughed. "I'm not usually a stupid person."

"No, but I've also never seen you so giddy about a client before."

"Giddy? I certainly have not been giddy," he protested with a small laugh.

"I don't know what else you would call it," Bruno replied. "All you talked about yesterday was how much you liked her friends, how cozy and nice you found her shanty. Oh, and let's not forget how hot she looked in a pair of jeans and the red blouse that exposed the tops of her shoulders. Face it, man. You are definitely smitten."

"I… I think I might be," Nick admitted. There was no question that he had been wildly attracted to her the night before last when he'd seen her so relaxed and open among her friends.

The timid, frightened woman he had first met was gone, taken over by a confident, strong woman who was obviously loved and cherished by her friends.

There was definitely no question he was wildly attracted to her. In truth, he couldn't remember ever feeling so physically drawn to a woman. The kiss they had shared had been amazing, and he couldn't help but look forward to a time when he could kiss her again. So yeah, he was definitely smitten and probably a fool as well.

"I just don't want you to get hurt," Bruno said. "You've already been through the wringer once with a client relationship gone bad."

Nick turned to look at his friend in the dim light from a nearby streetlight. "Do you really still believe Heather is guilty? Even with this drug connection taking shape?"

"It doesn't matter at this point whether she's guilty or not. What matters is she's a vulnerable woman who is depending on you. The power balance between you is off. It's possible any feelings she might develop for you will be born out of deep gratitude and nothing more, and once you win her case, she'll be gone from your life."

Nick frowned and once again directed his gaze toward the suspected drug house. After a moment, he returned his gaze to Bruno. "It's not that deep, bro." Just because he desired Heather, it didn't mean he was going to lose his heart to her. He simply refused to do that. It was just physical attraction.

Bruno raised his thick, black brow. "Whatever you say, dude."

NICK THOUGHT ABOUT Bruno's words the next morning as he drove to the police station. He believed the softness she had in her eyes when she gazed at him wasn't mere gratitude. He definitely believed the desire he had tasted on her lips was real and had nothing to do with the client-attorney relationship.

He'd spoken to her half a dozen times since the evening he had spent at her house. Some of their conversations had been light and easy, about things like how she was spending her time at home. They'd also had deeper conversations about the people they had dated in the past, among other subjects.

He was surprised she'd only had two fairly brief relationships before, and he'd shared about some of the women he had gone out with, however he hadn't told her about Delia. For some reason, he'd been reluctant to share anything about the only relationship he'd experienced where his heart had been truly broken.

Shoving all thoughts of romance past and present out of his mind, he parked in front of the police station and exited his car.

He needed to have a serious chat with the chief of police

about this whole drug connection. Now that he knew that it was possible Wesley had been into drugs, he intended to lean heavily on Etienne to look into it.

He walked into the lobby, and an officer he didn't know greeted him. The baby-faced young man wore a badge that identified him as J.T. Caldwell.

"I'm here to see Chief Savoie," Nick said.

"And you are?"

"Nick Monroe."

"I'll see if he's available right now." The officer disappeared through a door in the back of his area. A few moments later, he opened the door that led to the inner rooms.

"He's in his office," J.T. said.

"Thanks, I know where it is," Nick replied.

"Come in," Etienne's voice drifted out of the door at Nick's knock.

"You look like hell," Nick said once he was seated before his friend. Lines of stress were evident on Etienne's face, and his eyes appeared dull. The man looked utterly exhausted.

"Well, thanks," Etienne replied. He raked a hand through his thick, dark hair. "I haven't been getting much sleep lately, and to make matters worse another man has disappeared from the swamp."

"Willie Trahan," Nick replied.

Etienne looked at him sharply. "How did you know that? So far, we've managed to keep it out of the news."

Nick explained about sharing an evening with Heather and her friends, and them all talking about the disappearance.

Etienne released a deep sigh. "He's now listed as a missing person, but we all know this damned Swamp Stealer has taken him. So far five people are missing…three men and two women, and we still don't have a clue as to who this creep is or where he might be keeping these people. For all I know, they could all be dead or are being beaten and starved like Colette was."

"And I'm assuming she is still in the coma?"

"Yeah. God, I'm hoping she'll have some answers for us when she wakes up. Now, what can I do for you today?"

"How big is the drug problem here in Crystal Cove?"

Etienne gazed at him in surprise. "There's no question that we have a bit of a drug problem, but I wouldn't say it's huge. Why?"

"Word on the street is Wesley was not only using drugs but he was selling them as well. I now believe it was one of his drug connections who murdered him and set up Heather. I want you to reconsider the murder investigation, Etienne."

A deep frown cut across Etienne's forehead. "Nick, all you have right now is gossip and innuendo. I can't redo a murder case on that basis. Besides, right now I need all my manpower to find a missing man. Word on the street isn't good enough for this. Come back to me with some cold, hard facts about this drug thing and Wesley, and then I'll see about reinvestigating the case."

Disappointment swept through Nick. He'd hoped to get the police back involved with their powers that Nick didn't possess, but apparently that wasn't going to happen right now.

"If I were you, I'd talk to Radcliffe. Tell him your theory of the crime and see if you can convince him to drop the charges against Heather," Etienne suggested.

"Yeah, maybe I'll do that," Nick replied and got up from

his chair. "I'll talk to you later," he said and then left the police station.

*Talk to Radcliffe*. Yeah, right. Nick knew that would be a complete dead end. There was no way the prosecutor would drop the charges when there was so much direct physical evidence pointing at Heather. For him, this case looked like a slam dunk that would add to his résumé if he was successful in winning it.

Somehow, someway, they needed to find somebody who had firsthand knowledge about Wesley's drug abuse and connections. It was the only way he would for sure be able to save Heather.

Thinking of Heather as he headed back to his office, he called her number.

"Good morning, Mr. Monroe," her voice came over the line.

"Good morning to you, Ms. LaCrae," he replied. "And how did you sleep last night?"

"Like a baby," she replied. "And you?"

"Same. I've been thinking about this cooking thing, and I was wondering if maybe this Friday night you'd be up to coming to my place for a little cook-off."

"That sounds like fun, and by then I'm sure I'll be suffering badly from cabin fever and will welcome the change of scenery," she replied.

"Cabin fever that keeps you safe is a good thing," he replied.

"I know," she replied with a sigh.

"Friday night, how about I pick you up around six? I'll provide the food to cook, and we'll see who makes the best dinner. You can text me a grocery list, and I'll make sure you have everything you need."

"Sounds perfect," she said. "I look forward to it."

"Great, then I'll talk to you later," he said, and they ended the call.

He was definitely looking forward to the evening with Heather, but in the meantime, he needed to figure out a way to infiltrate the drug trade going on in Crystal Cove.

EVENING WAS TURNING into night, and Heather was preparing to go to bed. She turned on the battery-operated lamp on her nightstand and then changed from her day clothes to a comfortable lilac-colored nightshirt.

She got into bed and picked up the book she'd been reading over the past couple of days. It was a romance book, and lately it had been far too easy for her to imagine herself as the heroine and Nick as the hero.

She couldn't wait to see him again on Friday night. She'd missed seeing him over the past several days, even though they'd shared many conversations by phone.

Their relationship had deepened through those phone calls where they'd shared their past dating history, his disappointment over never having the kind of love from his parents that he'd needed as a child and her desire to one day have a family.

She had a deep belief in true love. Her parents had given her a beautiful picture in the way they had loved each other through the years until their deaths. She truly believed it had been grief that killed her mother. She had mourned so deeply at Heather's father's passing. Heather knew that her mother had just given up without the man she loved. Heather wanted that same kind of forever love for herself.

She read for a while, but eventually sleep beckoned and

she placed the book on the nightstand, and with a deep yawn, she turned out the light.

Shafts of moonlight drifted in through her window, dancing myriad shadows across her ceiling. The distant sound of water lapping and the bullfrogs' songs lulled her. She watched the shadows on the ceiling until her eyelids grew too heavy, and she succumbed to sleep.

She didn't know how long she had been asleep before she suddenly jerked awake. She bolted upright, her heartbeat thundering in her chest and a fight-or-flight adrenaline rushing through her veins. For several long moments, she didn't know what had awakened her. Had it been a horrible nightmare?

She turned on the battery-powered lantern next to the bed and looked around the room. Nothing seemed amiss. Maybe it had been a bad dream that had disrupted her sleep. She certainly had enough issues going on right now to produce a bad dream or two.

A loud boom sounded from her front door and then another boom at her back door. She jumped out of bed with a scream of fear lodged deep in her throat. Somebody was trying to break in!

She didn't need to know exactly who it was to be utterly terrified. It had to be the killer, and from the sound of it, he'd brought his friends.

Another loud bang against her front door dislodged the scream of fear that escaped her. She screamed long and loud as her brain tried to make sense of this. Oh God, she'd thought she was safe here. She'd truly believed he would never find her here in the swamp. But apparently, she had been wrong.

Frustration was added to the mix of emotions roaring inside her as she realized she'd left her purse, with her daddy's gun inside it, on the sofa in the living room. There was no way to retrieve it now. Any second, the front or the back door would come down and the men would be inside.

Once again, terror gripped her chest so tightly it was difficult to draw a breath. It held her inert in place as her brain struggled to find a solution. *Think. Think!* she commanded herself.

She couldn't even call for help because her phone was also in her purse in the living room. Damn, she had to do something. The sound of splintering wood let her know they were almost inside.

She locked the bedroom door and ran to her window and opened it. Once it was open, she began to scream again. The noise of her shrieks sent birds flying out of the tops of the trees and into the darkened skies.

The sound of more cracking wood filled the night, and then there was a faint shift in the air and she knew the door had been broken open.

Oh God, they were inside the shanty. Tears began to course down her cheeks as the first bang sounded against her bedroom door. There was only a flimsy lock on this door. It would easily be broken. They would be inside with her in the bedroom in a matter of seconds.

Sobbing, she tried to shove her dresser in front of the doorway. Bangs continued at the door, loud booms that echoed in her very soul.

"Hey, bitch, come on out," a deep voice yelled. "Come out and play with us." Ugly laughter followed the voice.

"Yeah, it's play time, and we're ready to play with you," another voice called out.

"Dead woman walking...that's what you are. But we want

to have some fun with you before we make sure you aren't walking or talking anymore." Again, laughter followed the voice.

She tried to ignore the jeers and taunts as she pushed and heaved on the dresser. She continued to sob, desperate to get the large piece of furniture in front of the doorway, but it was too heavy for her to move. The only thing she could do now was scream in abject terror.

She sank down on the edge of her bed, watching and waiting for the moment the door would come down and the men would be inside with her.

Raised voices drifted through her door. Wait...was that Louis's voice? And Travon? Oh God, had her neighbors come to help her? She jumped up off the bed and listened to the men shouting at each other. There was a scuffling sound, and then there was complete silence, except for the frantic beat of her heart.

A soft knock fell on her bedroom door. "Heather, it's safe now. You can come out." It was Becca, and Heather unlocked her door, opened it and then fell into her friend's arms, sobs of relief coursing through her.

Becca led her to the living room, where not only her neighbors Louis, Travon and Charles stood, but even Jackson, wielding a large, sturdy stick.

"I whacked one of them," the old man said. "I whacked him right over his damned head," he added proudly.

"Thank you," Heather said as she swiped the tears from her cheeks. She sank down on the sofa, and Becca sat next to her and put a comforting arm around her shoulders. The front door hung open, off the hinges, and the wood around it was splintered and broken.

"We heard your screams and knew you were in trouble.

There were three of them, Heather, and they were all wearing black ski masks over their faces," Louis explained.

"I tried to hang on to one of them so we could get an identification, but he managed to get away from me," Travon said with obvious frustration.

"I just thank you all for getting out of your beds in the middle of the night to help me," Heather said tremulously.

"You would do the same thing for any of us," Becca replied. "And now what we need to do is call the police and let them know what's happened here."

"My phone is here," Heather said and pulled her purse off the sofa and into her lap. Her fingers trembled as she took her phone out and punched in the emergency number. "We need the police," she told the dispatcher who answered. "Tell Chief Savoie that it's Heather LaCrae. Some men just broke into my shanty. I'll have somebody meet them at the parking lot to show them the way."

"That sounds like a good job for me," Jackson said once she'd hung up. "It's the one time I'll be happy to see the law."

He left the shanty, and for the first time, Heather released a tremulous sigh of relief. She was safe, but what now? "You're definitely going to need a new front door," Louis said.

"The back door is still intact," Travon said. "But your front door is a total loss. Louis and I can board it up for the time being after the police get here."

"Thank you. I don't know what I'd do without you all," Heather replied.

"You know we're all here for each other, Heather," Becca replied. She got up and went into Heather's bedroom. She returned with a robe for Heather to put on over her nightshirt.

"I'm going to try to find some boards for the front door,"

Louis said. "You guys stay here, and I'll be back in a few." The big man disappeared out the front door and into the darkness beyond.

"Who were those men?" Becca asked.

Heather released another sigh. "I believe at least one of them was the person who killed Wesley and tried to drug me to death."

"And now he's coming after you," Travon said with a frown. "He's afraid of you and what you might remember about him from the night in the bar."

Heather nodded and raised her finger to her mouth. Chewing her nails was a nasty habit and one she'd tried to quit. She'd started it when her father had fallen ill and she'd sat beside his bedside for hours on end. She only did it now when she was stressed, and she was definitely stressed out in this moment.

It took about thirty minutes for Jackson to finally walk back in, not only with three other police officers and the chief of police, but also with Nick.

The minute she saw him, she got to her feet and began to cry again. In four long strides, he was before her and gathered her into his arms. As she cried into the front of his shirt, she heard Travon explain about hearing her cries for help.

Finally, her sobs ebbed, and Nick led her back to the sofa, where he sat next to her and held her hand tightly in his. She was grateful for his support. The mere familiar scent of his cologne calmed her as she told Etienne her version of what had happened.

"I'm so sorry, Heather," Nick said softly when she was finished. "I was so sure you'd be safe here."

"I thought so, too," she replied.

"I'll have my men fingerprint the door frames to see if

we can lift anything," Etienne said. "You've all said they were wearing ski masks, but let's hope they were too stupid to wear gloves."

Louis returned and told her he had the wood necessary to board up the door. Meanwhile, she had fallen strangely numb. The sanctity of her home had been breached by a man who wanted her dead. Where could she go from here? Where could she hide? Who was this man who wanted to kill her? And what was going to happen now?

These important questions flittered through her head but could find no real purchase. It was as if her brain was on overload and had now shut down.

"Go pack a bag." Nick's deep voice penetrated through the fog.

She looked up at him in surprise. "What?"

"Go pack a big bag, you're coming home with me." He squeezed her hand and then released it. "Go on now."

She got up from the sofa and went into her bedroom. She pulled a large duffel bag from the bottom of her closet and opened it on the bed.

At the moment, the idea of staying at Nick's place was overwhelmingly appealing. Somehow, she knew instinctively that she would be safe with him.

The first thing she did was change out of her robe and nightgown and into a pair of jeans and a T-shirt. As she began to pull clothes out of her closet and pack them in her bag, she wondered how long Nick intended for her to stay with him.

Would it be just for a night or two? Yet, he'd told her to pack a big bag. Was that three outfits? Ten? She finally settled on a week's worth of clothing. She added in her toiletries and then zipped up the bag and carried it into the living room. Nick immediately got up from the sofa and took the bag from her hand. "Etienne, are we free to go?" he asked.

"Yes, we can finish up here without the two of you. If I need to speak to Heather again, I'll call and let you know," the lawman replied.

"Don't worry about your front door," Louis said. "Travon and I will take care of things here. You go on now and don't worry about any of this."

Once again, a deep gratitude for her friends brought tears to her eyes. "Thank you all," she said.

Nick threw his arm around her shoulder as they left the shanty. Despite the heat of the night, cold chills raced up and down her spine as she thought of what might have happened tonight if not for her friends. There was no doubt in her mind that if her friends hadn't intervened, she would be dead.

They didn't speak as they hurried down the paths to leave the swamp. Thankfully they encountered nobody and made it safely to Nick's car.

"You're safe now, Heather," he said once they were on their way to his house.

"Thank you," she replied. But for how long was she safe? She certainly wouldn't stay with any of her friends and bring this kind of danger to their doorsteps. It wouldn't take this person long to find her at the little local motel, so she didn't consider that an option, either.

Nick flashed her a long look. "Don't worry about anything, Heather. I've got you."

"I think I'm still in total shock," she replied honestly.

"It had to be terrifying to wake up and hear the sounds of people breaking into your home." His voice was soft with sympathy. "I'm so sorry that happened to you, and I'm so damned mad that I didn't see this coming."

They fell silent once again, and within minutes he pulled up into the driveway of a huge ranch house. It was too dark for her to see the color, but she instinctively knew it was beautiful. The garage door opened and he pulled in.

From the garage, he led her into a large, airy kitchen with attractive gray-and-black granite countertops. "Let's get you settled in for the rest of the night, and we can talk about things in the morning," he said.

From the kitchen, he led her down a long hallway and into the second room on the right. He flipped on the light switch, and a light on a nightstand came on.

The room was beautiful. The queen-size bed was covered in a royal blue bedspread, and the chest of drawers and dresser were rich polished oak. "You should be comfortable in here," he said as he set her bag on the floor next to the bed. "There's an en suite bathroom right there." He pointed to a doorway next to what she assumed was a closet door.

He walked over to where she stood and cupped her face with his hand. She turned her cheek into the warmth of the unexpected caress. "You're safe here. Now get some sleep," he said and then dropped his hand and headed to the bedroom door.

"Let me know if you need anything, otherwise I'll talk to you in the morning. Good night, Heather."

"Good night, Nick," she replied. He left the room and closed the door behind him.

Heather sank down on the edge of the bed, feeling as if she just needed a moment to breathe. She finally stood and opened her bag. She pulled out a fresh nightgown and then went into the adjoining bathroom.

It was also decorated in shades of blue, and she eyed the big tub longingly. If she got a chance before she had to leave here, she would love to take a bath.

However, that was the last thing she wanted to think about tonight. Right now, she just wanted to get into bed and forget that a man who wanted her dead had nearly succeeded tonight.

## Chapter Eight

Heather awoke slowly, the night that had passed filling her head. A cold chill swept through her as she remembered the events, but the cold slowly warmed as she also realized she was safe and sound in a bed in Nick's house. She was surprised she hadn't had nightmares all night long, but thankfully her sleep had been dreamless.

She turned over and checked the alarm clock on the nightstand. Last time she had looked at it, it had been a little after three, and now it was a quarter to eight.

Despite the relatively short night, she was ready to get up and face the day. Twenty minutes later, she was clad in a pair of jeans and a light blue T-shirt. She'd washed her face, brushed her teeth and hair, and when she was done, she opened the bedroom door and stepped out into the hallway.

The scent of coffee drifted in the air, letting her know Nick was awake and up. She walked into the large living room and looked around curiously. She hadn't noticed much about it last night when she'd come in.

A large, black overstuffed sofa sat opposite a fireplace, above which a huge television was mounted on the wall. A matching love seat made an L-shaped sitting area. The round coffee table was glass and shiny chrome and held an abstract silver sculpture in the center. There was also a little minibar built into one corner of the room. It was also a lot of chrome and shiny glass. The whole room exuded a quiet wealth and a classiness she found very attractive.

She walked on into the kitchen, where Nick stood at the stove with his back to her as he flipped bacon strips in his skillet. For just a moment, she didn't announce her presence but rather stood and drank in his appearance.

Nobody wore jeans as well as Nick did. They hugged his long legs and cupped his perfect butt. His white T-shirt stretched taut across his shoulders and exposed nicely muscled biceps.

"Good morning," she finally said.

He whirled around and cast her a grin. "Good morning to you. Coffee is in the pot, and I left a cup for you to use there on the counter. I wasn't sure what you'd want for breakfast, but no breakfast is really complete without bacon."

"Please don't go to any trouble on my account, just coffee is fine with me," she replied.

"Nonsense, everyone should start their day with a good breakfast," he said and turned back to the skillet. She walked over to the counter where the coffee maker sat and poured herself a cup of the hot, dark brew. There was a sugar bowl and a little pitcher of cream, and she added a bit of both to her cup.

"Have a seat," he said.

She sat at the large, round glass-topped kitchen table. "Your home is absolutely beautiful," she said.

"Thanks. Most of that is due to an interior decorator who helped me with it all. How did you sleep?" He began to take the bacon out of the pan and placed the crispy strips onto an awaiting plate.

"I slept surprisingly well," she replied. "What about you? Did you sleep okay?"

"I did." He slid the skillet off the burner, poured the excess grease into an awaiting can and then turned to look at her. "Now, one of the most important questions of the day... how do you like your eggs?"

"Any way is fine with me."

"Then how does a mushroom, red pepper and cheese omelet sound?"

"It sounds like a lot of work for you," she said.

He grinned, the dimpled smile causing a spark to shoot off in her heart. "It's no trouble, and I have to confess it's more for me than for you. I love my omelets."

She laughed. "Okay, then. I would love an omelet for breakfast."

"Great."

She watched silently as he went to the refrigerator and grabbed a red pepper and a carton of mushrooms. He washed and then began to dice up the vegetables. He added a couple leaves of sweet basil from the plant she had given him.

"I've never had a man cook for me before," she said once he had the egg concoction in the skillet.

"And I've never had a woman cook for me," he replied.

"Really? None of the women you dated in the past ever offered to fix you a home-cooked meal?" She looked at him in surprise.

"The women I dated were more interested in keeping up with the latest styles and going out to dinner than eating in."

"That's too bad," she replied.

The small chitchat was pleasant, but a bit of anxiety still twisted in her stomach as bigger questions than those about past dating experiences worked around in her head. Questions like how long would she be staying here? When he'd signed on to be her lawyer, he certainly hadn't agreed to her being a guest in his home indefinitely.

Within minutes the omelets were ready, along with the bacon and toast. "This looks delicious," she said as he sat down across from her.

"Dig in while it's hot," he replied. "How are you feeling after last night?" he asked, and then he crunched down on a crispy piece of bacon.

"I'm still in shock that it all happened. I thought for sure I was safe in my shanty. I just wonder how he found me," she replied.

"He had to have followed you in at some point," he replied.

"He's definitely persistent," she said darkly. She fought off a new chill. The idea of this man following her anywhere was horrifying. And what made it even more horrifying was she hadn't even known she was being followed.

"You have him scared," he said.

She released a small laugh. "Trust me, he has me scared, too."

"Well, you don't have to be scared any longer. I have a good security system, and you'll be safe here until Etienne gets the bad guy behind bars," he replied.

"But, Nick, we don't know when that might happen," she protested. "It could be days...weeks."

He reached across the table and covered her hand with his. "Heather, it doesn't matter how long it takes, you will stay here with me until your life is no longer in jeopardy. Bruno and I can keep you safe. In fact, he should be here in just a few minutes so we can go over logistics. Now, take that frown off your pretty face and finish your omelet. We've got you covered." He pulled his hand back.

"I don't know how I'll ever repay you for your kindness," she said.

He smiled. "You don't get it. Heather, I don't care about repayment for anything. I care about you, and I protect what I care about. Now finish eating before Bruno gets here."

Her heart swelled with relief at the knowledge that he'd allow her to stay here indefinitely. She certainly hadn't expected his kindness and his desire to keep her safe.

They finished the meal, and then she insisted on helping with the cleanup. As they worked to clear the table, their conversation remained light. They talked about favorite foods they liked to cook and various other recipes. He had just put the last dish into the dishwasher when a knock fell on the front door.

"That will be Bruno," Nick said. "Come on, let's move into the living room. Feel free to bring your coffee with you." He picked up his cup, and she picked up hers and followed him out of the kitchen.

She sank down in one corner of the sofa while he walked to the front door. She tensed slightly as Nick came back to the living room followed by the big private investigator. Surely Bruno would believe in her innocence now after what had happened last night.

"Heard you had some trouble last night," he said to her as he sat on the love seat.

"Definitely," she replied, fighting off a new chill as she thought of the night before.

Nick sat on the sofa close to her. "I've told her she'll be safe here until Etienne gets the bastard behind bars. But I'll have to depend on you to help me out with that."

"Whatever you need," Bruno replied without hesitation.

"I don't have a lot going on at the office right now, but I do have a couple of cases that will need some attention," Nick continued. "I don't want Heather left here alone, so I figured when I absolutely have to be in the office in town, you could be here with her."

"I can do that," Bruno replied.

"Is all that really necessary?" Heather asked, hating the fact that from the sounds of it the two men would be babysitting her. "Surely I'll be fine here alone when you need to be at the office," she said to Nick. "You said you had a good security system."

"But it's not infallible," he replied. "Heather, those men found you at your shanty deep in the swamp. They will have no problem finding you here," Nick replied.

His words shot a new chill up her spine. Of course, he was right. Those men probably already knew she was here. They were probably someplace nearby plotting her demise at this very moment.

"I'm in," Bruno said. "Just tell me when I need to be here, and I will."

Nick smiled at his friend. "I knew I could depend on you. I've got nothing going on for the next couple of days. What work I have to do, I can do from here. But there are a couple of clients who eventually I will need to meet in my office."

"Got it," Bruno said with a nod.

"I didn't even offer you a cup of coffee," Nick said. "Can I get you one?"

"Sure, I could drink a cup," Bruno replied.

Nick got up and left the room, and an awkward silence fell between her and Bruno. She took a sip of her coffee and then lowered the cup and eyed him. "Now do you believe I'm innocent of the charges against me?" she asked.

"Yeah, I think you're innocent," he replied.

She breathed a sigh of relief. For some reason, it was important that he believed her. However, she still felt a hint of disapproval wafting from the big man, and she didn't understand it.

At that moment, Nick came back into the room with a cup of the brew for Bruno. For the next few minutes, the two men talked about the case and the theories of who might be after Heather.

She sat silently and listened to the men talk about what her life had become. Murder and drugs. How had this ever happened to her? That night at the Voodoo Lounge, all she'd wanted was a relaxing drink after work, but instead she'd been set up by the real killer and now that killer was after her.

A new memory suddenly speared through her brain. "He was rather short but hefty, and he had dark hair," she said with sudden excitement. "I remember now...the man who had heated words with Wesley. But I don't know his name. I'd never seen him before."

"Okay, that's helpful," Nick said. "Would you recognize him if you saw him again?"

"Yes...yes, I believe I would," she replied.

"At least that helps us cut down the suspect list a bit. If that man killed Wesley, then we know it wasn't a tall blond," Bruno replied. "We need to see if we can somehow identify that man. I'll starting asking more questions of the people who were there that night. Surely somebody knows this guy and noticed the two men arguing."

"If they were arguing over drugs, then it's possible we'll

see this guy at that house we watched the other night," Nick said.

"What house?" she asked curiously.

"A house where it's rumored a lot of drug trafficking goes on," Bruno said.

"Maybe it's time we watch the house again and bring Heather with us," Nick said to Bruno. "In fact, we should plan to watch that house every night in hopes of seeing that man there."

"Sounds like a plan. If she can point out this guy, then I can work on identifying him," Bruno said.

"So, would you be up to that?" Nick asked her. His blue eyes gazed at her searchingly.

"I'm up for whatever gets the killer behind bars," she replied despite the new chill that danced up her spine. Surveilling a drug house for a killer seemed highly dangerous. What if they were spotted by the bad guys? They could all be killed.

Still, she would agree to almost anything to keep the warm light in Nick's eyes shining on her.

BRUNO LEFT A few minutes later, and Nick returned to his seat in the living room. "I've got to tell you, Heather. I admire how strong you've been through all of this. Most people would have crumbled into a million pieces, but you've stayed steady and strong."

She released a small laugh. "I'm not the type to curl up in a ball and cry, although I've certainly done plenty of crying into the front of your shirts."

He smiled. "And I haven't minded it a bit." He thought about those moments when he'd held her in his arms. Suddenly the memory of the kiss they had shared filled his mind. There was nothing he'd like more than to repeat that experience with her.

"I was thinking maybe tonight I could cook for you. I'll give you the home-cooked meal you've never gotten before," she said.

"I'd be a fool to say no to that," he replied.

"I'll have to see what you have here for me to cook."

"We can go into the kitchen and check it out right now," he replied. "Ready?" He stood.

"Ready," she replied. She also stood with her empty coffee cup in hand.

Together they went back into the kitchen, where she quickly rinsed her cup in the sink and then turned to look at him. He beckoned her to the refrigerator and opened the freezer door.

She looked inside and he stood just behind her. She smelled wonderfully good...of clean woman and the warm perfume he'd come to identify as specifically her own.

"I've got steaks and pork chops. There's a roast and chicken breasts among other things," he said, trying to ignore how her nearness affected him. He had to stop thinking of her as a desirable woman and instead think of her as a client and nothing more.

"I can make you some really good pork chops for tonight," she said and pulled the package of three chops out. He stepped back, and she closed the freezer door and set the package of meat on top of the counter to thaw.

He needed to get a little distance from her before he pulled her into his arms and kissed her until they were both mindless.

"I think I'll take care of a little work in my office. It's in the room across from yours. If you'd like, I can turn on the television in the living room for you."

"Oh, I would definitely like that," she replied. "I never get a chance to watch TV, and some of the women who come into my shop talk about what shows they are watching." It was easy for him to forget that she came from a place where electricity was a rare commodity, and she didn't have many of the things he took for granted.

"Come on into the living room, and I'll set you up with the remote," he said.

Minutes later, he walked down the hallway and then entered the room he used as a home office. The room was painted a soft light gray, and a large black desk held a computer and a fancy printer-fax machine.

He went to the desk and sank down in the comfortable leather chair. He leaned back and thought about everything that was going on with Heather's case.

Were they chasing down the wrong lead with the drug connection? Was it possible that the man Heather saw arguing with Wesley that night wasn't the killer at all? If the murder hadn't been about drugs, then what had it been about?

Beneath all of this was a simmering, inappropriate desire for his client. She'd worn her hair loose today, and from the moment he had greeted her that morning he had wanted to run his hands through the long, silky strands. Throughout breakfast, he'd been on a slow burn for her.

She was so different from all the other women he had dated in the past. She was far more down-to-earth and didn't seem superficial in any way. He would imagine she was a giver, and he'd mostly dated takers in the past.

He shoved thoughts of her out of his head and instead turned on his computer and pulled up his email. Within minutes he was immersed in the business of being a defense lawyer.

He didn't know how long he'd been working when Heather poked her head in the doorway. "I'm sorry to interrupt you, but I was wondering if you wanted me to make you a sandwich or something for lunch?"

He looked at his wristwatch and was shocked to see that it was almost one. "I didn't realize it had gotten so late. I'll knock off now and come to the kitchen." He saved the document he'd been working on and then got up and followed her to the kitchen.

"I have something to confess to you," she said as he pulled out sliced ham and cheese from the fridge drawer.

"What's that?" he asked. "And sit down, I've got this."

She sat down at the table. "I've not only been watching television, but I also took some time to snoop through your kitchen. In my own defense, I was looking for spices and all the items I need to make you a good meal."

He turned, looked at her and smiled. "I don't have a problem with that at all. In fact, I want you to familiarize yourself with the place you'll be calling home for a while."

He finished making the sandwiches and placed one in front of her and one for himself on the table. "Do you want chips with that?"

"No, this is fine for me." She smiled at him, that beautiful gesture that lifted her lips and sparkled in her lovely eyes. Oh, he could easily fall into the chocolate pools of her dark-lashed eyes.

"I didn't mean to interrupt you so you could fix lunch for me," she continued. "I could have taken care of myself, but I just thought you might want some lunch."

"I'm glad you did. Time got away from me. So how

was your television experience? What have you watched this morning?"

"I'd like to tell you I watched something highly educational, but I started watching the *Housewives* of something and immediately got hooked. The women are beautiful, but I've never seen such wasteful wealth. They fight about the most ridiculous things, but once I started watching, I couldn't look away."

He laughed and then sobered. "If you had their wealth, what would you do with it?"

She took a bite of her sandwich and chewed thoughtfully. "The first thing I would do is help all my friends in the swamp," she said after she swallowed. "I'd make sure all of them had good generators and cars. From what I see, you seem pretty well-off. What do you do with your excess money?" She flushed then. "I'm sorry, that is completely not my business and out of line."

"No, it's okay," he replied, not offended by her question at all. "I am pretty well-off, thanks to a trust fund and an inheritance from my grandfather. I'm incredibly lucky, and I try to give back in several ways. I defend many clients from the swamp pro bono. I also give generously to a couple of charities. The first one is a no-kill shelter for dogs and the second one is cancer. I lost my grandfather to pancreatic cancer, and I know you lost your father to cancer as well."

She nodded, the movement swinging her long, beautiful hair. "Were you close with your grandfather?" she asked.

"Very. He was the one person in my life who was always there for me, the person I could count on no matter what. He was my biggest champion." Talking about him brought forth a grief Nick rarely allowed himself to visit.

Even after all the years that had passed, Nick still missed the old man terribly.

"How old were you when he passed?" she asked softly, her big, doe-like eyes filled with sympathy.

"I was fourteen, and when he died it felt as if the very center of my world exploded, leaving me with nothing." He released a short laugh. "This lunch talk has gotten way too deep and heavy. Now, tell me more about these housewives you've been watching."

For the next half hour as they ate, she regaled him with the antics of five beautiful, wealthy women. He loved to watch her as she spoke. Her features became so animated, reflecting all her emotions, and he enjoyed every minute of it.

With each conversation he had with her, he felt more and more drawn to her not just physically, but emotionally as well. She was so open and warm.

But he wasn't about to allow himself to experience another Delia situation. No matter what happened between him and Heather, he intended to closely guard his heart.

After lunch, they watched a movie he thought she would enjoy. The romantic comedy made her laugh, which was exactly what he'd wanted it to do. The fact that she'd been through so much and still had her laughter was awe-inspiring to him.

"Maybe you should take a little nap," he suggested when the movie was over. "We'll plan our surveillance tonight between ten and two. Is that okay?"

There was no laughter in her eyes now as she gazed at him solemnly. "I guess tonight is as good as any night to start. The faster we identify this guy and prove he's the killer, the faster I'll be out of your house."

He realized he wasn't ready for her to get out of his house too quickly. So far, he was enjoying her company. His house...he had needed her energy and the conversation to battle the loneliness he'd felt when he was home alone.

She went to her room to nap, and he sat in the living room, realizing that he was a little tired himself. Last night, when he'd gotten the call from Etienne telling him that several men had broken into Heather's shanty, he'd immediately jumped out of bed, dressed and got on the road to get to her.

He'd been terrified of what they might find at her house. Had the men somehow assaulted her? Was she hurt...or worse? Guilt had ridden like a glowering passenger in his car. He'd been so sure she'd be safe there. Hell, he'd encouraged her to stay at the shanty.

The wild emotions, coupled with the time spent up in the middle of the night, now caught up with him. He leaned his head back and closed his eyes. His last thought was that having Heather here was a definite temptation, one he was determined to fight against.

## Chapter Nine

The next four days passed fairly quickly as Heather and Nick fell into a comfortable routine. He cooked breakfast for them in the mornings, and she cooked them dinner every night. Then late at night, she, Nick and Bruno would sit in front of the drug house watching for the man she was desperate to identify, but so far, no luck.

Tonight, it would be only her and Nick on surveillance. Since it was Saturday night, Bruno was headed back to the Voodoo Lounge to question more people about the night Wesley had been murdered. Hopefully, he would find some answers for them, answers that would help exonerate her of the charges against her.

Nick. Being around him had become an exquisite form of torture for her. As they had more conversations and got to know each other on a deeper level, her desire for him grew.

All she'd been able to think about was the kiss they had shared and how much she wanted him to kiss her again. There had been moments when she'd thought he was going to, but each time he quickly distanced himself instead.

It was just before ten when she changed the blouse she'd worn all day and pulled on a black tank top. It got quite warm at night sitting in the car without the air conditioning on.

She left her bedroom, and Nick was waiting for her in the living room. "Ready to go play detective again?" he asked.

He was clad in a pair of dark jeans with a black T-shirt, and his shoulder holster and gun were his only accessories. He looked slightly dangerous and incredibly hot.

"As ready as I can be," she replied.

A few minutes later, they left his garage. "First stop... our favorite convenience store," he said as he drove out of his driveway.

Each night, they stopped at the same convenience store to get drinks and snacks for the time they'd be sitting idly in the car. He pulled up in front of the store, parked and looked around.

"Okay, let's go get our goodies," he said as he unfastened his seat belt.

"I'll just wait out here. You know what I like," she replied. They bought the same items every night, so there was really no reason for her to go in with him.

"I'll be right back." He got out of the car and went inside the store, leaving behind the attractive scent of his cologne.

She looked around the area. There was only one other car in the parking lot, and that held a bunch of laughing teenage boys who she felt no threat from. However, there had been several times over the last few days when she'd felt like somebody was watching them. Nick had assured her she was just being paranoid, which he certainly understood.

Still, she felt as if she was holding her breath, just waiting for danger to find her again, and this time she was scared to death she wouldn't be so lucky.

Nick came back to the car, carrying a drink holder with

two sodas and a plastic bag filled with snacks. "I got the cheddar chips that we both like. I got your licorice and cinnamon bears, and I got the usual peanut candy bars and butterscotch disks for me."

"Then we should be all set for another four hours of surveillance and snacking," she replied.

"I think the kid behind the counter believes we're pot smokers and we get the munchies around this time each night," he said with humor as he handed her the drinks and the bag and then started the car.

"Oh, lordy, that's all I need, a rumor going around that I murder men and do drugs," she replied.

He laughed. "Don't worry too much about it. I have a feeling nobody would believe the kid anyway. Besides, what's a little pot smoking rumor when you're facing a murder charge."

"True," she replied. "Have you ever smoked it before?" she asked curiously as he drove out of the store's parking lot and onto the main road again.

"I tried it years ago, but it wasn't my thing. I don't like not feeling in complete control, so drugs just aren't in my life." He flashed her a quick glance. "What about you? Have you ever tried anything?"

"No. I've never had the desire to try any kind of drugs," she replied. "Although, I could become quite addicted to cinnamon bears."

He laughed once again. She loved the sound of his laughter. It was deep and rich and a sheer pleasure to hear. They then rode for a few minutes in a comfortable silence.

When they were just down the street from the drug house, he parked against the curb. They were close enough that from this vantage point they would be able to see who came and went from the house. The run-down place was definitely a blight to the nicer homes on the block.

"So, what deep topic are we going to delve into tonight to pass the time?" she asked once they were settled in. The drinks were in the holders between them, and the bag was in her lap.

He reached over and pulled out the cheddar-flavored potato chips. He ripped open the top of the bag and then held it out to her. "I was thinking maybe we needed to have a conversation about space aliens."

She laughed and grabbed a handful of the chips. "Okay, then space aliens it is."

"Do you believe in them?"

"I believe it is foolish for us to believe that we are the only people in the entire universe, so yes I do believe in them," she replied. "What about you?"

"I'm a believer. Do you think aliens are here on earth and walk among us?"

"No, I don't believe that," she replied. "Do you?"

"I don't know, I've definitely met a few people in town I'd consider real space cadets," he said.

She laughed. "I think that's different than space aliens. I imagine aliens would have to be highly intelligent to be here and conceal themselves among us."

"Do you think they're around with evil intent in their hearts? Do you think they're just waiting for the perfect moment to take over our world and then eat us as snacks?"

"I think that's a lot of hogwash. If they wanted to take over, they would have done it by now." She crunched on a couple of chips and then took a drink from her soda. "I don't lose any sleep worrying about an imminent alien invasion," she added.

"I sleep with an aluminum hat on every night so the aliens don't get in my head," he replied.

She laughed once again at the mental image of the very hot man with a silly aluminum hat on his head. "Does it have antennas, too?"

"Nah, I was afraid antennas would somehow call them to me," he replied.

"I'd like to see you in your hat sometime."

He grinned at her, his handsome features visible in the illumination from a nearby streetlight. "It's a very special thing for me to share. In fact, I've never shared it with anyone before."

He stopped talking as a car pulled into the driveway of the house and two men got out. Heather looked at them from the moment they left the car until they disappeared into the house.

"Neither of them is the man I remember arguing with Wesley," she finally said dispiritedly.

"That's okay. If he's in the drug trade, then hopefully he'll eventually show up here, and we'll be able to identify him," Nick replied.

"The trial date is coming closer and closer. What happens if I don't see this guy again? And just because he had a fight with Wesley, that doesn't necessarily mean he killed him." A deep anxiety tightened her stomach muscles, and she began to chew on her index fingernail.

He reached out and pulled her hand away from her mouth. "If you continue to chew on that nail, you're eventually going to eat your whole finger."

"I know, it's a terrible habit. I only do it when I'm really anxious."

"Well, don't be really anxious. Even if we don't identify

this man, even if we don't catch the killer, I've been working on a strong defense for you. I've got you covered. I've got you, Heather."

It was impossible to hang on to the anxiety when his blue eyes gazed into hers so earnestly, when his simplest touch eased the jumping nerves inside her and his voice rang with such authority and confidence.

They'd only shared a single kiss, but she found herself falling hard for him. For the past four days, they had essentially been living like husband and wife, except they didn't share a bedroom.

She looked forward to seeing him first thing in the morning, and she liked the fact that he was the last person she saw before she went to sleep. He often worked in his home office in the afternoons while she sat in the living room and watched television. Then they came back together for dinner.

It had become a comfortable routine although she missed her plants and her work. Lucy was opening the shop in her spare time and was taking care of watering the plants. While Heather appreciated that Lucy was trying to help her, she didn't even know what half the plants were.

Still, Heather wasn't used to having so much idle time. It gave her time to worry about what was to become of her. Would her life ever go back to what it had been before? Did Nick really have a strong defense? Would he tell her if he didn't?

Her thoughts were interrupted as another car pulled up in front of the house and two new men got out and went inside. Neither of them was the person Heather most wanted to see.

"Busy night at the drug house," Nick observed as the previous two cars left and another car pulled in, this one containing a young, thin woman. "A shipment must have come in. I'm surprised Etienne doesn't have some men out here watching the house or making some arrests."

"I'm sure all of his officers are tied up with the Swamp Soul Stealer's latest case," she replied.

"Yeah. It's too bad our police department isn't bigger so the police could be everywhere," he said. "But I know Etienne is doing the best he can with what manpower he has."

"Maybe it's time he gets a bigger budget," she replied. "Then he could hire more men."

"That needs to be brought up at the next town council meeting," he replied. "I'll make sure it is. I think it's been a while since we voted on more money for the police department."

Their conversation changed to all things strange and unusual. They talked about Bigfoot and the Loch Ness Monster. They broke into their candy stash, and she chewed the little cinnamon bears while he ate a peanut bar and then some of his butterscotch disks.

There was something intimate about two people sitting in a car in the middle of the night and talking about anything and everything that came to their minds.

There was a lull in the traffic for a little while, and then all of a sudden, the front door flew open and a man strode outside. He was a big guy, and he wore a shoulder holster and carried a big flashlight.

A new anxiety filled her as he began checking the vehicles parked along the curb. "Nick, you need to drive away," she said urgently. "He's going to see us. He's going to catch us."

"I can't drive off now. It would be too obvious. Just follow my lead."

When the man approached the side of their car, Nick

reached over and pulled her half over the console. He wrapped his arms around her and then took her lips with his.

Despite the fact that she was terrified, she couldn't help the flames of desire that were lit inside her by the unexpected deep kiss. She clung to his shoulders and prayed the man would pass them by.

Even though she had her eyes closed, a flash of light penetrated her eyelids, and she knew the man was shining his flashlight into the car.

Nick tightened his arms around her, and through his half-opened window, she heard the man chuckle and then sensed he moved on. Nick continued to kiss her for several long minutes. The kiss tasted of a heated desire and sweet butterscotch.

He finally released her, and she quickly looked outside and saw the man now on the opposite side of the street and heading back toward the house.

"That was a close call," Nick said.

"Far too close for me," she replied and fought the impulse to chew on her nail as a wave of anxiety swept through her. Even though the kiss had been very hot, the circumstances that had prompted it had been terrifying.

"I would assume he was looking for any cops who might be parked in the area and watching the place." Nick grabbed another candy bar from the bag on her lap and grinned at her. "Kissing you was a very hot way to avoid danger."

"I agree," she replied as the warmth of a blush filled her cheeks.

"He probably thought we belonged in one of the houses or were in the car because we are in the middle of a passionate affair."

"I'm just grateful the kiss worked, and he left us alone," she replied.

One thing was for sure, the kiss had confirmed to her that she was definitely falling in love with her defense attorney.

She now not only hoped that he would save her from going to prison for years, but also that he could save her heart by loving her back.

THE KISS WITH Heather had ignited an intense desire for her despite the circumstances surrounding the kiss. In that moment, she had tasted of hot desire and sweet cinnamon, and he'd wanted to take advantage of the situation and continue kissing her, but he hadn't.

The next day, Nick sat in his office in town knowing Heather was safe at his house with Bruno there to guard over things. Even though it was late Sunday afternoon, he had a client who should be coming in at any moment, but instead of focusing on that case, it was thoughts of Heather that filled his head.

Living with her for the past five days had been sheer torture. He wanted to take her to his bed so badly. His desire for her ached in his veins and half dizzied his head whenever he was near her.

The last time he'd felt like this about a woman, the end results had been disastrous, and he'd wound up with a very broken heart. Of course, he wasn't about to let that happen a second time. He was positive he could make love with Heather and not be in love with her. He just had to make sure if that happened, she was on the same page.

There was a knock on his door, and Sharon poked her head in. "Mr. Raymore is here."

"Send him on in," Nick said.

Michael Raymore was sixty-three years old. He was overweight and going bald, and this was the second time he'd been arrested for shoplifting from one of the higher-end stores in town. His defense this time was he had every intention of paying for the two bottles of expensive cologne that were in his pockets at the time he was arrested just outside the store.

Nick had needed to meet Michael in person and get the appropriate papers signed to defend the man. It was a relatively easy case, and the best Nick was hoping for was to get the man probation and a fine instead of any jail time.

"I'm on disability," Michael whined. "And I'm all alone and looking for a wife. A man has to smell good when he's meeting the ladies. But I intended to pay for the cologne. I just forgot they were in my pockets when I walked out of the store."

It would have been much easier to have a little sympathy if the man had stolen food, but that wasn't the case. The whole appointment only lasted thirty minutes, and then Michael left and Sharon came back into Nick's office. "Do you need me for anything else?" she asked.

"No, but I want to thank you for coming in on a Sunday," he said.

She grinned at him. "You can thank me when you write out my next paycheck."

He laughed. "You got it."

The minute Sharon was gone, he got ready to leave as well. Heather would probably be in the kitchen, preparing dinner. He hadn't asked her to take care of the evening meals, but she had insisted she take over that task as part of her payment to him. He had to admit it was a real treat for him, and each night the meals so far had been delicious.

The cook-off they had planned had gone by the wayside when she'd moved in with him.

He wondered how she and Bruno were getting along. During the nights of their surveillance together, Bruno had barely spoken to her. He hadn't been blatantly rude, but he'd definitely been rather cool to her. Not that it mattered. Heather was only a temporary pleasure in Nick's life. Within weeks, hopefully Heather would be back to her life, and he'd be back hanging out with Bruno and living his own.

He had to admit, he was going to miss her when she was gone. The thought surprised him. He would miss the sound of her musical laughter ringing in the air. He would miss her company in the evenings when they talked about all kinds of things. She was witty and intelligent, and he enjoyed all their conversations.

By the time he pulled into his garage, he'd shoved all those thoughts to the back of his brain. He parked his car, closed the garage door behind him and then entered into the kitchen.

The room was empty, and the air was redolent with the scents of cooking chicken. He left the kitchen and went into the living room, where Bruno sat watching television.

"Where's Heather?" Nick asked.

"Back in her bedroom. I think she's on the phone talking to one of her friends," Bruno replied.

Nick sank down on the love seat. "How did it go while I was gone?"

Bruno shrugged. "Fine. She's mostly been in the kitchen. She invited me to stay for dinner, but I declined."

"Why? You know you would have been welcomed."

"I know, but actually I have a dinner date," Bruno replied.

"Really? With who?" Nick asked curiously.

Bruno appeared to squirm slightly. "Uh… Sharon."

Nick looked at his friend in surprise. "My Sharon?"

Bruno grinned. "She's not your Sharon, but yeah. It's no big deal. We're just going to the café to eat."

"When did this all come about?" Nick asked, still surprised.

"On Friday I was just talking with her, and I thought it would be nice to take her out to dinner."

"She was just at the office with me, and she didn't mention anything about it."

"Yeah, well we didn't know for sure how you would react."

At that moment, Heather came into the room. As always, she looked stunning even though she was dressed casually in a worn pair of jeans and a coral-colored T-shirt. The coral color looked amazing against her slightly olive coloring. She smiled at him. "Hi, I didn't realize you were home."

"I'm home."

She laughed. "I can see that. Dinner will be ready in about thirty minutes or so."

"Something definitely smells delicious," he said.

"It's a cheesy chicken-and-rice casserole. I found the recipe online," she replied.

"Sounds good to me," he said.

"I hope it is. I asked Bruno to stay for dinner, but he said he had other plans."

"Yeah, he just told me that," Nick replied.

"Now, I'll just be in the kitchen, and I'll let you know when it's ready."

She left the room, but not before he smelled the scent of her evocative perfume. He turned to look back at Bruno, who was staring at him. "What?"

"Are you getting in too deep with her?" Bruno asked softly.

"Not at all," Nick replied quickly. "She's just a client who happens to be staying here with me temporarily."

Bruno stared at him for another long minute and then released a deep sigh. "I just don't want to go through it with you again. I had to pick you up off the floor after Delia, and you weren't yourself for months after that."

"This is nothing like that," Nick protested. "Trust me, my heart isn't in any danger. I like Heather, and I'm enjoying her company, but that's it," he assured his friend.

"Okay then." Bruno rose to his feet. "I'm going to head out of here. I need to change and get ready for my date."

"Thanks for today, and I hope you have a good time with Sharon," Nick said. "Just don't break her heart."

"Right," Bruno replied dryly. "Because I've always been such a heartbreaker."

Once he was gone, Nick went into the kitchen, where Heather was stirring something on the stove top. "Can I help you with anything?" he asked.

"No, just have a seat and relax," she replied. "Are you hungry?"

"Yeah, I am. I wasn't until I walked into the house and smelled dinner," he replied. The table was already set with two plates and the appropriate silverware.

He sat in the chair he always sat in to eat and watched her. She moved with a gracefulness that was attractive. "So, how was your appointment?" She moved a saucepan from the burner and then turned and looked at him.

"The appointment went fine. My newest client is a shoplifter, and Tommy Radcliffe is throwing the book at him for having two colognes in his possession that he didn't pay for when he walked out of the store."

"Your job will be to get him a lighter sentence?"

"That's it. How was your time with Bruno while I was gone?"

A small frown danced into the center of her forehead. "It was fine. I still get the feeling that he doesn't like me."

"I told you before, he's a cautious kind of guy," Nick replied.

"What does he think I'm going to do?"

*He's afraid you'll steal my heart and then dump me.* The thought remained in his head and wasn't spoken aloud. "I don't know, but he'll eventually come around."

"I hope so." She went to the oven and used mitts to take out a covered casserole dish. She set it on an awaiting hot pad in the center of the table. She then moved carrots from the saucepan to a serving bowl. Finally, she got from the refrigerator a fresh green salad and a bottle of ranch dressing.

She took the foil off the casserole dish to expose a bed of rice with several chicken breasts on top. "This all looks amazing," he said.

"Let's hope it tastes as good as it looks," she replied as she sank down in the chair opposite him.

"You are a very good cook," he said minutes later as he ate the food she'd prepared.

"I'm enjoying the novelty of having an oven," she replied.

"Do you miss your shanty?"

She nodded, her long hair gleaming richly beneath the light over the table. "I talked to Lucy for a while today, and it made me a little homesick. I'm also worried about all my plants. Lucy is watering the ones at my house and at the shop, but despite her good intentions, she really doesn't know what she's doing."

"If you want, we can go to the shop tomorrow, and you

can check things out." He saw the look of trepidation that immediately crossed her features.

"The last time we were at the shop things didn't go so well for us," she said.

"This time we'll take Bruno with us, and we'll be well prepared for anything." Nick smiled at her. "I got you," he said in an effort to ease her mind.

"And I appreciate that," she replied.

As they finished up the meal, they talked about past cases he'd had and some of the customers that frequented her shop. He helped her with the cleanup, and each time he inadvertently touched her, a tormenting desire shot through his veins.

By the time they sat side by side on the sofa to watch a movie, he felt as if he were on fire with his want of her. Apparently, she didn't pick up on his mood, but each unconscious movement she made only shot his desire even higher.

When she flipped strands of her dark, luxurious hair over her shoulder, it felt like an open invitation for him to wrap his fingers in it and pull her close. Every time she changed positions, a new waft of her scent filled his head.

He could scarcely pay attention to the movie as he was so captivated by her closeness to him. However, when a sad part of the movie played, he saw the spark of tears in her eyes.

"Hey, are you crying?" he asked and threw an arm around her shoulder.

She sniffled and released an embarrassed laugh. "That part was so sad," she replied and leaned into him. "Silly of me to cry over a movie."

"I don't find it silly at all," he said and pulled her closer into his side. "In fact, I find it quite charming."

She looked up at him and her eyes no longer held sadness, but rather an invitation, and at the same time her lips parted slightly.

He took the invitation by capturing her mouth with his. She immediately wrapped her arms around his neck and leaned closer to him. Her lips were incredibly pillowy, and when she opened them fully to him, his tongue danced in to swirl with hers. Just that quickly, he was completely lost in her.

He tangled his hands in her long, silky hair and continued the kiss until they were both breathless and panting. "Heather, I really want to make love to you," he finally said as the kiss ended.

"And I really want to make love to you," she replied, her eyes smoldering with unmistakable desire.

He stood and held out his hand to her. She hesitated only a moment and then slipped her hand into his. "But before we do this, I need you to understand I'm not promising you anything beyond this moment."

"I'm not expecting anything more than that from you," she replied half breathlessly.

She rose from the sofa, and together they headed down the hall to his bedroom. His heart beat a rhythm of excitement, and his blood rushed hot through his veins. Surely after this one time of letting go of self-control, she'd be out of his system for good, and they would go back to a strictly client-and-lawyer relationship.

## Chapter Ten

Heather got a quick glimpse of his large, beautiful bedroom. It was as if she'd stepped into her deepest, most desired fantasy. Being in Nick's arms was beyond heavenly. She tasted his desire for her in his kiss, and as he drew her closer and closer, she felt his desire for her in his obvious arousal that pressed against her.

It had been years since she had felt a man's arms around her and tasted this kind of hot hunger. It was exhilarating… intoxicating, and she couldn't get enough of it.

Their kiss lasted until he ended it and stepped back from her. His blue eyes simmered with fiery flames as he unbuttoned his white shirt and shrugged it off his shoulders and to the floor behind him.

Oh, a half-naked Nick was positively splendid. His broad chest was well muscled and gleamed in the twilight illumination coming through the nearby window. His chest tapered to a slim but muscular abdomen.

She reached out and ran her hands down his smooth, warm skin and then followed her hands with her mouth. She slid kisses down his chest for only a moment before he pulled her back into his arms for another long, breath-stealing kiss.

This time as he kissed her, he tugged the bottom of her T-shirt out of her jeans, and ended the kiss as he slid the garment up and over her head.

"Heather, you are so beautiful," he whispered as she stood before him in her lacy light pink bra.

"Thank you," she replied. Oh, she was ready for so much more. She wanted to be naked for him...with him. She wanted to feel her naked body intimately close against his own.

As he unfastened the top of his slacks, she unbuttoned the fly of her jeans. Once it was unbuttoned, she pushed them down and then off. By that time, he was only clad in his black boxers, and she was in a pair of lacy pink panties. He reached over and pulled down the top of the black bedspread, exposing white sheets and an invitation for her to get into the bed.

She slid into the sheets, and he followed her and then immediately pulled her into his arms once again. His bare skin met hers, and she thrilled at the way his warm body felt so close to her.

They kissed hungrily, their tongues swirling together and whipping their desire for each other higher and higher. She moved her hips against his, and he reached behind her and unfastened her bra. He plucked it off her and tossed it to the foot of the bed. She gasped in pleasure as his hands captured her breasts. His palms were so warm against them. He then rolled his thumb across her erect nipples, shooting pleasure from the throbbing tips to the very center of her. The pleasure only increased when his tongue flicked and toyed where his fingers had been.

She was lost in him...in the mindless pleasure that torched through her at his every touch. His scent surrounded her, the wonderful fragrance that spoke of safety and caring. She moaned with delight as his hands slowly moved down the length of her body and stopped at the waistband of her panties.

She wanted them off, and she wanted his boxers off, too. She was more than ready to be completely naked with him. He pulled her panties down far enough that she could kick them off.

Once she was naked, she moved her hands to the top of his boxers. "Take them off, Nick. I want you to be completely naked with me," she whispered breathlessly.

He immediately complied and then pulled her back into his arms and kissed her long and deep. Her body was now intimately close to his, and he was fully aroused. The kiss ended and his hands once again slid down the length of her body to the very center of her.

She gasped as his fingers began to dance against her sensitive skin and created a rising tension inside her. Higher and higher she climbed until she crashed down to the earth with a fierce orgasm. She cried out his name and clung to him until the exquisite moment finally ended.

But it still wasn't enough for her. She wanted more of him. She reached down and took his erection in her hand. It was hard, yet the skin covering it was velvety soft. He groaned as she moved her hand up and down in slow, even strokes. His erection grew even harder and bigger.

"Heather, I want you so badly," he said, his voice deeper than normal.

"Then take me, Nick," she gasped breathlessly. "Take me now."

She pulled her hand away from him, and he positioned himself between her open thighs. In the final light of day drifting through the window, his simmering blue gaze held hers for a long moment.

He slowly eased into her, filling her up as she once again gasped his name. For a long moment, he didn't move and then he began to pump into her, slowly at first and then faster and faster. She clung to his shoulders, meeting him thrust for thrust.

A new rising tension built inside her. Higher and higher she rode the waves of intense pleasure until she crested and shuddered with another powerful orgasm.

At the same time with a groan of her name, he found his own release. For several long moments, they remained locked together as they tried to catch their breaths.

Finally, he leaned down and captured her lips in a tender kiss. He ended the kiss and then rolled over to the side of her. "Wow," he said.

She laughed joyously. "Wow is right."

He leaned up on one elbow and gazed down at her with a frown. "That all happened so fast, we didn't even think about birth control."

"It's okay, I'm on the pill, and I haven't been with anyone for years, so you don't have to worry about anything else with me," she replied.

"And it's been well over a year since I've been with anyone," he replied, his frown gone.

"Really? I would think a successful man who looks like you could have a different woman every single night of the week," she replied.

He released a small laugh and then quickly sobered. "Well, I don't know about all that, but I quit dating a little over a year ago. When I was much younger, I had the dream of a wife and a couple of children, but I came to the conclusion that I'm better off all alone."

"But, Nick, that's so sad," she replied. He was such a kind, thoughtful man. She was sure he would make a wonderful husband and father.

"I guess you still have a dream of that one special man… marriage and eventually a couple of kids," he replied.

"Definitely, that's exactly what I want."

"Then I hope that's what's in your future." He leaned over and kissed her on the cheek then rolled out of the bed. "You can use my bathroom. I'll use the one in the hallway." He grabbed his boxers from the floor and then left the room.

She immediately got out of the bed and gathered up all her clothes and then went into the adjoining bathroom. The decor there was black and gold. His shower was big enough to accommodate several people at the same time and had four sprays coming out of the walls.

She could only imagine such luxury. When she showered, she only got a trickling spray of water, and it didn't last long. She cleaned up and got dressed. Her body was still warm in the aftermath of what they had shared, and her emotions were all over the place.

If she had believed herself to be falling for Nick, then the fall was now complete. She was in love with him, not that it mattered. He was obviously in a different headspace than she was. She was just a client who he happened to desire, and she'd do well to remember that.

She would have loved to spend the night in his arms. She would have loved to fall asleep with him spooned around her and with his warm breath caressing the back of her neck. But he wasn't inviting her to spend the night in his bed. Her heart squeezed tight with a sharp pain as her love for him buoyed up inside her. It was a love he obviously didn't feel for her and it was that thought that hurt her heart.

Once she was dressed, she went back into the bedroom. Nick wasn't there, so she went into the living room and sank down on the sofa. Minutes later, he joined her. He sat next to her on the sofa and pulled her close against him.

"Heather, I just want you to know that I consider what we just shared very special," he said. His eyes were warm and caring as he gazed at her.

Her heart constricted once again. "It was very special to me, too."

"But you do realize it should never have happened and shouldn't happen again. I would never want to take advantage of your vulnerability, considering our positions."

"Oh, Nick, you didn't...you couldn't take advantage of me. I wanted you, and it was as simple as that, and you obviously wanted me, too," she replied. "We are two consenting adults, and I wouldn't take back a minute of what we just shared."

"Still, it shouldn't happen again," he replied firmly.

"I'm not sure why, but okay. And I think on that note, I'll head to bed. These late nights of surveillance have finally caught up with me, and I'm really tired."

"I hear that," he replied and pulled his arm from around her. "I'm extra tired tonight myself, although the last of my energy was certainly well spent."

She laughed and stood. "Same. So, I'll just say goodnight now, and I'll see you in the morning."

"Goodnight, Heather," he replied.

"'Night, Nick." She left the living room and went into her bedroom. From there, she immediately beelined to the bathroom and started running the water for a bath. Next to the tub was a pretty container that held lavender-scented bath salts and a bottle of lavender bubble bath.

She sprinkled a little of both into the water, and then once the tub was full, she stripped naked and slid into the hot, scented water.

It felt absolutely heavenly. She leaned her head back and closed her eyes and thought about everything that had happened. No matter what, she would never, ever regret making love with Nick.

The whole experience had been beyond wonderful. Even though she had relatively little sexual experience, she knew he'd been a particularly caring partner. He'd taken her to heights of pleasure she'd never even known existed before.

If things went really badly for her and Nick couldn't keep her out of prison, then at least she would have this single memory to warm her heart on lonely, frightening nights behind bars.

MAKING LOVE WITH Heather had been even better than in his wildest imagination. She'd been so passionate, and her passion had fed his even higher than it had been. He'd thought having her once would get her out of his system, but the moment it was over, he wanted her all over again.

This morning, he'd awakened much earlier than usual and now sat at the kitchen table sipping a cup of coffee and thinking about his lovely houseguest.

There was no question he'd been developing feelings for her...deep feelings that were dangerous for him to have. Even if he fell in love with her and she professed to feel the same way toward him, he would never know if her love was real and not based in a wealth of gratitude. He still thought it was very possible that if he got her off the charges against her, she would walk out of his life without a backward glance.

It was definitely time he began to distance himself from her and maintain a more professional relationship with her. Thinking about the case against her made his stomach tighten with anxiety.

They still had nothing to take to Etienne to make him reinvestigate the case, and he still had no real evidence to show to a jury that she had been set up.

Jury selection started in less than three weeks. He had to make sure nobody with any prejudices toward people from the swamp was sitting on the jury.

Tommy Radcliffe had an easy tale to tell about the beautiful, poor swamp woman who had an affair with the wealthy, married Wesley. He would play up the fiction that Heather desperately wanted out of the swamp and Wesley was her ticket out. He'd make Wesley look like a choir boy whose only fault was being weak and unable to fight against Heather's wiles. Nick's fear was it was a tale that was far too easily believed.

He could argue she was too petite to kill the much bigger man, and Tommy would argue that anger and rage had given her the necessary strength to act in a murderous frenzy.

Nick could also argue the drug connection, but without any real evidence to back it up, it probably wouldn't fly. Although he would never tell Heather, the truth of the matter was Nick was worried.

He'd just poured himself a second cup of coffee when Heather came into the kitchen. Clad in a pair of jeans and a blue sleeveless blouse, and with her hair loose around her shoulders, she looked positively gorgeous. A lot of her beauty came from the fact that she didn't seem aware of just how pretty she was.

"Good morning," he greeted her.

She smiled. "Back at you," she replied as she headed toward the coffee.

"How did you sleep?"

"Like a baby," she said.

"I was thinking pancakes this morning."

She grinned again. "I like the way you think." She poured her coffee and then joined him at the table. "How did you sleep?"

"I slept fine. Are you hungry?"

"I'm starving," she admitted.

"You like sausage?"

"I do."

"Then sausage and pancakes it is." He got up from the table and began to work on breakfast. He was grateful that their conversation remained light and easy. He was particularly glad that there was no awkward rehash of what had happened between them the night before.

It didn't take him long to have a platter of sausage and a stack of pancakes ready. He placed both on the table and then added butter and warmed-up maple syrup.

"Eating pancakes is kind of like having dessert in the morning," she said after they started eating. "And you make a great pancake."

"Thanks. I could eat pancakes or French toast almost every day for breakfast," he replied.

"It's the maple syrup sweetness," she said.

A drop of the syrup clung to her lower lip, and he wanted nothing more than to lean across the table and cover her sweet-tasting mouth with his. Damn, this all would be so much easier if he had no desire for her, if he didn't like her so damned much.

They had just finished eating when a knock fell on his front door. "I'll be right back." He got up from the table, grabbed his gun from the nearby counter and then went to answer.

It was Bruno. "Why didn't you just let yourself in?" Nick asked. "You have a key, and you've always let yourself in before."

"You know I don't like to do that," Bruno replied. "Especially now since you have a woman living here with you."

"What do you expect? To walk in and see her sitting on the sofa naked?" Nick replied in amusement.

"Don't give me a hard time, bro. I haven't even had my coffee this morning. Besides, I come with news."

Nick raised a brow curiously. "Good news?"

"Give me a cup of coffee, and I'll tell you all."

"Come on in. Heather and I were just finishing up breakfast." Nick led his friend into the kitchen.

"Good morning, Bruno," Heather said.

"Good morning to you," he replied and beelined to the coffee maker.

Nick returned to his chair at the table. "You want some pancakes?"

"Nah, I'm good." Bruno poured himself a cup of coffee and then joined them at the table. "You guys go ahead and eat, and I'll do the talking."

"We're finished eating, so talk," Nick said.

"Okay, as you know, last night I took Sharon to the café for dinner," Bruno began.

"Oh, that's nice," Heather said. "She seems like a wonderful woman."

"How did things go between the two of you?" Nick asked.

A hint of a smile lifted a corner of Bruno's mouth. "I enjoyed it, and I think she did, too. Anyway, after dinner we decided to go to the Voodoo Lounge and have a drink. We sat at the bar because we didn't intend to be there that long."

He paused and took a drink of his coffee. Nick fought the urge to hurry the man along and get to the point. Bruno said he had news, but Nick still didn't know if it was good news and something that might help Heather's case or bad news that would hurt her.

"Anyway," Bruno continued, "we were sitting at the bar, and we got to visiting with a couple who was sitting next to us. The conversation went to the night of the murder, and they told me they were there that night and they saw Heather being helped out the back door by a squat, dark-haired man."

"Finally, witnesses we can use," Nick exclaimed with excitement.

"Thank God," Heather said tremulously.

"Slow down, I haven't finished yet," Bruno said. "I asked them if they'd told the cops what they saw concerning Heather, and they told me that they hadn't because they didn't want to get involved. When I asked for their names, they declined to give them to me and left soon after that."

"So, we don't have their names," Nick said as a deep disappointment slammed into his chest.

"Oh, boss of little faith," Bruno replied with a full grin. He pulled a small notepad from his T-shirt pocket. "The bartender was more than happy to tell me that Sharon and I were visiting with regulars Paul and Anette Darnel." He handed Nick a page from the notebook with the names written on it.

"I've always said you're the best," Nick said to his friend.

"But if they don't want to get involved, then what good are they?" Heather said softly. "I mean, apparently they were ready to let an innocent woman go to jail."

Nick frowned. "We'll take this information to Etienne and see if this is enough for him to reopen the case. I'll also subpoena them, and they will have to talk at trial. Good work, Bruno."

"Thank you for working so hard on my behalf," Heather said.

"No problem," Bruno replied.

"Let's talk about the plans for the day," Nick said, still excited at the prospect of having witnesses that worked in his defense case.

"What's the plan?" Bruno asked.

"The first thing we'll do is have a little chat with Etienne, and after that Heather needs to go to her store to water some of the plants there. I would like you to go with us."

"My time is yours," Bruno replied.

Nick leaned over and grabbed one of Heather's hands in his. "This is the first real break we've gotten in the case." He grinned at her, squeezed her hand and then released it.

"I'm afraid to get too excited for fear I'll just be let down," she replied.

"I'm hoping to find more people to substantiate the fact that the killer took you out the back door," Bruno said. "If there were two who saw that, then there are probably ten. It's just a matter of me finding them and getting their names."

"Why would nobody come forward to tell the police that? Why not tell the police the next morning after they heard I'd been arrested for the murder?" Heather asked.

"My guess is that the guy who took you outside that night

looked like a real bad guy. The witnesses who saw him might have been afraid of retribution if they came forward."

"What a sad state of society it is," Heather said with a shake of her head.

"It's the times we live in," Nick replied. "Good people are afraid to get involved with anything crime related. It's how women get beat up in a public place and nobody steps up to stop it."

"I would hope the people of Crystal Cove were different," Heather said.

"People are people no matter where they live," Bruno replied.

"Let's get the kitchen cleaned up so we can get on our way," Nick said as he stood. "Bruno, feel free to help yourself to another cup of coffee."

Heather helped with the cleanup, and within twenty minutes they were all ready to go. Bruno sat in the passenger seat of Nick's car, and Heather sat in the back seat. He knew his partner would be watching in all directions for any trouble approaching their car.

As Nick drove toward the police station, he hoped like hell this was enough to finally get the lawman to reinvestigate the case. If not that, then he hoped Etienne would talk to Tommy Radcliffe about dropping the case against Heather.

It was a matter of justice, and as prosecuting attorney, Tommy should want to see real justice done. Now that they had witnesses to corroborate Heather's story, Tommy should want to do the right thing and get the real killer behind bars. And that wasn't Heather.

However, Tommy had always been a bit of a grandstander, and this was the case he'd been yearning for—it had garnered a lot of publicity, and he would probably be playing to a full house of people attending the trial.

When they reached the police station, Etienne was in his office. "Let's make this quick," he said once they were before him. "I just got word that another person has disappeared in the swamp."

"Who?" Heather asked, obviously worried about her friends there.

"Clayton Beauregarde," Etienne replied.

"Do you know him?" Nick asked Heather.

"Yes. His wife is Lillie, and they recently had their first child," Heather replied, her dark eyes simmering with sadness.

"According to Lillie, last night he left his place to make a quick run to the grocery store. Unfortunately, he never came home." A muscle ticked in Etienne's tense jaw. "Now, what's up?"

Bruno explained about the couple he had met the night before and how he had gotten their names from the bartender. "They're witnesses to the fact that Heather was half carried by a man out of the back door," Nick added. "This is proof that there was somebody else in that alley the night that Wesley was murdered."

"Then use them as witnesses for your case," Etienne said, obviously distracted by the crime at hand.

Nick knew he wasn't going to get anywhere with Etienne, at least not today with a new man missing from the swamp. "I know you're busy right now, so we'll get out of your hair. But maybe in a couple of days you can sit down with me for a talk."

"Great, now if you'll excuse me, I was just on my way out," Etienne said.

Within minutes, they were all back in the car and headed to Heather's shop. "I think you're on your own from here on out," Bruno said, voicing what Nick was thinking.

"What does that mean?" Heather asked.

"It means that we can't depend on Etienne to reinvestigate the case or do much of anything else. We'll just have to take our chances at trial," Nick replied. He looked in his rearview mirror. Heather was chewing on her nail, obviously apprehensive.

Nick hadn't realized just how much he'd hoped Etienne would immediately reinvestigate the case until now, when he feared that wasn't going to happen. Nick didn't blame Heather for being anxious. For the first time since he'd taken her case, he was really anxious, too.

## Chapter Eleven

Another week passed and the closer her trial got, the more Heather worried about what was going to happen to her. Still, despite her concerns, spending time with Nick only made her feelings toward him deepen.

She awoke early on Sunday morning in Nick's bed. Apparently, he had awakened even earlier as she was alone in the bed that smelled of his cologne. Instead of getting up, she rolled over on her back and thought about the week that had passed.

Nick was spending more time in his home office working on her case, and Heather continued to cook their evening meal. Bruno had found two more people who had seen Heather being "helped" out of the back door by a rough-looking man. Unfortunately, like the first couple, these people also indicated they didn't want to get involved.

However, Nick had the names of the four people, and after finding out their addresses, he intended to seek subpoenas so they would have to testify for the defense.

"I got you," Nick kept telling her, and when she gazed into the depths of his beautiful blue eyes, she believed him. She also believed he was developing strong feelings for her. She felt it in his touch and saw it in his eyes when he gazed at her. There was a softness...a genuine caring there, and it warmed and excited her.

Then there had been last night. The two of them had gone on their surveillance duty while Bruno had gone to the bar. It had been another uneventful night, and when she and Nick had gotten home, they had shared a kiss. It was supposed to be a simple, good-night kiss. But it quickly became something much deeper, much hotter, and just that quickly they were out of control and had wound up in his bed.

She stretched, satisfied as a gator after eating a full meal. It had been Nick who had invited her to spend the night in his bed, and it had been beyond wonderful to fall asleep with him spooning closely around her and his arm around her waist and holding her tight.

Suddenly, she couldn't wait to see him. She got out of his bed, quickly made it and then went into her own bedroom to get dressed for the day.

By the time she left her bedroom, the scent of bacon and coffee wafted in the air. "Hmm, smells like breakfast," she said as she entered the kitchen.

Nick turned from the stove and grinned at her. "I figured that would get you out of bed."

She laughed. "You know I love your breakfasts."

"Almost as much as I love your dinners," he replied. "How about omelets this morning?"

"You know I especially love your omelets." She grinned at him and then poured herself a cup of coffee and sat down at the table. She watched him work, comfortable in the silence as he prepared the omelets.

He didn't speak again until he had breakfast on the table. As they ate, they talked about the latest on the Swamp Soul Stealer case. Clayton Beauregarde had yet to be found, although a bag of groceries had been found on the ground not far from his shanty.

"The heartbreaking thing is he was so close to being home...so close to being safe when he was taken," Heather said.

"Yeah, that makes it that much more disheartening," Nick agreed. "I'd like to know how he manages to disable these people so quickly. Nobody ever hears anything. No screams...no calls for help...nothing."

"I know Etienne has pinned a lot of his hopes on Colette Broussard waking up and being able to tell him who the monster is and where he's keeping all the people he kidnapped, but what if, God forbid, Colette never wakes up?"

Nick shrugged. "Who knows? I know Etienne is doing everything in his power to find this creep, but from what I hear, the creep isn't making any mistakes."

"If you were to guess, would you think it's somebody from town or somebody from the swamp?" she asked.

He frowned thoughtfully. "It would help if we knew the motive. There are days I think it has to be somebody from town who is prejudiced against the swamp people. Then there are other days I think that only somebody from the swamp could sneak around and kidnap people and take them somewhere deep enough in the swamp where nobody can find them."

"I don't want to believe it's somebody from the swamp, but I'll admit there are a lot of things that point to that," she replied.

"How many people does that make now who are missing?" Nick asked.

"Six. Six souls that have been lost," she replied. "And

that's not counting Colette, who for all intents and purposes is also a lost soul."

"It's wild that this is going on and nobody knows who the bastard is. Now, we'd better change the subject while we finish eating, otherwise we'll both wind up with a bad case of indigestion," he said.

"I agree," she replied.

While they finished their meal, they small-talked about an upcoming celebration Crystal Cove was having. Each year the town had a street fair with booths selling food and people offering handmade items for sale. There was also a carnival with a Ferris wheel and other rides to delight small children and adults alike.

She had always heard it was a great time with neighbors visiting and laughter ringing out in the air. There were gator wrestling contests and baking competitions and a host of other fun things.

"I've never been to the fair before," Heather confessed as they cleared the dishes.

"Really? Then we'll have to plan to go together to this one," he replied. "Why haven't you been before?"

"I figured it wasn't much fun to go alone and all my friends usually had other plans. Then I was nursing my father and taking care of my mother."

Would she really be free to enjoy life after the trial? "It's possible we'll still be in trial when it happens."

"Trust me, trial will be adjourned through the course of the fair. Even Judge Cooke will want to enjoy the festivities. But I have a feeling this is going to be a very short trial, and then we'll celebrate our success by going to the fair," he replied, confidence ringing in his tone.

She looked at him with more than a hint of worry. He

grabbed one of her hands. "Take that look off your face right now," he said. "How many times do I need to tell you that I got you?"

"Apparently many times," she replied with a small laugh.

He squeezed her hand and then released it. "By the way, I meant to tell you that you make a really good cuddle buddy."

She laughed once again. "I can say the same thing about you."

His gaze held hers for a long moment. "I wouldn't mind it if you wanted to snuggle with me again tonight."

Her heart lifted and flew with happiness. "I would love to snuggle with you tonight, but only if you wear your aluminum hat for me," she added with an impish grin.

It was his turn to laugh. "Okay, it's a deal."

After breakfast, he disappeared into his office, and Heather sank down on the sofa to watch television. But it was hard to concentrate with the utter happiness that danced in her heart and filled her head.

He had to care about her. Surely a man who wasn't interested wouldn't invite her to his room for the night and wouldn't make plans to see her after the case was over.

He'd told her he planned to be alone for the rest of his life, but maybe he'd come to that decision because he hadn't found the right woman. And maybe…just maybe she was the right woman for him. At this thought a shiver of delight rushed through her.

She knew with certainty he was the right man for her. She wanted to be with him for the rest of her life. She wanted to spend her days with him and sleep in his arms every night. She longed for a family, and she would give Nick as many babies as he wanted.

Her feelings for Nick had nothing to do with loneliness

or gratitude, although she would always be grateful to him for everything he had done and was doing for her. Without him she would probably be dead by now.

At noon Nick came out of his office for some lunch. He made them ham-and-cheese sandwiches, and while they ate, he seemed slightly distant and distracted. He ate quickly and then returned to his office.

Early afternoon passed, and then it was time for her to start cooking dinner. Tonight, she was trying parmesan-encrusted pork chops. Once again, she'd gone to the internet to find a recipe. She was making mashed potatoes, creamed corn and corn muffins as well.

She enjoyed cooking with all the conveniences Nick's kitchen had to offer. It was so different from cooking at her shanty. A wave of homesickness struck her. There was no question that she missed the swamp and her cozy little shanty.

She spoke on the phone fairly regularly to Lucy, but she missed seeing and talking to some of her other friends as well. If she and Nick became a real couple, she would still want to spend time in the swamp. She wasn't sure how it would work between them, but she believed one way or another, things would work out. After all, love conquered all.

It was around five and dinner was ready when Nick came back into the kitchen. "Oh, I was just on my way to tell you dinner is ready."

"The delicious smells called to me," he replied and took a seat at the table. "You've been spoiling me with all these wonderful meals each night."

"I've told you before, I like cooking for you," she replied as she took the pork chops out of the oven. The rest of the meal was already on the table. "At least you're complimentary." She set the chops in the center of the table and then took her seat opposite his.

"I can't help but be complimentary. Your food is always excellent."

"Dig in while it's hot."

They both filled their plates and began to eat. Once again, he was quiet and appeared distracted. Was he worried about the case? Jury selection was right around the corner, followed quickly by the trial. "Is everything all right?" she finally asked.

"Yeah, it's fine. I have a new client coming in tomorrow, and I've been spending my time today getting all the information I can on the case."

"So you'll be in your office in town tomorrow?"

He nodded. "And Bruno will be here with you while I'm gone."

"I'm surprised we didn't see him today. He usually pops in at some time during the day," she said.

"I talked to him on the phone this morning. He had nothing new to report."

"I was hoping he'd find more people who saw that man take me out the back door." She took a drink of her water, swallowing against her disappointment.

"Hopefully, he will find more people before trial. But if we only have the four witnesses, that should be enough to cause reasonable doubt."

There was a confidence in his tone that soothed her fears. She had to believe that he was going to get her off the charges against her. She refused to believe any other scenario. Besides, she believed in Nick.

They finished their meal, and after cleaning up, they moved to the living room, where they watched a movie, and then it was bedtime. He hadn't mentioned any more about her coming into his bedroom to snuggle.

He headed for his bedroom, and she went to hers. She pulled on her nightgown and then washed her face and brushed her teeth. She went back into her bedroom and pulled down the covers, disappointed that she apparently wasn't going to end her day by cuddling with Nick.

She had just slid into the sheets when he called out to her. "Heather...are you coming in here?"

She practically leapt out of the bed. "Yes, yes I am," she replied. She grabbed her purse off the nightstand and hurried toward his bedroom. Since the night the men had broken into her shanty, she'd been carrying the purse everywhere she went. She would never be caught without her daddy's gun again.

She took one step inside his bedroom and dissolved into a fit of giggles. He sat up in bed, bare chested but wearing a ridiculous aluminum cap on his head. It even had a small bill, making it resemble a ball cap.

She dropped her purse on the floor and fell to the bed as she continued to laugh. "That's hysterical," she said amid giggles.

He looked at her in mock indignation. "Please do not make fun of the item that keeps me safe in case of an alien attack."

"You are such a goof ball," she said.

"Please don't let anyone know. It would ruin my tough-guy reputation," he replied with a wide grin. He swept the hat off his head and placed it on the bed.

"Your secret is safe with me." She picked the hat up and examined it. "When on earth did you have time to make this?"

"I sneaked a roll of foil out of the kitchen after breakfast, and then I spent part of the afternoon fashioning it just for you. I had to do something to hold up my end of the bargain."

"The bargain?"

"You know, the one where I got to snuggle with you, but the payment for the pleasure was letting you see me in that hat."

"Oh, that bargain." She got out of bed and carried the hat to the dresser. "I'm just going to set it right here, so if you feel the presence of aliens, you can easily grab it." She immediately went back to his bed and joined him beneath the sheets.

He turned off the bedside lamp and then pulled her into his arms so he could spoon her. He swept her hair aside and then kissed her on the nape of the neck. "Goodnight, Heather."

"'Night, Nick," she replied. She snuggled into him. This was the way to go to sleep…with laughter in her heart and the man she loved holding her tight. She would gladly exchange the sound of waves lapping against wood and the croak of bullfrogs for the sound of Nick's even breathing next to her.

She awakened the next morning once again alone in the bed. Nick had apparently gotten up again without waking her. The smell of fresh coffee wafted in the air as she left his bedroom and went to her own to get dressed for the day.

There was a lightness in her heart as she went into the kitchen and greeted him. He stood at the stove, cooking sausage patties. "Sausage and waffles," he said.

"Sounds delicious," she replied as she poured herself a cup of coffee. "Is there anything I can do to help?"

"Yeah, you can pour us each a glass of orange juice," he replied. Lordy, but the man looked so hot in his jeans and a white T-shirt. "Other than that, I've got everything under control."

She poured the juice and then sat and watched as he poured thick batter into an awaiting waffle maker. "I'm planning on leaving here around ten this morning. My appointment with the client is at ten thirty, and I should be home by noon."

"So Bruno will be on babysitting duty again," she said.

"He's never had such a beautiful baby to guard," he said with a grin that flashed his dimples and caused a new warmth to cascade through her.

After breakfast, Nick went back to his bedroom to change his clothes for his meeting in town. When he came back into the living room, he was clad in black slacks, a gray dress shirt and a black suit jacket that she knew hid his holster and gun. He also wore an attractive gray-and-black tie.

"You look all ready for business," she said. He looked ridiculously handsome with a faint aura of danger. She stepped up in front of him and straightened the knot of his tie.

"Thank you," he said.

She smiled up at him. "I can't in good conscience let you go out in public with a crooked tie."

He returned the smile. "And I love that about you."

She stepped back from him, and at that moment there was a knock on the door. It was Bruno, who greeted them both and then sank down on the sofa.

"Bruno, you want coffee or anything to drink?" she asked.

"Nah, I'm good," he replied.

"I should be back around noon," Nick said to his friend.

"Whatever, I'm here for as long as you're gone," Bruno replied.

Minutes later, Nick was gone and Heather sank down on the love seat. "Nick depends on you a lot," she said.

"He's a good man. I depend on him, too."

"He's a wonderful man," Heather replied tremulously. "How did the two of you meet?"

"We met when Nick was in fifth grade and I was in third grade," Bruno said. "At that time, I was a scrawny little kid who got picked on a lot. Meanwhile, everyone liked Nick. He was popular, got good grades and was already a handsome dude. Anyway, one day a couple of older guys were punching around on me, and Nick stepped in. He told them I was one of his best friends, and I was to be left alone."

"Did it work?" Heather asked.

Bruno offered her one of his rare smiles. "Like a charm. We became great friends after that. Then by the time junior high rolled around, I had a big growth spurt and could handle myself without his help."

"It just goes to show again what a wonderful man Nick is," she replied.

Bruno stared at her for a long moment. "You think you're in love with him, don't you?"

Heather's heart quickened. "I don't think so... I know so. I'm in love with him." It felt great to finally admit her feelings out loud. "I am completely in love with him."

Bruno frowned. "Look, Heather, I don't want to see you get hurt, but Nick is fairly unavailable when it comes to love."

Her heart felt like it suddenly stopped beating. "W-what do you mean? He has seemed very available to me."

Bruno shrugged. "You're a beautiful woman living under his roof."

The implication was that Nick was just taking advantage of her. As she thought of all the deep conversations she and Nick had had...all the laughter they had shared, she just couldn't believe it. She knew Nick cared about her on a much deeper level. In fact, she believed he was falling in love with her, too.

"It's more than that between us," she finally said in protest.

Bruno leaned forward. "Nick will never again trust a woman enough to get married, especially if that woman is a client of his."

"But, why?" she asked and stared at the bald man inquisitively.

"Has he told you about Delia?" He leaned back again.

She frowned. "Delia? Who is Delia?"

"So he hasn't told you about Delia Hunter." She shook her head. "She was a client of his several years ago."

"What about her?" she asked in confusion. What would an old client have to do with the here and now and what was on going on between her and Nick?

"Ask Nick. It's not my story to tell," Bruno replied. "I'm just telling you this because I don't want to see you get hurt, and I don't want my friend to get hurt."

"I would never...could never hurt Nick. I owe him so much for everything he has done for me."

"Are you sure your love for him isn't just a huge amount of gratitude?" He looked at her long and hard. "I would think in these circumstances it would be easy to mistake the two."

"Trust me, what I feel for him isn't simple gratitude," she replied. "It's so much more than that."

"See how you feel about things once the trial is over," he replied. "And now I'm done talking about it," he replied. "I already said too much as it is. Why don't you turn on one of your shows to watch until Nick gets back here."

She turned on the television, but there was no way she could concentrate on a show when so many thoughts were racing in her head.

She knew her heart where Nick was concerned. She was definitely grateful to him, but aside from her gratitude, her love for him continued to grow each and every day.

Was Nick just using her because she was pretty and available? Because she was swamp and therefore easy to use and then eventually discard when this was all over?

She found that hard to believe. Nick just wasn't that kind of man. He was an honorable man who would never use a woman like that. Or did he have her completely fooled? Still, there was one question that whirled around and around in her head. Who in the heck was Delia Hunter?

NICK WAS UNIMPRESSED with his new client. He'd already overheard Brett Mayfield talking crap about Heather and people from the swamp when he'd been in the café. Now the man needed representation due to a bar fight that saw him arrested.

The fight had occurred in a seedy bar located on the west side of town. Nick had never even been in Ralph's Brewery, where the parking lot was usually filled with big motorcycles and pickup trucks.

Once again Tommy Radcliffe had thrown the book at the man, charging him with assault and battery for beating down a man. From what Nick had learned, it was a typical bar fight with fists thrown by a lot of boozed-up hotheads.

"Radcliffe is just picking on me," the big man whined. "I was only defending myself. That crazy Dax Patrick came at me. I don't even know what he's doing in Crystal Cove. He's a creep and an outsider and doesn't belong here."

"I'll see what I can do to get the charges changed to a misdemeanor," Nick replied.

"I got money. I can afford to pay a big fine. That's the only reason why Radcliffe charged me and not that creep Dax. Besides, I wasn't the only one throwing fists that night. There were a lot of men throwing down."

"Let's get this all taken care of." Nick had the man sign the appropriate paperwork. "From the notes I got from your arraignment, the trial is set for a month away. However, I'm hoping we won't have to go to trial. I'll be in touch with you in the next couple of days," he said as Brett stood to leave.

"And I'll be waiting to hear from you," Brett replied and then left his office. Brett was a big meathead, hotheaded and ready to punch people, especially when booze was added to the mix. Still, Nick was fairly sure it would never get to trial. He would call Tommy in the next day or two and see what they could work out. He imagined Tommy would be okay with a large fine paid by Brett.

Sharon knocked on his door and then came into his office. She had been keeping the office open for new walk-in clients while Nick had been working from home.

"Heard you had a date the other night," he said to her and gestured to the chair in front of his desk.

"I did." She sat. "Do you mind? About me and Bruno?"

"Why on earth would I mind?" he asked.

"I wasn't sure if you were okay with us fraternizing with each other outside of work hours," she replied.

"Even big-muscled bald guys need love," he replied with a grin.

She laughed. "It's not that deep yet. It was just one date, although he did invite me to get ice cream with him tomorrow night. Uh...did he say anything to you about me?"

"No, he's playing it close to his chest. You know how he is, Sharon. He doesn't talk much and especially not about his feelings. But I would say the fact that he asked you out again means he enjoyed your company."

Her cheeks pinkened. "I really enjoyed his company, too."

"Speaking of feelings, how are things going between you and Heather? It must be difficult sharing your space after living alone for so long."

"She makes it incredibly easy. She's the perfect houseguest, and we get along great." Too great, he thought to himself.

"Are you ready for trial?" Sharon asked.

"Yeah, in fact I'm going to be sending you a lot of things in the next week or so to prepare for the big day."

"I stand ready to serve," she replied.

"That's good because you know I depend on you," Nick replied. "And now I'd better get out of here. I've got Bruno with Heather, and the two of them still aren't very comfortable with each other."

He stood, along with Sharon. She returned to her desk in the front, and he left the office. As he drove home, his thoughts were filled with Heather.

He had been so determined to distance himself from her, but he'd failed at that miserably. When he smelled her perfume all day long and enjoyed every minute he spent in her company, it was damned difficult to deprive himself of her.

Besides, it wouldn't be long now before her trial was over.

At that time, she would return to her life and her shanty in the swamp, and their time together would be over.

His chest tightened as he thought about no longer having her in his world. He couldn't be in love with her because he refused to believe in love again. He would never trust in a woman's love again, especially a client's love. Fool me once, shame on you. Fool me twice, shame on me.

He just wanted to enjoy her now, and then he would let her go so she could find a man who was emotionally available to her…somebody who wasn't in charge of her future… a man she wasn't grateful to.

As always when he drove down his street, he looked for potential danger. This quiet that was going on right now from the killer felt loaded. The closer they got to trial, the more dangerous he would be. If he was afraid of what Heather might testify to, then he was going to make a move to silence her permanently and soon. Somehow, they all had to be ready for it.

Unfortunately, Etienne and his men hadn't found any clues or leads to follow about the men who had tried to break into Heather's shanty. So, nothing had come from that investigation.

He saw no strange cars and nobody to give him pause on the street, and so he pulled into his garage, parked and closed the door behind him.

He had to keep her safe, and he had to get her off the charges. At this moment in time, he wasn't sure what was going to be more difficult.

He got out of his car and went inside to find Bruno and Heather in the living room. They were watching a show on television, and the moment she saw him she reached for the remote and hit the pause button.

"That was quick. How did your meeting go?" she asked.

"It went fine." He pulled on the knot of his tie and unfastened it. "How are things here?" He looked at Bruno and then back at her. He sensed a weird kind of tension in the air.

"Things are fine, except she's got me watching some reality show," Bruno replied and immediately stood. "Now that you're home, I'll just get out of here. I'm assuming we're doing surveillance duty tonight."

"That's the plan," Nick said as he walked his friend to the door.

"Okay, then I'll see you tonight." With that, Bruno left.

Nick walked back into the living room. "I'm going to go change into more comfortable clothes, and then I'll be right back," he said.

"Okay," she replied.

He changed into jeans and a gray T-shirt and then returned to the living room. He sank down on the sofa next to her and smiled. "Anything exciting happen while I was gone?"

"No, nothing, but in just a few minutes I need to get into the kitchen and put dinner in to cook."

"And what culinary delight are you making for dinner tonight?"

"Smothered steak and potatoes, corn and salad."

"Hmm, sounds delicious. You know if you ever tire of making the evening meals, I can take over."

"No, I really enjoy cooking for you. However, I must say that your freezer is getting fairly empty, and tonight will be the last of the fresh lettuce."

"I'll make a grocery order tonight and have it delivered tomorrow."

She looked at him in surprise. "The store will do that? Bring groceries to your doorstep?"

He laughed. "They will if you pay extra for the pleasure of home delivery."

"I wonder how much it would cost to get groceries delivered to me in the swamp."

"Probably a lot," he replied.

"You're probably right," she said. "If you order some fish, I can fix my awesome fried fish for dinner one night."

"Awesome fried fish, now that sounds like a plan," he replied.

She smiled. "On that note, I think I'll get busy in the kitchen."

"It's awfully early for you to start cooking dinner," he observed.

"I know. I'm mostly just doing some preparation work, and then I'll actually cook it all later this afternoon," she explained.

"And I'm going to go do a little work in my office," he replied. "So I'll just see you later."

"Later," she echoed. They both got off the sofa. She headed for the kitchen, and he went down the hall to his office. For the next two hours, he got most of the information he would need to defend Brett Mayfield and then worked on his opening statement for Heather's trial.

He'd hoped that Heather's trial would never happen. He'd hoped the charges would be dropped, but it looked like nothing was going to stop it now.

The opening statement was one of the most important things in a trial. It told the jurors what his case was and how they were going to prove Heather's innocence. He'd been writing and rewriting it for the past week, needing to make sure he got it all exactly right.

He'd had the subpoenas served on the four witnesses

who saw Heather with the man going out the back door. He would like to have an interview with each of them before trial, but he'd called them all, and they told him they didn't want to talk unless they had to and that would be under oath.

He was starting to feel as if all the cards were stacked against them. Etienne was too busy with the other big crime going on, Tommy was being a stubborn jerk and witnesses didn't want to talk. At this point, what else could go wrong?

By the time Heather called him for dinner, his stomach was growling with hunger and he was ready to knock off for the day. He went into the kitchen, where she was placing dinner on the table.

"Hmm, smells good," he said as he sank down in his chair at the table.

"This is something I cook occasionally for myself at home since it's a skillet dish," she replied.

She joined him at the table, and they began to eat. The steak was incredibly tender, as were the chunks of potatoes and mushrooms. It was all covered with a thick, flavorful gravy.

"This is really good," he said.

"Thanks," she replied succinctly.

Something was off. She was unnaturally quiet through the meal. Even though he tried to make small talk with her as they ate, she appeared distracted and distant. Her energy felt low, and even when he tried to get her to laugh by saying something silly, her response was lackluster.

With everything that was going on in her life, she certainly deserved to have an off day. But it bothered him. He wanted to know what was going on in her pretty head. He wanted to somehow make it better.

He waited to say anything to her until dinner was done

and the dishes were cleared. They moved into the living room and decided on a movie, but before he hit Play, he leaned over and took her hand in his.

"Heather, is anything wrong? You were unusually quiet through dinner. You seem preoccupied. Are you worried about anything? Is there something I can do to help?"

Her eyes were unusually dark as she held his gaze for a long moment. "No, I've just been thinking about what's going to happen. Even if you win my case, I'm trying to figure out exactly how I'll pick up the pieces of my life. Will there be some people in town who believe I'm guilty of something even after my trial? Will people maybe think I conspired with that guy to kill Wesley? Will anyone ever shop at my store again?"

"Whoa," Nick said and squeezed her hand tightly. She was obviously getting more and more upset with every sentence she spoke. "Honey, when this is all over and you've been found innocent, there's no question in my mind that you will easily be able to pick up the pieces. You are such a strong woman, Heather. I know you'll be fine, and people will return to getting their fresh herbs from you. Something else will come along for people to talk about. Please believe me, you're going to be just fine." He gave her hand another tight squeeze, and then he released it.

She let go of a tremulous sigh and then held his gaze for another long moment. "Who is Delia?"

Shock sat him upright at the name from his past. As Heather held his gaze expectantly, he realized he was going to have to tell her about his painful love story.

## Chapter Twelve

Heather saw the utter surprise that overtook his features, and then he released what sounded like a weary sigh. "I guess my partner has a big mouth," he said.

"He just mentioned her in passing and I was naturally curious," she replied. She was more than curious. She needed to know about the woman who, according to Bruno, kept Nick from ever wanting to commit to anyone else.

He broke his gaze from hers and instead stared off into the space just above her right shoulder. "She was a client of mine, and she'd been charged with breaking and entering into an apartment and badly beating the woman inside. Apparently the two had heated words with one another over a fender bender in the grocery store parking lot. She insisted she was innocent of the charges against her, and I immediately believed her. She was a beautiful woman, and in the two months before her trial started, we grew very close."

"You were in love with her," Heather said softly.

He looked back at her and slowly nodded his head. "Yeah, I was. I thought she was the one...the woman I'd been waiting for. I wanted to marry her and build a future with her. I wanted her to have my babies. She seemed to want the same things, and I was sure when her trial was over, we were going to have a very happy life together forever."

He gazed away from her again and cleared his throat. "Anyway, that didn't happen. I won at her trial, and she was cleared of all charges against her. It was then she confessed to me that she'd only acted like she was in love with me so that I would work my hardest to get her off. She told me she was grateful for all my hard work, and then the next day she left town with another man. And that's the story of Delia."

"She broke your heart badly," Heather said softly.

Once again, he looked at her. "Yeah, she did," he agreed.

She felt his pain. It emanated off him in waves and dulled the blue of his eyes. She hurt for him, and now she understood what Bruno had said…about Nick being emotionally unavailable to another woman, especially one who was his client.

"Nick, I'm so sorry that happened to you, but not all women are like her," she said.

He released a small, dry laugh. "Logically I know that, but the heart remains wary."

"I could never pretend to love a man no matter how high the stakes were for me," she said fervently. She leaned toward him, fighting her impulse to touch him in some way.

"It was an evil thing for her to do, but, Nick, you shouldn't close your heart off to giving and receiving love because of her."

She wanted to say so much more to him. She wanted to bare her heart and soul to him. She desperately wanted to tell him that she was deeply in love with him. But this wasn't the time for that…not now when his heart was so heavy with memories of a past betrayal.

"I'm so sorry that happened to you, Nick. You didn't deserve that," she finally said.

He smiled at her and reached out to touch a strand of her hair. "You're a very nice woman, Heather."

She returned his smile. "I'm glad you realize that."

He dropped his hand and cleared his throat once again. "Ready to watch another show?" he asked. "We have plenty of time before Bruno gets here for surveillance."

"Sure," she replied, although she could think of many other ways to pass the time before surveillance. She'd like to stroke the side of his face until the darkness in his eyes lifted. She wanted to take him in her arms and hold him tight. She wanted to kiss him with enough passion that he would forget Delia's name.

Instead, she focused on the crime drama he'd put on for them to watch. She'd been watching it for several minutes when a remembered scent filled her head.

"Spearmint," she suddenly said. "The man who carried me out into the alley smelled of beer and spearmint. I just remembered that."

He paused the show and turned to her. "And Etienne found spearmint gum wrappers in a parking space across the street from your shop on the day we were shot at."

"So it was likely the same man. Oh, I wish I could remember more about that night," she said miserably.

"I know you're doing the best you can. Heather, even if you don't remember another single thing, we might have enough evidence to beat the charges. We have four witnesses who corroborate the fact that a man was in that alley with you and Wesley, and that's a real game changer."

"I just want the man who killed Wesley, the man who has

tried to kill me, behind bars," she replied. "He needs to go away for the rest of his life for what he's done."

"I definitely agree with you, and once the charges against you are dropped then Etienne will have no other choice but to reopen the case. He'll find this guy, and justice will be served."

"I hope so," she replied fervently.

He put the show back on, but her thoughts whirled around and around in her head, making it impossible for her to focus on the drama taking place on screen.

Her thoughts continued to be tangled in her head as they parked at the drug house for another night of surveillance. Bruno and Nick talked softly about past cases they'd worked on, and she tried to sort out all the information she'd gained about Nick.

That Delia woman had apparently done a real number on his head. She understood now why Nick would be so wary about getting involved with another client again.

And yet they were involved. He could pretend he didn't care about her, but Heather knew better. Despite what Delia had done to him, Heather believed he had healed and his heart was once again open.

Was he afraid she was another Delia just pretending to care about him, and once he won her case, she would dip out of his life forever? All she could do was continue to show him her love and hope it broke through any doubts he might have about her.

She wouldn't speak the actual words to him until her case was over. Then he would know for sure that her case had nothing to do with her love for him.

These thoughts were interrupted as a car pulled up to the house. She leaned forward with anticipation and then slumped back in the seat as a young woman got out of the car.

Heather popped a little cinnamon bear in her mouth and chewed the sweet. This whole thing felt like such a waste of time. They really had no clue if the man they sought was part of the drug world. They had no idea if he would eventually come to this run-down house. They could be spinning their wheels all for nothing with these surveillances.

They were only guessing that he fought with Wesley that night over drugs and money owed. The two men might have been fighting over something else altogether. So far, Bruno had found nobody who was willing to talk to him about Wesley's drug abuse.

"They're all afraid of self-incrimination," Bruno had said. "Apparently the drug problem among the upper crust here in Crystal Coves is a dirty little secret."

It was now close to midnight, and the moon shone down a beautiful illumination. Suddenly a wave of homesickness struck her and tightened her chest.

She missed seeing the moonlight dance on the dark swamp waters at night. She also missed seeing the early morning sun painting everything with a golden gild. There was no place as beautiful as where she lived, with its vivid green colors and the lacy Spanish moss. When this was all over, she'd dance on her porch and breathe in the scents of home. And if things didn't work out with Nick, she'd mourn deep and long over the fact that he was gone from her life.

The door to the house flew open, and two men stepped out on the rickety front porch. They were both big men, and they were armed.

Oh God, she thought. If they decided to do a street patrol

now, it wasn't going to end as well as it had last time, unless Nick decided to plant a big kiss on Bruno.

"Something is about to happen," Bruno said, his voice low and taut.

"Yeah, but what?" Nick replied, his voice also filled with tension.

Heather leaned forward and started chewing her nail as nervous tension filled her. The men remained standing outside, obviously on some kind of guard duty. But what or who were they guarding?

About fifteen minutes later, a car pulled up out front. Heather watched the man who got out of the car. "It's him," she exclaimed with excitement. She leaned forward and gripped Nick's shoulder. "That's the man who carried me out of the back door that night."

"Are you sure?" Nick asked.

"I'm positive," she replied and squeezed his shoulder.

Bruno raised the fancy camera he always had with him on surveillance nights and began to take photos until the man disappeared into the house.

"I mostly got pictures of his back. I'm hoping to get better ones when he comes back out of the house," Bruno said.

"Then we'll have the pictures to take to Etienne," Nick replied with his own excitement.

The man was only in the house for about ten minutes and then he exited. Once again, Bruno's camera clicked and whirred, only stopping when the man disappeared into the car. The two guards immediately went back into the house.

"I'll see if I can get a picture of the license plate," Bruno said, and he took more photos as the man drove off.

"Finally, some success," Nick said.

"About time," Bruno replied.

Excitement winged through Heather's blood as well. The time spent here had been a success, and soon the man would be identified.

"Now we can get out of here. We'll go to my place and have a celebratory drink." Nick started the car.

"Sounds like a plan to me," Bruno said.

Heather really hoped Bruno had gotten some good photos and they could find out the man's name. She was certain he had killed Wesley in that alley and had tried to kill her. Hopefully Etienne could get him into custody, not only to once and for all prove her innocence, but also to make sure the man would never try to kill her again. Or anyone else.

They got back to the house, and Nick made drinks for them all. Heather sipped on the whiskey and soda while Nick and Bruno looked at the pictures in the camera.

"Boom," Nick said at one point. "That's a perfect one for us to get him identified." He moved away from Bruno. "Can you have these all printed out by morning?"

"I can. How about I plan on meeting you here around nine in the morning with the prints?"

"That would be great, and you can stick around here while I take them to Etienne?" Nick asked.

"Definitely." Bruno downed the last of his drink and stood. "I'd better get out of here now so I can have things ready in the morning."

Nick set his drink down and also stood. "I'll walk you out."

A moment later, Nick returned to the room and smiled at her. It was one of his full-dimpled smiles that rushed a sweet heat through her. "What a great night," he said.

"Definitely," she replied.

"There's only one thing that would make it better."

"And what's that?" she asked.

"It will make it a perfect night if I can fall asleep next to you."

She smiled at him. "I totally feel the same way."

"Then let's go to bed." He held out a hand to her and pulled her up and off the sofa. She grabbed her purse, and then together they headed down the hallway.

Minutes later, Nick was spooned around her, sound asleep. Surely, she was making ways into his heart. Bruno was wrong about his friend. She believed Nick was open and ready to love again, and she truly believed Nick loved her.

To think this was all temporary and just a dream that would end hurt her heart. They were about to catch the killer, and that would exonerate her, but in the end, would she be left all alone and brokenhearted?

"This is a photo of the man who was in that alley with Heather and Wesley," Nick said the next morning as he handed Etienne one of the photos they had taken the night before.

Etienne took the photo from him. He frowned and looked back at Nick. "And how do you know this?"

"Heather positively identified him as the man who took her out in the alley. He was coming out of the drug house on 22nd Street. We've had the house under surveillance for some time now, figuring he might show up there," Nick explained.

"Dammit, Nick, don't you know how dangerous that might be?" Etienne gave him a dark, disapproving look.

"I had Bruno with me," Nick replied.

"I don't care. It was still damned dangerous," Etienne said.

"But successful," Nick said with a grin.

Etienne released a deep sigh and then looked at the picture. "I don't recognize him. I don't suppose Heather remembered his name?"

"I don't think she ever knew his name. According to her, she didn't speak to him before all this happened. And I'll bet you a dollar when you find him you'll discover he chews spearmint gum."

"I'll give copies of this to my officers and see if we can get a name on this guy."

"Can you also show it to the four people I've subpoenaed? They won't talk to me right now, but I'd like to get confirmation from them that this is the man they saw helping Heather out the back door at the Voodoo Lounge that night."

"I can do that," the lawman agreed.

"Anything moving on the Soul Stealer case?"

Once again Etienne frowned. "Nothing. I swear this man moves like a ghost through the night. He manages to take control of people without a sound and then whisk them away without leaving a single clue behind."

"And still no movement from Colette."

Etienne shook his head. "Nothing. I've been spending my nights in her hospital room, holding her hand and talking to her. I'm hoping the human touch and the sound of my voice will somehow assure her and call her back to consciousness." He released a dry, slightly embarrassed laugh. "I know it sounds stupid."

"Not at all," Nick replied. "And for everyone's sake, I hope it works." Nick couldn't stand the idea of Heather returning to the swamp with this madman at work. He couldn't stand the idea of anything bad ever happening to her again.

"I'll just get out of here and let you get back to work.

You'll call me if any of your officers find out the identity of this guy?"

"Definitely, and if your witnesses all identify him as the man who took Heather out into the alley, then I'll encourage Tommy to drop the charges against her, and I'll reopen the case."

"That's definitely music to my ears," Nick replied and stood. "Then I'll talk to you later."

"Later," Etienne agreed.

Nick walked out into the late morning sunshine feeling more optimistic about the fact that Heather's case was probably never going to trial. While he was confident that, in the end, he would have been successful in getting her off, having the charges dropped was now in the best interest of justice.

He fully expected to get a phone call from Tommy in the next day or two telling him the charges against Heather had been dropped and the case had been reopened.

As he was walking to his car, he passed a jewelry shop and had a sudden desire to go in and buy something for Heather in celebration. He entered the shop and was greeted by Mollie LeBlanc.

"Hey, Mollie, it's nice to see you again," he said, remembering her from the night he had met all of Heather's friends. "But I thought you clerked at the grocery store."

"I did, but I quit to come here and work. I figured the odds of meeting the wealthy man who is going to marry me and get me out of the swamp were better selling jewelry here instead of ringing up fish at the grocery store."

He laughed. "Has it worked yet? Have you met that special wealthy guy?"

"Nah, but a girl can always hope. Now, what can I get for you today?"

"I wanted to look at your gold necklaces," he said. Heather didn't wear a necklace presumably because she didn't have one. He could only imagine the beauty of the gold against her beautiful olive skin.

"Is this for you?" Mollie asked.

"No, actually it's for Heather," he replied.

Mollie's eyes widened. "Oh, that's so nice. She will love it." She cast him a sly smile. "Is there a special reason for the gift?"

"We've become good friends, and she's been through so much, so I just wanted to do something nice for her," he replied, hoping no gossip would follow this purchase.

Mollie led him to a glass display case that held an array of gold necklaces. There were different sizes and lengths to consider. After some thought, he finally settled on one, and once Mollie had placed it into a gift box, he left the store.

*What are you doing, man?* He asked himself as he drove home. What in the hell was he doing with Heather? He was in love with her. The realization suddenly hit him like a ton of bricks over his head.

Oh God, he'd tried to keep his heart away from her. He'd tried to shield himself from the very emotions he now realized he harbored deep in his heart for her.

But he had no willpower where she was concerned. He thought it was all about desiring her physically. But he now realized he wanted to spend each and every minute during the day with her and to wrap her in his arms every night. He wanted to laugh with her for the rest of his life. He'd been a stupid fool.

Yes, he was in love with her, but he would never trust

that she loved him back. Oh, she might believe herself to be in love with him, but he would never believe that her love hadn't grown out of deep gratitude and would disappear once she was finally safe and free.

This was the beginning of the end. Their time together was growing to a close. Within days, she could potentially go back to the swamp. She didn't know it, but she would take his heart with her.

He would never let anyone know the depths of his love for her and how badly he would mourn when she was gone. He would hide his feelings deep inside. He had known better than to mix business with pleasure, but he'd allowed himself to blur those lines, and now he would pay the consequences for that.

The necklace he'd bought her would be a goodbye gift, and maybe when she wore it, she would occasionally think of the lawyer who had helped her out when she had no other place to go…the man who had believed in her innocence despite all evidence to the contrary.

He pulled into his garage and pocketed the gift box. When he walked in, Bruno and Heather were in their usual places in the living room.

"How did it go?" Bruno asked him.

"Better than expected," he replied and sank down on the sofa next to the big man. "Etienne is going to have all his officers flashing the photo around town to see if they can get the man's name. He's also going to encourage Tommy to drop the charges against you," he said to Heather.

"That would be amazing," she replied, a happy light dancing in her eyes.

"Yeah, that means within the next few days you could be back in your shanty and resuming your life again," he said.

"That would be nice," she replied, although Nick could have sworn the sparkle in her eyes dimmed a bit. Still, it could have just been a trick of the light.

"It will be nice for us all to get back to our own normal lives," Bruno said.

"Amen to that," Nick added.

Moments later Bruno had gone, and Nick and Heather were alone again. "While I was out, I bought you a little present," he said.

Her eyes widened. "A present for me? Why?"

"Because I wanted to and as a celebration of sorts," he replied. He got up and pulled the gift box out of his pocket. He took the lid off and crouched down beside her so she could see what was inside.

"Oh, Nick...it's beautiful, but I can't accept that from you," she protested.

"And why not?" he asked.

"Because it's obviously expensive, and I already owe you so much," she said.

"So you would take away my pleasure in giving you a gift? Come on, Heather. Don't take away my joy. Besides, it will look beautiful on you, and I wanted you to have something from me when this is all over." He unfastened it and took it out of the box. "Now, move your hair aside so I can put it on you."

She swept her long mane aside, and he fastened the necklace on her. "There," he said as he stepped back from her. "Just as I figured, it looks beautiful on your skin."

She touched the necklace with her fingertips. "Thank you, Nick. I'll wear it always."

He simply couldn't help himself. He pulled her up and off

the sofa and into his arms. She immediately molded herself to him and wrapped her arms around his neck.

"I can't believe it's almost over," she said softly. "It's been a nightmare, and yet it's also been a wonderful dream all at the same time."

"I agree, but even wonderful dreams have to come to an end," he said and released his hold on her. He had to stop touching her…stop wanting her before he got in any deeper. It was just a matter of days before she went back to her life in the swamp, and their time together would end.

It was best that way. She deserved a man who would love her without restraint, and he told himself it simply wasn't going to be him. Soon after, he went into his office and she went into the kitchen. He heard the ding of a message on his phone, and when he opened it, it was an alert to let him know his groceries were arriving.

He had requested contactless delivery, and ten minutes later he watched out the peep hole of the front door as a young man lined up the plastic bags on his porch. He recognized the man as someone who had delivered to him before.

When he was gone, Nick cautiously opened his door, his gun at the ready. Until Etienne had the bad guy in custody, there was still the possibility of danger. This would be a perfect opportunity for somebody to rush his door.

He gazed all around the area, and seeing nobody anywhere around, he quickly pulled the bags inside and then closed and relocked the door. He carried the bags into the kitchen. "Special delivery," he said as he placed the groceries on the kitchen table.

He'd decided to keep things as light and simple as possible after the emotional morning. He'd let her know in so many ways now that an ongoing relationship between the two of them wasn't going to happen, that this magic they had going on between them was, indeed, coming to an end.

He'd hoped to get a phone call from Etienne telling him the man in the photo had been identified, but by dinner time that still hadn't happened.

She'd fixed another delicious meal. The roast was tender and served with rich brown gravy. Mashed potatoes and a vegetable medley rounded out the supper.

"I'm definitely going to miss your cooking," he said.

"I'm sure you'll be just fine cooking for yourself," she replied.

They fell silent for a few minutes as they focused on eating. He couldn't get a read on her mood. She was quiet and appeared pensive. He had a feeling he'd hurt her with all his talk of her going home.

The very last thing he'd ever wanted to do was hurt Heather. But he'd warned her that he wasn't in the market for a wife. He'd told her early on that he wasn't promising her anything.

He couldn't help it that their relationship had deepened and grown. She would eventually realize he did her a favor by making her go. She would eventually realize that any feelings she had toward him were tangled up with feelings of gratitude.

It was possible she was ready to go home, back to the swamp that she loved. It was possible she was more than ready to leave here…leave him. After all, she'd never told him she was in love with him. Maybe he was just a conceited jerk for believing she might be.

"Are you okay?" he finally asked.

She looked up at him and smiled. "I'm fine. I'm just a bit tired."

"Just think, there's no more need for middle-of-the-night surveillance, so tonight we can go to bed at a reasonable hour and get a good night's sleep."

"That sounds absolutely wonderful," she replied.

They finished eating and then cleaned up the kitchen and went into the living room. "I thought that maybe tonight instead of watching a movie, maybe I could teach you a little chess," he suggested.

"That sounds like fun. But I'm only interested on one condition. You teach me chess for an hour, and I teach you how to dance for an hour." She cast him an impish smile. Oh, he loved it when her eyes sparkled with humor and she looked so happy.

He laughed. "Okay, it's a deal." He got his chessboard out of a cabinet that was set against one wall.

She watched as he set it all up on the coffee table. "My father used to play chess with a couple of his buddies when I was younger," she said. "I always thought it looked intriguing, but he never taught me to play."

"I find it intriguing," he replied. "It's definitely a game of strategy."

"Then that explains why you like it," she replied. "As a lawyer, I'm sure you're all about strategy."

He laughed. "Maybe a little bit."

He then began to explain to her how the game was played and how the different pieces moved. Just as he suspected, she was a quick study. After a half an hour of explaining how each piece moved, they began to play their first game.

He easily beat her. The second game, she made several smart adjustments to her play, but once again he beat her. But by the third game, he had to work hard to win against her. They quit playing after he won the fourth game.

"You wait and see, I'll beat you when we play again," she replied boastfully as they cleared off the game from the coffee table. "Okay, I now know how to play chess, so it's time to see how you dance. Can you put on some music for us to dance to?" Her eyes shone merrily.

He got up and turned his stereo on. It immediately piped an oldies song through the house. She remained sitting on the sofa, her eyes bright. "Why don't you show me how you would dance to this, and then I'll know how much work I have ahead of me."

"Okay." He intentionally moved as awkwardly as he could, flailing his arms and legs around and setting her into a bout of giggles. "Stop," she cried between laughs. "Please stop...you're doing that on purpose."

"Then get up and show me how it's done," he replied.

She rose to her feet and took his hands in hers. "Just sway and get a feel for the music," she instructed.

He swayed with her, and then she showed him several steps and they began to dance. He was never going to get a job as a professional dancer, but after several fast songs he felt good about the fact that at least he wouldn't make a total fool out of himself on the dance floor in the future.

Then a slow song came on, and he pulled her into his arms. "This, I know how to do," he said softly. She fit so perfectly against him, and the sweet scent of her hair...of her...dizzied all his senses.

When she looked up at him, he took her lips in a tender kiss, and then he released her. "I think that's enough dancing for one night. I don't know about you, but I'm ready for bed."

"Me, too," she agreed. "Am I sleeping in your room?"

He should tell her no, start the distancing that needed to happen right now, but she definitely was his biggest weakness. Even if they didn't make love, he loved falling asleep with her in his arms.

"I would love for you to sleep in my bed," he replied, helpless against his own desire for her.

It would soon be all over, but for tonight he would sleep with her in his arms and cherish the moments he had left with her.

## Chapter Thirteen

Heather snuggled into Nick's arms. He had already fallen asleep, but despite her tiredness, she was finding sleep elusive. This had been the most difficult day she'd spent with Nick. He'd broken her heart in a million different little ways, and she'd had to fight hard to hide it.

He'd made it very obvious that he had no intention of continuing to pursue a relationship with her once this was all over. Somehow, she had hoped that he would profess his undying love for her, and they would live happily-ever-after. But that hadn't happened, and she knew now it wasn't going to happen.

She would return to her shanty all alone, and it was going to take her a very long time to get over loving him. And it was only when she was back in her familiar shanty that she would allow her tears of heartbreak to fall.

She would cry long and hard for the man she loved who didn't love her back. Yet, until today, she'd been so sure that he loved her. Oh, he hadn't said the words out loud, but it had been in the way she caught him gazing at her when he thought she wasn't looking. She'd felt his love every time he touched her in the simplest way. The necklace had felt like a gift of love from him. But apparently, it had been a present of goodbye. She'd been wrong to believe that he loved her as he'd made it clear throughout the entire day that he was letting her go.

She must have drifted off to sleep because a jarring siren noise awakened her. Nick was immediately up and out of the bed. "Somebody is breaking in," he yelled as he grabbed his gun from the nightstand. "Stay in here and call Etienne."

Her heart banged against her ribs in an accelerated rhythm as the siren continued to blare through the house. "No, Nick," she yelled as he peeked outside the door.

Even the siren couldn't hide the sound of a gunshot. Oh God, they were not only in the house, but they were also firing bullets in the direction of their bedroom.

She didn't have to be a rocket scientist to guess who it was, and right now she and Nick were trapped in the bedroom at the end of the long hallway. Eventually it would be easy for a man or men to creep down the hallway and get into this room where she and Nick would be sitting ducks.

She jumped off the bed and retrieved her phone from her purse. She quickly made the call to the police station and then pulled out her daddy's gun.

The house was dark except for the moonlight that drifted through the windows. Nick slid out into the hallway, and the sound of gunfire went off. One…two…three shots. Oh God, had Nick been hit?

On trembling legs, she ran to the doorway and peeked out. "Nick," she screamed as she saw no sign of him. Was he lying on the floor in the darkness? Bleeding to death or already dead from a gunshot wound? "Nick," she cried once again in desperation.

"Stay there, Heather," he yelled back. He'd apparently made it into the bathroom next to the bedroom. Another shot rang out, the bullet splintering the doorjamb next to where she stood. She screamed and stepped back into the bedroom.

Her fear tightened her chest, making it impossible for her to draw a deep breath. She panted, her abject terror, not just for herself, but also for Nick, ripping through her very soul.

The siren screeching overhead only added to the melee. What was Nick doing? Why had he left the bedroom? Was he trying to be some sort of hero? Facing the bad guys before they could get to her? He could be killed attempting to save her. The very last thing she wanted was a dead hero… a dead Nick. The very thought horrified her.

She gripped her gun more firmly in her hand. More gunfire sounded, and once again she peeked out of the room and down the hallway. The air there was smoky and smelled acrid from the gunpowder.

"Nick," she screamed once again, needing to assure herself he was still alive.

"I'm here," he yelled back from the same position.

As Heather watched the hallway, she saw a dark figure in the distance. She raised her gun and fired at him. She wasn't going to just sit on the bed and allow Nick to be killed by a thug who wanted her dead. She would do whatever she could to help Nick.

She stepped back into the room as answering gunshots fired back. "Heather…cover me," Nick yelled just loud enough for her to hear. Once again, she leaned out of the room and began to shoot as Nick quickly left the bathroom and raced across the hall into his office.

She suspected his plan. He wanted to back them up farther away from the bedroom where she was located. She now believed there were two shooters. Their guns sounded slightly different. She knew with certainty one of them was the man who had killed Wesley.

Her nerves had calmed a bit beneath a steely resolve to make sure she and Nick walked out of this madness alive. She breathed slowly, in through her nose and out through her mouth. She wanted to weep and scream, but she could fall apart later. Right now, Nick needed her to keep her head about her.

She looked out again and saw a figure rushing toward Nick's office. She closed her eyes and fired four shots, one right after the other. When she opened her eyes again, she saw a dark figure on the floor. Smoke swirled in the dark air, making it impossible for her to discern if it was Nick.

Oh God, was it Nick? Had she inadvertently shot him? Her heart seemed to stop beating. Had she accidentally killed the man she loved?

Then the man began to scream in pain. A shudder of deep relief rushed through her. Thank God it wasn't Nick. She lowered her gun, her knees weak with fear and the unknown.

The screaming siren overhead suddenly stopped, and the house was silent except for the man she had shot. "Get me an ambulance," he cried. "Dammit, I'm hurt and I need some help here."

"Don't trust him, Nick," she yelled. "It could be a ruse." At that moment, the sound of other sirens pierced the night. It was the sound of approaching police.

Heather sank to the floor as a rush of deep relief flowed through her veins, although she still tightly gripped her gun and watched the doorway.

Within minutes, all the lights in the house were turned

on, and police filled the place. She got back up to her feet, although her legs were still shaky.

It wasn't until Etienne disarmed the man in the hallway, with the bright lights gleaming overhead, that she finally saw who she had shot. It was him...the man who had killed Wesley.

She raised her gun. Now he was the sitting duck, and there was nothing more she would like to do than put a bullet in his evil heart. Her hand began to shake, and she finally lowered the gun. She couldn't shoot him. She wasn't like him.

She tossed the gun on Nick's bed and then left the room.

Nick met her in the hallway, and she collapsed in his arms, crying the tears she'd held in during the entire ordeal. He held her tight against him, stroking her back. "It's okay, Heather. We're safe now. It's finally over."

He led her to Etienne, who stood over the man who was bleeding and groaning and moaning from a wound in his lower thigh. He was also now handcuffed. "That's him, Chief Savoie. That's the man who took me out into the alley...that's the man who murdered Wesley," she said, still clinging to Nick.

"Shut up, you bitch," the man said, spitting the words out with rage.

"I'm not going to shut up," she replied angrily. "You killed Wesley, and you drugged me and tried to set me up."

"You were the perfect patsy," he exclaimed with a nasty laugh. "You were as dumb as a box of rocks that night, leaving your drink unattended like you did."

"Did Wesley owe you money? Did he take a bunch of drugs from you and not pay up?" Nick asked.

"Nobody steals from Dax Patrick," he exclaimed fervently. "I don't give a crap if you're some lowlife junkie on the street or some big-ass business man thinking he's smarter than me. Nobody steals from me and gets away with it."

"I've called for an ambulance, and as soon as it arrives, he'll be taken out of here. He'll go directly from the hospital to the jail. We also picked up two men attempting to flee from the scene, and they are also now in custody." Etienne offered Heather a tired smile. "You won't have to worry about this creep or any others ever again. They're all going away for a very long time."

In the light, the evidence of the gun battle was apparent in the holes in the walls. Tearfully, she looked up at Nick. "I'm sorry I shot up your house."

"Oh, honey." He squeezed her tight against him once again. "You can shoot up my house anytime," he said with a gentle smile.

It took another thirty minutes or so for the ambulance to arrive and whisk away the wounded, although the house was still full of police officers.

Heather and Nick had moved into the living room, where they had been questioned by Etienne. "Thank God your security system woke you up," Etienne said. "Otherwise, you would have been shot in bed."

"It did what it was supposed to do," Nick agreed.

They were left alone for a few minutes, and then Etienne approached them again. "I hate to tell you both this, but you're going to have to find other accommodations for the rest of the night. This is now a crime scene, and we'll need to process it and do a full investigation."

Nick frowned and looked at her. "I suppose we can get a room at the motel."

"That isn't necessary," she replied. She took Nick's hand in hers and held his gaze. "Come to my shanty, Nick. We'll be safe there now." There was nothing she would like more than to invite him into her world as he had invited her into his.

An hour and a half later, Heather unlocked the back door to her shanty and they entered. "Wait here," she said, stopping him just inside the door. She went ahead of him and turned on several of the battery-operated lights to illuminate their way through the dark place.

Nick followed her and when he reached the living room, he sank down on her sofa and she sat next to him. "I'm exhausted yet wired at the same time," she said.

He laughed. "I feel the same way. Nothing like a little gunfight in the middle of the night to wake you up."

"I was so terrified, Nick," she confessed.

"Want to know a little secret?" he asked.

"Sure." Her gaze held his.

"I was more than a bit scared myself," he replied. "But in a gun battle, I'd definitely pick you as my partner."

"I never want to be in a gun battle again," she replied.

He released a deep sigh, and they both were quiet for several long moments. "It's nice here," he finally said. "It's so peaceful."

"It is," she agreed. "It's part of what I love so much about it."

"I think I'm ready for some sleep now," he said. "There's at least a couple hours of night left before morning."

"I'm ready for bed, too." She stood and held out her hand to him. He took it and also rose from the sofa. She led him into her bedroom, and she immediately turned on the light next to the bed.

The last time she had been in here, she'd been screaming for her life, hoping somebody, anybody, would come and help her against the three men who had broken in. A cold chill streaked up her back at the memory, but it couldn't persist against the fact that she had survived that night.

They had each packed a hasty bag at Nick's before they left. The bags were left unopened as he stripped down to his boxers and she pulled on a nightgown from her dresser drawer. Then, together, they got into the bed.

He immediately pulled her against him, and she relaxed into his arms. "We made it, Heather," he said sleepily. "The bad guy is in jail, and your innocence has been proven now without a shadow of a doubt."

"All's well that ends well," she replied, even as an overwhelming sadness tugged at her heart. This would probably be the very last time she slept in his arms. There was no more reason for her to stay in his home.

As she listened to his soft, rhythmic breathing mingling with the sound of bullfrogs croaking their nighttime songs, she finally fell asleep.

She awakened before Nick and quietly slid out of bed without waking him. She went into the bathroom to wash her face and then headed for the back porch to start her generator.

The plants in her kitchen looked good and healthy, letting her know that Lucy had taken good care of them while Heather had been gone. She pulled out her coffee maker and got it working and then grabbed from one of the cabinets the two-burner stovetop she cooked on.

This morning, she could cook Nick breakfast because he wouldn't know how things were done in the swamp. She checked her cooler, grateful that somebody had kept ice in it to save the items inside. Thank goodness for good friends, she thought. She was truly blessed in that aspect of her life.

She pulled out a carton of eggs, a package of shredded cheese and a stick of butter. She placed them all on the counter, and by then there was enough coffee to pour herself a cup.

She sank down at the table and sipped the hot brew, her thoughts filled with Nick. She had a feeling that today was going to be goodbye, and her heart already hurt at the very thought.

There was no other reason for her to remain in his home now. She was no longer in danger from anyone and no longer needed his and Bruno's protection.

He would probably take her back to his place to pack up the last of her things and then would bring her back here to begin their lives apart. Her heart squeezed tight, and hot tears pressed at her eyes. She swallowed hard against them. The last thing she wanted was for Nick to see her cry over him. He'd seen her cry over many things already, but she refused to let him see her cry over him.

She'd been a fool to think that a man like Nick could ever really love a woman like her. In the end, she was simply a swamp rat he'd desired but didn't love.

At that moment, he walked into the room. He was dressed in a pair of jeans and a light blue T-shirt. "Good morning," he said with the smile that always warmed her heart.

"Good morning. Sit and I'll pour you a cup of coffee, and breakfast is coming right up," she replied. "Although breakfast won't be as elaborate as what you're used to."

"To be honest, I wasn't expecting anything." He sat at the small table, and she got him a cup of coffee.

"How did you sleep?" she asked and pulled her skillet from a cabinet. She also got out her toaster.

"Like a baby," he replied. "What about you?"

"The same." She stayed focused on making the breakfast of scrambled eggs and toast. She didn't want to look at him for too long because she feared her heartbreak would explode right out of her.

As they ate breakfast, they talked about the night that had passed. "I'll be interested to find out who this Dax Patrick really is. I realized after I heard that name that I'd heard it before."

"Oh really, where?" she asked curiously.

"My latest client was involved in a bar fight with him. My client told me at the time that Dax was not from around here and was an outsider. I'd like to know what specifically brought him to Crystal Coves to deal drugs."

"I certainly had never heard of him before. I still don't understand why he used me as a fall guy in the murder," she said.

"I understand why. Like he basically said, you were a woman all alone and vulnerable. The truth is you just happened to be at the wrong place at the wrong time," he replied.

"So, just like you suspected, Wesley was killed over drug money," she said.

"Which just goes to show that dabbling in drugs can be very dangerous," he replied.

They finished breakfast and she cleaned the dishes, insisting his help would be more of a hindrance in the small space.

Once that was finished, Heather returned to the bedroom

while Nick sat on the sofa waiting for her. She dressed and then returned to the living room.

"I just spoke to Etienne," he said. "The police stayed all night at my place, and it's now clear for us to return." He stood and at that moment Heather realized she didn't want to go back to his place.

"I'll just stay here," she said. She couldn't go back to the space where she had been so happy with him and not completely lose it. "I grabbed most of my things from there last night. Any clothes I have left there you can donate to a charity."

He looked at her in surprise. "Are you sure?"

She nodded. "I'm positive."

"Then…uh… I guess this is goodbye," he said slowly. He bent down and picked up the small duffel bag he'd brought with him the night before.

"Nick, I'm in love with you." The words blurted out of her. She was unable to hold them in any longer. She needed to say the words to him before he left for good.

He dropped the duffel back to the floor and stared at her. "I'm madly, crazy in love with you," she said and took a step closer to him. "Nick, I don't want this to be goodbye. I want to spend the rest of my life with you. I want to have your babies and build a family with you."

"Heather, I'm sure you're just grateful to me," he finally replied as a deep frown creased his forehead. "Considering everything we've been through, it would be easy to mistake gratitude for love."

"You silly man. Don't tell me how I feel. Of course, I'm grateful to you, but that has nothing to do with the deep love I have for you," she replied.

"I just think you're confused," he said, obviously uneasy.

"Dammit, Nick. I'm not confused," she said with a touch of anger. "I am deeply in love with you."

He stared at her for several long moments. "How can you love me?" he finally said. "I'm unlovable. Delia certainly didn't love me. Hell, my own parents didn't love me enough to stay home from their fancy dinners and jet-setting lifestyle to spend time with me," he said sharply.

It was her turn to stare at him, suddenly seeing the depths of his childhood neglect in the darkness of his eyes. "Oh, Nick, that only speaks to something being wrong with your parents, not anything wrong with you."

She took another step toward him. "You are a kind and caring man. You're intelligent and you have a great sense of humor. What's not to love? And I think if you look deep in your heart, you'll discover that you're in love with me, too." Her heart pounded in her chest, and she felt as if this was the most important moment of her life.

She saw it then…a flash of emotion in his eyes that gave her hope. It was there, love shone bright from his eyes, and then he looked away from her, and when he gazed at her once again, it was gone.

"Heather, you're a beautiful, intelligent woman. Sure, I enjoyed your company. We had a crazy physical attraction to each other. Despite everything that was going on, we had fun together, but I'm not in love with you."

"You're lying," she exclaimed. "You do love me, Nick. Why don't you see that we belong together? I'm not your parents, and I'm definitely not Delia. I'm a woman who will love you with all my heart for the rest of your life."

"I… I don't know what else to say to you."

She studied his features, already memorizing them for

when she wouldn't see him again. "What are you so afraid of, Nick?" she finally asked desperately.

"I'm not afraid of anything," he protested and once again averted his gaze from hers. "I'm sorry, Heather, but I'm just not in love with you."

There was nothing left for her to say. Apparently, no words she could speak were going to change his mind. She watched dully as he once again picked up his duffel bag. "I'm sure we'll see each other around town," he said. She followed him into the kitchen and to the back door.

"Goodbye, Heather," he said and then walked out of the back door and out of her life.

She went back into the living room and collapsed on the sofa, unable to hold back her tears any longer. She'd won in that she wouldn't have to stand trial for murder, and she had survived all the attempts to kill her. But she'd lost the most important thing of all... Nick.

"GIRL, YOU NEED to get out of this shanty," Lucy said to Heather almost two weeks later. The two of them sat on Heather's sofa, and another day was slowly coming to an end. Her trial date had come and gone. Etienne had called her to let her know all charges against her had been dropped and that the three men arrested at Nick's house had also been the three who had broken into her shanty.

"I've been busy," Heather protested. "I've had things to do around here."

"Like what?" Lucy challenged her.

"Well, for one thing, I had to get a new front door put on." Heather had hired Brett Mayfield to take care of the job. He was one of the few handymen in town who would come to the swamp to work.

"That was done over a week ago. Why aren't you going into your shop?"

Heather released a deep sigh. "I'm planning on going in tomorrow. I just haven't felt like doing much of anything lately."

"You've got to pull yourself together, Heather. I know that man broke your heart, but you can't let this break your spirit," Lucy said softly.

Heather released another sigh. "I know and I'm going to pull myself together starting tomorrow."

"You swear?" Lucy eyed her dubiously.

Heather laughed. "I swear."

"The town fair is in three days. Are you planning on going?" Lucy asked.

Heather's heart constricted at thoughts of the fair. She had thought she'd be going with Nick, but that certainly wasn't happening now. "I don't know. I would imagine it's not much fun to go by yourself."

"I wish I didn't have a date. I would have much rather gone with you instead of with Arnie Foray."

"Arnie is a very nice guy, and you'll have a good time. I'll just stay home that day and enjoy the solitude," Heather replied.

"That's the problem, Heather. You are getting way too much solitude," Lucy said.

Heather laughed. "I promise that won't be the case starting tomorrow." Her laughter died, and she stared at her friend. "Can you keep a big secret?"

"You know I can. We've kept each other's secrets safe since we were kids. So, what's the secret?"

Heather swallowed hard. "I... I think I might be pregnant."

Lucy's eyes widened. "Wha...what makes you think that?"

"I'm three days late, and normally I'm never late." Heather reached up and touched the gold necklace she still possessed, then dropped her hand back to her lap.

"How on earth did you allow that to happen?" Lucy asked. "I thought you were on the pill."

"I am." Heather frowned. "You know I was on those heavy antibiotics right before everything happened. And then with everything that was going on, I forgot to take my birth control pills several times."

"Oh, Heather," Lucy replied. "What will you do if you are pregnant?"

"I'm not going to follow in the footsteps of poor Marianne," she said.

For a moment she remained silent as she thought of tragic tale mothers in the swamp used to warn their daughters about sleeping with town men.

She placed a hand on her flat belly. "If I am pregnant…"

"If you are, then are you going to tell him?" Lucy asked.

Heather frowned thoughtfully. "I don't know. I certainly don't expect anything from him. This is my issue, and I haven't thought yet about telling him. Besides, I could be wrong about the whole thing and I'm not pregnant. I might just be late."

"The first thing I'm going to do in the morning is bring you a home pregnancy kit. One way or another, you need to know. I'll make sure you have plenty of time to pee on a stick before we both have to go to work," Lucy said.

LATER THAT NIGHT, Heather was in her bed and thinking of the possibility that she might carry Nick's child. She would never, ever get pregnant on purpose in an attempt to trap him. It was only in the last couple of days she'd thought about how many birth control pills she'd missed over the past couple of weeks. There had been more than several missed pills. She'd been out of her element and not in her normal routine, and that was the only excuse she had for the lapse.

This baby—if he or she truly existed—had been an accident, but Heather would love and nurture it with utter happiness and joy. The baby was wanted, and she would try to be the best mother she could be.

The next morning, true to her word, Lucy was at her door with a bag from the pharmacy in town. "I bought two for you to take. Just to be sure." Heather sat on the sofa next to Lucy as she took them out of the bag, and together they read the instructions.

"Well, they look easy enough," Lucy said. "So go pee, and then we'll wait and see the results."

A few minutes later, Heather came out of the bathroom, the two test sticks in her hands. She set them on the coffee table, and nervously she waited for the results to show.

"Well, congratulations," Lucy said a few minutes later when both tests indicated Heather was, indeed, pregnant. "You know I'll be here to support you through it all," Lucy said.

"I know." Heather reached out and gave her a big hug. "Thank God for good friends."

A thrill rushed through her, followed by a sweet rush of heat. In nine months' time, she would be a mother. The joy was only tempered by the fact that Nick hadn't loved her.

Later that morning, she opened up her shop. She spent part of the morning watering all the plants and the rest of the morning dusting and doing general cleaning.

She was happy when Mrs. Albertson came in. Marigold

Albertson was as colorful as her name. The older woman had been a regular customer of Heather's before she'd been charged with murder.

"It's so nice to see you back here where you belong, Heather." She reached up and adjusted the colorful floppy hat she wore on her silver-blue hair. "You have to be glad to have all that nastiness behind you. Of course, I never believed any of it about you."

"Thank you, Mrs. Albertson. I appreciate that."

"And now I would appreciate some fresh parsley and oregano and a bay leaf or two. The weather is cooling off a bit, and so I'm ready to make some of my soups."

"That sounds lovely," Heather replied as she moved to the display that held those herbs.

Minutes later, Marigold went happily on her way, and Heather sank down on the stool behind the register. Pregnant. She still couldn't believe it. It was a piece of Nick she would always have with her.

She still didn't know if she would tell him or not. On the one hand, she felt like it was none of his business since he'd kicked her to the curb. But the other part of her thought he had a right to know, and he had a choice of whether he wanted to be in the child's life or not.

She didn't know how long she'd been sitting there when she saw him—Nick. He approached her door, and her breath caught in the back of her throat. Had Lucy told him about Heather's pregnancy? No, Lucy wouldn't betray her that way.

He walked into the door. "Good morning, Heather," he said.

She stood from her stool. "Uh...good morning to you,"

she replied. Oh, why was he here? Just seeing him again stabbed her like a sword into the very center of her heart.

However, he looked like hell. His blue eyes were dull and lines of what appeared to be sheer exhaustion traced down the sides of his face. He was clad in jeans and a gray T-shirt. Still, her heart squeezed tight at the very sight of him.

"It's good to see you back here where you belong. I was wondering when you were going to open your store again."

"Are you here for the plants I owe to you?" she asked, grateful that her voice was calm and even and not displaying any of the emotional turmoil whirling around inside of her.

He shifted from one foot to the other, looking incredibly uncomfortable. "Actually, I'm here to ask you a very important question."

"And what's that?" she asked curiously.

"Have you now realized that what you felt for me was a lot of gratitude and nothing more?" His gaze held hers intently.

"Absolutely not. My love for you hasn't stopped. I'm in love with you, Nick, and it's going to take me a very long time to get over loving you. I'm not sure I ever will get over you, so why are you really here?" This was killing her... seeing him again.

"Because Bruno has told me I've been a miserable bastard without you, and it's true." He took a step toward her. "I've been absolutely miserable without you, Heather. I think about you all the time, and it's an ache in my heart that never, ever goes away."

Her heart began to beat in an accelerated rhythm as she continued to stare at him. What was he saying? What did this mean? He took a step toward her. "Heather, I fought against it, but the truth is I'm madly in love with you. I want to spend the rest of my life with you."

Tears welled up in her eyes. This time they were tears of joy. "Are you sure, Nick?" she asked tremulously. "You have to be very sure."

"I've never been so certain of something in my entire life." He took another step toward her. "But I was so afraid that you'd realize you didn't love me. You were right—I was afraid to take a chance on you."

"You have nothing to be afraid of. I love you, Nick, and nothing is going to chan..." She didn't get the full sentence out of her mouth before he had her in his arms and his lips took hers in a tender, loving kiss that brought tears to her eyes.

The kiss ended, but he still held her close and gazed deep into her eyes. "I don't have a ring, but, Heather LaCrae, would you be my wife...would you marry me as soon as possible and build a family with me?"

"Yes, oh yes, Nick," she replied, joy exploding through her veins and warming her heart...her very soul. He kissed her once again, and in the kiss, she tasted his unmistakable love.

They finally stepped apart from each other, but he held her hand tightly. "We have a few things to work out," he said.

"Like what?" she looked at him curiously. She was in the very best dream of her life, and nothing he could say would take away her happy glow.

"Like swamp versus town," he replied. "I know you love your shanty. How about we spend weekdays in town so I can work, and then we spend weekends at the shanty?"

"That sounds perfect," she replied. But she had a secret

to share with him, and she wasn't sure how he was going to take the news. However, now was the time.

"Nick...when you talked about building a family, how soon did you want that to happen?"

"Whenever you're ready." He gazed at her adoringly. "You've given me back the dream I'd once had of a wife and family, and I'm excited about having both. Why? When do you want to start working on a family?"

Nerves suddenly fluttered through her. "Now," she said. "In fact, we not only already started, but your family is going to increase by one in about nine months."

He looked at her in confusion. Then she saw the exact moment he realized what she'd said.

"You're pregnant?" he asked.

She nodded. His eyes widened, and a huge smile curved his lips. "For real?"

"For real," she replied, a new happiness rushing through her as she saw the shining from his eyes.

"Life doesn't get any better than this. I'm going to be a husband and a father. Heather, I'm so excited about the life we're going to have together. Thank you for loving me," he said humbly.

"Thank you for loving me back," she replied.

He pulled her against him once again. "I got you, Heather. I got us." He kissed her once again, the kiss one of promise. It promised love and laughter and a lifetime of happiness.

ETIENNE SAT NEXT to the hospital bed. It was almost midnight, and the hospital was quiet. He held Colette's slender hand in his and watched her breathe in and out. Over the last couple of months, he'd watched her bruises slowly fade and her skeletal body gain weight.

She was a beautiful woman, and with the medical treatment she'd been receiving, much of her natural beauty had returned. Her cheeks had some color, and her long, dark hair was once again shiny.

"Colette, it's safe now for you to wake up," he said softly. "Nobody is going to hurt you again."

He'd been talking to her for the past hour as he'd done night after night, hoping she would crawl out of the darkness that she clung to. The Swamp Soul Stealer had three women and three men and presumably was holding them someplace deep in the swamp. He would continue to kidnap people from the swamp unless he was stopped.

Etienne hoped like hell that Colette held the key to catching the man. But before she could help, she had to wake up. "Colette, you're safe now. You don't need the darkness anymore. You can come to the light." He squeezed her hand lightly, hoping for any kind of response, but there was none.

He would be back here the next night and the night after and for as long as it took to coax the sleeping beauty awake.

\* \* \* \* \*

# CANYON KILLER

## CINDI MYERS

For Susan

## Chapter One

"I love my family. I really do. But sometimes they annoy me almost beyond bearing." The infant in Bethany's arms stared up at her with wide blue eyes, then blew a bubble. Bethany laughed. "Yeah, why am I complaining to you? But give it twenty years or so, and you'll understand. Families are wonderful, but sometimes..."

She shifted the infant, Joella, to her other arm and turned back to the computer at the front desk of Peak Jeep Tours and Rentals. The message blinking there, from her mother—who also happened to be her boss—informed her that Mom had made a dentist appointment for her for the following month. As if Bethany, at twenty-three, wasn't capable of making her own appointment. She was tempted to call and cancel it, but in the small town of Eagle Mountain, Colorado, there really was only the one dentist, and she liked him.

She sighed, closed the message and turned her attention back to the baby.

"Uh, Bethany, is there something you've been keeping from us?"

She looked up from admiring the infant to find her brother Dalton regarding her with a quizzical expression.

She had three brothers, and Dalton was the youngest, two years younger than Bethany. Tanned, with a scruff of a beard and a faded Alpine Adventures T-shirt stretched across his broad shoulders, he looked as if he had lived in Eagle Mountain all of his life, instead of only two months. Locals still looked *her* up and down and said things like "You're not from around here, are you?" And she had lived here nine months. It really wasn't fair.

"She belongs to a couple who booked a Jeep trip up to Portnoy Basin," she said and smiled down at the baby again.

"Are we offering free babysitting with our tours now?" Dalton leaned over and snagged a handful of jelly beans from the bowl on the corner of the desk.

"They thought they would be able to take her with them." She settled Joella into her carrier and tucked a soft yellow blanket around her. "I had to explain we couldn't allow an infant, even in a carrier, in an open-topped Jeep on a rough four-wheel-drive road."

"And they talked you into watching her." Dalton chuckled. "You're such a sucker."

"It's not as if she's much trouble," she said. "And the trip was her mom's birthday present. She was really looking forward to it."

"Sucker," he repeated. "I'm going to see what I can find for lunch."

Dalton moved past her, into the back room, as the front door opened and a man entered—tall, twentysomething, bronzed, chiseled features and close-cropped hair, aviator sunglasses, dressed in khaki cargo pants and a button-down shirt with the sleeves rolled up to reveal muscular forearms. Your basic gorgeous, outdoorsy type this town seemed to be full of.

Bethany smiled broadly. "Hello. How can I help you?"

"I need to rent a Jeep," he said.

"Great." She returned to the desk and pulled up the Jeep rental form. "How long would you be needing it? We rent by the hour, but the daily rate is a better deal."

He moved in closer. He smelled like leather and some exotic spice. Expensive. "I need it for a couple of months," he said. "Until the project I'm working on in town is finished."

"Oh." She looked back up at him. He had removed the sunglasses to reveal blue eyes, fine lines at the corners. "Most people just want to take them into the mountains for a day or two."

"I need it for at least a couple of months," he repeated.

"Sure. We can do that." Bethany forced her attention back to the form. It was either that or keep staring at him like a smitten teen. "Since you want it for that long, I could offer you a ten percent discount." That wasn't an *official* policy, but it made sense to her. And it wasn't as if Mom and Dad were going to fire her for trying to please a customer.

"Thanks." He handed over a matte black credit card. The kind that screamed *high credit limit*.

"I'll just need your name and contact information."

"Ian. Ian Seabrook."

She filled in his name and the address and phone number he rattled off, copied off his insurance and driver's license information, then checked the board to see what was available. They had a couple of their usual blue rental units available. And a brand-new black one. The black one wasn't officially in the rental pool yet. Dalton and his twin, Carter, were lobbying hard to put it in the tour fleet so they could drive it. But hey, Ian looked like he would take good care of it. She grabbed the keys off the hook.

The door opened and Carter came in. He and Dalton weren't identical twins, but they looked enough alike that people who didn't know them well sometimes got them confused. Carter was an inch taller and five minutes older and a little beefier than Dalton. "Whose Porsche is that parked out front?" he called.

Ian turned to look at him. "It's mine."

"Are you taking a tour with us?" Carter leaned back against the desk, focused on the newcomer.

"Mr. Seabrook is renting a Jeep," Bethany said. She inserted Ian's credit card into the card reader.

"Seabrook." Carter straightened. "Ian Seabrook?"

"Yes." Ian accepted his credit card from her.

"You're the guy who bought Humboldt Canyon and closed it to climbing." Carter turned to his sister. "Some of the guys were talking about it at the last search and rescue meeting. Humboldt was a popular climbing spot, and this guy closed it and is going to develop it."

"I'm going to build a via ferrata," Ian said.

"What's a via ferrata?" she asked.

"It's Italian for *iron way*," Ian said. "It's a climbing route with steel cables, platforms and walkways. It will be open to the public."

"It's a tourist attraction." Carter spoke with a sneer.

"Like this Jeep tour company." Ian slipped his credit card back into his wallet.

*Touché.* Bethany bit back a grin. Carter definitely deserved that comeback. "It sounds like a lot of fun," she said.

Actually, anything to do with climbing scared her, though training with search and rescue was helping her conquer that fear. So far she had been content to help the really skilled climbers with their gear, but she had taken a couple of training sessions navigating some less technical terrain. She had joined search and rescue when she'd first moved to Eagle Mountain to push herself out of her comfort zone, and it was definitely doing that.

"It sounds to me like a rich guy looking to make a profit off something that used to be available to everyone for free," her brother said.

"Carter!" She glared at him. "Nobody asked you."

She wouldn't have wanted to be on the receiving end of the look Ian sent Carter. "Why don't you wait and see what I do before you pass judgment?" Ian said.

Joella chose that moment to start crying. Bethany rushed to the carrier and picked up the baby. "Sorry," she said, raising her voice to be heard over the wailing. She bounced the infant in her arms as she returned to the desk. "Let me finish up the paperwork and get you on your way."

"Cute." Ian leaned closer. He smiled and extended one finger. The baby immediately fell silent and grasped his finger.

Uh-oh. Call her a cliché, but she couldn't think of anything more devastating than a good-looking guy smiling at a baby. She blamed evolution, stirring up all those hormones. He looked up and met her gaze. Yep. Devastating.

"How old is she?" he asked.

"I don't really know." One-handed, she grabbed the paperwork from the printer tray. When she turned back, she caught his puzzled look and laughed. "I'm watching her for a couple of customers."

He accepted the paperwork. "Thanks. Um, I didn't get your name."

"It's Bethany. Bethany Ames."

"She's my sister." Carter still looked out of sorts. "Don't get any ideas."

Her face heated, but she stayed calm. "Ignore him," she said to Ian. She handed him the keys. "It's parked at the end of the row. Let me know if you need anything else."

"Thanks. I'll check it out, then come back in an hour or so to pick it up."

"Then I'll look forward to seeing you again." She put a little extra warmth behind her smile. She wasn't dating anyone, and no matter what Carter said, Ian Seabrook seemed really nice.

He nodded and left.

As soon as the door closed, Carter turned on her. "*Let me know if you need anything else*," he simpered. "Honestly, Betty. You sounded pathetic."

Her brothers only called her Betty when they were annoyed with her. "And you sounded out of your mind."

"What are you two fighting about?" Dalton came in, a half-eaten sandwich in one hand.

"Ian Seabrook was in here, and Bethany was flirting with him," Carter said.

"I wasn't flirting."

The door that led to the back office opened again, and their mother entered. Trim and athletic, with blond, curly hair and freckles, Diane Ames could probably pass for ten years younger than fifty-two. She stared at Bethany. "What are you doing with a baby?"

"She's the Hendersons'—on the ten-a.m. tour. They didn't realize they couldn't take her with them."

"You could have refunded their money and suggested they hire a babysitter," Carter said.

"And have them leave disappointed or even angry?" Bethany smiled at Joella. "Besides, she's no trouble."

"When they come back, ask them to give us a good review on social media," Dalton said.

He was the business's IT and media manager, in addition to one of their tour drivers. Carter maintained all the Jeeps. Everyone wore multiple hats in a small business like theirs.

"Did I hear a customer in here just now?" Mom walked over to the desk and bent over the computer screen.

"A guy rented a Jeep for two months," Bethany said.

"Not just a guy," Carter said. "Ian Seabrook."

Dalton let out a whistle. "Let's hope nobody vandalizes the Jeep. A lot of people around here are really upset with him."

"Who is Ian Seabrook?" Mom asked. "Why are people upset with him?"

"He's, like, a billionaire who bought Humboldt Canyon and closed it to the public. He's going to build a climbing area for tourists."

"Is he really a billionaire?" Bethany asked. He had looked so ordinary. Well, gorgeous and ordinary.

"The son of a billionaire," Dalton said. "His dad owns Seabrook Holdings, one of those big companies that buy up little companies, drain them dry, sell them off, then move on."

"He seemed very nice," she told her mother.

"Which Jeep did you rent him?" Carter asked.

"The black Wrangler."

"The new one?" He loomed over her. "Why did you do that?"

"It was purchased for the rental fleet," she said.

"That wasn't for certain," Carter said.

"I think a man who owns a Porsche knows how to take care of an expensive vehicle," she said.

Her brother's lip curled in disgust. "Like you're such a good judge of character."

"What's that supposed to mean?" she snapped.

"You thought Justin was a great guy, too."

Justin Asher, Bethany's former fiancé. The man who had waited until the invitations had been sent and all the nonrefundable deposits paid before he'd decided she wasn't the woman for him.

"Carter, that was uncalled for," Mom said.

He looked at the floor. "I'm sorry," he said. "But the new Jeep? And to a guy like Ian Seabrook?"

"Just because he has money and he's starting a new business doesn't make him an awful person," Bethany said.

"It does if he closes off land people have been using for free for decades," Carter said.

"Both of you, stop arguing," Mom said. "People are here for the one-o'clock tour." She nodded toward the front window, where they could see half a dozen people getting out of two vehicles. "Boys, get the Jeeps ready."

Grumbling to themselves, Carter and Dalton exited. Mom and Bethany started checking in new arrivals. As soon as they were out the door the morning tour returned, and they had to see to them. The Hendersons were thrilled with the trip and happy to see Joella and to hear that she had been a perfect angel in their absence. They promised a good review online and left a generous tip.

By the time Mom and Bethany were alone again Mom had apparently forgotten about Ian. "Your dad and I have chiropractor appointments this afternoon," she said. "You shouldn't run into any problems, but if you do, you can always call us. And don't forget to lock up after the last tour returns."

"I'll be fine, Mom." Bethany wanted to remind her that she had been working for the company since before they'd bought out the previous owners, but thought better of it. Nothing she said could get past this image her family had of her as flighty and irresponsible. For some reason she had never ceased to be their silly little girl, despite all evidence to the contrary.

She said goodbye to her mom, and settled in to file paperwork, confirm reservations for the next day's tours—and possibly daydream about a certain blue-eyed billionaire.

## *Chapter Two*

Obviously word had gotten around town about what Ian was up to. As soon as he'd put up the Closed to the Public sign at the head of Humboldt Canyon, he'd expected to get some criticism, and it didn't really bother him. He had a thick skin. But he had been pretty steamed at that guy at the Jeep place for bad-mouthing him in front of Bethany. At least he hadn't let his temper get the better of him and gone off on her brother.

She'd been cool about the whole thing. She'd even come to his defense, which didn't happen that often. He had noticed right away that Bethany had that pretty girl-next-door vibe going for her. Then he had seen her with the infant, and the disappointment he'd felt had taken him by surprise. A baby meant there was probably a partner somewhere. Then she'd revealed she'd just been babysitting, and the relief he'd felt was all out of proportion to the moment.

She wasn't the type he usually went for. That was his first clue that there was a lot more going on under the surface than he was ready to acknowledge.

Traffic came to a stop. Eagle Mountain didn't have any traffic lights, but he could see a big truck up ahead backing out of an alley. He waited, window rolled down to catch the breeze. Hard to believe it was July, the weather was so pleasant.

A leggy blonde woman on the sidewalk stopped to stare. "I like your car," she called.

Ian nodded. A person didn't buy a car like this and expect to be inconspicuous. But he hadn't counted on just how noticeable the Porsche would be in a small town like Eagle Mountain. He hadn't bargained for how big of a pain it would be, either. Not only did the town not have traffic lights, it didn't have much pavement. And the roads in and around Humboldt Canyon were narrow, winding, steep and rocky. About ten minutes after arriving to oversee the Eagle Mountain Via Ferrata, he'd realized he needed a Jeep. But Eagle Mountain didn't have car rental companies, either.

They did, however, have a Jeep tour company that also rented Jeeps. Now all he had to do was get a lift back into town to pick up his new ride.

Traffic started moving again, and he turned off onto the county road that led to Humboldt Canyon. He had to slow down when the pavement ended and carefully steer the low-slung Porsche the rest of the way. He pulled up to the RV that would be his new home/office for the next few months and looked around. No sign of George, the guy he had hired as sort of a general handyman to get things ready for the major construction. George's pickup truck, which Ian had been counting on for a ride back into town, was nowhere in sight.

A note on the door of the trailer provided an explanation: *Gone to Junction for parts.*

Junction was an hour away. Ian didn't know how long ago George had left, but he figured it would be at least a couple of hours before he made it back. Peak Jeep Tours closed at three.

He went inside and sat at the desk in what would have been the RV's living area, which he had turned into an office. Another note was on the desk, this one written on cardboard that looked like it had been ripped from one side of a beer carton, three-inch-high letters written in black marker: NO VIA FERATA. There was an obscenity after the word *no*, and they had misspelled *ferrata*.

George had left a sticky note beside it. *Found this on the front gate.*

Ian tossed the sign into the trash and sat back. He needed that Jeep, and he couldn't leave the Porsche on the street in front of the rental place all week. As soon as people found out it was his...no telling what they'd do. He tried to think of anyone else in town who might help him, but he had only been here one day and didn't know anybody.

Bethany's smiling face popped into his mind. He didn't really know her, but at least she'd been friendly. She had been obliging enough to babysit a customer's infant, so maybe she would help him out, too. He pulled out his phone and punched in the tour company's number.

"Hello, Peak Jeep Tours. How can I help you?" She sounded every bit as friendly on the phone as she had in person.

"Bethany, this is Ian Seabrook. I need a favor."

"Hey, Ian. What do you need?"

"I'm looking for a way to get the Jeep I rented out to my place," he said. "The guy I was counting on to give me a ride had to go to Junction. If I drive back to town, can you follow me to my place in the Jeep? I'll see that you get home safely."

Silence.

Right. What young woman would agree to drive to an isolated location with a guy she didn't know?

"You can bring your brother along if you like," he added. Ian didn't like him, but he wanted to put her at ease, and he really needed that Jeep.

"That's okay, Ian. I'm happy to help you. But I will leave a note for my folks, telling them where I've gone. And you don't have to drive all the way back here to guide me. Just tell me where you are, and I'll meet you."

"Great. Do you know where Humboldt Canyon is? I have a trailer set up there."

"Sure," she said. "You'll have to wait until I get off at three thirty."

He checked his watch. Another hour, but he didn't really have a choice. "I'll see you then. And thanks a lot."

Ian spent the next hour reviewing communications from the design team and answering emails from his contacts in various locations overseas. He wasn't someone who had trouble focusing—he had been accused of being too single-minded at times. But he kept checking the time and trying to calculate how long after three thirty it would be before Bethany got here.

Finally he heard the Jeep's approach on the rough road and was waiting in front of the RV when Bethany rolled up and parked next to the Porsche.

"I can see why you wanted a Jeep," she said as she climbed out of the driver's seat. "But hey, this is gorgeous." She turned her back to him to look up at the canyon walls.

He came to stand beside her and joined her in admiring the view. The canyon walls rose straight up over two hundred feet, the jagged rock in rich shades of orange, red and purple. Dark green conifers jutted from the rock in places, while in others yellow and lime-green lichen glowed in the afternoon sun.

Bethany smiled up at him. One of her upper front teeth was crooked, the slight imperfection appealing in a way he couldn't quite put his finger on. "Tell me about this via ferrata," she said.

"The idea is to have a route of walkways, rungs, ladders and platforms that people can follow as they make their way up and along the canyon walls," he said. "The iron road. It's challenging but doable for most people, especially if they hire a guide to coach them along—which we'll recommend they do. It's a way to share my love of climbing with other people. A via ferrata is set up so that people who wouldn't normally be able to experience the sport—people of all different ages and abilities, even with certain disabilities—can climb, with the right gear and assistance. They started out in Europe and have spread to the United States. They're really popular, and this is the perfect place for one."

"We have a big climbing community around here," she said.

"Are you a climber?"

She shook her head. "But I volunteer with search and rescue, so I'm starting to learn. It's not required for the work we do, but it comes in handy. Fortunately we have a number of skilled climbers on the team."

"Search and rescue? That's amazing. What kind of calls have you been on?"

"All kinds," she said. "We get cars that go off the road in the canyons and crash, lost hikers, people who get hurt on the trails and can't get down under their own power. Falls in the mountains. And we get our share of climbing accidents."

Ian had experienced a couple of bad falls—fortunately

nothing that had resulted in permanent injury. "The locals are lucky to have people like you on call," he said.

"Do you know many of the local climbers?" she asked.

"I've met some of them. I know a few of the local guides. Most of my climbing has been in Europe and Asia, though. I spent six months last year in Tibet."

"My brothers said you're a billionaire. Is that true? Or is that a really rude question to ask?"

Her smile was so disarming, he couldn't be offended. "My dad is a billionaire," he said. "I'm not in his league." Time to change the subject. "If you're not in a hurry, I could show you around."

"I'd love that."

"Are you up for a little hiking? The trails can get rough."

"I'm ready." She extended one foot to show that she was wearing hiking boots.

"Then let's go. I'll show you the general route for the via ferrata."

He led her up a rocky path he had hacked out with a machete the day before. "This first section will feature a rope bridge, then there will be some iron rings set into the cliff face to traverse, then a platform where people can catch their breath and enjoy the view."

"It sounds just challenging enough to be fun," she said.

"That's the idea." He leaned down to help her onto a large boulder.

"Where did you live before you came to Eagle Mountain?" she asked. "I mean, before Tibet?"

"I grew up in Upstate New York, but I haven't lived there for fifteen years. Mostly I've traveled. Before I came here, I was living in Maine, near Mount Katahdin," he said. "What about you? Have you always lived in Colorado?"

"No, I've only been here nine months. I'm originally from Vermont."

"What made you decide to come to Eagle Mountain?"

"I came here to take a job at the Jeep rental place where I work now," she said. "My parents came to visit and ended up buying the business and moving the whole family here."

"How many are in the whole family?"

"My mom and dad and my three brothers."

"Do they all work with you?" he asked.

"The younger ones—the twins—do. You met Carter. His twin is Dalton. My older brother, Aaron, is a sheriff's deputy."

He couldn't imagine what that would be like, surrounded by family. "I'm an only child, and my folks divorced when I was pretty little. I don't see them much now that I'm grown."

"Oh, I missed them all when they weren't here, but it would be nice if they weren't quite so involved in my life."

"I guess I could understand that." They detoured around a washout in the cliff face. "There was some flooding this spring and a mudslide that took out a big section of the cliff," he said. "We'll have to reinforce this area and put in some drainage."

"Are those caves up there?" She pointed to a shadowed area high above them.

He stepped back and looked in the direction she indicated. "I think you're right. The mudslide must have opened up some pockets in the cliff face."

"It looks like there's a ledge up there. I think we could get to them."

Before he could say anything, she was already headed up the slope, scrambling around rocks, squeezing past trees, steadily gaining altitude.

He hurried after her. "Careful!" he called as one foot slipped, sending loose dirt rolling toward him.

"I'm fine!" she called, and kept going.

He stepped onto the ledge right behind her. The rock shelf was scarcely a foot wide, so they had to turn sideways to make their way along it. A rush of cooler air greeted them when they reached the opening to the first, largest cave.

"Wow, look at this." She stepped under the overhang.

Ian followed, bending down to avoid hitting his head.

"I wish we'd thought to bring a flashlight," she said.

He pulled out his phone. "We can use this." He directed the beam from his flashlight app onto the walls of the cave, estimating the space to be about five feet tall and six feet wide, with an undetermined depth. Jagged rock around the opening showed fresh scarring, as if pieces had broken off in the mudslide.

"I wonder how far back this goes," Bethany said and started deeper into the cave.

"The rock could be unstable," he called, even as he followed her. She might not have been a climber, but she didn't lack nerve—he'd give her that.

"Shine the light back here," she said. "I want to see how far this goes."

Ian moved in behind her and directed the light over her shoulder, onto a wall of rock. "It looks like it stops right here." He swept the light down across the floor.

"What was that?" She put her hand on his arm. "I thought I saw something white. Swing the light back that way."

He moved the light more slowly, back across the floor, and focused the beam on a strange tableau. It took a moment for the scene to register.

Bethany clutched him more tightly. "Is that…a skeleton?"

## Chapter Three

Bethany averted her gaze, then forced herself to look back. Working with search and rescue meant facing difficult things, she told herself. After the initial horror of realizing there was a human skeleton on the floor of the cave, curiosity took over, and she was able to study the scene before them more closely. "It's not one skeleton," she said. "It's two." There were definitely two skulls, side by side at one end of the tangle of bones.

"It looks like they're...embracing?" Ian asked.

"Are we sure they're even real bones? Maybe it's just a prank." She started forward, but Ian held her back.

"I don't think they're fake." He pulled her farther away.

"What's that around them?" she asked. "Rags or a blanket?"

"Maybe their clothing, rotted away."

"Which would mean they've been here a long time." That would also explain why there wasn't more of them left and no smell of decay, just a mustiness to the air.

Ian tugged her arm again. "Let's go back down and call the sheriff. There's no cell reception in here."

She had little memory of the journey down, her mind still back in that cave, picturing what looked like two Halloween decorations, cuddling like lovers. How could that be real?

When they were back at the trailer, Ian called the sheriff's department to report that he had found what looked like human remains in a cave in Humboldt Canyon. His voice was calm, though she noticed his white-knuckled grip on the phone.

He ended the call and looked at her. "They'll be right here. We're supposed to stay put and wait."

"I still think they're not real," she said. "Someone must have put them up there."

"You mean to scare me off?"

She shrugged. "My brothers said people are upset about you closing the canyon to the public."

"I don't think they were fake," he said.

"How can you be sure?"

He shook his head but didn't answer. They fell silent, seated on opposite sides of the desk in his office. Waiting.

Not much time had passed before the crunch of tires on gravel propelled them out of their chairs and outside.

A Rayford County Sheriff's Department black-and-white SUV rolled to a stop in front of them. Bethany tensed. Only one thing could make all of this more awful.

The driver's-side door of the vehicle opened, and Sergeant Gage Walker stepped out. The sheriff's brother was familiar to her from search and rescue calls, and she relaxed a little as he came toward them.

"Bethany, what are you doing here?"

A second deputy had emerged from the passenger side of the vehicle. She let out a groan. Her older brother, Aaron, followed behind Gage, a scowl making him look fierce. Like Bethany, Aaron had inherited their dad's dark curls, which he kept clipped short.

After four years with the Waterbury, Vermont, police

department, he had agreed to help his parents and brothers move to Eagle Mountain and ended up accepting a position with the Rayford County Sheriff's Department after one of their long-time deputies had left to run a family business.

She ignored his question and turned away.

Gage nodded to Bethany, then addressed Ian. "You called in about human remains."

"We climbed up to those caves to look around." He pointed out the caves, high on the opposite cliff wall. "We found two skeletons. They look like they've been there a long while. Just bones and rotting clothing."

Gage squinted up at the caves. "How did you get up there?"

"There's a trail," Ian said.

"Then let's go see."

Ian led the way, Gage and Aaron close behind. Bethany trailed after them.

Aaron stopped and turned to her. "You need to stay down here."

"No." She kept walking, prepared to push past him if necessary.

"Let her come with us," Gage said. "We'll need to get her statement, and I might have questions."

She resisted the urge to stick out her tongue at Aaron. Childish, maybe, but if he was going to be the big brother bossing her around, it was so tempting to slip into the role of bratty little sister.

No one said anything on the climb up. The various implements attached to Gage's and Aaron's uniforms rattled together as they moved. By the time they reached the top, both men were sweating. Bethany remembered that they would be wearing ballistics vests. Aaron had let her try his on one time—it had been heavy and hot. She felt a stab of sympathy for her brother, though she didn't say anything.

"In here." Ian led the way along the ledge to the cave. He stopped at the opening and pointed.

Gage moved in first, followed by Aaron. The beam of a flashlight bounced off the rock walls. Ian and Bethany moved in a little closer.

"The bones look old," Gage said. "The clothing is rotted away. That takes years in this climate." Still holding the flashlight beam on the bones, he looked back at Ian. "This isn't as popular as Caspar Canyon, but climbers have been coming out here for years. How did no one find this before now?"

"I don't think these caves were visible before that mudslide a few weeks ago," Ian said. He pointed at the slide path, still evident above and below the cave opening. "This whole section of the cliff sheared off in that slide, revealing these caves. This is the largest, but there are two others."

"Have you looked in them?" Gage asked.

Bethany gasped. "Do you think there are more bones?"

"We didn't look in them," Ian said.

"Aaron, check out the other two caves," Gage said.

Her brother moved past. The rest of them focused on the skeletons once more.

"If this was all covered by rock and dirt, how did the bones get here in the first place?" Gage asked.

"Maybe there was a smaller opening?" Bethany speculated. "They could have climbed in and gotten trapped." She shuddered at the thought.

"There are holes in both skulls." Ian pointed. "I didn't get a really good look, but I thought I saw something metallic in the skull on the left. Like a bullet."

Gage moved nearer, keeping close to the cave wall until he was beside the bones. He shone the light on the skulls. Now Bethany could see a small, round hole in both—above the temple in one, in the middle of the forehead in the other. Gage nodded. "I think there is a bullet in there."

Bethany looked at Ian. "You didn't say anything about a bullet before."

"I didn't want to upset you."

"Ian. I work search and rescue. I've dealt with more upsetting things." A child in pain was a lot tougher to deal with than these dry, long-dead bones.

"Sorry," he said.

Aaron returned. "The other two caves are empty," he said. "Neither of them are as large as this one."

"Let's go back down, and I'll call the coroner and we'll get your statements," Gage said.

Back at the trailer, Gage made a phone call, then sent Aaron to take Ian's statement. He turned to Bethany. "Tell me what happened."

"Ian rented a Jeep from us," she said. "I agreed to deliver it. He offered to show me around, so we decided to hike around the area. We found the caves, looked inside and there were the bones."

"Whose idea was it to go into the caves?" Gage asked.

"Mine. I don't think he'd noticed them until I pointed them out."

"What do you know about Ian Seabrook?"

What did she know? He was good looking. He drove a Porsche. He seemed to like babies, and he seemed to like her. "He's planning to build a via ferrata here in the canyon, and I guess that's upset some people in town," she said.

"His father is a billionaire. And I guess he's a really experienced climber?"

Aaron emerged from the trailer, where he had been interviewing Ian. "We've got to wait for the coroner," Gage said to him. "Take your sister home, then come back here." He tossed Aaron the keys.

"Come on," Aaron said and headed toward the SUV.

Bethany looked back to the trailer. "I should say goodbye to Ian."

"We have to go." He slid into the driver's seat and started the engine. She was tempted to return to the trailer and refuse to leave, but she wouldn't have put it past Aaron not to pick her up and put her into the SUV, which would be beyond embarrassing, so she climbed into the passenger seat.

Aaron didn't wait until they were out of the canyon before the grilling began. "What are you doing with that guy? You don't know anything about him. For all you know he murdered those two people," he said. "You should have waited and had Carter or Dalton deliver the Jeep. It's dangerous for a woman alone with a strange man. Don't you have any sense?"

"If you think Ian had anything to do with those two people who probably died a hundred years ago, you need to go back to Law Enforcement 101," she said.

"You still don't know anything about him. You shouldn't have come out here alone."

"If I'm never supposed to be alone with a man, how am I going to date?"

"Now you're saying this was a date?" he said. "With a guy you met, what, five minutes ago?"

"Listen to yourself! You're being ridiculous."

Aaron's face was red. He didn't look at her as he turned

onto the county road. "You don't know what it's like, getting a call about two bodies, then finding your sister on scene. For all I knew when we showed up, there was a murderer nearby."

She hugged her arms across her chest. "Obviously whoever killed those two is long gone. And you don't need to worry about me. Or Ian. He's a nice guy."

"He's good looking and he's rich. That doesn't mean he's a nice guy. He sounds pretty ruthless to me, finding a way to make money off of something that was free to everyone for decades."

"I'm not going to talk to you when you're blathering nonsense like this."

Bethany looked away. She understood why the climbers were angry with Ian, but hearing him talk about the via ferrata, how it would allow people who weren't serious climbers to enjoy challenging themselves, she had felt his excitement. Just because you made money off of something didn't mean it was a bad thing.

"I'm not going to tell Mom and Dad about this," Aaron said.

Just when she was ready to stay angry with him, he did something like this. "Thanks," she said.

"I'm not doing it for you. I don't want to upset them."

"Nobody needs to be upset. I'm a grown woman. I'm perfectly capable of looking out for myself."

He shook his head but wisely said nothing. She sat back, fuming.

Even Aaron must've seen that she had never been in danger today. She was curious about the bones and a little sad about the people who'd died, but they had nothing to do with her.

THE RAYFORD COUNTY CORONER turned out to be a stout older man named Butch Collins, who scrambled up the path to the caves with more agility than Ian would have expected. Ian followed Butch and Gage up the trail, half expecting one of them to tell him to go away, but they didn't. He stood outside the cave while they went inside to reexamine the bones, and tried to think how those two people had ever gotten up here. Maybe more of the cave opening had been exposed years ago.

Butch and Gage emerged from the cave. "The bones are quite old," Butch said as he stripped off nitrile gloves. "I'll know more once I've done some tests, but I'd guess they've been in that cave for several decades at least. There's some evidence of gnawing by rodents, but apparently no large animals could get to them. If we can learn their identities maybe we'll have a better idea how they ended up there."

"Once we have a few details about age and gender, we'll search missing persons," Gage said. "If we get some names, we can look for dental records. Barring that, we're lucky to have a top-notch forensic facial reconstructionist in the area. She could recreate the victims' faces, using their skulls, and that might help us identify them. But that kind of work is expensive, and it takes time. We'll start with the simplest approach first. Even with names, finding the murderer is going to take real luck."

"I'm supposed to start construction soon," Ian said. How long was this going to hold things up?

"We'll get a team up here to examine the area for evidence," Gage said. "Depending on what we find, you should be able to clear the area, though it may be a few weeks."

"I could shift the work to the other end of the canyon for the time being," he said.

"That would be good," Gage said. "Just keep people away from here until we've finished our investigation."

They followed Butch down the trail and met the investigative team at the trailer. "We're going to be here a while," Gage told Ian. "You're free to go home."

"This is my home, for now," he said. "I live in the rest of the trailer."

"The trailer isn't part of the crime scene, so you can stay here, but you'll have to keep out of our way."

"Of course," he said.

"Bethany mentioned some in the climbing community aren't too happy with your plans for the canyon," Gage said. "Have you had any trouble?"

"A few nasty notes. A few remarks from people." The sign left on his gate today had been typical. "Nothing that felt like a real threat."

"Not much of a welcome to town."

"I can deal with it." He studied the man in front of him. Gage Walker came across as a straight shooter. "Do you know Bethany well?"

"Not well. We've run into each other on a few search and rescue calls."

"Her brother didn't seem too happy about her being here with me."

"They're a close family."

"I met one of her other brothers when I rented the Jeep. They come across as a little overprotective."

"I have two daughters," Gage said. "Having a job like mine, where you see all the terrible things people do to each other, it feels like there's no such thing as overprotective."

Ian couldn't argue with that. "Do I need to be worried about those two skeletons?" he asked. "I mean, whoever killed them is probably long gone, right?"

"Probably," the sergeant said. "I'd like to know what happened to them, but I don't know if we ever will. It's hard to investigate a murder so long after the fact. The best we can do is try to identify them. At least then we might give their families some closure." He glanced toward the cliff face, which now had a line of people making their way up the trail and swarming around the caves. "We'll be out of your way in a few hours, I expect. If we have any questions, we'll let you know."

Ian went back into his office and tried to focus on work, but his mind kept replaying the events of the afternoon. Not just finding the bones, but being with Bethany. She had left without saying goodbye. She probably never wanted to see him again. Nothing to put a damper on a budding friendship like a couple of skeletons.

## *Chapter Four*

"So were they dry bones, like a Halloween skeleton, or was there rotting flesh and stuff?" Carter sat across the dinner table from Bethany and helped himself to mashed potatoes.

"I'm trying to eat," Bethany said. Though she didn't have much of an appetite. Her dream of keeping the afternoon's discovery from her family had been shattered when Carter and Dalton had burst in to report they'd heard about the find from fellow search and rescue volunteers Ryan and Eldon, who had seen the parade of sheriff's department vehicles headed toward Humboldt Canyon and gotten the details from a 911 dispatcher Ryan knew.

"I don't like the idea of you being involved in any of this," Mom said from one end of the table.

"I'm not involved in anything," she said.

"You and Ian Seabrook got friendly really fast," Dalton said.

"He rented a Jeep and I delivered it," she said.

"And stuck around to take a hike with him. Where he showed you a couple of human skeletons." Carter made a face. "Not my idea of a fun date."

"It wasn't a date. And it was my idea to go up to those

caves, not Ian's," she said. "He was just as shocked as I was to find those bones up there."

"I think you should stay away from the whole thing." Her father, a tall, broad-shouldered man whose dark hair showed slashes of silver at the front, looked up from his hamburger steak and gravy. "From what your brothers tell me, this young man doesn't have the best reputation."

"He's only been in Eagle Mountain two days," she protested.

"All the more reason to stay away from him," her mother said. "We don't know anything about him."

"He talked about his plans for the via ferrata," she said. "I think it's going to be something a lot of people will enjoy."

"People who have no business climbing, you mean," Carter said.

"Who are you to say who can climb and who can't?" Bethany countered.

"That's enough, children," their mother said.

Bethany pushed back her chair. "May I be excused? I have a search and rescue meeting."

"So do we." Dalton pushed back his chair, and Carter did as well.

Bethany didn't wait for her brothers. She headed out in her Subaru and arrived at search and rescue headquarters ahead of them. Then she sat in the parking lot for a few minutes and pulled herself together. Time to put aside her frustrations over family and lingering upset over the afternoon's events. She was here to focus on her search and rescue training and learning how to better help other people.

The large training room was already filling up by the time she made her way inside. "Hey, Bethany," her best friend, Chris, greeted her. The two friends embraced.

"It's been ages since I've seen you," Bethany said.

"I know. But I've been so busy with the wedding and Serena and everything." Chris and her fiancé had recently adopted a little girl and were getting ready for their wedding this fall. As happy as Bethany was for them, she couldn't help but feel her friend was slipping away. Chris had other priorities now, some of which Bethany could admit she envied.

But she was determined not to reveal any of that. She turned to greet the other volunteers around her. Across the room, she heard Carter and Dalton arrive. They were quickly surrounded by other young men in the group.

Bethany turned her back on them. She still resented that her brothers had decided to join SAR—something that, until their arrival, had been one thing she didn't have to share with her family. But they were good volunteers, fit and capable, so she couldn't very well protest their acceptance into the group. All she could do was focus on her own training and being the best team member she could be.

"Bethany, you have to tell us about the bones they found in Humboldt Canyon." Eldon Ramsey, a big, burly guy who was originally from Hawaii, cornered her as she was grabbing a cup of coffee from the urn on a side table.

"Um, there's not a lot to tell," she said. "Except they looked like they had been in that cave a long time."

"I heard there were two bodies." Ryan Welch, Eldon's best friend, joined them. "Is that true?"

"Yes. Well, more skeletons than bodies."

"And they were murdered?" Ryan pressed. "How?"

"I'm not sure I should talk about it," she said. "And I don't really know anything." She turned away, spooning too much sugar into her coffee.

"Maybe this will stop construction on the via ferrata," someone she couldn't see said.

"We should be so lucky," someone else said.

"It might make Seabrook think twice about his project." That was Carter's voice, as familiar as her own.

"Some folks are talking about organizing a protest," Eldon said. "If enough people show up to picket, maybe he'll realize how unpopular his closing the canyon is."

"I didn't even know the canyon was for sale," Caleb Garrison said.

"I think the old guy that owned it died and his heirs decided to sell," Ryan said.

"Whoever bought the property probably would have closed it to climbing," Sheri Stevens said. "Everyone is worried about liability these days."

"At least Ian is doing something that will allow more people to enjoy the canyon," Bethany said. "A via ferrata sounds like fun."

"It sounds like a way for a lot of inexperienced people to get hurt," SAR Captain Danny Irwin said. "Anybody who pays the fee can do those courses, whether they know what they're doing or not."

"Ian said he's going to recommend people hire a guide," she said. "And there will be safety equipment."

"Sounds like you've gotten pretty friendly with Ian Seabrook." Chris nudged her. "Pretty fast work there, considering he's only been in town for a couple of days."

Bethany tried to fight down a blush, aware that everyone was looking at her. "I've just talked to him," she said. "Maybe if some of you would do the same, you wouldn't be upset about what he's doing."

"He has a reputation in the climbing community," Sheri said. "And it's not all good."

"What do you mean?" Bethany asked.

"He's one of the top-ranked climbers in the world," she said. "But there's bad blood between him and some of his competitors. There was an incident with Tyler Grey in Indonesia last year."

"I remember hearing about that," Eldon said. "Tyler accused Seabrook of moving some anchors he'd set."

"And there was that trouble two years ago in Mongolia," Ryan said. "Seabrook organized an expedition to Khüiten Peak and bailed at the last minute. A lot of people had made plans, and he left them hanging."

"That doesn't sound like the Ian Seabrook I met," Bethany said. Though really, they had only been together for a couple hours. He'd made a good impression on her, but still...

Danny checked his watch. "We'd better get started, or we'll be here all night."

They returned to their seats, and Bethany tried to focus on the review of best practices for transporting injured persons. But she was aware of curious looks and whispered comments from those around her. The image she had of Ian—of a thoughtful guy with good intentions—was so at odds with the picture they had painted of him. Was he really a selfish braggart who ran over others to get what he wanted?

And if their impression of Ian was closer to the truth, was she yet again attracted to the wrong man?

IAN HAD AN appointment two days later with the county to finalize the permits for constructing the via ferrata. He hated all this behind-the-scenes bureaucracy but had learned to gut it up and plow through. He intended to be as physically involved in the construction as he could, but first he had to jump this hurdle.

"Your building permits appear to be in order," the woman at the clerk's office told him. "Here's the inspection schedule that must be completed throughout the construction process. And you'll need to have final approval from the county commissioners before you can open for business. Has anyone from the commissioners' office contacted you?"

"No. They should have a copy of my business plan," he said. "What else do they need?"

"They may have questions for you."

"Fine. How can I get in touch with them?"

"You'll need to contact the chair, Walt Spies. His office is across the hall."

Ian accepted the schedule from the woman and crossed the hall to the office labeled County Commissioners. The woman at the front desk informed him that Walt Spies wasn't in. Ian left his number and returned to his Jeep.

He headed toward the canyon, anxious to get started. He slowed as he passed the Peak Jeep Tours office. He should stop and say something to Bethany, see how she was doing after the shock of the other day. As he hesitated, a Jeep pulled up to the office and Carter Ames got out. Ian pressed down on the accelerator and sped by. He had caused enough friction between Bethany and her family.

As he neared the turnoff for the canyon, he was surprised to see a number of cars and trucks parked along the side of the road. His hands tightened on the steering wheel. Had people come to gawk at the place where the skeletons had been found? They couldn't ignore the signs he had posted, which meant they were deliberately trespassing.

At the end of the road, his way was blocked by a crowd of people milling about. He inched the Jeep forward, but they pushed in close. "No via ferrata!" they chanted. They leaned over, glaring into his windshield. "Open Humboldt Canyon!" others shouted.

He tapped his horn, but they pressed in closer. Finally, he shut off the vehicle and shoved open the door. "You people are trespassing on private property," he said. "If you don't leave, I'll have to call the sheriff."

"We have a right to peacefully protest!" a woman shouted.

"Not on my property!" Ian pushed through the crowd. He wanted to get a better look at the situation before he called for help.

The demonstration seemed to be concentrated at the entrance to the canyon, right outside the gates. So, technically not on his property. At least thirty people milled about, some with signs, others focused on a man who had climbed into the bed of a truck, bullhorn in hand.

Now that he was away from his Jeep, people didn't appear to recognize Ian. They probably assumed he was another protester. He took advantage of that and hung back as the man with the bullhorn began to speak.

Unlike many of those gathered to demonstrate, this man was older, with a deeply lined face and stooped posture. He wore jeans, boots, a snap-buttoned shirt and a straw cowboy hat. His voice, amplified by the bullhorn, echoed around the canyon. "We're here today to protest the privatization of a public asset," the man boomed. "We're here to take back Humboldt Canyon!"

Cheers rose up from the crowd. Ian leaned down to address a petite brunette beside him. "Who is that?" he asked.

"That's Walt Spies," she said.

"The council chair?" Ian remembered the name.

"I think so. I know he owns a ranch near here."

"We're here to peacefully exercise our right to free speech," Walt said. "Our goal is to make it very clear to Ian Seabrook that him and his via ferrata are not welcome in Eagle Mountain!"

More cheers. Ian's stomach clenched. He moved toward the pickup. He had every intention of grabbing that bullhorn and telling everyone here exactly what he thought of them.

"Mr. Seabrook. Do you have something you'd like to say to us?" Walt leaned over the side of the pickup bed to address Ian.

Ian was startled that Walt had recognized him. But a simple online search would have brought up his picture. "You've all had your say. Now you need to leave," he said.

"Do you still intend to go through with building a via ferrata here?" Walt asked. "Despite the public's objections?"

"A couple of dozen people with signs don't necessarily reflect the opinion of everyone," Ian said.

"What about those two skeletons you found?" Walt asked.

He frowned. "They don't have anything to do with the via ferrata."

"You don't think they're a sign that you should leave well enough alone?"

"I don't believe in signs," Ian said.

"Maybe you should," Walt said. "The universe doesn't look kindly on disturbing a grave."

The crowd pressed in around him, but Ian remained focused on Walt. He didn't like the man, but considering his position in the county, Ian needed to tread lightly.

"I'm leaving the mystery of what happened to those two people to the sheriff," he said. "I'm focused on building an attraction the whole town can be proud of."

"We were proud of this canyon before you came along," someone shouted.

"No via ferrata!" someone else shouted. The crowd took up the chant. "No via ferrata. No via ferrata!"

Ian turned and stared at them, struggling to keep his face expressionless. He couldn't remember when he had felt so helpless—and so alone.

Two men ran toward him, and he braced himself for an attack. "Mike is hurt!" the first to reach him yelled, not at Ian but at Walt Spies. "Mike Addison is hurt. He fell and is hanging by one rope. We need help—quick!"

## Chapter Five

Bethany was at work Friday afternoon when her phone alerted with a message asking for search and rescue volunteers. "Mom, I need to go," she said. "Someone is hurt."

"Oh no." Her mother frowned. "Carter and Dalton are both leading tours."

"They're probably out of cell range right now anyway. But I can go." She hurried out the door.

She kept her gear bag in the back of the Subaru and had only to change into sturdy boots—also tucked in the car—to be ready to roll.

The scene at search and rescue headquarters was organized but tense. "We've got an injured climber in Humboldt Canyon," Sheri said. "Danny is at work, so I'm stepping up to command."

Bethany helped load gear, then got a ride with Grace Wilcox and two others in Grace's car. Chris wasn't here today, she noticed. Probably busy with family.

They were getting ready to leave when Carter and Dalton raced in. "Just in time," Dalton said as he crowded in beside Bethany. Up ahead, Carter found a place in Ryan's truck.

"I thought Humboldt Canyon was closed to climbing," Bethany said as they headed out.

"I heard there was a group organizing a protest there today," Dalton said. "Carter and I were going to go, but we couldn't figure out how to get out of work."

"Why aren't you at work now?" she asked. "I thought you were leading a tour."

"We were almost finished when we got the alert," he said. "So we raced back to the office." He chuckled. "We gave those tourists the ride of their life."

"You'd better hope no one complains."

"They won't. They loved us. When we told them we had to get back to save someone's life, they cheered us on."

She believed that. Carter had yet to meet a person he couldn't charm. "*You're* not saving a life," she said. "It's the whole team."

"Right. But we didn't want to miss out."

She was surprised to be greeted by a crowd at the entrance to the canyon. Tony Meisner, at the wheel of the specially outfitted Jeep that served as the search and rescue vehicle, had to blip the siren to get people to let them through.

They parked at the base of the cliff and piled out of the vehicles. Bethany stopped to gaze up at the figure caught like a fly in a tangle of ropes near the top of the cliff. A short distance away, a white banner had been plastered to the rock. No Via Ferrata it declared, in slightly crooked lettering.

"We tried to haul him up, but then we were afraid we were hurting him more." A lean, narrow-faced man in climbing gear was talking to Sheri when Bethany moved in to help unload gear.

"Tell me what happened." Sheri stared toward the suspended climber.

"Mike had just finished hanging the banner and repositioned to start down," the other climber said. "I think an anchor must have pulled out? All I know is that one minute he was fine, and the next he was falling. The belay did its job and held, but somehow his arm became entangled in the line. I don't know if his arm is broken or what, but when we tried to haul him up, he screamed and passed out. Now he's just hanging there."

Sheri turned to the others. "Ryan and Tony, I want you to climb up to Mike from the canyon floor, one on either side. I'm going to descend from the top, along with a litter. Once we've assessed Mike's condition, we'll cut him free, maneuver him into the litter and bring him up."

"You'll need a couple different riggings up top," Ryan said.

"Eldon, you and Caleb work on those," Sheri said.

"Dalton and I can help," Carter said.

"Bethany, you and Grace and Anna help up top with the ropes." Sheri assigned others to be in charge of other gear, and still others were tasked with keeping the crowd away from the cliff.

"Do you know how to get to the top of the canyon?" Ryan asked her.

"There's a dirt road that heads up that way, but you have to park and hike through the woods," Sheri said. "We'll take the Beast." She opened the passenger door to the rescue vehicle. "Pile in, everybody."

Bethany was climbing into the back of the Beast when a commotion rose up behind her. "What do you people think you're doing?" Ian shouted.

He wasn't addressing the rescuers but the crowd of onlookers. "You're all trespassing," Ian said. "The sheriff's deputies are on their way now."

"Our friend is up there, hurt," one man protested.

"And he wouldn't be hurt if he hadn't been climbing illegally," Ian said. "Search and rescue are here now. The rest of you need to leave."

"He wouldn't have been up there if you hadn't closed off the canyon," someone else shouted. "We have a historic right to be here."

"You don't have a right to anything," Ian said. His face was flushed, his hands clenched in fists at his sides. Sunglasses hid his gaze, but Bethany could hear his anger.

The climber lunged at Ian, who fought back. Eldon and Ryan moved in to separate them.

"Everybody calm down." Eldon said as he dragged Ian away. "Leave the crowd control to the cops."

The climber was still shouting as Ryan and another man tried to calm him, but Ian immediately quieted. He looked over and saw Bethany but quickly looked away before she could react. The sight of him facing the crowd of angry protestors alone sent an ache through her. She wished she could go to him, to let him know he had at least one other person on his side.

"Come on—we need to go," Grace said.

They had to travel less than a mile to reach the spot overlooking the injured climber, but it took the better part of an hour to do so. Once they reached the parking area on the narrow dirt forest road, they had to unload a mountain of gear from the vehicle. Bethany and the others staggered under the weight of ropes, pulleys, break bars, anchors, pitons, a winch, the parts for a wheeled litter and other first aid gear.

Another thirty minutes passed as they assembled a spiderweb of ropes anchored at various points along the top ledge and fed through pulleys. Caleb and Eldon worked together, talking of DCDs, tie-offs, belays and jiggers. Bethany and Grace laid out what seemed like miles of brightly colored climbing ropes and passed them to Carter and Dalton, who relayed them to Tony and Caleb.

"What's a DCD?" Bethany asked Grace.

"Descent control device," she said.

"Like a brake bar or certain kinds of hitches," Caleb said.

"How do you keep track with so many ropes?" Bethany asked as lines crisscrossed at the top of the cliff.

"Every rope has a specific purpose," he said. "If you know the purpose, you can remember how to set it up to work most effectively."

"How did you learn to do this?" She handed him the end of a coil of climbing rope, which he fed through a brake bar.

"There's an organization called Rigging for Rescue that teaches seminars on this stuff," Caleb said. "Week-long hands-on practice. It's pretty intense stuff. Eagle Mountain Search and Rescue footed part of the tuition for me to attend this spring. Ryan and Eldon went, too. And Tony has taken several advanced courses. I think Danny and Sheri have, too." He tested his knot.

Sheri joined them, having donned a climbing harness and helmet. "How's it going?" she asked.

"We're ready when you are," Caleb said.

The radio mounted to her shoulder crackled, and she keyed the mike. "Go ahead."

"Ryan and I are with Mike," Eldon said. "He's in and out of consciousness. He hit his head when he fell. He says he was wearing a climbing helmet, but it must have come off.

His right arm is caught in the ropes and I think it's broken, but the head injury is the real problem. He's not really able to assist much with the rescue. We're going to set some anchors and rope him to those so he's not swinging by his belay rope."

"I'm headed down, and the litter will be right after me," Sheri said.

"Grace and Bethany, I'm putting you on the litter," Caleb said. "It will be light and pretty easy to lower down. Just try not to bang it into the cliff face too much."

"What if we drop it?" Bethany asked.

"You won't drop it. As soon as Sheri is down safely, I'll show you what to do."

Bethany leaned over the edge to watch Sheri descend. The tall, lithe blonde was a fast, agile climber who made difficult pitches look easy. Even wearing a bulky pack with first aid supplies, she seemed to float down the face of the cliff. Only the trickle of gravel from the occasional foothold and the quiet grunts as she worked the ropes betrayed any sign of effort. Eventually she stopped just below the injured man. She spent a few minutes talking quietly with Ryan and Eldon, then she signaled for the litter to be lowered.

Other volunteers had assembled the lightweight aluminum litter, which broke down for easier transport. They had fastened lines to either end and a guide line in the middle. Bethany focused on not getting anything tangled as she and Grace carefully lowered the whole thing until Sheri could reach up one hand and grab hold. Then, with Ryan and Tony's help, they maneuvered the litter until it was beneath the injured climber.

"Hold steady while we get him secured," Sheri instructed

over the radio. "We're going to have to cut his ropes, but we need to make sure he doesn't fall when we do."

"We can send down a sling if you need it," Caleb radioed back.

"Do that," she said. "I think I'm going to have to stand in it to take care of him. There's no ledge or other good foothold in this section of wall."

Bethany looked over the edge again, fighting a slight sensation of vertigo. She could see the tops of the rescuers' helmets in the nest of ropes below. They all seemed so calm and focused. She wasn't sure if she would ever be able to dangle on the end of a rope a hundred feet above the ground and remain so serene.

"We've got him on a safety line and cut his arm free," Sheri radioed a little while later. "I need to splint the injury before we maneuver him into the litter. Tony's going to get the air splint from my pack. Mike could use some pain meds, but we're short medical personnel today."

"He'll feel better once the arm is splinted," Caleb said. "And the ambulance will be here soon."

Another long wait. This was the hardest part of rescue work, Bethany thought. You couldn't rush, but every minute that passed meant more suffering for the injured person.

A siren's wail drifted up from below, gradually growing louder. An ambulance drove into the canyon and parked at the base of the cliff. Bethany noticed that several sheriff's department vehicles had also arrived and the crowd had thinned out. She wondered where Ian was. He had been so upset. What a terrible thing to have happen in what was essentially his home.

"We have Mike secured in the litter," Sheri radioed. "We're ready to bring him down."

"We've got him now." Caleb and Eldon moved in to take over handling of the litter.

Sheri had positioned herself underneath the litter to guide it to the ground and keep Mike calm. Ryan and Tony waited until she was on the ground before they began their own descent. The team at the top of the canyon watched as Mike was transferred from the litter to a gurney and loaded into the ambulance. As soon as the doors were closed, they moved in to disassemble the delicate network of ropes and equipment.

By the time they drove away from the cliff, there was no one left in the canyon. Sheri had sent the other rescuers back to headquarters. They spent another hour unloading and stowing gear.

"Good job, everybody." Sheri came in to report as they were preparing to leave. "Mike has a concussion and he may need surgery to repair the damage to his arm, but he's going to be okay."

"Did anyone retrieve the banner he was hanging?" Bethany asked. She had just remembered it.

"You mean the sheet that said No Via Ferrata?" Sheri asked. "I think we left it up there."

"It'll give Ian Seabrook something to think about," Ryan said.

Bethany opened her mouth to argue, but Carter took her by the arm. "We need to get home," he said.

She glared at him, but he only shook his head. "This isn't your fight," he said quietly.

She was too tired to argue, drained by the day's exertions and the turmoil of her emotions. And maybe Carter was right. What was Ian to her but a good-looking man she had spent a few hours with? For all she knew, he blamed her for finding those skeletons on his property, drawing attention he didn't need or want.

ALL THAT NIGHT, Ian kept replaying the events of the day, from his first sight of the protesters to Walt Spies's taunts about disturbing the dead to the injured climber dangling from the cliff. He hadn't handled any of it well. As the first rays of the sun lit up his bedroom, he lay on his back and stared at the ceiling. He knew what his father would do. Phillip Seabrook would order up a fleet of armed guards to protect the property. Then he'd find a way to cajole or outright bribe the proper county officials into approving the project.

Ian didn't want to bully his way into acceptance. But he didn't want to waste time trying to change the minds of people who had already condemned him. Which left the people out there who hadn't yet made up their minds.

He showered and shaved, then headed into his office. George was waiting for him. A stocky, bow-legged man whose résumé included everything from bull riding to well digging, George seemed a good choice to handle all the jobs associated with this project that Ian wasn't equipped to do.

"I stopped in to tell you I'm quitting," George said.

"Why are you quitting?" he asked.

"I could deal with the nasty signs and people giving me the stink eye when they found out who I worked for. Then that business with the skeletons happened, and I was pretty creeped out. Then yesterday, with that climber getting hurt...that was the last straw. Maybe Walt Spies is right and this project is cursed. Whatever. I don't want any part of it."

Ian's first instinct was to argue that George wasn't thinking straight. He was letting people he didn't even know drive him away from a good job. But did he want someone working for him who didn't really want to be there?

"I'll send your last paycheck to the bank in a few days," Ian said. "Good luck to you."

"You need that luck a lot more than I do," George said and left.

Ian couldn't even muster any anger over this latest setback. The only thing to do was move forward. He disagreed with his father about a lot of things, but that was one bit of his dad's advice that he had found useful. Do the next thing.

With that in mind, he grabbed the keys to the Jeep.

The first thing he saw when he stepped outside was the banner the protesters had affixed to the cliff. No Via Ferrata, in crooked black letters on what must've been a bed sheet. One corner had come loose and rippled in the breeze. He would have to figure out how to get it down—or maybe the wind would do the job for him. Right now, he had more important things to do.

His first stop was Peak Jeep Tours. Bethany's smile when he walked in made him feel at least two inches taller. "I came to apologize for my behavior yesterday," he said.

"You don't have anything to apologize for," she said.

"Yes, I do. You and the rest of the search and rescue team were there to help that climber, and I distracted you, almost brawling with that protester. I should have waited for the sheriff's department to handle the crowd."

"I don't blame you for being upset," she said.

"Not everyone is as understanding as you are." He came to stand beside her desk. "How are you doing? That was an impressive rescue yesterday. It looked intense."

"The people on the ropes were doing all the hard work. I was just there to assist."

"Still, that's an important job, too."

She nodded. "It takes the whole team. That was something I learned really quickly."

He looked around the office. "Are you here by yourself?"

"I am. Dad is having a root canal and Mom drove him. Carter took one of the Jeeps to a glass place for a new windshield, and Dalton is leading a tour."

"Do you have a minute to talk?"

She swiveled her chair toward him. "Of course."

"I want to offer you a job."

She stared. "Um, what kind of job?"

"Administrative assistant. I need help juggling everything to do with this construction project. After that, I'll need someone I can trust to run the via ferrata in my absence."

"Won't you manage it?"

He shook his head. "My main focus is still climbing. And I have other projects I need to check in on. All that involves a lot of traveling. I rarely spend more than a few months in one place. I need someone here to keep an eye on the everyday operations."

"And you want me to do that? I don't know anything about climbing or via ferratas."

"I'll teach you what you need to know." He bent down beside the desk so that he was more at her eye level. "I've seen how good you are with people, and you're calm under pressure. I'll pay you more than whatever you're making here."

"Wow." She sat back. "I don't know what to say."

"How about yes?"

"I'll have to think about it," she said.

He stood. "That's fair enough." The door opened and a couple entered. He moved away. "Let me know when you decide."

Ian hurried out, feeling more optimistic than he had before he'd walked in. He had one person on his side at least.

His next stop was the sheriff's office. A trim woman with short white hair, red eyeglasses and red hoop earrings greeted him. "Good morning, Mr. Seabrook. What can I do for you?"

"How did you know my name?" he asked.

"You were pointed out to me in town the day before yesterday, and you have a face a woman doesn't forget."

Had she just *winked* at him? He blew out a breath. *Okaaay.* "I'd like to speak to Sergeant Walker."

"Let me see if he's available."

A few minutes later, Gage Walker entered the lobby. "Hello, Ian," he said. "Come back here."

"I wanted to know if you had found out anything more about those two skeletons."

Gage leaned into an open door. "Aaron. Ian Seabrook is here. Let's bring him up to date."

Aaron Ames gave Ian a wary look, then followed him and Gage across the hall to another office. "Sit down," Gage said, as he settled behind the desk on one side of the small room. "Aaron, close the door."

He did so, then leaned back against it, arms crossed.

"We have a good lead," Gage said. "We're waiting on dental records to confirm the identities."

"Do you have any idea who killed them?" Ian asked.

"None," Gage said. "But we're looking into it." He shuffled through the papers on his desk and pulled out a couple of eight-by-ten black-and-white photographs. "I had the local historical society pull these photos of Humboldt Canyon as it looked approximately fifty years ago. This is from a newspaper story at the time about a local canyoneering club."

Ian examined the photographs, which depicted half a dozen young people, some at the base of the cliff and some halfway up the steep slope.

"I think in here is where those caves are located." Gage pointed at an area above the climbers. "You can see it's just an area of underbrush. No sign of the caves."

"So they didn't show up until the mudslide took out part of the slope," Ian said.

Gage nodded. "This is a photo taken about ten years ago. It's actually from a previous attempt to sell the property that didn't go through." He passed over a second photo, this one devoid of people, and pointed out the same area at the top of the photo. "A lot of the brush had been cleared away or died off by this time. There's some shadowing here that might be openings to the void below. They might have been there before, obscured by the brush."

"And what—those two just crawled in there?"

"We don't know. But maybe when we confirm their identity, we'll know more."

"Is it still okay if I proceed with construction?" Ian asked.

"Go ahead. I think we've gotten all from the site we're going to. Have you had any more trouble?"

"No. I'm hoping that climber's accident made the protesters think twice about their misguided efforts." He stood. "Will you let me know when you find out the identity of these people?"

"Why do you want to know?" Aaron asked.

Ian turned toward him. "They were found on my property. I'd like to know their names. I think most people would."

Aaron looked like he wanted to answer, but he glanced at Gage, then pressed his lips more firmly together.

"We'll keep you posted," Gage said.

"Thanks."

His final stop of the morning was at the city offices. "Is Walt Spies in?" he asked the woman behind the desk.

"May I ask who's calling?"

He looked past her to the frosted-glass door of an office with Walt's name in gold on the front. He could make out a shadowy figure inside. "Tell him Ian Seabrook wants to speak with him."

The door to the office opened and Walt stepped out.

Ian moved toward him. "We need to talk," he said.

Walt looked him up and down. He was at least six inches shorter than Ian and almost fifty years older, but he did his best to look intimidating. "I don't think we have anything more to discuss."

"I think it will be worthwhile for you to listen to me."

Interest sparked in his eyes, and he opened his office door. "Come in."

Walt settled behind his desk and didn't say anything. Ian waited. He was good at this game, had seen his dad use silence to his advantage many times. Blowhards like Walt liked the sound of their own voice too much to keep quiet for long.

"So what do you want?" Walt asked at last.

"You're head of the county commissioners," Ian said.

"Yes."

"So you'll be voting on the operating permit for the via ferrata."

"I will."

"Then I want to invite you and the rest of the county commissioners to come to the canyon. See what I have planned there. See how it's going to benefit this community."

Walt leaned forward. "And what's in it for me if I do?"

"You'll be making an informed vote. One based on facts, not just public opinion."

He laughed. "You don't know anything about politics, do you, Mr. Seabrook? Public opinion is all that really matters."

Ian remained silent. Walt sobered. "I've been doing my research on you. Your father has made billions in business. I figured he taught you a few tricks."

"What do you mean?"

He rubbed his thumb and forefinger together. "When you said it would be worthwhile for me to listen to you, I thought you were going to offer up cash. Isn't that the way your old man does it?"

"You thought I was going to bribe you?"

"Aren't you?"

"No." Ian stood. "The offer still stands to come see for yourself what I'm doing."

"I don't have to do that. If the voters don't like it, then I don't like it. And something else I don't like is people coming in here and trying to change the way we do things. People move here because they like our way of life. They like being able to drive out to a canyon and climb or hike there."

"They have plenty of public land where they can do those things," Ian said. "Humboldt Canyon is private land, and it always has been."

"Private land that climbers were allowed to use."

"What do you think would have happened to that land if I hadn't purchased it?" Ian asked.

"That doesn't matter because *you* purchased it and you're trying to change things. I'm on the side of the people who are against that." He stood. "Quit while you're ahead, son. That's my advice."

"You didn't do enough research when you looked into me," Ian said. "If you had, you'd know I'm not a quitter."

## Chapter Six

At dinner with her family Saturday, Bethany picked at her plate and half listened as Dalton regaled them with the story of a woman on that afternoon's tour who had been shocked to discover there were no coffee shops in the high country and the only restroom was a pit toilet beside the road. "She may never forgive her husband for signing her up for the tour," Dalton said. "But he tipped me twenty bucks, I think for putting up with her."

"It always pays to be nice to people, no matter how difficult," Mom said. "Bethany, did anyone interesting stop by the office this afternoon?"

Bethany fumbled her fork. For a moment she wondered if her mother had heard about Ian's visit. But no, Mom's bland expression showed she was merely repeating the trick she had used when they were small, of asking each child to contribute something about their day. "As a matter of fact, Ian Seabrook stopped by," she said.

"What did he want?" Carter asked.

"He offered me a job."

She had to fight back a grin at the silence that followed.

"A job doing what?" her father asked. One side of his

face was swollen from his dental work, but he still managed to look stern.

"Administrative assistant now, but transitioning to manager of the via ferrata when it opens," she said.

"It's never going to open," Carter said. "The climbers are organizing to speak against it at the county commissioners' meeting. The county will never approve an operating permit."

"I hope you turned him down," her mother said. "It doesn't sound like a good opportunity at all."

"I told him I'd think about it." Bethany focused on her plate, too afraid to let them see her disappointment. She had hoped that the announcement that a man like Ian—a person who could hire anyone—had offered her a job managing a big concern like the via ferrata would have impressed them, if only a little. Maybe it would have helped them to see her in a new light, as a mature woman with talent and intelligence.

"You have a job," her father said. "You don't need another one."

"I'd like to find something with a little more potential for advancement than working the front counter at the family business," she said.

"When your father and I retire, you and the boys will take over the business," her mother said. "That day will be here sooner than you think."

The last thing Bethany wanted was to run a business with Carter and Dalton. Her brothers would always team up against her when any decision had to be made, yet they were sure to leave her the bulk of the paperwork *because you studied accounting and we're more people-oriented.* That last part was true, but it didn't mean she wanted to be the office drudge. Ian was offering her the opportunity to run her own office.

"I don't have to decide anything right away," she said.

"You heard your brothers," her mother said. "It sounds to me like this Ferrari thing, whatever it is, doesn't have much chance of succeeding. And then where would you be? We'd have to hire someone to fill your position, and you'd be unemployed."

*Right. Because no one else would hire poor little Bethany.* "I'd find a job, Mom. I'm not incompetent."

"I didn't say that, dear. But things aren't always as easy as you think. One of the reasons your father and I decided to buy this business was to offer you and your brothers security."

"Aaron is doing all right without your help," she said.

"Aaron may not want to be a cop forever," her dad said. "Twenty years and he'll be eligible for a pension, and then what will he do? He can help with the Jeep tours."

He sounded so pleased and proud. Bethany offered him a smile. "That's really sweet of you, Dad."

"Sweet. And smart. So see? You don't need another job."

Why were families so hard? Everything her parents did for her, Bethany knew they did out of love. She'd needed a job, so they'd made one for her. She'd needed a place to live—*Here's an apartment right here.* How could she make them understand that all she really wanted was to make her own choices and stand on her own feet? If she failed, she liked to believe that she was strong enough to get up, dust herself off and move on. All she wanted was the chance to try.

Bethany shoved back from the table. "I have to go. I'm meeting Chris at Mo's."

She and Chris had a tradition of meeting at Mo's Pub on Saturday nights to catch up on the week. Originally they had spent the time bemoaning their single status, but that had changed since Chris had met Rand Martin, a gorgeous trauma surgeon who had won her heart. Together they had adopted a nine-year-old girl who'd escaped from a cult in the area. The child, Serena, and plans for her upcoming wedding were keeping Chris busy lately.

"I can't stay long," Chris announced as she slid into a booth at Mo's across from Bethany. She swept her blue-dyed hair out of her face, the bright colors of her full-sleeve tattoo flashing in the overhead light. "Serena has that flu bug that's going around, and I hate to leave her too long."

Bethany stuffed down her disappointment. A sick child trumped a dateless friend any day of the week. "Poor kid. I hope she feels better soon. What else is new with you?"

"Not a lot. Except I've decided to take a leave of absence from search and rescue. I have too much else to deal with right now."

"I'm sorry to hear that, but I understand." Because that was what friends did, right? They understood. "I'll miss seeing you."

"You'll see me plenty," Chris said. "After all, you're my maid of honor. By the time the wedding rolls around, you'll be sick of me."

Bethany forced a smile. She wasn't losing her friend. She was only losing that closeness of knowing she could call any time and Chris would be there for her. Chris had other priorities now. She listened to Chris's description of her hunt for the perfect bridesmaid's dress and remembered her own excitement before her wedding-that-didn't-happen. And then Chris was standing.

"I'm sorry. I really have to go," she said. "I'll talk to you soon."

Bethany watched her leave, then stared at the half-eaten plate of nachos they hadn't really shared. If things had worked out with Justin, she could have offered advice and maybe a few funny anecdotes for her friend. She would be moving ahead with exciting plans for her own life instead of just being…stuck.

She wasn't stuck, she scolded herself. She was moving, if not very fast. She had a new job offer. And an interesting new man in her life. Possibilities. The trick was to keep from screwing things up.

IAN SPENT SUNDAY setting pins in the canyon walls to mark where the various features of the via ferrata would go. He didn't have to do this himself, but it felt good to get out his climbing gear and stretch his limbs. He scouted interesting routes up the face of the cliff, stretching for hand-and footholds, the familiar smell of sun-warmed rock flooding him with memories of so many other climbs, from the first scrambles in the White Mountains of New Hampshire to his summit of El Capitan in Yosemite on his twenty-first birthday.

He had gone on to establish new routes and lead climbing expeditions all over the world, but even the most extensive expedition was reduced to the simple act of the next move and then the next, relying on his body to carry him up and up, testing his nerve and his limits, believing he would always reach the top.

Late afternoon, he was resting on a ledge halfway up the cliff after driving in a pin to mark the beginning of a walkway that would jut from the canyon wall when a Rayford County Sheriff's Department SUV crawled down the road into the canyon and parked in front of the trailer. A deputy exited.

"Up here!" Ian shouted and waved, catching the deputy's attention. "I'll be right down."

He was down in a matter of minutes and walked over to meet Aaron Ames.

"I heard you were a big-time mountain climber," Aaron said by way of greeting.

"It's been my focus the last few years."

"So why come to Eagle Mountain and do this?" He gestured toward the wall Ian had just descended.

"I saw my first via ferrata in France. I was struck by how it brought so many different people to challenge themselves in the mountains. I wanted to recreate that kind of community."

"I see that banner is still up there."

Ian looked over his shoulder at the sheet the protesters had hung. Only two sides remained fastened, so the cloth draped, a limp flag. "I thought I'd see how long it would stay up there," he said. "Not much longer, I don't think." He turned back to Aaron. "What brings you here?"

"We've identified the remains found here."

"Come in and let's sit down."

Inside the trailer, Ian filled a glass with water from a pitcher in the refrigerator and drank it down. "Would you like some?" he asked Aaron. "Or I could make coffee."

"Nothing for me, thanks."

Ian sat at his desk, and Aaron took the chair opposite. "The couple in your cave were Abby and Gerald Boston," Aaron said. "They were a newly married couple who disappeared from Eagle Mountain almost fifty years ago. Their families thought they had left town and cut ties with everyone. If they were planning to leave, they didn't get very far."

"How were you able to identify them so quickly?" Ian asked.

"We got lucky. Gerald's driver's license was in a rotting billfold beneath the body. Since he was from Eagle Mountain, we contacted the local dentist. He's the son of the dentist who cared for the Bostons," he said. "We were able to get his dental records from storage and confirm the identity. From there, we obtained his wife's records and confirmed the second skeleton belonged to her."

"Fifty years. And no one knew what happened to them?"

"We found a relative still living in town—a nephew. And we talked to the nephew's dad, who lives in Phoenix. They all said Gerald had talked of making a fresh start someplace new. When he and Abby disappeared, the relatives assumed that's what they had done."

"Any idea who killed them?"

"None. We recovered the bullets that killed them, but it was a common caliber. Any other evidence like DNA rotted away a long time ago. We'll probably never know what happened to them."

Ian nodded. "It's strange to think they were up there all those years and no one knew it."

"Bethany says you offered her a job."

The abrupt shift in conversation didn't surprise Ian. He had been expecting it ever since he'd seen it was Aaron in the sheriff's cruiser. "I did."

"Why her?"

"She's smart, friendly and calm in a crisis. She's dependable. I need someone like that."

Aaron narrowed his eyes, as if weighing the truth of Ian's statement. "You saw all that in her?"

"She volunteers with search and rescue. That takes courage. Dedication. Hard work. I saw her in action when that protester was hurt. She's respected by the other team members."

"She shocked us all when she moved down here and joined search and rescue."

"Maybe because you only saw her as your little sister. But she's not so little anymore."

"That's what worries me," Aaron said. "She's still naive about a lot of things. She's not used to high rollers like you."

Ian laughed. "I'm not a high roller. I'm just a rock jock."

"You drive a Porsche. That's a high roller in my book."

"I drive a Jeep now."

"I don't want to see my sister hurt. I think she might be a bit infatuated with you. That could end badly."

The words reverberated through him, as if he'd hit his elbow on a jagged rock. He resisted the urge to ask for details—what did Aaron mean by *infatuated*? Had Bethany said anything about him? What did she think of him? Instead, he kept his voice neutral. "I'm not going to hurt her. It was a legitimate job offer."

"And if she turned you down?" Aaron asked.

"I like to think we'll still be friends."

Aaron didn't comment, but he didn't seem as hostile as he had before. "Call us if you find any more bodies," he said after a pause.

The comment surprised a laugh. "I hope not."

Aaron cracked a smile. "Me, too."

Ian followed him outside. "Will you continue to investigate Abby and Gerald's murders?" he asked.

"We'll do what we can, but with so little to go on, it won't be a priority."

"That's understandable, I guess." He looked up at the caves. "Still, it would be good to know what happened to the—"

The crack of a rifle cut off his last word. The window behind them shattered.

"Get down!" Aaron shouted and dove for the SUV.

BETHANY GUIDED HER Subaru around a deep pothole on the road to Humboldt Canyon. She hadn't called to let Ian know she was coming. She hadn't even been sure about it herself until she had turned onto this road. She still didn't know what to tell him regarding his job offer, but she wanted to talk to him. Maybe they could laugh over her parents' reaction to the news that someone had offered her a new job.

She braked to avoid hitting a rabbit that raced across the road in front of her—a snowshoe hare—big white feet standing out from its summer-brown body. She was about to speed up again when a pickup truck shot from a narrow side road she hadn't noticed before. The truck skidded in front of her, fishtailing wildly before the driver regained control and rocketed past her.

*Some people*, she thought and continued cautiously toward the canyon.

Her mood didn't improve when she pulled up to Ian's trailer and saw a black-and-white sheriff's department SUV parked next to Ian's Jeep. She pulled in beside it and looked around but saw no one. Maybe Ian was inside with the sheriff's deputy. She started to open the car door to get out.

"Bethany, get down!"

Aaron's voice cracked with anger, but she heard the fear behind his words. He peeked out from behind the SUV.

She stared at him, confused. "What?"

"Get your head down. Someone just shot at us from the cliff."

She ducked her head below the level of the door but turned to look up toward the cliffs. All was still. Then she carefully eased open the driver's door. "Where's Ian?" she asked.

"I'm under the Jeep," he said.

"Stay in the car and stay down," Aaron ordered.

His radio crackled, and he said something she couldn't make out. Bethany sat with her body twisted awkwardly and folded forward, her head pressed against the steering wheel. She tensed, waiting for a gunshot or a shout or anything but the ticking of her car's engine as it cooled.

"I think whoever was up there is gone," Aaron said.

She turned her head and saw that her brother had emerged from behind the SUV, so she started to straighten up. "Stay down!" he barked.

Ian scrambled from beneath the Jeep and moved, crouched down, to her side. "What are you doing here?" he asked.

"I came to see you." She glanced toward her brother, who was talking on the radio again. "What's going on?"

Aaron was off the radio now. He moved toward them. "Bethany, what are you doing here?"

"I came to see Ian. What is going on? Why are *you* here, Aaron?"

"Ian and I were talking. Someone took a shot at us." He looked over his shoulder. She followed his gaze and saw the shattered window on Ian's trailer.

That had her up and out of the car. "Are you okay?" she asked Ian.

"I'm fine."

"I'm fine, too," Aaron said.

"I can see that," she said. "And at least you're wearing a ballistics vest." She turned back to Ian. "Who was shooting at you?"

"We didn't see them," he said.

"They had to have been up on the other side of the canyon," Aaron said. "Though I don't know how they could get up there."

"There's a dirt road," Bethany said. "Just a track, really. We used it to get to the cliff top to rescue that climber. You have to park and walk about a hundred yards." Fear jolted her. "I may have seen the person who shot you. Or seen their truck."

"What?" Ian asked.

"Who was it?" Aaron asked.

"I didn't see the driver, but as I was coming up here, a white pickup truck came shooting out onto the road from that dirt track. He was going so fast, he lost control for a minute, then straightened out and flew by me. I wondered why someone would be driving so recklessly on that rough road."

"Can you describe the truck?" her brother asked.

She frowned, trying to remember. "It was just a truck. White. Two doors, I think."

"Ford, Chevy, Dodge or Toyota?"

"I don't know." She gave Ian an apologetic look. "I'm not a car geek. I don't notice them much."

"Someone's coming," Aaron said as the crunch of tires on gravel reached them.

Ian stepped in front of Bethany. "Stay behind me," he said.

The car turned out to be another sheriff's department SUV. Deputy Jamie Douglas parked next to Aaron's vehicle and got out. "I got your call about the gunshots," she said. "Is everyone okay?"

"Just one gunshot," Aaron said. "And we're okay. It took out a window." He indicated the shattered glass. "I'm pretty sure they're gone now. Bethany just got here, and on her way in she was passed by a white truck driving erratically. She said it came from a dirt road that leads up to the other side of the cliff. That's the direction the shooter was firing from."

Jamie moved over to the window and examined it. "Can I go inside?" she asked Ian.

"Of course."

She went into the trailer and emerged a few moments later with a plastic evidence bag. "I found the bullet. Remington .223." She showed it to Aaron.

"Let's take a look up on the cliff top," he said. He and Jamie returned to her cruiser and drove away.

When they were gone, Bethany wrapped her arms around Ian. "I'm glad you weren't hurt," she said.

He held her for a moment. He felt good. Solid. Sexy, too. On that thought, she pulled away. She had no idea how he felt about her, and she didn't want to come on too strong.

"Come inside," he said.

He didn't say he felt vulnerable standing in the open, but in his place, she would have. She followed him into the trailer, where he grabbed a broom and began sweeping up the glass. She fetched a trash can and helped him clean up the area. Only then did they sit, side by side on a love seat on the end wall.

"It's good to see you," he said. "I was worried that the shooter was still around."

"Thank goodness they left." She angled toward him. "What was Aaron doing here?"

"He came to tell me they've identified the two bodies we found in the cave."

"Already? Who were they?"

He told her about the newlyweds who had disappeared fifty years before. "And their families really thought they had left without bothering to ever get in touch?" she marveled.

"I guess. They supposedly have a nephew who lives here in town. The sheriff spoke to Gerald's brother. They couldn't think of anyone who would have wanted to kill the couple."

"What a mystery." She sat back. "It's such a sad story."

"Yeah, but at least they died together," he said.

"In each other's arms. Still, it must have been horrible." If she kept thinking about it, she was going to depress herself. "When I saw Aaron, I was afraid he came to warn you away from me."

"He did that, too." Ian's eyes met hers—a little bit teasing, a little bit fond. "I think I persuaded him to let you make your own decisions."

"Thanks."

"And have you made a decision?"

"I want to make sure you're going to get county approval to open to the public before I say yes to the job," she said.

He nodded. "It's not the answer I wanted, but it's probably a smart one."

"I could still help you out. In my spare time."

"I'd rather, if you aren't going to work for me, you'd go out with me."

Bethany stared at him, aware that her mouth was open. She probably looked like a stunned trout. She closed her mouth and tried to muster some composure. Sure, she really liked this guy, but what did he see in her? "After my brother told me who you were, I looked you up online," she said. "You've dated models. Actresses."

"I went out with one actress. One time. As for the models..." He shrugged. "They're not that special."

"Still, why do you want to go out with me?"

"For one thing, you're not impressed by me," he said. "Or at least you hide it well. You're smart, and you're not afraid to stand up to people, even your own family, and say what you really think. Do you know how rare that is? That first day I met you, when your brother was giving me a hard time, you defended me. And you didn't even know me. That made an impression." He leaned closer. "You're also beautiful, and I'd really like to kiss you."

"Yeah. I'd like that, too."

He slid one hand behind her neck, his fingers rough but warm. She leaned into him, and their lips met. Oh, yes, the man knew how to kiss—soft and firm, receiving as well as giving. The sensation moved through her, like ripples in a pond, warmth and awareness and anticipation flowing down her body.

He lifted his head and smiled down at her, a smile full of heat. She reached up to kiss him again, but the rattle of the door had them pulling apart.

Aaron and Jamie entered. "We found a bullet casing," her brother said. "Same caliber as the bullet that took out your window. Someone has been up there, but they're long gone."

"We spoke with the workers at the end of the canyon,"

Jamie said. "They didn't even hear the shot over the sound of their equipment. And none of them saw anything."

"Why fire just one shot?" Ian asked. "They had us pinned down. They could have kept shooting."

"Maybe they just wanted to frighten you," Jamie said. "Warn you off."

"It frightened me at first," he said. "Now it just makes me angry."

Aaron turned to Bethany. "I don't want you working out here," he said.

"I've already told Ian I want to wait until the via ferrata is up and running." And after that kiss, she might still turn him down, in favor of a different relationship.

*Early days*, she reminded herself. *Don't rush things. Just enjoy yourself.*

Aaron nodded and turned to Ian. "Maybe you should think about moving into town."

"I'll think about it. But I'm going to be here all day working anyway. If someone is out to get me, they'll know where to find me."

"I can't believe people are getting so upset about one canyon," Bethany said. "There are so many places around here to climb."

"Maybe this isn't about the via ferrata," Aaron said. He rubbed the back of his neck. "I mean, a bullet seems a lot more personal to me. Have you made any enemies, Ian?"

"There are people who don't like me," he said. "But nobody who would want to hurt me."

"This place was for sale before you bought it," Jamie said. "Did you beat out another buyer? Someone who might be upset that they didn't get the property?"

Ian's expression hardened. "I did beat out someone," he said. "And they were plenty angry about it."

"Who?" Aaron asked. "We should try to find out if they're behind this harassment."

"You won't find out anything," Ian said. "If he's responsible, he knows how to cover his tracks."

"Who is it?" Bethany asked.

He looked at her, eyes filled with pain. "My father. Phillip Seabrook can't stand for anyone to get the best of him. Not even his son."

## *Chapter Seven*

Ian wished he could take back the remark about his father as soon as he had uttered it.

"Are you serious about your father being responsible for trying to kill you?" Aaron asked.

"The shooter didn't really try to kill either one of us, did he?" Ian looked at the shattered window. "He broke the window and left. He was trying to frighten us, not murder us."

"You can't be sure of that," Aaron said. He took out a note pad. "What's your father's contact information? We'll need to talk to him."

"No—forget I said anything. And don't spread word of this around town. It's just a broken window." He moved to the door and opened it. "I need you all to leave now."

Aaron was going to argue, but Jamie said, "Call us if you see or hear anything suspicious."

When they were alone, Bethany moved closer to Ian. "Can I ask you something?"

"What is it?"

"You said your dad wanted to buy the canyon. What was he going to do with it?"

"He wanted to open it up for mining. Studies have shown traces of copper and tellurium in similar rock formations. He planned to strip out the rock, crush it and extract as many precious minerals as possible."

"He would have destroyed it!" she said.

"I couldn't see that happen. I have money of my own, from my grandmother and from investments I've made. I used some of it to make sure I made the highest bid for the canyon."

She clutched his arm. "Ian, you saved it! People need to know that."

He covered her hand with him. "Don't tell anyone."

"Why not?"

"Because half of them won't believe you and at least some of the other half will decide I'm working on my father's behalf and using the construction of the via ferrata to test the ore or something. Then there will be people who decide mining would be a better use of the property and put pressure on me to use it for that. It's not the kind of attention I want."

"All right. I won't say anything."

His eyes met hers, searching. "You need to go home now," he said. "I know we both thought it would be safe for you here, but clearly it isn't."

"I'm not the one someone fired at," she said.

Ian put his hand on her shoulder. "I would never forgive myself if anything happened to you. Even if whoever is doing this is only trying to harass me, accidents happen—like that climber who fell the other day. I can't risk you being injured."

She looked away, but not before he saw the hurt in her eyes. "I want to see you," he said. "But I'll need to come to you."

"All right," she said. "But you have to stay in contact and

let me know you're all right. I care about what happens to you, too."

"You're a caring person," he said.

She gripped his arm, her fingers surprisingly strong. "You're not just anybody, Ian. Not to me."

Before he could think how to reply, she released him and hurried away. He stared after her, heart pounding. Other people had told him he was important to them at various times in his life—other women. People who depended on him. But he had never believed them the way he believed Bethany.

BETHANY KEPT HER promise not to say anything about Ian's father or about what had happened in Humboldt Canyon on Sunday. The sheriff's department had apparently also managed to keep quiet about the incident because all talk at the regular search and rescue meeting Wednesday was of the rescue of the climber Mike Addison, with those who had been on the scene providing a play-by-play for those who hadn't been able to participate.

Talk of the protests at Humboldt Canyon naturally led to debate of the pros and cons of the via ferrata. While most of the skilled climbers—those who spent much of their spare time on the cliffs around town—disliked the idea of the via ferrata, Bethany was gratified to hear a few defenders.

"I had a chance to try out the via ferrata over in Telluride," Danny said. "It was a blast."

"It will just bring more unqualified people onto the cliffs," Ryan groused.

"It also might bring more people to the sport," Sheri said. "Once they get a taste of it, they might want to pursue it more seriously."

"It could mean more business for local guides," Bethany said, remembering what Ian had said about encouraging people to hire someone to escort them through the course.

"I met Ian Seabrook years ago, climbing Katahdin," Tony said. "He had a good reputation in the local climbing community." He shrugged. "Of course, that was years ago."

"I really think he wants this to be a positive thing for our community," Bethany said.

"Bethany just wants the via ferrata to go through because Seabrook offered her a job," Carter said.

Her face heated as everyone turned to look at her. "Nothing's decided yet," she said. "He just mentioned it. And Carter had no business bringing it up."

He held up his hands. "Hey, nobody said it was a secret."

Dalton rested one hand on Carter's shoulder. "If you get the job, promise you'll ask Ian if I can drive his Porsche."

"That is a sweet car," Caleb said.

"The Porsche is in storage somewhere in Junction now," Bethany said. "Ian said it wasn't practical to drive here."

Which led to a discussion of the merits of different sports cars. Had that been Dalton's intention all along? He was generally more thoughtful than Carter, though sometimes the two paired up to tease her.

But eventually the conversation turned back to the via ferrata. "I heard Walt Spies is leading the push to turn down the operating permit for the via ferrata," Carrie Andrews, a local architect, said.

"Why is Walt against it?" Sheri asked. "He's not a climber."

"His ranch borders that property," Tony said.

"Then I'm surprised he didn't try to buy the place," Carrie said.

"Maybe he did," Ryan said.

"Let's get started, everyone." Danny directed their attention to the front of the room. "In light of last week's rescue operation to retrieve an injured climber, we've decided this week's training will include an overview of the equipment involved and the roles of team personnel in a rescue pickoff," he continued. "Next Saturday, we'll meet up in Caspar Canyon to practice what we're reviewing tonight. It's important for everyone to be familiar with the equipment and roles in a rescue like this, even if you aren't a part of the pickoff team. Your handout includes a list of terms you'll need to memorize. There will be a written test on Saturday."

Bethany studied the handout. She recognized a few of the terms—*belay, anchor,* and *twin tension lines* were familiar to her. But others she didn't remember hearing before. She listened intently as Tony described each item on the list, showed slides that demonstrated the various equipment in use, then passed around examples of the various items.

By the time the evening ended, Bethany's thoughts were as tangled as climbing ropes, extending in every direction. As she tucked away the handout to study later, she reminded herself that no matter how chaotic a rescue rigging appeared, it was actually very organized.

Dalton appeared beside her. "Come on—we're ready to go," he said. She had ridden to the training with her brothers.

Bethany shouldered her backpack and followed them into the parking lot. She was startled to see the black rental Jeep idling out front. As she jogged over to it, Ian opened the driver's door and got out.

"Ian, what a surprise." She stopped in front of him. She wanted to throw her arms around him but was aware of her brothers right behind her and most of her fellow volunteers looking on.

He glanced around at all the people, then turned to her. "I had to make sure you were okay," he said. "I stopped by the rental office and no one was there, so I went to your parents' place. They told me you and your brothers were here."

"Why wouldn't she be okay?" Carter put a hand on Bethany's shoulder.

Ian looked pained. He took a folded piece of paper from his pocket and handed it to Carter. Bethany looked on as her brother unfolded the note. Printed in block letters was the message LEAVE HUMBOLDT CANYON ALONE OR NEXT TIME I'LL AME MY SIGHTS ON BETSY.

"My name isn't Betsy." Bethany sounded and looked much calmer than Ian felt as she studied the note. "And they misspelled *aim*."

"I think they're trying to make a pun on our last name," Dalton said. He was reading over Carter's shoulder.

"Where did you find this?" Carter asked.

"It was tucked under the wiper blade on my Jeep when I came out of the Cake Walk Café tonight," Ian said.

A dark-haired man with an air of authority shouldered his way through the crowd gathered around Ian's Jeep. "What's going on?" he asked.

"Jake is a deputy with the sheriff's department," Bethany explained.

"I found this note on my Jeep." Ian took the note from Carter and handed it to Jake. "I came here to make sure Bethany was all right."

The deputy read the note. "Where were you parked?"

"In the alley behind the Cake Walk Café."

Jake nodded. "From what I remember, that alley is pretty dark. I can ask around, but I don't think the chances are good that anyone saw whoever put this on your Jeep." He turned to Bethany. "Who calls you Betsy?"

"No one."

"Dalton and I call her Betty sometimes," Carter said. "But only because we know she doesn't like it."

"Someone who heard your name once or twice and didn't really know you might get mixed up and think it was Betsy." A petite redhead woman joined them.

"This is Hannah, Jake's wife," Bethany said. "She's a paramedic with Eagle Mountain EMS."

"Why would someone leave a note threatening Bethany on your Jeep?" Jake asked.

"Someone must have seen us together," Ian said.

"But we haven't been together," she said.

"You came to the canyon Sunday afternoon," he said. His heart pounded. Had the person who'd fired at him and Aaron still been there when Bethany had arrived? Watching them?

"Bethany, has anyone threatened you directly?" Jake asked.

"No."

"It might be nothing," he said. "But considering someone has already shot at Ian once, it would be a good idea to play it safe."

"Someone shot at you?" Carter shouldered through the crowd that had gathered to stand beside Bethany. "When? Who?"

"Sunday afternoon," Ian said.

"And you were there?" Carter's face was red, his voice raised. "Bethany, you need to stay away from the canyon and from Ian."

"You can't tell me what to do," she countered, then she turned on Jake. "You need to find out who's making these threats. Have you looked at Walt Spies?"

"Why Walt Spies?" he asked.

"He owns land next to Humboldt Canyon," she said. "Maybe he wanted to buy it and Ian beat him to the punch. And he's leading the protests against the via ferrata."

"Leaving vague notes like this doesn't seem like Walt's style," Jake said. "But we'll keep an eye on him. In the meantime, let us know if you notice anyone following you or anything at all happens to unsettle you." He held up the note. "Can I keep this?"

"I don't want it," Ian said.

"So many people have handled it at this point that we won't be able to recover fingerprints or DNA, but maybe the handwriting will tell us something," Jake said. "If nothing else, it could be evidence when we do find who's threatening you."

The crowd began to disperse. "We need to go," Carter said.

"You two wait at the car," Bethany said. "I want to talk to Ian."

"Bethany." Her brother looked stern.

She glared at him, and after a moment, he backed off. "Don't be too long."

When they were alone, Bethany moved closer to Ian. He started to apologize for putting her in this predicament, but she put a finger to his lips. "I'm not going to stay away from Humboldt Canyon, but I'll only come in the daytime."

"I don't think it's a good idea for us to be seen together," he said. "That's what made you a target in the first place."

"I don't care what some jerk thinks of me," she said.

"But as long as we're in public, they can't do anything to me." She put her arm around his waist and laid her head on his shoulder.

His arm went around her automatically and pulled her close. He wasn't convinced she would be safe with him, but how much more would he worry if he couldn't see her? "All right," he said. "As long as we're in public, we can still see each other. I can come to the office."

"Or to my house."

He suppressed a groan. "Your brothers already don't like me. And when I went to your parents' house looking for you tonight, they didn't seem too happy to see me, either."

"Once they know you better, they'll learn to love you."

Ian wasn't so sure about that, but for her, he was willing to give it a try.

"Come by the office tomorrow afternoon," she said. "I want your help with something."

"What's that?"

"I want to try to find out more about Abby and Gerald Boston. Maybe the historical society has old newspapers we can look through. If they were newlyweds, there should have been a wedding announcement."

"That probably won't tell us anything about who might have murdered them," he said.

"No, but I'd like to know more about them."

"Yeah. I would, too. All right, I'll see you tomorrow." He bent and kissed her lightly, aware that her brothers were probably watching. But he had spent a lot of years not caring what other people thought of him. No need to change now.

BETHANY HAD NEVER visited the Eagle Mountain Historical Society—or any historical society, for that matter. The

Victorian-era cottage two blocks off Main Street housed a museum focused on local history as well as an archive of documents, books and photographs related to the area's past.

"This is so cute," she said as she and Ian stopped just inside the doorway to admire a wall display of household items from two centuries before, carefully labeled for modern visitors—a button hook, butter churn, collar stays, bed warmer and ink well.

"Hey, Bethany."

She turned and was surprised to see fellow search and rescue volunteer Caleb Garrison. "Caleb! How nice to see you. Do you know Ian Seabrook?"

"I've heard of you." He offered his hand to Ian, and they shook. "Caleb Garrison."

Bethany noticed the name tag pinned to his shirt. "Do you work here?"

"I'm a volunteer. My day job is teaching history, but it's my hobby, too. Have you visited the museum before?"

"No," she said. "And I'd love to tour it some time, but today we're here to do some research in the archives."

"Sure." He led the way across the hall. "The archives room was added a few years ago. Much better than the basement where everything was stored previously. What can I help you with?"

"We're looking for anything we can find about Gerald and Abby Boston, who lived in Eagle Mountain fifty years ago."

"Can you tell me anything else about them?" he asked. "Do you know what jobs they held or if they had any children?"

"I don't think there were any children," she said. "All I

really know is that they were newlyweds who disappeared not too long after their wedding."

"Let's start with the census records. That will give us more information about their families." He moved to a table in the center of the room and opened a laptop. "We used to keep census records on microfiche, but now they're digitized online. You can search by name and location and should find a match pretty quickly. When did they live here?"

She glanced at Ian. "We're not sure," she said. "They died fifty years ago. Approximately."

"No problem. Let's start with 1970 census and work forward from there." Caleb typed rapidly, then turned the screen toward them. "I think this is the man you're looking for. Gerald Boston, born 1949, death date unknown."

Bethany met Ian's gaze. She turned back to studying the computer screen and gasped. "This says he was married to a woman named Katherine Berringer." She leaned closer. "Born 1950, died 1985. Only thirty-five years old. But that would have been after Gerald died."

"Maybe Katherine's middle name was Abigail?" Ian suggested.

Bethany shook her head. "This shows her middle name as Elizabeth."

"Maybe it's a different Gerald Boston," Ian suggested.

"This is the only one on record living in Eagle Mountain in 1970," Caleb said. "Let's try the 1980 census." He typed again, then shook his head. "No Gerald Boston here."

"Try Katherine Boston or Katherine Berringer," Bethany suggested.

More typing. Caleb nodded. "Katherine Boston was living here then. The same address as before."

"Maybe she was a first wife," Ian said. "Can we find out if Gerald was divorced?"

"You can request that information in writing from the state archives," Caleb said. "Though without a specific date, that might take longer to find."

"What about marriages? Can we find out if there's any record of Gerald marrying Abby?"

"Marriage records after 1960 are private," Caleb said. "Though if there was an announcement in the paper, you might find it there."

"How do we do that?" Ian asked.

"Follow me." He led them to the far end of the room and a shelf stacked with oversize folders. "These are all the issues of the *Eagle Mountain Examiner* prior to when they began digitizing them, about 2010." He reached up and pulled a volume off a shelf. "This is 1975. Even then, the paper only came out once a week, so you should be able to get through them fairly quickly."

"I'll take 1975," Ian said and reached for the folder.

Bethany took the folder for 1976, and they moved to a large worktable in the center of the room and began flipping through the papers. Bethany scanned the pages of newsprint, stopping to marvel at photographs of young women in short skirts and men with long hair and sideburns. "Did you know you could buy a hamburger for thirty-five cents in 1976?" she asked.

"You're supposed to be looking for a marriage announcement," Ian said.

"Sorry. You're right." She flipped faster, scanning the pages and forcing herself not to stop to read the articles about local politics or school events.

Halfway through the folder, she realized there was a section at the center of each issue of the paper that listed events that had taken place in the previous week, from birthdays of people in town to anniversaries, funerals and marriages. She scanned this column closely, learning that *Patsy Lehring turned six years old Friday, celebrating with a family party with cake and ice cream.* And *Pete and Donna Farber celebrated twenty-four years of wedded bliss on Tuesday.*

"I think I found it," Ian said.

Bethany moved over to stand beside him. His finger hovered over the page, pointing to an item. She leaned forward and read, "'Gerald Boston and Abigail Simpson were wed in a civil ceremony at the Rayford County Courthouse last Wednesday afternoon, Judge Patrick Simmons presiding.'" She grinned at Ian. "That's it. Katherine must have been George's first wife."

"Would she hate him enough to kill him?" he wondered.

"Find what you need?" Caleb rejoined them.

"Yes," Bethany said. "But how can we find out more about Katherine Berringer Boston?"

"We could start with a web search of the name." He moved to the laptop. After a few moments of typing, he shook his head. "I'm not finding anything. And the census records show she lived here most of her life. She never remarried and apparently didn't have any children."

"Aaron said George's nephew still lives in town," Ian said. "Maybe we can find and talk to him." He checked his phone. "But I really need to go now. I have a teleconference."

"I'll do a little more research online at home and see if I can find Gerald's nephew," Bethany said.

They thanked Caleb and left the museum. "Have you heard from any more protestors?" she asked.

"Nothing. What about you? Anyone suspicious hanging around? Any odd phone calls or notes left on your car?"

"Nothing. I think that note was just someone's lame idea of trying to get your attention. I haven't felt like I was in danger for even one minute."

"I hope you're right."

"And I hope all of this will blow over," she said. "It's so silly anyway."

He studied her for so long that she grew warmer in the heat of his gaze. She put a hand to her cheek. "What are you staring at?"

"I want to tell you to stay away from the canyon for your own good, but I'm beginning to realize you're going to do what you want to anyway."

"You're a smart man." She smiled. "And admit it—you want to see me, don't you? And you want to show off what you're doing in the canyon."

He leaned down and brushed his lips across her cheek, sending a thrill through her. "Yes, I want to see you. And yes, I want you to see what I'm doing. But be careful."

"Always." Careful with her person. Not always careful with her heart.

## Chapter Eight

On Friday, Bethany woke with a heavy feeling in the pit of her stomach. She picked up her phone and stared at the date, and the black feeling intensified. One year ago today she was supposed to have stood in front of friends and family and declared her love to Justin Asher, the man she had believed she would spend the rest of her life with.

Instead, she had spent the day in tears, she and her mother packing up wedding gifts to be returned to the well-wishers who would never hear her vows. Her wedding dress had been packed away, never worn, in an archival box now relegated to her parents' attic.

She allowed herself a few tears in the shower, then headed downstairs. This was just a day, like any other day. She wasn't going to spend it in mourning.

But when her mother greeted her at the office with a hug, her face solemn, Bethany almost broke down. Dalton and Carter avoided the office altogether, although when she went outside she caught them glancing at her with the same expression they might have worn if a bear had wandered into the office.

*I'm fine!* she wanted to scream at them. Then again, that might not be very reassuring.

By the time the day ended, she was jumpy and irritable enough that everyone was leaving her alone. She debated retreating to her apartment for a bubble bath and a bottle of wine—or maybe just a pan of brownies. When, instead, she received a text from search and rescue, it was like being pricked with a pin, some of the pressure of the wound she had been nursing all day relieved.

The call was for a missing hiker. "Craig Boston is seventy, six feet, one inch tall, with long gray hair and blue eyes." Deputy Ryker Vernon read off the description from his phone to the volunteers who gathered at a local trail head. "He left home wearing navy hiking pants and a black T-shirt and carrying a blue daypack. He may also be wearing a red windbreaker and a Houston Astros ball cap. He left home this morning a little after eight a.m. and told his neighbor he intended to hike the Bridle Reins Trail at the base of Mount Wiley. We've verified that his car is at the trailhead parking area."

"Any history of medical problems or dementia?" Danny asked.

Ryker shook his head. "The neighbor says no. He hikes every week. Her words when I talked to her were, 'He could out-hike you any day of the week, Deputy.'"

This brought a few laughs from the assembled searchers, but they quickly sobered. Danny spread out a map on the hood of the search and rescue Jeep, and they gathered around him.

"The trail gains eight hundred feet in elevation in the first mile, traveling pretty much straight up the slope," he said, indicating a highlighted route on the map. "There's a split at the one-mile point where the Laughing Johnny Mine Trail comes in from the east. It's possible to take that trail up, connect with the Silver Chip Trail and make a loop back to a point two miles up the Bridle Reins Trail.

"It's eight miles round trip," Danny continued, "but if Mr. Boston is the hiker his neighbor says he is, he might have taken that route. Or he may have continued straight up the Bridle Reins Trail, which ends at an overlook at about the three-mile point. The last section of the trail is less well-defined. It's possible he got off the main path and ended up somewhere he didn't want to be. Maybe even cliffed out." He raised his head. "We'll divide into teams of three and search all the possibilities."

Bethany was assigned to a team with Caleb Garrison and Grace Wilcox. "I wonder if Craig Boston is Gerald Boston's nephew," she said as they started up the trail. Their assignment was to hike the Laughing Johnny loop from the west. Carter and Dalton were in the group that would hike from the east.

"He might be," Caleb said. "When you find him, you can ask him."

"Who is Gerald Boston?" Grace asked.

"He's one of the people whose skeleton was found in that cave in Humboldt Canyon," Bethany said.

"He and his wife," Caleb said. "A sad story."

"They were murdered, right?" Grace asked. "I remember now."

"Yes. I'd like to ask Craig about his relative, provided he's in any shape to talk."

Caleb led the way, setting a brisk pace up the trail. Bethany did her best to keep up, though the steep pitch soon had her panting. She reminded herself that if Craig was injured or ill, they needed to reach him as soon as possible. Focusing on this idea—and the possibility that he might provide some answers to the mystery of what had happened to Gerald and Abby—kept her going.

After they turned onto the Laughing Johnny Mine Trail the path became less steep, and Bethany was able to catch her breath. They halted for a drink, and she gratefully pulled out her water bottle.

"How is Ian?" Caleb asked.

"He's okay. Busy with construction."

"Have you seen it yet? The via ferrata?"

"Not yet." She didn't elaborate.

They continued up the trail. "Craig!" Caleb shouted. "Mr. Boston!"

"Mr. Boston!" Bethany echoed. But no answer came.

They had been hiking about an hour when the trail was blocked by the massive trunk of a fallen fir. The trunk was almost as wide as Bethany was tall, and dozens of branches poked up from it like porcupine quills.

"We'll have to go around," Grace said.

"Which is probably what Craig Boston did," Caleb said.

"He might have lost the trail and been unable to get back," Bethany said, remembering their training on the behavior of lost persons.

"Let's look for any sign he came this way." Caleb moved to one side of the tree, while Grace and Bethany moved around the other side. Bethany studied the ground, looked for a crushed branch or a foot impression in the leaves or even a thread from a piece of clothing caught on a branch. Grace walked ahead of her, doing the same.

"Over here." Grace stopped and pointed to the low-hanging branch of a young spruce that had been broken off. "It was probably hanging down in his way. He's pretty tall, right? So he broke it off." She raised her voice. "Caleb, we've found something."

He examined the broken branch and agreed it might be an indication that Craig had headed this way. They moved more carefully through the underbrush now, watching for signs that Craig had passed this way and for hazards such as holes, uneven rocks or sudden drop-offs.

"How far have we walked?" Bethany asked after they had been walking a while.

Caleb checked his handheld GPS. "About one and a half miles."

"Would he have come this far off course?" she asked. "Wouldn't he head back toward the trail? He was just trying to detour around the tree."

"He might think he was heading toward the trail," Caleb said. "It's easy to get turned around out here."

"We've found people who were miles away from where they were supposed to be," Grace said. "And some of them we've never found, even though it seemed impossible that they could have disappeared so quickly."

"Let's hope this isn't one of those cases," Caleb said.

They continued through the woods, stopping to call Craig Boston's name, listening for a response. After another twenty minutes had passed, Grace halted and said, "I thought I heard something."

Bethany held her breath, straining to hear anything besides her own pounding heart. Then a new sound cut the stillness, a distant voice that might have been crying, "Help!"

"This way," Caleb said and struck out to their left. "Craig! Craig Boston!"

"I'm here!" came a stronger shout.

They were nearly on top of him before they saw him. He was lying behind another downed tree, almost hidden by its still-green foliage.

"Am I glad to see you," he said when they clambered over the trunk to join him.

"Are you Craig Boston?" Caleb asked.

"Yes." He grimaced and gripped his calf. "I got caught up trying to climb over this tree and fell. I think my ankle is broken."

"We're with Eagle Mountain Search and Rescue," Grace said. She knelt beside his head. "We're going to take care of you."

Caleb radioed that they had found Craig and gave the rest of the team the GPS coordinates for their location. Meanwhile, Grace and Bethany gave the injured man water and cut away some of the tree limbs so he could rest more comfortably. "We're going to have some people here soon with a splint for your ankle and a litter to get you down to an ambulance," Caleb said.

"I feel so stupid," Craig said. "I've been hiking these trails for years, and I know better than to put my foot down anywhere I can't see clearly."

"Accidents happen to even the most experienced, prepared people," Grace said.

"How did you know to look for me?" he asked.

"Your neighbor called 911 when you were late getting home," Caleb said.

"She worries about me, hiking alone at my age. I guess this time her worries were justified."

"I'm going to put some cold packs on your ankle to help bring down the swelling," Caleb said. "When the nurse gets here he'll fix you up with a proper splint and something for the pain. That will help you feel a lot better. Are you having any other pain? Any trouble breathing or chest pains?"

"No, it's just the leg that's bothering me."

Bethany had learned that it could be helpful to distract alert patients with conversation while they waited for help to arrive. "Mr. Boston, are you related to Gerald Boston?" she asked.

"Call me Craig. Why do you want to know?"

"I'm one of the people who found his, um, remains. In the cave in Humboldt Canyon."

He studied her more closely. "What is your name again?"

"Bethany. Bethany Ames."

He looked lost in thought.

"Are you Gerald's nephew?" she asked.

"I am," he said. "Gerald Boston was my uncle, but he was only a few years older than me."

"I'm sorry for your loss," Bethany said. "That must have been hard, learning what happened to him all those years ago."

"It was, and it wasn't," Craig said. "The family story was that he and Abby had run away, but I never believed he would vanish like that without saying anything. He and my dad were close."

"Do you mind telling me something about him and Abby?" she asked. "I've been really curious."

"I didn't know Abby all that well. But Gerald was head-over-heels in love with her. She was a pretty thing, very sweet."

"I read that he had been married before."

"Where did you hear that?" His voice was sharp.

She drew back. "I visited the historical society, trying to

find out more information about them. I wanted to know them as more than bones in a cave."

He calmed a little. "Yes, Gerald was married before. His first wife, Katherine, never forgave him for divorcing her. But they'd known each other only a short time before eloping. Then he learned how unstable she was. She drank to excess almost every day, lied about everything and flew into jealous rages over imagined slights." He shook his head. "Gerald thought they would both be happier divorced. He met and married Abby, but Katherine continued to plague him. We thought that was the reason he and Abby supposedly left town—to get away from Katherine."

"Do you think she would have been angry enough to kill them and hide them in that cave?" Bethany asked.

Craig sighed. "I can't help thinking she had something to do with it. Except Katherine had a disability, and it prevented her from walking very far. Gerald always said that was why she was so bitter. She blamed him for the accident that injured her leg, but Gerald said she was drunk and fell out of a car she was riding in with another man. The car tire crushed her leg," he explained. "The other man—we had no idea who he was, though there were rumors about Katherine being seen around town with a man who wasn't her husband—drove off and left Katherine lying by the side of the road. After that, she used a crutch even to walk across the room.

"I can't see how she would ever have gotten up to that cave or overpowered Gerald and Abby, who were both young and fit," he said, "but maybe she and the other man—whoever he was—were in it together."

"Such a sad story," Grace said.

"It is," Craig said. "The sheriff's department said they

would investigate the murder, but I don't see how they're going to find out anything after all this time."

A shout from a short distance away distracted them all. "Here comes the rest of the team," Caleb said.

Bethany moved over to make room for Danny, who quickly assessed Craig's condition. "You'll need X-rays to confirm, but I don't think the ankle is broken," he said. "Probably just a bad sprain. I'm going to splint the ankle and give you something for the pain, then we'll get you down off the mountain."

While Danny tended to Craig, the others assembled the wheeled litter, then moved their patient into it. "Are you ready for your ride down the mountain?" Carter asked.

"More than ready," he said, a little drowsily. His features had relaxed and some of the color had returned to his face as the pain medication did its work.

The litter had one large wheel in the center, which made it easier to navigate the narrow hiking trail but required volunteers at each corner to support it and guide it over rough spots. Volunteers took turns on litter duty, which was more tiring than Bethany would have expected, since it required supporting part of the patient's weight as well as maneuvering over rough terrain without a clear view of the ground. But they had all practiced the job, and the trip down the mountain went smoothly. An ambulance was waiting when they arrived at the trail head, and paramedics transferred Craig into it and drove away.

"Another job well done," Carter said as he and Dalton caught up with Bethany in the parking lot at search and rescue headquarters. "I'm starved."

"Let's get pizza," Dalton said. "You want to come, Betty?"

She glared at him for using the nickname she despised. "No, thanks." She clicked her key fob to unlock her Subaru.

"Where are you off to in such a hurry?" Carter asked.

"None of your business," she said, then got into the car and started it before they could quiz her further.

Yes, she had promised to stay away from Humboldt Canyon, but she wanted to see Ian's face when she told him what she had learned from Craig Boston.

## *Chapter Nine*

Ian met her at the door of his trailer, brow furrowed. "Bethany? Is everything okay? What are you doing here?"

"I came to see you." She hurried up the steps. "And before you say anything—I have a good reason to be here. Let me in and I'll tell you."

She was prepared for him to argue, but instead he ushered her inside and locked the door behind them. "What's going on?" he asked. Good. He didn't appear angry, only concerned. Maybe a little worried on her behalf.

Bethany moved to the sofa and sat. "Search and rescue got a call late this afternoon about an overdue hiker," she said.

"Did you find him?

"We did. He had a sprained ankle, but he's going to be fine." She patted the cushion beside her. "Come sit down and I'll tell you all about it."

He sat. "Guess who the hiker was?" she asked.

"A celebrity? Some famous actor or something?"

"No, he was Gerald Boston's nephew."

"No kidding? Did you ask him about Gerald and Abby? Or is that kind of thing not allowed in search and rescue?"

"We're encouraged to make conversation when the patient is alert, in order to take their mind off their troubles and pass the time. We had to wait for the rest of the team to show up with the litter and the first aid supplies."

"So you figured talking about his dead relatives would be a good distraction?"

She made a face. "He didn't mind at all. And I did tell him I was sorry for his loss." She flushed. "I know some people think I'm impulsive and even rude at times, but I always figure I should be upfront with people. And in this case, I learned a lot of interesting stuff."

"Such as?"

"Craig—his name is Craig Boston, which is how I guessed he was the nephew we'd heard about—he said Gerald really loved Abby and that she was pretty and sweet and very different from Gerald's first wife."

"Katherine."

Bethany nodded. "Katherine sounds like a real piece of work. She drank and told lies and was very jealous. And apparently she ran around on Gerald, because Craig said there were a lot of rumors about her being seen in the company of another man," she explained. "And while she was with that man, she fell out of a car he was driving. The wheel of the car ran over her leg, and he drove off and just left her there! Can you imagine? Craig said instead of blaming the other man for her accident, she blamed Gerald. After the accident, she had to walk with a crutch and couldn't go very far."

"So she couldn't have killed Gerald and Abby."

"Craig didn't think so. But he said he wouldn't be surprised if Katherine's unknown boyfriend had been involved. He had no idea who the man might be. He said the sheriff's office promised to investigate, but he doesn't think, after all this time, they'll find the killer."

"Abby could have been the original target," Ian said. "Maybe a jilted lover, or just some guy who was obsessed with her, who was upset that she married Gerald and decided that if he couldn't have Abby, no one would."

She sat back and chewed her thumbnail. "You're right. I should have asked him more about Abby. By then the other SAR members had arrived, and they needed to get Craig ready for transport to the ambulance."

"Maybe we can talk to him again sometime."

"Maybe so. Have you been back up to the caves since we found them?"

"No. The sheriff's department had people up there for a couple of days, taking photographs and collecting anything that looked like evidence, though I don't think they came up with much. After that, I never went back up there."

"I'd like to go up there again to look around," she said. "Not that I think I would see anything the sheriff's deputies missed, but now that I know more about Gerald and Abby, I can better envision their situation."

"Won't that just make you sad?"

"A little. But I want to see."

"It's too late tonight."

"I know that, silly." She leaned her head on his shoulder and sighed.

"Rough day?" he asked.

"A little."

He waited a beat, then asked, "Want to talk about it?"

Did she? Maybe. "Today was supposed to be my wedding day. Well, not today, but this date a year ago."

He grew very still. Maybe not even breathing. She raised her head and looked at him. "I'm not pining over him—my former fiancé," she said. "Just, well, grieving what might have been." She could have been married by now. Maybe even planning for children.

"What happened?"

"He changed his mind about wanting to marry me. But he waited until one month before the wedding—after we had made all the reservations, hired the caterer and the photographer and the DJ. After we'd sent the invitations. We'd already had one wedding shower. I had wedding gifts at my house. It was humiliating."

"That's tough," Ian said. "But maybe better to know that about him before you were legally tied."

"Oh, yes. I'm sure it was. But I wasn't thinking about that when I was calling people and canceling, and hearing we couldn't get our deposits refunded. Or when I was returning gifts and being asked over and over 'What happened?' I couldn't help translating that question as 'What did you do wrong?'"

"I'm sure you didn't do anything wrong."

She blew out a breath. "Maybe not. But Justin was such a great guy. I mean, that's what everyone said. Even after I told them he had called off the wedding, at least sixty percent of the people said, 'But Justin is such a great guy.'"

"Justin sounds like a grade-A jerk."

She laughed—at the words themselves and the fierceness with which he said them.

He pulled her close once more. "Where does this guy live? Next time I'm in the area I could stop by his house and punch him."

"Thanks, but you don't have to do that."

"I think it would feel pretty good."

"You feel good." She snuggled closer. For maybe the first time since Justin had told her he didn't love her enough to spend the rest of his life with her, she felt truly grateful for his decision. If he hadn't dumped her, she wouldn't be here now with Ian.

He took her hand in his and kissed her knuckles. One by one, brushing them with his tongue, like flames licking along her body.

Bethany tilted her mouth to meet his, his lips caressing, carrying a heat that flowed through her. She slipped her arms around his waist, reveling in the feel of his body, all taut muscle and masculine angles.

His fingers threaded through her hair, cradling her head as he deepened the kiss, his tongue tangling with hers, gentle and teasing. His other hand slid down her body, his palm tracing the fullness of her breast and the curve of her waist and hips. She gripped his hips and then his buttocks, bringing him closer still.

Ian moved his lips to kiss her neck and then her ear. "I want to make love to you," he growled.

"I want to make love to *you*," she echoed.

"Let's go into the bedroom." He moved back enough to take her hand.

She was too focused on him to register more than an impression of the bedroom—dark colors, a big bed, the soft glow of the lamp he switched on beside the bed. He pulled his shirt off, revealing a sculpted chest and ridged abs.

Her heart pounded and she was hot all over. Yes, she was definitely wearing too many clothes.

He apparently had the same thought and moved in to slide his hands beneath the hem of her Eagle Mountain Search and Rescue T-shirt. She lifted her arms, and he tugged it over her head, then reached around to unhook her bra. "Nice," he said as he tossed it to the floor, and she wasn't sure if he meant her choice of undergarment or her naked breasts, the nipples taut with both arousal and the sudden draft.

They finished undressing, and Ian led her to the bed. Once there, he lay back and beckoned her. She didn't move in close right away, preferring to sit back and admire him. How had she never appreciated the benefits of climbing before? "I've fantasized about you naked, but the real thing is even better," she said.

"Mmmm." He sat up and cupped her breasts. "Even better," he murmured, then drew one taut peak into his mouth.

Arching her back, Bethany laughed. He looked up at her. "What's so funny?"

"I'm just so happy." She wrapped her arms around him, and they fell back together on the pillows.

"I love that I don't have to guess how you're feeling," he said. "Because you always tell me."

"Some people see that as a flaw." She kissed her way along his jaw. "But right now I'm feeling like I don't want to wait any longer."

He leaned over her to reach into the drawer of the bedside table. She kissed his chest, then slid lower, kissing her way down his body. He groaned but stayed still on his hands and knees as she moved down…down.

"You keep that up, and this is going to be over before we've really started," he said after a moment.

With feigned reluctance, she slid up to lie beside him and watched as he rolled on the condom. A flutter of nervousness passed through her. This man had dated actresses and models, athletes with perfect bodies like his own. What was he going to think of her?

He rolled over and took her in his arms. "Come here, beautiful," he said.

He kissed her, and in that moment she did feel beautiful. Desirable. His every movement communicated how much he wanted her. She relaxed and focused on enjoying the moment—on giving and receiving pleasure with a man who was helping her to trust again.

IAN TOLD HIMSELF not to rush. They had waited for this moment. He wanted to enjoy it. One thing he had already learned about Bethany was how much she could surprise him. She was so open with her feelings—so willing to laugh and to risk being awkward or different from everyone around her. In lovemaking, that translated to a contagious enthusiasm. As they moved together and came to know each other's bodies, he found himself feeling more sheer joy than he had in a long time. He didn't have to impress her or live up to some myth of the perfect partner.

With her, it was enough to caress and hold, to give and receive all the pleasure they could find. When he finally moved into her she accepted him with an openness that pulled at him, somewhere deep inside. Though his instinct was to close his eyes, to keep her from seeing how much she moved him, he forced himself to keep them open, to keep looking into her eyes, seeing his own desire and need and satisfaction reflected back at him.

Bethany's climax shuddered through him, and she cried out her pleasure, uninhibited and delighted. His own climax overtook him, and he shouted her name, something he had never done before. She had vanquished his famous reserve, tearing aside the aloofness that had earned him a reputation as someone who was hard to get along with.

"Do you know how special you are?" Ian asked as he cradled her to his side moments later.

"I've always been different," she said. "I used to think it was a bad thing, then I decided every one of us is set apart from others in some way. When I started to embrace my quirkiness I felt better about myself, even if not everyone understands me."

"I don't have to understand you to appreciate you." He'd almost said *love*—but that was too soon. Ian couldn't remember using the word with anyone, even his parents.

But here with her, in this moment in the darkness, hearing her heart beat against his side, feeling the sigh of her breath across his chest, he felt closer to knowing the meaning of love than at any other time in his life.

## Chapter Ten

Bethany awoke to the insistent jangle of her phone. She groped for it on the bedside table and levered up onto one elbow, squinting at the bedside clock as she did so—7:00 a.m. "Hello?"

"Bethany?" her mother asked. "Where are you? Are you all right?"

"I'm fine, Mom. Why are you calling me?"

"I came in to open the office and went upstairs to your apartment to say hello, and it was obvious you hadn't been home all night."

She sat up, suddenly a lot more awake. "You went into my apartment?"

"I had to make sure you were okay. You could have fallen in the shower and hit your head. Your bed was still made and yesterday's breakfast dishes were still in the sink."

"How do you know they were yesterday's breakfast dishes?"

"Because they were there when I went up yesterday to borrow a cup of rice. You really should transfer your rice from the plastic bag to a glass jar, you know. Mice or bugs can get into the plastic."

"Mom! You can't take things from my cabinets without asking first."

"Don't be ridiculous. I'm your mother. And don't try to change the subject. Where are you?"

"I'm at Ian's."

Long silence. "You're sleeping with him now?"

"Mom!"

"I'm just trying to determine how serious you are about this man."

"When I'm ready to share that information, I promise I'll tell you."

"I don't think it's safe for you to be there with him."

*Because of Ian, or because of other people?* But she didn't ask. She didn't really want to know the answer. "I'm fine, Mom."

"When are you coming home?"

"My work shift starts at ten. I'll be there then."

"Your father isn't going to like this."

"Then don't tell him. I have to go, Mom."

"Why? Is something wrong?"

"Ian is waiting." She ended the call. Let Mom imagine what he was waiting for.

Ian was coming out of the bathroom when she exited the bedroom. He was freshly shaved and smelled of mint and soap. "Good morning," he said. "I didn't wake you, did I?"

"My mom woke me."

"Is everything okay?"

"She went up to my apartment this morning—just to make sure I was okay, she says. And she noticed I hadn't come home last night. Because she was in there yesterday, too, and saw the dirty dishes in the sink. I have no privacy!"

"I'm sorry. That is aggravating." He wrapped his arm around her, and she leaned into him briefly.

Then she straightened. "I'll survive. But it's just as well she woke me. I have to be at work at ten, and I want to revisit the cave first."

"I'll go with you," he said. "Let's have breakfast first."

She hurried to get cleaned up and dressed, and met him in the kitchen, where he handed her a mug of coffee. She drank deeply. Nothing like that first cup to improve her mood.

They ate toast and peanut butter, finished their coffees, then stepped outside. Bethany breathed deeply of the cool morning air, the scent of evergreens detectible beneath the construction dust. She followed Ian across the canyon. Colored stakes and paint marked the location of various structures, mazes of scaffolding rose up in several places and bridges and platforms were beginning to take shape.

"Will the via ferrata extend this far?" she asked as they approached the trail up to the caves.

"I originally thought it would, but the engineer determined the soil is too unstable in this area. That's probably why the mudslide did so much damage. We'll stick to the areas with more stable rock formations."

They climbed toward the cave. The trek seemed easier this time, the trail better defined than before, she supposed, because of all the trips various law enforcement personnel had made back and forth to the Bostons' unfortunate gravesite.

At the entrance to the cave, Ian switched on a flashlight and played its beam across the floor. The opening itself was smaller than she'd remembered, dark and musty and swept clean.

"You say this wasn't here when you purchased the property?"

"No. The sheriff's department has pictures taken fifty years ago that show a lot of trees and underbrush here. The cave openings might have been in there somewhere, but they weren't obvious in the photos. We think the mudslide last month took out a good chunk of hillside and revealed these openings."

"Then how did Gerald and Abby get in here?"

"They may have crawled in to hide from someone. Or been forced in here at gunpoint, then shot."

She shuddered. "I'd really like to know who Katherine's boyfriend was," she said. "If he was ruthless enough to run over her and leave her lying in the road, he might not balk at murder."

"If Gerald's nephew doesn't know his name, I don't see how we'll figure it out," Ian said.

"I want to try again at the historical society," she said. "I'll bet those old newspapers have more about Katherine. They probably would have reported the accident that injured her leg. Maybe we can find out more about her. And we can look for information on Abby's family as well. Maybe they were locals, too."

"It would be interesting to know more about them," Ian said.

"Let me see." She took the light from him and directed the beam along the walls, then shifted it to the floor. The impressions of many shoes showed in the dust, along with drag marks and flat areas where the deputies had set equipment. Something glinted in the light on the floor of the cave. She moved to examine it more closely. "Ian, look at this."

He came to stand beside her. Spotlighted in the beam of the flashlight was a thin gold band.

She bent and picked it up. "It looks like a wedding ring."

Bethany studied the ring. "Maybe it was Abby's?" Ian sounded doubtful.

She shook her head. "Look at this place. The sheriff's department swept it clean. How could they have missed this?"

"We'd better take it to them."

She looked around the cave once more. "Do you think someone was here after the police left?" she asked. "Someone who left this?"

"I haven't seen anyone unfamiliar around here," Ian said.

"They could have come here while you were busy supervising the construction or running an errand in town. If they parked somewhere else and slipped in on foot, it would be possible."

"But why even come here?" he asked. "And why leave this ring?"

"I don't know." She pocketed the gold band. "But I'm interested in hearing what the sheriff's department has to say."

AARON EXAMINED THE thin gold band Bethany had handed over when he'd first met up with her and Ian at the sheriff's department. "There's no inscription or anything," he said. "It could belong to anyone."

"But does it belong to Abby Boston?" Bethany asked. "Did the investigators somehow overlook it when they were collecting evidence from the cave?"

He shook his head. "I don't think so. They were very thorough."

"Was Abby wearing a ring?" Ian asked.

Aaron frowned. "I'll have to check."

"Then do it," Bethany said. "This could be important."

He left the room. Ian and Bethany sat side by side at the table, the only sound the ticking of a clock as each minute advanced. "I never spent so much time in a sheriff's office before this," she said. "Or any law enforcement office."

"Where did Aaron work before he came to Eagle Mountain?" Ian asked.

"Waterbury, Vermont, police. But I never visited him at work."

The door opened and Aaron returned, followed by Gage. "Abby Boston was wearing her wedding ring when we found her," Gage said. "A gold band with an inset of diamonds." He held up the plain band Abby had found. "Where *exactly* did you find this?"

"It was on the floor of the cave," she said. "The beam of my flashlight caught it, very near where the skeletons were. I think it would be hard to miss, especially if you were trained to look for evidence."

"We've got photographs taken at the scene," Gage said. "None of them show a ring like this."

"Do you think someone came to the cave after your investigators went away and left this?" Ian asked.

"Have you seen anyone hanging around?"

"No. But there are a lot of construction workers coming and going these days. It wouldn't be too difficult for someone to slip in on foot."

"Why leave a wedding ring?" Aaron asked. "Even one this small and plain would be worth something."

"I could make up a hundred stories about why someone would leave a wedding ring at the site where two lovers died arm in arm," Bethany said.

"You could?" Ian sounded surprised.

She was aware of all three men staring at her. Did they not have any imagination? Or see the romantic possibilities? "Maybe someone's own marriage ended and they felt sympathy for Abby and Gerald," she said. "They left the ring as a symbolic gesture."

"Or maybe they just wanted to confuse all of us," Aaron said.

"We'll keep this and see if anyone comes looking for it," Gage said. "I don't think we can do more than that."

"What about the man Katherine was seen with?" she asked. "The one who left her lying hurt after she fell out of the car?"

"When we interviewed him, Craig Boston said he didn't know who he was," Gage said.

"If he left her after his car ran over her, I can't imagine they were ever close again," Aaron said. "Why would someone like that kill Abby and Gerald? And don't say you can think of a reason because whatever it is, it's as illogical as your ring story."

"I didn't say the ring story was true," she said. "And people do behave illogically. Every day. Especially when it comes to strong emotions like love."

"If you find out anything else, let us know," Gage said. "Thanks for bringing in the ring." He turned to Ian. "Have you had any more trouble out at your place?"

"Things have been quiet," Ian said. "I think everyone is waiting to see what happens at the county commissioners' meeting to discuss the operating permit for the via ferrata."

"There's still a lot of opposition to the project," Aaron said.

"As the project takes shape, I think more people will see how it will be good for the community and for climbing," Ian said. He offered a hand. "Thanks for your help with all of this."

Aaron hesitated, then shook Ian's hand. Ian and Gage exchanged handshakes as well.

"I think you're winning Aaron over," Bethany said when they were outside again.

"Maybe he's accepting that his sister can make her own decisions."

She took his arm. "Wouldn't that be something?" She wanted to tell him that she had made some decisions about him—that she might be falling in love. But an uncharacteristic caution held her back. As impulsive as she was with some things, she had learned the hard way to guard her heart.

BY THE FOLLOWING FRIDAY, the via ferrata was beginning to take shape. The contractors had set anchors and supports all along the canyon wall for walkways and platforms and begun drilling for setting iron rings and ladder rungs into other sections of the course. The sound of drilling and hammering reverberated through the canyon all day, but as the sun set the clamor ceased. Ian walked through the construction area, assessing that day's progress and anticipating what was to come.

The construction crew didn't work weekends. Ian rose early Saturday, planning to inspect the previous day's progress, then maybe find somewhere to climb. Though he and Bethany had talked almost every day, he hadn't seen her since the previous Saturday. He had been working late every day, pulling the via ferrata project together. A Friday dinner date had been canceled by a summons for search and rescue volunteers to help look for a lost child who had wandered away from a local campground. The boy had been found safe after midnight.

Today, Bethany had a climbing clinic for search and rescue in Caspar Canyon. As much as he would have liked to see her and cheer her on, he thought it best to avoid that area, especially given the animosity of some of the hardcore climbers to him and his project.

Yesterday afternoon, the construction crew had installed the supports for a catwalk two-thirds of the way up the canyon wall, to be reached via a series of iron rings embedded in the rock face. The support system consisted of short lengths of iron beams inserted in thirty-six-inch-deep holes drilled in the rock, set with concrete. The contractor had suspended scaffolding from the top of the cliff to facilitate the work, and this was still in place. The workers had used a boom truck to lift them up to the scaffolding, but Ian settled for free-climbing, finding easy hand-and footholds in the rough rock.

There were seven supports for the ten feet of walkway. Ian stepped onto the first one, testing its sturdiness before stepping fully onto it. He grinned. These things weren't going anywhere.

Movement down below caught his eye. He looked down to see a figure moving around in front of the trailer. "Hey!" he shouted.

The figure started and looked up at him. From here, it looked like a kid. "What are you doing here?" Ian called.

"I just wanted to look around!"

"You need to leave."

The kid didn't answer but turned and ran back toward the gate. Ian waited to make sure he had left, then moved forward to the next support. He could extend one arm to touch the rock wall to steady himself, but he didn't need to. He moved to the next support and looked down. It was a long way to the bottom, but he had never been afraid of heights, and he had certainly been in more precarious positions with much farther to fall.

He stepped onto the fourth support, and fear gripped him as it wobbled. As it gave way beneath him, he leaped to the fifth support, only to find himself falling, his screams echoing through the canyon.

## *Chapter Eleven*

Saturday found Bethany at Caspar Canyon with search and rescue, contemplating a spiderweb of ropes and miscellaneous hardware arrayed at the top of the cliff. "We're going to run a couple of scenarios today to teach you more about working with rigging for rescue work," Tony told the gathered volunteers. "You'll learn some terminology and safety rules and get a feel for the kind of scenarios you might encounter—situations some of you have already encountered. We'll have a volunteer play the role of injured climber, and Ryan and Eldon will be in charge of the rigging."

Carter stepped forward. "I volunteer to be the injured climber."

"Thanks," Tony said. "But Grace is going to fulfill that role." He gestured to the equipment laid out in front of them. "Bethany, can you hand me a DCD?"

She scanned the array of tools and selected the descent control device and handed it to him.

"Good job," he said. "You've been studying the list of terms we gave you."

Bethany nodded. She didn't want to be the person who made the wrong choice in a real emergency or the one who couldn't find what a fellow volunteer needed at a critical moment.

"Grace is going to climb down and pretend to be injured," Tony explained. "Then it will be up to us to set the proper rigging in order to send someone down to rescue her."

Grace, in harness and helmet, began her descent. Halfway down the face of the cliff, she stopped. "What do I do now?" she called up.

"Call for help," Ryan said.

"Help! Help!"

Bethany bit her lip to keep from laughing. Grace sounded like the victim in the local melodrama.

"What's wrong?" Tony called down.

"I've hurt my ankle."

"Can you put weight on it?" he asked.

"No. It hurts too bad. Help!" Grace added a note of hysteria.

The volunteers gathered around Tony. "We're going to set up a rigging that will allow us to lower and raise a sling," he said. "Rigging makes use of various systems of pulley, ropes and other equipment to work around obstacles, multiply force or allow safer access. Today you'll see some examples and learn some terms, but it can take years and more advanced courses to become proficient. You won't be called on to set rigging by yourself, but we want everyone to be familiar with the terms so that you can assist in rope rescue if needed."

Thus began two hours of tying knots, affixing various equipment and discussing angles, degrees of force and a lot of other terms Bethany was sure wouldn't stick in her head. But as she watched and listened, and occasionally assisted, she began to connect certain actions with specific results and the ropes became less confusing spiderwebs and more beautiful, and practical, designs.

She approached Tony when they were packing up to leave the canyon. "I want to do more of this," she said.

"More climbing?"

"Not so much the climbing as the rigging," she said. "I love seeing how everything fits together. It makes sense to me."

He nodded. "Watch for the announcement of beginner rigging for rescue clinics, and sign up for one," he said. "We can always use more volunteers with that training."

On the ride back to SAR headquarters, Bethany sat between Carter and Dalton. "Today was great," she said. "I may have found my search and rescue specialty."

"You don't like to climb," Dalton said.

"I'll get better at climbing," she said. "But this isn't about climbing. It's about using the tools to help climbers."

"I think you should leave that kind of thing to people with more experience." He patted her knee.

She glared at him, but he was already looking in another direction. Never mind. She wasn't going to let her brothers dampen her enthusiasm. She couldn't wait to tell Ian about today's discovery. He could help her with the climbing aspects. It would be something they could do together.

IAN WAS FALLING, arms flailing, desperately trying to grab hold of something but only grasping air. He slammed into unyielding rock, and pain ripped through his body. His fingers instinctively closed around something—part of the scaffolding? So much pain, white hot, stealing his breath. His grip loosened as consciousness faded. Sliding into empty air once more...

He emerged again, like a diver breaking the surface of the ocean. He was on his back on some hard surface. The ground? No. His legs dangled unsupported. He forced open his eyes, trying to see past the gray fog. Red rock. Blue sky. Where was he?

"Hey! Hey, mister!"

He turned his head toward the side but could see nothing. He tried to respond, but the words emerged as a groan.

"I'm gonna go for help. Hang on."

Another groan, then he slipped beneath the fog again...

Sun burned his face, but the rest of his body was icy. So cold. He ought to be numb, but pain gripped him like a vise. What had happened? A fall, but where was he climbing? Red rock and hot sun. Was he in Yosemite? Morocco? He couldn't remember.

Where was his team? Had they abandoned him? Had they left him here to die?

BACK AT SEARCH and rescue headquarters, the volunteers unloaded their equipment and stored it away. They were almost done when their phones starting going off with alerts from their first responders app. "Injured climber at Humboldt Canyon," Grace said as she read the same words on her phone.

"Another protester?" Ryan asked.

"Maybe," Tony said. "Let's get all the equipment back out and loaded up. The emergency dispatcher has already contacted EMS, and they have an ambulance on the way."

Bethany sent a text to Ian: Headed your way. What's going on?

She didn't get an answer, but he was probably busy with

whoever was injured. She wouldn't allow herself to think it might be him.

The ambulance was waiting in Humboldt Canyon when the search and rescue team arrived. Captain Danny Irwin also met them.

Hannah Gwynn walked over to meet them as they exited their vehicles. "He's up there, on the ledge," she said.

Bethany followed Hannah's pointing finger and spotted the crumpled figure on a narrow ledge halfway up the canyon. From this distance, she couldn't tell much about it. "Who is it?" she asked.

"We don't know yet," Hannah said. "We called up to him, but he didn't answer. We checked him out with binoculars, and we're pretty sure he's still breathing."

Danny turned and began hauling gear out of the Beast. The others pitched in to do the same, though Bethany kept looking back at the small figure. "Where's Ian?" she asked.

Hannah turned to her. "Is he supposed to be here? We haven't seen him."

"He lives here." Bethany felt sick and stared back at the figure on the ledge. Could that be Ian?

"Who called this in?" Grace asked.

"They refused to identify themselves," Hannah said.

"What's that hanging above the ledge?" Tony asked. He had come to stand beside Danny, who was scanning the scene with binoculars.

"I think it's some kind of construction scaffolding." Danny handed the binoculars to Tony. "One end is collapsed, like maybe our guy fell from above it and it broke when his body slammed into it."

"Ouch." Sheri had moved in on Danny's other side. "Hitting the scaffolding could have caused more injuries."

"But it also would have slowed him down, maybe changed the angle of his fall," he said. "We need to figure out the best approach to get to him."

After a brief consultation, they elected to send Danny and Tony up to the ledge. As an RN, Danny could assess the man's injuries and try to stabilize him. Tony could help transfer him to a litter.

"That ledge doesn't look wide enough to hold anyone else," Sheri said. "You'll need a sling. I'll take care of that." She turned and started calling for the equipment they would need.

Bethany tried to focus on helping, but once the climbers started up the canyon wall, all she could do was watch.

Carter moved in beside her. She stiffened, bracing herself for some barbed remark about Ian. Instead, he put his arm around her shoulder. "If it is Ian, he's in good hands now," he said. "You know Danny and Tony will do everything they can to save him."

She bit her lip to keep from crying, unable to speak. But she leaned against him, grateful for his comforting presence.

SOMEONE WAS SHOUTING. Noise reverberated off the rock. Ian couldn't make out the words. He didn't have the strength to answer. He closed his eyes and drifted away again...

"Ian. It's Tony Meisner. We met climbing Katahdin years ago. I'm with Eagle Mountain Search and Rescue. We're here to help you."

Ian focused. On breathing, though it hurt to do so. On opening his eyes and pushing back the fog. A weathered, bearded face leaned over him. That face receded, replaced by a second, a blond man. "I'm Danny," the man said. "I'm a nurse. I'm going to assess your injuries and try to make you more comfortable."

Another groan. He had to do better than that. "Thanks," he whispered. Had they even heard him?

"It looks like you fell from above," Danny said. "Maybe hit the scaffolding on the way down and landed on this ledge. Does that sound right?"

Did it? He couldn't remember. "Where...where am I?"

"Humboldt Canyon. Eagle Mountain, Colorado."

Concentrate. Why was that familiar? The via ferrata! His via ferrata! Memory returned. "The catwalk supports failed," he said, speaking slowly and carefully enunciating each word. He wanted to be sure they understood. "Someone sawed through them."

"What catwalk?" He thought Tony asked this.

"Up...above."

They all looked up, but all he could see was the broken catwalk, jagged pieces hanging over them.

"Where are you having the most pain?" Danny asked.

Everything hurt, but when Ian focused, he could identify the source of the worst of it. "Ribs," he said.

"Does it hurt to breathe?"

"A little."

"You may have cracked a few ribs, but your oxygen levels are good. No blood from your head. Do you think you hit it on the way down?"

"Maybe," Ian said.

"He was smart enough to wear a helmet. That saved him a lot of grief," Tony said.

"They'll run tests at the hospital to make sure," Danny said. "But there's no obvious swelling or bleeding, and his pupils are normal." He addressed Ian once more. "We're going to put you in a cervical collar. Then I'll give you something for the pain."

Any attempt to move him hurt, but Ian gritted his teeth and endured it. He had been here before—in Yellowstone, where he'd fractured his arm in two places in a fall, and in Africa, where he'd broken both ankles. He had recovered and climbed again.

A needle in his arm, then warmth flooding through him. The pain was still there but distant. Separate from him somehow. "Your legs and arms look okay," Danny said. "You're a lucky man. We're going to get you into a litter now. Lie still. Let us do all the work."

A flash of panic as they lifted him into the air, but that quickly faded as the litter embraced him and they roped him in. "We're ready to go," someone said, and they began to float, this man he didn't know—Danny—literally embracing him as they gently descended.

Then he was on the ground, the ropes released. Other people moved in to check his vital signs and examine his injuries.

"Ian? Ian, it's Bethany."

She leaned over him, the freckles standing out against her pale skin. He tried to smile at her, but he couldn't control his face. "You're going to be okay," she said.

*I am.* He didn't know if he said the words out loud or not.

"Let's get him to the ambulance," someone said. Then he was moving again, and the fog descended once more.

DEPUTY JAKE GWYNN responded to the call for assistance from the sheriff's department. The search and rescue crew surrounded his SUV as soon as he parked it. Bethany stood at the edge of the crowd, curious, but most of her focus still on Ian. He had looked so pale and helpless, strapped into that litter, wrapped up like an infant in a cradleboard. Was he really going to be all right? How long before she could see him again?

"What happened here?" Jake asked.

"The 911 dispatcher got a call about a fallen climber in Humboldt Canyon," Danny said. "Ian Seabrook was apparently up on some supports for a catwalk that was being built as part of his via ferrata project. The supports gave way, and he fell, hitting some scaffolding on the way down and landing on a narrow ledge. He may have some broken ribs. Maybe other injuries—we can't be sure until he has a more thorough examination at the hospital."

"I climbed up and took a look at those catwalk supports he was talking about," Tony said. "It looks like someone cut through the last three. They left just enough metal connected to make them look intact, but any weight would cause them to give way."

"How would anyone know he would go up there?" Jake asked. He looked to Bethany. "Was anyone else supposed to be here this morning?

"I don't know," she said. "Yesterday he mentioned the construction crew was finishing up the supports for the catwalk and then they were taking off for the weekend. They'd let the concrete set over the weekend, then finish the catwalk construction on Monday."

"Did he have anyone else working with him?" Sheri asked. "An assistant or anything?"

"His assistant quit right after the trouble with those protesters," Bethany said. *I was supposed to be his assistant.*

"What was he doing up there on the catwalk?" Danny asked.

"I don't know," she said again. "Maybe he just went for a climb?"

"He probably climbed up there to check out the construction," Sheri said. "It's something I would do."

"Maybe the sabotage wasn't aimed at Ian," Carter said. "Maybe it was just meant to slow down the construction of the via ferrata."

"Who called 911?" Danny asked. "I don't think Ian could have done it in his condition."

"The dispatcher said it sounded like someone young," Jake said. "Maybe a teenager."

"Maybe the kid cut through those supports as a prank, then when he saw Ian fall, he panicked and called for help, then ran," Ryan said.

"It would take a torch and some time and muscle to cut through those supports," Tony said. "That doesn't sound like a mere prank."

"We'll try to track the caller down," Jake said. He looked up toward the broken scaffolding. "It would take a lot to cut through iron or steel like that. You'd think Ian would have heard the commotion and come out to see what was going on."

"Maybe they did it at night, when he was asleep," Carter said. "And maybe they found some way to muffle the noise."

"You don't know anyone who would do this kind of thing, do you?" Jake asked. "Maybe you heard someone talking about sabotaging the construction?"

Her brother paled. "Me? No! I mean, I've heard plenty of people complaining about the canyon being closed and about Ian buying it. And someone already took a shot at him."

"You'd think he would quit while he's ahead," Eldon said. "He's got plenty of money—why does he need to build a tourist attraction to make more?"

Bethany turned on him. "You're all wrong about him. Ian

isn't doing this because he's greedy or selfish or any of the reasons you think. He's doing it because he wants to share climbing with other people. And because his dad was going to buy the canyon and destroy it for mining."

"Wait. Ian bought the canyon so his *father* wouldn't destroy it?" Carter asked. "So he, like, used his dad's own money to get the better of him?"

"Ian has his own money," she said. "He doesn't need his dad's."

The silence stretched. People began to drift away, back to the search and rescue vehicles.

"Let me know if you do hear anything," Jake said.

He turned away, and the rest of the crowd dispersed. Bethany intercepted her brother. "You'd tell me if you heard of someone trying to hurt Ian, wouldn't you?" she asked.

"What? Of course!"

She wanted to believe him, but Carter was good at keeping things to himself when it suited him. "Tell Mom and Dad I went to the hospital in Junction to see Ian," she said. "I don't know when I'll be back."

"Do you want me to go with you?" he asked.

"No." The thought of facing the possibility of a horribly injured Ian filled her with dread, but this was one time when her family couldn't help her.

## Chapter Twelve

"We've taped your ribs, which should help you be a little more comfortable. Ice and anti-inflammatories and rest until they heal."

Ian looked up from the emergency room bed at the young doctor standing beside him. "How long will that be?"

"At least a month. Maybe longer. If your symptoms don't resolve within six weeks or they worsen, contact your doctor."

A month was a long time to be limited in what he could do, but Ian knew from previous injuries that if he wanted to climb again, he had to obey doctor's orders. "I'm a fast healer," he said.

The doctor's look said he wasn't impressed. "You've got a lot of bruising that will be pretty sore for a few days, and you've got six stitches in your right thigh from a jagged tear," he said. "You should see your primary care physician to have those removed in a week to ten days." He patted Ian's shoulder. "You're a very lucky man. We wouldn't be having this conversation if you hadn't landed on that ledge."

"I guess not." He didn't call it luck that he had fallen in the first place. Someone had tampered with those catwalk supports, he was sure.

"I'm going to discharge you. You're free to get dressed, though you'll need someone to drive you home."

The doctor was on his way out of the room when two men in uniform entered. Sergeant Gage Walker and Deputy Aaron Ames approached Ian's hospital bed.

"How are you feeling?" Gage asked.

"Better than I was when they brought me in here," Ian said.

"Are you up to talking about what happened and answering a few questions?" Gage asked.

"I'll try," he said. "Everything between the fall and arriving here at the hospital is a blur."

"Can you tell us what happened?"

"I climbed up to take a look at the supports the construction crew had just set for the catwalk. I was walking on the supports when one of them gave way and I fell. I'm sure someone cut through the supports deliberately. The first couple were fine, but the ones at the end wouldn't hold me. Has anyone taken a look at them?"

"One of the search and rescue people said he looked at them, and he agreed with you they'd been cut," Aaron said.

"Did you see anyone else in or around the canyon that morning?" Gage asked. "Anyone who might have tampered with the supports?"

Something niggled at the back of Ian's mind. He tried to bring it into focus. "There was someone…a kid." He sat up straighter, the memory clearer. "I had just stepped onto the supports when I looked down by my trailer and saw this kid. I told him he needed to leave, and he did."

"When you say a kid, how old do you think?" Gage asked.

"It was hard to tell from that distance. Maybe a young teen. Fourteen? Fifteen?"

"Had you seen him before?" Aaron asked.

"No."

"Someone—the dispatcher said it sounded like a young person, maybe a teenager—called 911 to report a climber had fallen in Humboldt Canyon," Gage said. "Do you think it could have been the same person?"

"Maybe." Another memory surfaced, dim and mixed up. "I thought I heard someone shouting at me after I fell. But everything was pretty fuzzy by then. I was in and out of consciousness, I think."

"We'll try to find this kid and see what he has to say," Gage said.

"Why would a kid cut through those supports?" Aaron asked.

"It wouldn't have been easy," Ian said. "He'd have to climb to the scaffolding and bring something to cut them with—a torch, maybe."

"Did you hear anything unusual last night or early this morning?" Gage asked.

"No. But I'm a pretty sound sleeper."

"Have you had any more threats?" he asked.

"No," Ian said. "It's been quiet."

"We weren't able to learn any more about the note threatening to harm Bethany Ames," Gage said.

"We're keeping Bethany safe," Aaron said.

"That's what I want, too," Ian said. He met Aaron's gaze, and the deputy was the first to look away.

"Is there anything else you can tell us?" Gage asked.

"Hello?"

Ian turned toward the door, and there was Bethany, still in her search and rescue uniform, her hair in two braids, framing her face. She glanced at Aaron and Gage. "I didn't mean to interrupt."

"We were just leaving," Gage said.

"What are you doing here?" Aaron demanded.

"I came to see Ian." She sent her brother a defiant look, then strode over to Ian's bed, bent and kissed him on the lips.

STEAM WASN'T EXACTLY coming out of Aaron's ears, but he definitely looked uncomfortable, Bethany thought, as she perched on the side of Ian's bed.

"We have to go," Gage said, and Aaron reluctantly followed.

"That was the best medicine I've had all day," Ian said. "Even if you kissed me to get a rise out of your brother."

"That wasn't the only reason—I promise." She patted his hand. "How are you feeling?"

"Better. They're kicking me out of here. I need to get dressed."

"Need any help?" The look she sent gave him something to think about beside his aches and pains.

"I think I can manage. But I could use a ride back to the canyon."

"I can do that."

"Thanks." His expression sobered. "I'm sorry you had to see me like that, though. It must have been a shock."

"It was." She cleared her throat. "The paramedics told us they were pretty sure you were still breathing, but until someone could climb up there, we didn't know how bad off you were. What did the doctor say?"

"I've got a couple of broken ribs and a few stitches in my thigh. Nothing that won't heal in a few weeks."

"What happened? Tony said someone cut through some supports where you were climbing."

"I think so. No idea who, though."

"Is that why Aaron and Gage were here?"

"Yes. They wanted to find out what I knew."

"Why would someone cut the catwalk supports?" she asked. "They couldn't have known you would climb up there."

"No. But the construction crew would have been up there to finish the work. One of them might have been hurt or even killed. Even if they had noticed the damage right away, it's going to set back the project—probably a few days. They'll have to remove the damaged support, cut new ones and install them."

"This isn't peaceful protesting," she said.

"No. Someone really wants this project to stop. If we learn why, maybe we can figure out who's responsible."

"I still think Walt Spies is suspicious," she said.

"I can't see him climbing up to cut those beams," Ian said. "He must be at least seventy."

"There are plenty of seventy-year-olds in this town who are in great shape. Craig Boston was on a challenging trail when he injured his ankle the other day."

"I can't see why Walt would go to so much trouble. He's in a position to vote against the project—and probably to influence other commissioners to join him. He doesn't have to risk his own safety to attack me and my project."

They fell silent. Bethany weighed the wisdom of saying what was on her mind, then decided she had to go for it. "What about your dad? You said he was upset that you outbid him for the property."

"He was. He is. He hasn't spoken to me since it happened,

but that's not unusual. Unlike your family, mine isn't close. Dad pretty much disinherited me when I chose climbing over a job in the family business. It's one reason my grandmother bypassed him and left all her money to me. But it was something else for him to resent."

"Would your father hire someone to sabotage the via ferrata—as a way to get back at you or to force you to give up? Then maybe he could buy the property and mine it?"

"I don't know. I hate to think of it, but maybe he would."

"I'm sorry." Bethany rubbed his hand again. "I have a confession to make," she said. She had to get this out before she lost her nerve. "Promise you won't be angry with me."

"Why would I be angry?"

"I told some people—well, search and rescue volunteers and Deputy Jake Gwynn—the reason you purchased the canyon. I mean, I told them you wanted to build the via ferrata so all kinds of people could enjoy climbing. But I also told them about your dad wanting to destroy the canyon by mining it and how you bought it to save it."

Ian closed his eyes and said nothing. He was so pale, his features sharpened by suffering.

"I'm sorry," she said. "I shouldn't have told you like this, when you're in pain. I know I promised not to tell anyone, but I couldn't stand there and have them all thinking you were only building the via ferrata out of greed or selfishness. I wanted them to know you're not like that."

He opened his eyes again. "It's okay," he said. "I know you meant well."

"Do you want me to leave now?"

Ian took her hand. "No. Stay." He even managed a smile. "It's okay. Really. I doubt anything you said will change very many people's minds. I learned that when I got into competitive climbing. People believe what they want to believe about you, all evidence to the contrary."

"I overheard some climbers talking one day. They said you had a bad reputation in the climbing community."

His expression darkened. "I like to think I have a good reputation with most people in the climbing world, but I have my enemies, and they like to tell unflattering stories. What did you hear?"

"Something about you moving someone else's anchors?"

"Tyler Grey. I didn't move his anchors, but he's convinced that I did. He set a route, and I climbed it a couple of days after he did. There were no anchors then, and I said something to him about it. Because I pointed out they were missing, he jumped to the conclusion that I had removed them."

"So who did remove them?"

"There was a group of environmentalists in the area at the time who were lobbying hard for legislation to prevent the installation of permanent anchors in climbing areas. My guess is one of them removed the anchors, but I don't know for sure. But Tyler spread the story that I had taken them, and his friends believed him. I didn't waste a lot of breath defending myself, and some people took that as an admission of guilt."

"There was something else about bailing on an expedition you organized."

He groaned.

"Are you okay?" She stood. "Should I call a nurse?"

"I'm just disgusted that story is still around."

She sat again. "What happened?"

"I did organize an expedition to climb Mount Khuiten, in Mongolia. And I did drop out at the last minute. Because my mother was in a car wreck and ended up in the hospital. People always leave out that part of the story."

"Why would they do that?"

"Some of them lost a lot of money on airfare and stuff. I offered to reimburse them, but that wasn't good enough for some of them. Money can do a lot of good things, but it can also make people mean."

"Do you think any of them could be behind what's going on in the canyon?"

"I doubt it." He sighed. "I'll make some calls, see if I can find out what Tyler and a couple of others who had it in for me are up to, and I'll try to get a read on my dad's attitude toward me these days. There's something else I've been thinking about, though."

"Oh, what's that?"

"Maybe these threats and vandalism and even the shot that was fired at me and Aaron aren't related to the via ferrata at all but to us finding those skeletons," he said.

"Gerald and Abby have been dead fifty years."

"That doesn't mean whoever killed them isn't still alive. They've gotten away with murder for years because everyone who knew the Bostons thought they had moved away. I start work in the canyon and find those skeletons, and all of a sudden the killer might be discovered."

"It wasn't your fault that cave opened up. The mudslide a few months ago did that."

"Right. But maybe there's something else in the canyon the killer doesn't want to come to light."

"Or maybe they've heard we've been asking around about Abby and Gerald," she said. "That might explain why I was threatened, too."

"Or maybe the culprit really is a disgruntled climber who doesn't want me to build the via ferrata."

"Let's hope the sheriff's department comes up with something." She stood. "I'll step out for a few minutes so you can get dressed. Then I'll take you home."

While he was focused on seeing the via ferrata project through to completion, she would do a little more digging into the history of the area and the people associated with it on her own.

WHEN IAN'S PHONE rang Monday afternoon, he debated not answering it. He was almost at the point where he couldn't deal with one more thing. But he knew better than to think ignoring this particular caller would give him any peace. He clicked to answer. "Hello, Dad."

"I heard you're up to your elbows in alligators with this iron road project of yours." Phillip Seabrook had a sharp, clipped way of speaking, emphasizing each word and talking a little louder than necessary. "I called to see if you were ready to cry uncle and let me bail you out."

"You heard wrong," Ian said. "Everything is going smoothly."

"Ha! Don't ever try to beat me in a poker game, son. You're a terrible bluffer," he said. "I can read, you know, and that little newspaper in Eagle Mountain reports that the locals have been protesting against your climbing playground and one of them almost died. Not to mention two skeletons found in a cave up there before you even broke ground. You've had enough bad publicity already to sink this project. I'm offering you a chance to get out while you're ahead. Go back to climbing mountains in Peru."

"No, thanks, Dad." He tried to sound snide, but no one could layer on the disdain like his old man.

"You haven't even heard my offer."

"Whatever it is, I'm not interested."

"You won't get an offer like this from anyone else," Phil said. "Of course, I'll give you less than you paid for the place, but that's to be expected since the property has a negative history now, what with finding dead bodies and people being almost killed."

*I was one of those people*, he wanted to point out but didn't. "If you think people in Eagle Mountain are going to welcome your mining project more than they've welcomed my plans for a via ferrata, you're dreaming," he said.

"The difference, son, is that I don't care what the locals think. I'll promise a lot of jobs and deliver on that promise, and I'll be sure to contribute a lot of money to every local cause. They'll hate me for a while, but by the time I'm done pouring on the cash, they'll love me. I'll own them and I'll own their politicians, and I'll be even richer from all the rare earth metals I'm going to pull out of the ground."

"What happens when you've mined all the metals from the canyon?" Ian asked.

"I'll throw more money their way to do what they want to about cleaning up the problem, and I'll move on."

"I'm staying right here," Ian said.

"You're so transparent," Phil said. "I can sense your disapproval through the line. But you're not any better than I am, deep down. You're building your own climbing playground in the canyon and deigning to share it with the locals. At least the things I do feed more than my ego."

"Why are you calling about this now, Dad?"

"Isn't that clear? I thought you'd be ready to sell out."

"But why call today? Did you know I just got out of the hospital?"

"The sheriff's deputy who contacted me might have mentioned it. Did you really think I'm the one behind your accident?"

The sheriff's department was leaving no stone unturned in their search for the person responsible for the vandalism. "I don't know, Dad. You always said you did whatever it takes to succeed."

"That doesn't include harming my own son, even if you don't have sense enough to give up on a bad idea. Sell out to me and go back to roaming the world. There must be a few peaks you haven't climbed yet. Or you could finally wise up and come to work for me."

They were back to an old argument, one Ian would never win. "I have to go, Dad." He didn't wait for an answer and ended the call.

His hands were shaking. He laid aside the phone and tried to focus on his breathing. He shouldn't let his dad get to him like this. But it still galled that while his father had raised him, he didn't know Ian at all.

He tried to focus on the computer screen and the presentation he was making to the county commissioners when they considered his operating permit. Despite a few setbacks, Ian thought the via ferrata would be ready in a couple of weeks. But his dad's voice crowded out everything else.

*If I didn't know better, I'd suspect you weren't even my son.* The incident that had prompted this outburst? Ian's winning the top prize at a regional climbing competition when he'd been fifteen. Though he and his dad had had their share of disagreements over Ian's devotion to climbing by that point, Ian had been sure his father, who liked nothing better than beating out the competition, would appreciate that he had come in first.

According to Phil, climbing rocks—even if the rocks were mountains—was a pastime for kids and losers. Phil had wanted Ian to come to work for him, to learn the ins and outs of dealmaking and leveraged buyouts, gamesmanship and climbing to the top of the business heap, by any means possible. When Ian had said he wasn't interested, a wall had gone up between father and son that Ian had never succeeded in scaling.

He knew his dad would never love climbing. Ian only wanted the man to respect that the sport was important to him. Climbing had introduced him to the sensation of conquering something greater than himself, triumphant yet also humbled by the vastness of creation. He wanted to introduce others to that feeling. He wanted to shape Humboldt Canyon to a purpose yet respect it. That was something his father could never understand.

## Chapter Thirteen

Bethany had offered to bring dinner for herself and Ian Monday evening and to help him with any paperwork relating to the via ferrata project, but he'd turned her down. "I wouldn't be very good company right now," he'd said. "I'm going to rest and take it easy."

She'd wanted to tell him that she saw through this transparent attempt to keep her away from Humboldt Canyon but held her tongue. He probably did need to rest and recover from his injuries, and she had things she wanted to do.

An attractive, middle-aged woman who introduced herself as Brenda greeted Bethany at the historical society. "I'd like to look through some older issues of the *Eagle Mountain Examiner*," Bethany said. "From the 1970s."

"Of course." Brenda led the way to the archives. "Is there something in particular I could help you find?"

"It's for genealogical research," Bethany said. She had decided not to mention Gerald and Abby. She didn't want to explain her admittedly far-fetched theory that their deaths fifty years ago might be linked to Ian's troubles in Humboldt Canyon today.

"Here are the older issues of the paper." Brenda showed

her the large folders. "Let me know if I can help you with anything else."

Bethany selected a folder and carried it to the worktable at the center of the room. The newspaper pages were yellowing and fragile, filled with images and articles from a time that she knew only from old television shows and movies. Eagle Mountain appeared on the page like a fictional small town, full of smiling cheerleaders, winning basketball players, hand-shaking city councilmen and women showing off flowers they had grown or prize-winning recipes. She saw no people of color, no females in positions of leadership and no mention of crime or controversy.

After pages of such blandness, the shock of a headline about a house fire, complete with accompanying photos of a building ablaze, startled her.

"Fire Destroys Newlyweds' Home," declared the bold headline. *The home of Mr. and Mrs. Gerald Boston was consumed Wednesday evening in a blaze authorities suspect was the work of an arsonist.*

Bethany checked the date. This had to be near the time Abby and Gerald had disappeared.

She turned her attention back to the newspaper. *The couple escaped with only the clothing on their backs. They were asleep when the fire woke them and were able to escape out their bedroom window. The sheriff's department has no suspects at this time.*

She flipped through the issues of the paper that followed but found no further mention of this mysterious fire. Chin in hand, she tried to remember what else Craig Boston had told her about Gerald. She selected the folder for the previous year's issues of the newspaper and flipped through it. Long minutes passed as she searched each issue, only the rustle of dry newsprint and a distant clock striking four interrupting her reading.

She stopped when she located a small headline: "Local Woman Injured When Car Tire Crushes Her Leg."

*Katherine Boston, 24, of 126 Bluebell Court, was hospitalized Friday after an accident in which the tire of a vehicle she had been riding in crushed her leg. Mrs. Boston says she was exiting the vehicle when the parking brake failed and the car moved forward. The momentum pushed her to the ground, and the tire rolled over her right leg and crushed it. She was found shortly after by her husband, Gerald Boston, and rushed to the hospital.*

Bethany frowned. The article almost made it sound like Katherine had been driving the car. Or maybe Gerald. No mention of another man or if Katherine had been drinking.

She continued to search the papers and stopped again on a very small legal notice: *A divorce was granted to Gerald F. Boston and Katherine E. Boston of Eagle Mountain.*

Had her injury, possibly while intoxicated and possibly while out with another man, been the last straw for Gerald? Less than a year later, he had married Abby, and shortly after that, someone had set fire to their house. And not much later, the couple had disappeared. According to Craig—and the lack of any mention in the newspaper in the weeks after their disappearance seemed to back this up—everyone assumed they had simply left town. No one suspected murder, and their killer's secret had laid buried for five decades.

Brenda entered the room. "We're going to close soon. Did you find what you were looking for?"

"I think so, yes." Bethany closed the folder and stood. "Thanks for your help."

Outside, clouds had rolled in, darkening the sky except

for the occasional flash of lightning. She hurried along the empty sidewalk, the threat of rain apparently having chased most people indoors. It was downright eerie, being out here by herself.

Then she realized she wasn't alone. Other footsteps echoed behind her, though when she turned to look back, the sidewalk was empty. The hairs on the back of her neck rose, and she held her breath. But only the throb of her own pulse sounded in her ears.

She shook herself and continued down the street. The weather had been beautiful when she'd left her apartment earlier, but her decision to walk to the historical society didn't seem like such a great one now.

That echo again—definitely footsteps.

Bethany whirled around and caught a glimpse of someone disappearing into an alley. "Who's there?" she called.

No answer. She started toward the alley, then thought better of it, a vision of herself being yanked into that narrow, dark space sending her hurrying in the opposite direction.

When she reached Peak Jeep Tours she was relieved to see Dalton out front, washing off one of the Jeeps. "Trying to get the worst of this mud off before the storm," he said as he directed the hose nozzle toward the mud-caked rear tires.

Any other time, she might have pointed out the rain would likely wash off the mud, but she didn't have the energy for that now. She tried to slip past him, wanting to call Ian and tell him what she had learned at the historical society.

"Where have you been?" Dalton asked over the gush of water.

"Shopping," she lied.

"What did you buy?"

"Nothing." She watched in silence as he continued to rinse mud from the Jeep. "Can I ask you something?"

He shut off the water and turned to her. "Go ahead."

"You seem to be okay with Ian. Why is Carter so against him?"

"He doesn't really hate Ian," Dalton said. "I think he's a little envious because Ian's getting all the attention from the local women that he used to get."

"He's *jealous* of Ian?" In a way, it made sense. Carter was good looking and charming, and when he had first moved to Eagle Mountain, every woman in town had seemed to go out of her way to stop by the tour company to introduce herself. He'd kept a busy social calendar for months, but come to think of it, he didn't seem to be going out as much anymore.

"He'll get over it," Dalton said. "It looks to me like Ian isn't interested in those other women. They'll figure that out soon enough and be back to fawning over Carter."

"You really think Ian is the reason Carter hasn't been dating as much lately?"

"It doesn't matter what I think," Dalton said. "It's what Carter thinks. He got used to all the attention when he first came here, and now it's disappeared. It's probably because the novelty of a new guy in town wore off or because he dated everybody in the small-town dating pool. But it's easier to blame Ian. Plus, Carter would give his left ear to have a car like Ian's Porsche."

"What about you?"

"Nah, I'd rather have a Jeep."

"You're a new guy in town, too," she said. "And you're Carter's twin. Why aren't the women fawning over you? Or are they?"

"Nonidentical twin. I don't have Carter's smooth-talking charm. And I don't really want to juggle a bunch of women. One is enough for me."

"Any particular one in mind?" she asked.

"No. But I'll know when I meet her. Until then, I'm keeping my options open." His expression sobered. "But seriously, Bethany, be careful with Ian."

"What do you mean?"

"I don't think he's a bad guy, but you don't really think he's going to stay with you, do you?"

"You don't think I'm good enough for him?" It was a good thing her brother had moved away because if he hadn't, she would have been tempted to kick him.

"You have to be realistic," he said. "You want the house and family and living happily ever after right here in Eagle Mountain. Ian has spent his adult life traveling the world, dating supermodels and conquering mountains. He's not going to be happy with the kind of life you want. You two might have fun for a while, but he's going to leave, and then you'll be hurt." Dalton spread his hands wide. "I don't want that. You've already been hurt once. Don't set yourself up to go through that again."

She wanted to tell him that wasn't going to happen. Ian had said he could depend on her. Didn't that mean she could depend on him? But the truth of Carter's words was like a rock in the pit of her stomach. She was famous for letting her feelings overrule logic. Was she making the same mistake with Ian?

"We found the kid who called 911 the night you fell," Gage said. He'd invited Ian into his office Tuesday to update him on the latest in their investigation of the vandalism in Humboldt Canyon. "He said he was there that day because he wanted to see the via ferrata, figured he could sneak in and take a look after the construction workers left. He didn't know you were living there."

Ian scratched the back of his head. "I can't really see a kid cutting through the supports on that catwalk. How old is he? How big is he?"

"Not big, and not that old—twelve," Gage said. "We don't think he's responsible for the vandalism. He was pretty terrified when we questioned him. His mom and dad came with him. They seemed like good parents, and he's a good kid."

"I owe him for calling in the accident. No telling how long I would have lain there if he hadn't."

"How are the ribs?" the sergeant asked.

Ian shifted. "They're okay." He had dealt with worse. "Did this kid see anyone else lurking around that day?"

"He says he didn't." Gage sat back, studying him for so long Ian began to feel uncomfortable.

"What is it?" he asked.

"We talked to your father," Gage said. "He said he was in Paris the night you were injured...and for four days prior to that."

"He called me."

"Did he say anything you want to share with me?"

"He told me to quit while I was ahead and offered to buy me out. About what I expected from him."

"Is it possible your father hired someone to harass you into giving up on the via ferrata project?" Gage asked.

Ian had spent too many hours asking himself this same question. "Anything is possible with my dad. He's known for being ruthless when it comes to his business dealings.

And he and I don't see eye to eye on most things. But I'm still his son. He doesn't want me dead."

"Do you think someone else wants you to quit and they're behind these attacks?"

"Maybe. But I don't know who." Another question he had wasted too much time trying to answer. "What about Walt Spies? Did you talk to him?"

"Walt was at a planning commission work session that afternoon into evening."

"So we have no idea who's doing these things."

"You could set up cameras," Gage said. "That might help you see if anyone is messing around."

Ian groaned. "I feel like an idiot for not thinking of that before." He pulled out his phone and scrolled to his notes app. "I'll see about getting some installed."

"Let us know if you see anything of interest," Gage said. "Have you had any more problems at the job site or at your trailer?"

"No. The catwalk is repaired. The construction foreman says it's stronger than ever. We should have most of the structures complete by the end of next week. Then it's a matter of installing pit toilets, a building for a welcome center and gift shop, and delineating a parking area. As soon as the county approves my operating permit, I'll advertise for employees."

"You seem pretty sure the county is going to grant the operating permit."

"They don't have any real reason not to."

"Reason and politics don't always mix. Even locally." Gage stood. "Thanks for stopping in. We'll keep looking into this, but so far we don't have much to go on."

Ian left the sheriff's department. The conversation hadn't

reassured him that he and the via ferrata were safe from further damage. He would only brood on the possibilities if he returned to the canyon. He needed something to take his mind off himself—he needed to see Bethany.

Bethany and her mother were reviewing something on the computer when Ian entered the tour company office later that afternoon.

"Hello, Mr. Seabrook," Mrs. Ames said. "Can I help you with something?"

"Hi, Ian," Bethany said. "I was going to call you when I got off work. I'll be done here in a few minutes." She focused on the computer, typing rapidly.

"You're going out?" Mrs. Ames asked her.

"We are." She glanced at Ian. "Right?"

"Right."

Yesterday she had called and suggested they get together. She had hinted at news to share but refused to reveal more, saying, "I want to tell you in person."

Bethany hit a few more keys, then stood. "Let me grab my purse."

She exited the room, leaving Ian alone with her mother, who folded her arms across her chest and scrutinized him. Ian tried to think of something to say but drew a blank. He wasn't used to trying to impress others. His family name or his fortune, his car and even his climbing prowess were usually enough to make a good impression. What could he say that would reassure Mrs. Ames that he was a good person?

"I know some people think we're overprotective," she said. "But Bethany is our only daughter. She almost died when she was born, and that made her even more precious to us. If you have children one day, you'll understand."

"I think a lot of Bethany," he said. "I would never do anything to hurt her."

Mrs. Ames's expression didn't soften, though she did uncross her arms. "You'd better not," she said.

"I'm ready." Bethany hurried into the room, headed for the door. "Bye, Mom. See you tomorrow."

Ian might have been imagining things, but he would have sworn he felt Mrs. Ames's gaze drilling holes in his back as he followed her daughter to his Jeep.

"I overheard what Mom told you," Bethany said as she buckled her seat belt. "I can't believe she dragged out that story about me almost dying."

"I'm sure that was very traumatic for your parents," he said.

"I'm twenty-three. You'd think they'd be over it by now."

"I can't blame them for loving you. I'd have given anything when I was growing up if my parents paid that much attention to me."

"But you're an only child, right? Weren't you spoiled rotten?"

He shook his head. "My parents were too involved in their own lives to waste much effort on me. I had nannies, then went to boarding school and summer camps. My grandmother was the only person who was close to me."

"I'm sorry."

The pity in her voice tore at the long-buried hurt he didn't like to examine too often. "Don't feel sorry for me," he said. "I learned to be independent from a young age. But watching my parents also made me think how I'd treat my own children differently."

"I'm sure you'll be a good father," she said.

He didn't answer. It unsettled him even more, talking

about children with her. As if they were discussing their own children. The idea wasn't an awful one. She would make a good mother. One day. In the future. After he had established the via ferrata and returned to traveling around the world to climb.

That had always been the plan—to spend a few months in Eagle Mountain, getting the project off the ground, then move on to another location, even another country. He wasn't ready to settle down in one small town.

But the thought of leaving Bethany set his heart racing. He couldn't decide which upset him more—the thought of never leaving or the thought of never seeing her again.

Ian cleared his throat. "What would you like to do?"

"Let's go to the cemetery."

He thought he was getting used to Bethany's quirks—her impulsivity and outspokenness, and her sometimes imaginative view of a situation. But this caught him off guard. "Is there something at the cemetery you want me to see?"

"We can walk around and talk there and not be disturbed. It's a beautiful place."

"So is the park."

She grinned. "And I want to look for Katherine Boston's grave."

"Why?"

"I'll tell you when we get there."

"Okay." He shifted the Jeep into gear. "To the cemetery."

## Chapter Fourteen

Bethany gave Ian credit for not freaking out when she'd suggested an afternoon at a graveyard. He'd even waited until they'd turned into the parking area for the cemetery before saying anything else. "Now do you want to tell me why we're here?" he asked.

She told him about her visit to the historical society and what she had learned about the accident that had damaged Katherine's leg as well as the fire at the newly wed Gerald and Abby's home.

"If they went missing only a short time after someone tried to burn down their house, why wasn't law enforcement more suspicious when they disappeared?" Ian asked. "Why didn't they at least investigate the possibility of foul play?"

"Maybe because the family said Abby and Gerald had talked about moving to get away from Katherine's harassment," Bethany said. "I wonder if the sheriff questioned Katherine about the fire. I know she couldn't walk long distances, but maybe she could have set the fire?"

"I don't know if they have records going back that far, but we could ask," Ian said.

"I also found the official notice of Gerald and Katherine's

divorce," she said. "It was granted six months after Katherine's leg was injured, a year before Gerald married Abby."

"We know Gerald remarried," Ian said. "Did Katherine?"

"If she did, I didn't find any mention of it. But we know there were rumors she had a boyfriend—someone who could have set that fire for her and maybe even have murdered Gerald and Abby." Excitement zinged through her. "I wonder how we could find out if she was seeing anyone special."

"When did she die?" he asked.

"Nineteen eighty-five."

"There might be something in her obituary, maybe mention of a close male friend."

"Why didn't I think of that?" Bethany said. "I'll have to go back to the historical society."

"There's no guarantee he would be listed in the obituary if they never married," Ian said. He turned into the parking area for the cemetery. "And she died ten years after Gerald and Abby. If she did have someone acting on her behalf to exact revenge, that person might have been out of the picture by then."

Eagle's Rest Memorial Park was a tree-shaded expanse of ground near the river, dotted with grave markers and monuments. Ian and Bethany stopped just inside the entrance and stared at the neat rows of graves. "How are we going to find her?" she asked.

"I guess we start walking and reading," he said and led the way down the nearest aisle between graves.

They located Katherine Boston's headstone after only fifteen minutes. Beneath her name and dates of birth and death was a single word: *Beloved*.

"Whoa!" Bethany gripped Ian's arm. "Beloved of whom? A lover?"

"Or a relative or friend," he said. "*Beloved* can mean a lot of things."

"Who's buried nearby?" she asked. "That might give us a clue."

They scanned the graves to either side. One was a family of five named Creech, the dates of their deaths ranging from 1916 to 2018. On the other side was a man named Davies and his wife.

"Maybe she was Davies's mistress?" Bethany asked.

"Except he died a year before she did." Ian pointed out the date. "His wife died two years later, but I doubt she would have agreed to put her husband's mistress next to him or order a grave marker with the word *beloved*."

"I see what you mean." She returned to stand in front of Katherine's grave. After a moment, she straightened. "I just realized something," she said.

"What is it?" Ian asked.

"Whoever loved Katherine, that person is still alive."

"How do you—" Then he saw the flowers laid at the base of the marker. A bouquet of daisies, still fresh.

It stood out in the row of otherwise unadorned graves. Bethany knelt and checked the wrapping around the bouquet. "No indication of a florist," she said. She looked around. "Let's check that building over there. Maybe there's an attendant or something."

Before they reached the building, they encountered a man by a shed, filling a lawnmower with gasoline. "Do you work here?" Bethany asked.

The man straightened. He was very tall—six inches taller, if not more, than Ian, who was at least six feet. He had long arms, long legs and a long face with deep lines alongside his mouth. "I'm the caretaker," the man said. "Can I help you?"

"We were visiting a grave," Bethany said. "Katherine Boston. She's over there." She pointed toward the row that contained Katherine's site. "And we noticed fresh flowers on her grave. Do you know who brought them?"

"Why do you want to know?" the man asked.

"Um, so I can thank them," she said. "It's such a nice thing to do."

The caretaker didn't say anything.

"Do you know who put the flowers on Ms. Boston's grave?" Ian asked.

"Don't know," the man said and picked up the gas can once more.

"Have you seen anyone around her grave?" Bethany asked. "With or without flowers?"

The man shook his head and returned to pouring gas into the mower.

Ian took her arm. "Let's go."

Back at the Jeep, Bethany could scarcely contain her agitation. "I'm sure Katherine is the key to this mystery," she said. "She was the woman scorned. Craig said she hated Gerald enough to kill him."

Ian unlocked the Jeep, and they got in. "It's a big step from resenting a former spouse to murdering him and his new wife in a remote canyon," he said. "We know Katherine couldn't have committed the crime herself. And we don't know if she really had a friend who would have helped."

"The logical part of my mind knows you're right." She grinned at him. "And yes, I do have a logical part of my mind."

"I never said you didn't."

"Thank you for that, but I know I tend to rely more on impulse and instinct. I can't shake the feeling that Katherine is involved in the murder somehow."

"It happened such a long time ago," Ian said. "Without DNA or some other conclusive evidence, you'll probably never know what happened for certain."

"Maybe not, but I think it's important for us to try to find out."

He angled his body toward her. "Why is it important?" he asked. "I really want to know."

She glanced at him, then looked back at her hands, clenched in her lap. "This is going to sound silly…"

"Tell me and let me decide that," he said.

She drew in a deep breath. "The way Gerald and Abby died was so horrible—all alone in that cave. And no one even looked for them for fifty years. Then we found them. That connects us with them, in a weird way. I think if we could find out who killed them, even if that person is long dead and can't be punished for the crime, it would be a way of finally laying them to rest. Of giving them the peace they deserve."

"That's very sweet of you, to want to do that for them," he said.

"And maybe silly. But there's another reason to look for their killer. Maybe an even more important one."

"What's that?" he asked.

"You said it before—the vandalism and the attacks on you might not be because someone is opposed to the via ferrata project," she said. "Maybe you've been targeted because you uncovered the killer's secret."

"I was only speculating. So you really think their killer is still alive and here in Eagle Mountain?"

"Why not? They would be older now—in their seventies or even eighties. But they could still be worried you'll find out their secret and they'll go to prison. It's reason enough to threaten you."

"As far as I know, the sheriff's department doesn't have a single suspect in Gerald and Abby's murder," Ian said. "I can't see the murderer has anything to worry about."

"Except that all these years, no one has even known there was a murder. The killer was perfectly safe. Now people are starting to ask questions. At least...you and I are asking questions. That's making the killer nervous. If they can shut us up, maybe they can make this all go away." She frowned. "I'm not saying that makes a lot of sense, but someone who would kill two innocent people and leave them in a cave for fifty years has to be a little unbalanced."

He went very still. "If what you're saying is true, you could be in real danger," he said.

"So could you. So *are* you. Someone already tried to shoot you, and you could have been killed, falling off that catwalk."

"Someone shot *at* me. And at your brother, the cop. And only broke a window. That doesn't seem like a very serious attempt at murder to me. And the catwalk was more likely to injure one of the construction workers than me. Whoever sawed through those supports couldn't have known I would climb up there. I didn't even know I would until I did it."

"The only thing that's happened to me is someone sent a lame note." She didn't mention the feeling yesterday that she was being followed. That had probably just been her imagination.

He didn't answer, only looked at her with a pained expression.

"What? Why are you looking at me like that?" she asked.

"I can't decide if I need to tell you to stay away from me for your own safety or if it would be better for me to keep you close. At least then you'd have someone trying to protect you."

"I have an entire overprotective family, remember?"

"No offense, but I'm not sure how much defense they would be against a killer."

"Is there something else about you I need to know? A black belt in karate or training as a Navy SEAL that you neglected to mention?"

He pulled her close. "Haven't you figured out that I'm incredibly stubborn? I don't give up when it comes to scaling mountains, and I won't give up going after anyone who tries to hurt you."

Bethany had read about how love made people weak in the knees, but she had never experienced it before. If Ian hadn't been holding her upright, she might have slid right out of her seat. "I never feel safer than when I'm with you," she said, the words just above a whisper.

He kissed her, a kiss full of so much passion and tenderness and *need* that she wanted to wrap herself around him and never let go. When he broke the kiss and looked into her eyes, she said. "I choose option B."

He blinked. "What were the options again?"

"Staying with you." She stroked one finger down his cheek, feeling the afternoon stubble against her skin, an erotic sensation, as if that same stubble was brushing against every nerve. "Let's go back to your place," she said. "Now."

IAN WANTED TO figure out why sex with Bethany was so different. It was passionate and intense and satisfying, but it was different. For one thing, she talked while they made love. Not in an annoying way. She made him talk, too, about things he hadn't spent much time verbalizing to anyone— what they liked to do in bed. What they didn't like to do. How they thought about life and themselves.

And Bethany made him laugh. She had a wicked sense of humor that was sweet with a spicy kick. She made bad puns and told risqué jokes, and somehow that turned him on even more. She made sex fun. When they lay together afterward, her head on his shoulder and his arm around her, he thought he might know what people meant by the word *bliss*.

"I'm hungry," she said. "What do you have to eat?"

Ian tried to think what was in his refrigerator. "Probably not much," he said. "We could go out to eat."

"I don't want to wait that long." She sat up and reached for her shirt. "Let's see what you have."

What he had was a can of tomato soup, some slightly stale bread and a lot of cheese. He was still protesting that they should go out while Bethany was opening the soup and making sandwiches. Ten minutes later, they were eating grilled cheese and hot soup.

"Sorry I couldn't offer something better," he said. "I don't cook much."

"This is perfect." She grinned at him. "This whole evening is perfect."

After they ate, they wandered back into the living room/ office. He was going to suggest they watch a movie when she sat down at his desk. She studied the notes he had made on a legal pad. "What are these?"

"I was playing around with some ideas for the public areas of the via ferrata. I want to highlight the history of the area." He leaned over her and indicated some sketches he had made. "There are places that will take photographs and transform them into weatherproof plaques. I remember that the historical society had a lot of photographs related to the area. The sheriff's department showed me one of some climbers in the canyon fifty years ago. I'd like to find more photos like that or even of ranchers or anyone who visited the canyon decades ago.

"I could affix the photos to the walls at different rest stops along the climbing route," he continued. "People could read about the people in the photos. It would be something unique to this area."

"That's a brilliant idea." She slid into the desk chair and studied the drawings more closely.

Ian reached over and pulled up a website showing the kinds of plaques he was considering. "What do you think of these?"

"I love it. I could go back to the historical society next week and look for more photos for you."

He moved in behind her and put his hands on her shoulder. "I've been feeling guilty about asking you to help me while you're still working for your family," he said. "You deserve your free time."

"I don't mind helping. And I like learning more about the business."

He knew she wasn't just saying that. Bethany brought enthusiasm to everything she did. "Have you thought any more about coming to work for me?" he asked. "I need a smart person I can rely on."

"To run the place while you're away."

He had said those words himself, so why did hearing them now make him feel like he had swallowed stones? "Even if I'm here, I need a good manager," he said. "You'll have a lot of freedom to make decisions. My dad and I don't agree on a lot, but he taught me to hire good people, then let them alone to do the job they're skilled at."

"Do you really think that would work—me being your employee?" she asked.

"We'd find a way to make it work."

"I want the job," she said. "But I think I should wait until you have an opening date for the via ferrata before I tell my folks. They'll need time to find someone else to do my job."

"I'm willing to wait."

Bethany turned back to the desk. There wasn't anything significant about the conversation, but the air suddenly felt ten degrees cooler.

She rifled through a stack of invoices. "Do you want me to enter these on your books? I recognize the accounting program you're using."

"That would be great."

She nodded and began sorting the invoices from miscellaneous notes, flyers and receipts. She studied a hand-written note. Ian leaned over her shoulder and read the note. "You can toss that," he said. Weeks ago, he had been looking up flights to Argentina on a passing whim.

"Are you thinking of going to Argentina?" she asked. Her voice sounded strained.

"I was thinking of spending next winter there, climbing. But I haven't decided yet." He silently cursed himself the moment he said the words. He hadn't decided anything for sure. At the time, Argentina had sounded great. He hadn't been there in years. But now, with the via ferrata just starting and with this new relationship with Bethany, he was in no hurry to leave Eagle Mountain.

*I should tell her that*, he thought. "I—" he began. And his voice failed.

"I'll bet Argentina is great," she said. She gave him a big smile. "You'll have to send me pictures."

She turned away, and the moment was lost. Never mind. He had plenty of time to figure out how to tell her what she was coming to mean to him.

## Chapter Fifteen

*Ian isn't like Justin.* Bethany reminded herself of this over and over in the next few days, as she kept replaying their conversation about Argentina. He wasn't pretending he wanted to stay with her forever only to yank that dream away at the last minute. Ian was being upfront with her. This was his life. He wasn't a family man. He didn't come from that kind of background. She knew what she was getting into. If she wanted to be with him now, these were the terms she had to accept.

Did that make her a strong woman or a fool for willingly walking toward pain instead of protecting herself and running away?

Maybe a little of both. She wanted to be strong and she wanted to guard her heart against hurt, but she didn't know how to pull away from Ian when being with him felt so good. Not just making love to him, but talking to him. Laughing with him. Enjoying the way he looked at her, as if he truly *liked* everything about her, just as she was. He thought she was smart. Capable. Brave. He laughed at her terrible jokes and kissed her as if he never wanted to stop. Who would ever want to pull away from that?

All she knew to do was keep moving forward, enjoying the good feelings for as long as they lasted.

While Ian focused on overseeing the last of the construction in Humboldt Canyon, Bethany paid another visit to the Rayford County Historical Society. "I'm looking for an obituary and some photos," she told Caleb.

"You'll have to search the newspaper archives for the obituary," he said. "Do you know when the person died?"

"I do."

"That will make it easier. Let me show you our photography index." He led the way to a computer in a back corner. "You can search our photo collection by the name of a person or place," he explained. "We have thousands of photographs, most donated by area families, as well as some of the old newspaper archives. Your search will pull up a call number and a brief description. Give me that information, and I'll pull the photos for you."

"This is going to be easier than I thought," she said.

She typed in her search terms and came up with a list of possible photos. She gave these to Caleb, then turned her attention to issues of the *Eagle Mountain Examiner* from 1985. She found the obituary for Katherine Boston, accompanied by a grainy black-and-white photo of an older woman with short hair and a stern expression.

*Katherine Berringer Boston was born in 1950 in San Antonio, Texas, the beloved daughter of Jacob Berringer, a successful merchant, and his wife, Nina Leon Berringer. The family moved to Eagle Mountain, Colorado, when Katherine was ten, and she quickly became known as a local beauty. Many a man competed for her attention until she met the love of her life, Gerald Frankline Boston, of Denver, Colorado. After her marriage to Gerald, Katherine became involved in all the social organizations in town, including Eastern Star, the Women's Club and the Arts Guild.*

*Tragedy struck the couple when Katherine was injured in an automobile accident, which left her unable to walk without difficulty for the rest of her life. She never fully regained her health and finally went to her reward. Internment at Eagle's Rest Memorial Park, Eagle Mountain.*

Bethany reread the words. No mention of Katherine and Gerald's divorce. Anyone reading this would think they'd had a happy marriage. There was no list of survivors, either. No mysterious lover who might have committed murder on her behalf.

"Here are your photographs." Caleb returned with a shallow tray full of envelopes, each envelope containing one or more photographs.

As she had hoped, her search for Humboldt Canyon had produced a trio of shots of climbers from the 1960s, complete with bell-bottom jeans, striped rugby shirts and long hair. "Their equipment looks pretty primitive compared to what we use today," Caleb said as he laid out the photos on the table in front of her.

"No helmets," she said. "And is that one guy barefoot?"

He peered more closely at the photo in question. "I think he is. They're obviously having a blast."

She also found some undated scenic shots taken in winter, showing icicles on the cliffs and snow deep on the rocks. "Can I get copies of all of these?" she asked.

"Sure. It takes a few days to a week to get them produced."

"No hurry," she said. "I'll probably want some of these others, too."

"I'll go get the price sheet while you finish looking."

Her searches for Abby Boston and Katherine Boston or Katherine Berringer yielded nothing. She had better luck with Gerald Boston. At the last minute, she did a search for Walter Spies. One of the photos associated with Walt was the same as a photo she had requested of Gerald.

The first photo of Gerald showed a young man with side-parted brown hair long enough to touch his shoulders and a thick moustache. He was pictured with a group of men labeled as employees of Atlas Mining. She didn't recognize any of the others standing with him.

The next photograph showed a group of three men and three women dressed in jeans and T-shirts, standing with several saddled horses against a backdrop of rock. Someone had written a list of names in the margins of the photo in blue ink: *Walt S., Gerald B., Craig B., Abby S., Kate B., Susan M.*

Bethany leaned over the photo, trying to bring the small image into better focus. Walt S.—that had to be Walter Spies. He had been a handsome young man—square jawed, sandy haired and blue eyed. He held the reins of a big black horse, the woman identified as Susan M. on the other side of the horse. Next to her stood Gerald with a brown-and-white horse, Kate B. beside him. Katherine Berringer? Or was she already Katherine Boston? Next to her was Abby S. The future Abby Boston? Then a roan horse and Craig Boston—floppy blond hair and wire-rimmed glasses. The girls all had long hair with feathered-back sides and wore lots of eyeliner.

Here was proof Walt Spies had known Craig and Abby. But hadn't Craig said Abby and Gerald had met after his divorce? Had she misunderstood? If Kate B. and Katherine Boston were the same person, then Gerald had known Abby while he'd still been married.

"Here. This might help." Caleb handed her a magnifying glass. "It can help with some of these older, blurry shots."

Bethany thanked him and examined the photo again but found nothing of interest. None of the women's hands were positioned where she could see a wedding or engagement ring, and all of them were looking at the camera, not at each other.

The other photographs of Walt were from newspaper ads for his campaign for county commissioner and a couple since he had taken office. Bethany requested a copy of the group photo and left the building mulling over the afternoon's revelations.

She was crossing the street, headed back toward her apartment, when someone called her name. She turned to see Craig Boston moving toward her.

Bethany waited for him to catch up. "Hi, Craig. You look like you're getting around pretty good."

He leaned on his cane and frowned down at the walking boot. "I'm doing okay. The physical therapist says I'm ahead of schedule, but I've always been pretty stubborn. What have you been up to?"

"I just came from the historical society. I found the greatest photo of you and Gerald and some others. You were riding horses. I wish I had it here to show to you. The museum is making a copy for me. Do you remember that day? Walt Spies was with you, too."

He scratched his cheek. "Can't say as I do. When was this?"

"Sometime in the midseventies, I'd guess. There was a woman identified as Kate—could that be Katherine?"

"I think sometimes people did call her Kate. Who else was in the picture?"

"Someone named Susan and a woman identified as Abby S.—could that be Gerald's Abby?"

"I doubt it. If he was with Katherine, Abby wasn't in the picture yet." His face brightened. "I think that must be Abby Smith. I went out with her a few times. Never anything serious."

"Who was Susan M?" she asked.

Craig shook his head. "I don't remember. Maybe Walt's girlfriend at the time? He had a lot of them."

"He was a ladies man?" She could see that. Even in that photo she had recognized a certain rugged sensuality.

"I guess so. Not me. I never had good luck with women. But hey, I'd love to see that photo when you get a copy."

"I'd be glad to show it to you."

"Did you find anything else interesting at the historical society?"

"Ian is looking for photos of people enjoying the canyon—early hikers and climbers and miners—to display at the via ferrata. I found a few things like that."

"So you're helping him with this via ferrata project? How's that going?"

"It's going well. He's going to be ready to open soon."

"Provided he gets approval from the county."

"I think he's winning people over. Now that they can see the course they're getting excited about it. It's going to be a good thing for the community."

"Well, good luck with that," he said. "I'll see you around."

She watched him hobble away. His earlier comment—about not being good with women—saddened her. That photo had showed a smiling young man who had a bright future before him. Now he was old and alone. Had he made the choice not to marry, or had someone broken his heart?

Bethany turned and started walking again. Craig's personal life was none of her business, but the romantic in her couldn't help but wonder about his story. That was what had led her to dig into Gerald and Abby's lives. She wanted to know what had brought them to their tragic end, as if figuring that out could inform how she lived her own life.

THE NEXT WEEKS passed in a blur full of packed days at Peak Jeep, training once or twice a week with search and rescue, call-outs for auto accidents and injured climbers, and not nearly enough time with Ian, since he was busy also. But one Monday in late July, he called her. "Are you free one afternoon this week?" he asked. "The via ferrata is finished. I want you to see it."

"That's wonderful! We can get together this afternoon."

They agreed he would pick her up at four o'clock, and she ended the call. "What are you looking so happy about?" her mom asked.

"Ian's coming to pick me up after work. The via ferrata is finished."

The lines on her mother's forehead deepened, but she said nothing.

"Don't look like that, Mom. Ian is a great guy."

"And I can see that you really care for him. You've always been so quick to give your heart. I'd hate to see you hurt again."

Bethany started to protest that Ian wasn't going to hurt her, but she already knew that wasn't true. He probably wouldn't mean to hurt her, but when he moved on from Eagle Mountain, she was going to be left with a hole in her heart. "I'm old enough to know that life isn't all fairy tales and happy endings," she said. "But I'm enjoying being with Ian right now."

She was waiting when he pulled up to the Jeep rental office, and they headed for Humboldt Canyon. "I can't believe it's finished already," she said.

"There are a few things I need to do before we can open to the public, but the climbing route is complete. I can't wait to see what you think."

She told herself she would act impressed, even though, as a non-climber, she might not share his excitement.

Ian parked by the trailer and led her to a cleared-off space deeper into the canyon. "Here is where we'll have the welcome center," he said. "I'm going to bring in a modular building once I have approval from the county. That will be trimmed out with rustic wood and rock to look like it's been here for decades. Once climbers register, they'll attend a mandatory safety briefing and sign a liability waiver and an agreement to wear the safety equipment at all times and abide by the rules."

He walked to a section of canyon wall behind the welcome center site. "Over here will be a practice area for anyone who wants to familiarize themselves with basic techniques before they tackle the course. I'm thinking we'll have some field days for kids, too, where they can get an intro to climbing and try out some of the simpler features."

"That sounds about my speed," Bethany said. She followed him along the canyon wall to a rock wall studded with iron pins.

"The main route begins here. You'll start by clipping onto the safety cable there." He indicated a steel cable. "Cables run the length of the route, and at every transition point you'll clip onto a new section of cable. In case of a fall, the cable will catch you."

He led her through the canyon, pointing out iron ladders, rungs, bridges and cabled walkways. The route took climbers up steep pitches and along narrow ledges.

"It looks like a pretty challenging climb," she said.

"The idea is to give people a challenge but make it as safe as possible." He glanced down at the dress and sandals she was wearing. "I should have thought to tell you to bring jeans and boots and could have given you a guided tour."

"We'll do that some other time," she said.

"I've sent off the photographs you chose to be made into plaques," he said. "I'm going to attach the plaques to the wall at various transition points. People can read about the history of the area."

"Everything looks great," she said when they reached the end of the route. She squeezed his arm. "People are going to be so excited once they see this."

"I'm going to throw a party to thank everyone who has helped to bring this together," he said. "The construction crew, county officials, law enforcement, search and rescue, local climbers. I already contacted Danny about having search and rescue tour the route, maybe even do some training here to familiarize yourselves with the layout."

"Have you heard anything from the county about your operating permit?" she asked.

"There has to be a public hearing and an official vote before they can award the permit," he said. "I've been speaking with the commissioners and county officials. They seem receptive at least. And I'm going to make a presentation to the commissioners at the hearing."

"You'll impress them, I'm sure." At least, he would impress everyone except Walt Spies. But Walt was only one vote.

Ian put his arm around her. "I want to take you to dinner to celebrate," he said. "I made reservations at Spruce Lodge."

Spruce Lodge was a new inn high in the mountains with a restaurant that was already becoming known for fine dining. The restaurant itself was small and rustic, with stone-and-cedar walls and subtle lighting. White linen cloths and shining silver added to the atmosphere of elegance.

This was the kind of place Ian was used to dining in, Bethany thought as she studied the menu. A place where price was no obstacle. "This is amazing," she said a short time later as she cut into her steak.

"It's good, but I enjoyed soup and sandwiches with you just as much," he said.

On the drive back to the canyon, he took her hand. "Can you stay for a while?" he asked.

"I can stay all night." As long as he was here, she didn't want to miss a moment.

THE ROAD INTO Humboldt Canyon was dark, without a single streetlight or glow from the window of a home to cut the night's blackness. Once in the canyon, only a thin band of stars overhead provided any illumination beyond the narrow swath of the Jeep's headlights. When Ian pulled up to the trailer and cut the engine, the silence of the place closed around them, as confining as the darkness. He reached over to take Bethany's hand, wanting the feel of her close by, but she jerked forward and gasped. "What is that?" she whispered.

He stared out the windshield at the bulky figure that emerged from the shadows at the side of the trailer.

The Jeep's lights switched off, and it was like being plunged into a pit. Ian held his breath, ears straining. The crunch of gravel being compressed by heavy footsteps sent a jolt of fear through him.

Bethany let out a whimper, then made scrabbling noises. "What are you doing?" Ian whispered.

"I'm looking for something to use as a weapon. Whatever that thing is, it's headed this way."

Ian turned the key in the ignition, and the headlights spotlighted the figure approaching. Not a bear or a monster, but a man.

Ian was out of the car before he even had time to think. "Walt Spies, what do you think you're doing, lurking around my home?" he shouted.

"Stop!" Bethany ran past Ian and kicked Walt in the shin. "Get out of here!"

The old man bent double, swearing. "I could charge you with assault!" he shouted.

Ian took hold of Bethany's arm and gently pulled her away. Seeing the old man looking so helpless had calmed him. "What are you doing here, Walt?" he demanded.

Walt Spies straightened. The harsh light deepened the lines on his face and left his eyes in shadow, giving him the appearance of a Halloween mask. "I came here to talk to you," he said. "I didn't expect to be attacked."

"What are you doing lurking around in the dark at this time of night?" Bethany asked. "And then to come stalking toward us without saying a word? What were we supposed to think?"

Walt ignored her. "We need to talk," he said to Ian.

"What do you want to talk about?" Ian asked.

"I came to warn you of trouble ahead if you keep moving forward with this project," Walt said.

"Is that a threat?" he asked.

"Not from me, but someone has it in for you. If things keep escalating, someone is going to end up dead."

"That sounds like a threat to me," Bethany said.

Walt reached behind him, and Ian stepped in front of Bethany. "What are you doing?"

"I want to show you this." He pulled a folded sheet of paper from his back pocket and thrust it at Ian.

Ian took the paper and unfolded it. "'Stop the via ferrata, or you're next,'" he read. "Where did you get this?"

"Someone left it in my mailbox this afternoon," Walt said. "My home mailbox."

"Have you shown this to the sheriff?"

"No. I thought you should see it first."

Bethany looked over Ian's shoulder. "It's typed. Anyone could have written that. You could have written it yourself."

"Why would I do that?"

"To shift suspicion away from you," she said. "We know you're opposed to the via ferrata. Maybe you're behind all these 'accidents' that keep happening around here."

"I don't have time to waste with games," Walt said. He took a step closer. "Look, I don't like this via ferrata project because it's going to bring more traffic to a county road we can barely maintain as it is. It's going to bring a lot of tourists to an area without the facilities to take care of them. You might think a couple of portable toilets and a soft drink machine will be enough, but people are going to want indoor plumbing and a snack bar. They'll want paved parking and lights at night. This beautiful canyon is going to turn into an amusement park, and I don't want to see that."

"I agree that the canyon is beautiful," Ian said. "I want people to appreciate that beauty. I have no intention of installing a bunch of lights or a restaurant. If my facilities aren't enough for people, then this obviously isn't the place for them."

"At the rate things are going, you might not get a chance to find out whether it's enough," Walt said. "Someone is going to a lot of trouble to keep your via ferrata from ever opening. I'm worried about you, son."

"Thanks for your concern," Ian said. "Now, you need to leave."

Walt turned and stalked into the shadows. After a moment, an engine roared to life. Headlights illuminated and he jolted down the drive toward the county road.

Ian put his arm around Bethany. "Let's go inside," he said.

She followed him into the trailer and dropped her backpack onto the sofa in his office/living room. "That was weird," she said. "Why was he even out here, waiting in the dark like that? He could have called you on the phone."

"Maybe he thought it would be more intimidating to deliver the message in person."

She looked him up and down. "You're several inches taller and a lot younger than he is. Did he really think he was going to scare you?"

"He's tougher than he looks," Ian said. "When he grabbed my arm it was like being in a vise."

She moved in and wrapped her hands around his biceps. The muscle bulged there, honed from years of climbing. "I still think he was being foolish, coming here at night like that."

"I can't believe you kicked him." He pulled her closer and grinned at her.

"He frightened me," she admitted. "And when I'm afraid, I fight back."

"Good for you." Ian rubbed her back, then looked thoughtful. "I wonder if maybe we frightened him, too. Or, at least, caught him by surprise."

"Oh! You mean, maybe he wasn't waiting for you, but he was up to no good and we interrupted him?"

"I don't have any proof of that, but did you notice how he parked his truck some distance away from the trailer—farther back in the canyon where it really couldn't be seen by anyone driving in?"

"He hasn't made any secret of being opposed to the project," she said. "I've always thought he could be behind some of the things that have happened."

"The sheriff says he has an alibi for every time something has happened," Ian said.

"He was here when that climber was injured."

"Mike falling was an accident," Ian said.

"Maybe that's what gave the vandal the idea to cause trouble," Bethany said. "They saw how much trouble it caused and thought it might be a way to stop the via ferrata."

"I need to tell the sheriff's department about the note Walt showed me," he said.

"I don't believe for a minute that anybody but Walt wrote that note," she said. "He's just trying to cover his tracks."

"I'll let the deputies decide about that." He squeezed her shoulder.

She smiled up at him, and the band that had been tightening at the base of his neck from the moment they'd seen Walt emerge from the darkness loosened a little. He would worry about the man later. Right now, he and Bethany were alone, and he planned to take advantage of the opportunity.

Ian leaned down and kissed her. "I don't want to think about the via ferrata or anything else right now," he said.

"What via ferrata?" She wrapped both arms around his neck and arched toward him. "Kiss me like that again, and I'll forget my own name."

"That sounds like a challenge to me." So he kissed her again and did his best to make them both forget about everything but this moment, in each other's arms.

BETHANY WAS LOST in a haze of desire and pleasure. She and Ian were still standing in Ian's living room, but they might have been floating on a cloud. Being with him was so amazing. How had she gotten so lucky? She pulled back enough to smile up at him, then frowned. "What's that noise?" she asked.

"What noise?" He nuzzled at her neck.

"A crackling sound, almost like a campfire." She pulled out of his arms and looked around. Ian didn't have a fireplace. She sniffed and caught the definite scent of woodsmoke.

"Something's burning." Ian moved to the middle of the room, looking around. Just then, the smoke alarm began blaring.

"There!" She pointed toward the other end of the trailer. "In the kitchen."

Ian started walking that way, but she caught the tail of his shirt and pulled him back. "We have to get out of here," she said.

"You're right." He moved to the door and tried to pull it open, but it wouldn't budge.

Panic climbed her throat. "What's wrong?" she asked. "Why won't it open?"

He shook his head. "The back door," he said. He started that way, but the heat from flames licking up one wall of the trailer drove him back. Bethany stared as fingers of fire swept up the paneling, until the whole kitchen was aflame.

She pulled out her phone and stabbed out *911*. But when she put the phone to her ear, she heard only silence.

"No signal," Ian said, staring at his own phone.

"How could they both not be working?"

He shook his head. "It doesn't matter. We have to get out of here." He tried the door again, and when he couldn't open it, he slammed his shoulder against it. The whole trailer shook, but the door didn't budge.

"The windows!" Bethany ran to the window and tried to open it. But it also refused to move.

"Stand back!" Ian shouted. He picked up the desk chair and hurled it at the window. It hit the middle of the glass, making a small crack, then bounced to the floor. Smoke was pouring into the room now, choking them. He coughed and picked up the chair again. This time he kept hold of it, battering it against the window until the glass shattered.

Cool air rushed in, and the heat of the fire intensified, fed by fresh oxygen. "Get out!" he shouted.

Bethany moved to the window and began pulling away shards of glass. Ian tore off his shirt, wrapped his arm in it and began punching at the glass, clearing it from the frame. "Go!" he shouted again. "I'll be right behind you."

She tried again to crawl through the window, but it was too high in the wall for her to get her leg over the sill. Desperate, Ian lifted her by the waist and pushed her through. She screamed, falling, and he dove out after her.

## Chapter Sixteen

The ground was cool, and Ian pressed his face to it, even as he wrapped both arms around Bethany and rolled her farther away from the fire. She clung to him, shaking with sobs.

"Shhh. You're okay." He kissed the top of her head and tried to soothe her.

After a while, she quieted, then pushed herself away from him and into a sitting position. "I'm okay," she said and looked back toward the fire.

Only a few minutes had passed, but the trailer was almost fully engulfed now, the structure folding in on itself as the blaze roared. The stench of burning metal and rubber and wood filled the air, and the light from the flames bathed them in a ghastly, flickering light.

"Ian, you're hurt!" She put a hand to his forearm.

He flinched and touched his own hand to the blisters rising on his skin. The backs of both hands were blistered, too. He looked away from the sight. "Are you okay?" he asked.

"I've got a few cuts from the window glass. They're not too bad." She indicated some scratches on her arms, blood beading along one of them. "And my hair and clothing are a little scorched."

Hearing her words shook him out of the stupor he had

been in since first seeing the blaze. He stood and reached down to pull her up. "We need to get out of here," he said. "Whoever set the blaze might still be in the area. Or they might come back. Come on."

They jogged to his Jeep. He fumbled for the keys in his pocket. His fingers didn't want to work right. But at last he had them and pressed the fob to start the vehicle. They climbed into the seat, and he put the vehicle in gear.

He was backing up while she was still grappling with her safety belt. The idea that whoever had set the fire might still be here, waiting for them, made his skin crawl. All he could think about was getting away.

"Why don't our phones work?" she asked again. "They're not landlines that someone could cut."

"No, but here in the canyon I rely on Wi-Fi calling," he said. "It works via a satellite dish. If someone destroyed the dish, the phones wouldn't work."

"Do you think that's what happened?"

"Someone tampered with the front door so it wouldn't open," he said. "They didn't want us getting out of there or getting help."

He gripped the steering wheel more tightly, only dimly aware of the pain, too focused on his rage at the arsonist. They could have died in that fire. Bethany could have died.

"As soon as we get a signal, I'll call 911," she said.

Ian stretched out a hand and touched her shoulder. He wanted to stop the Jeep and pull her close to comfort her, but he didn't dare. He didn't trust whoever had done this not to come after them.

When they reached the highway into town, he slowed and pulled out his phone. Though Bethany had offered to report the fire, he wanted to talk to the operator himself.

When his call was answered, he identified himself and reported the fire. "Tell the sheriff I'm pretty sure the fire was deliberately set," he said.

"Where are you now, sir?" the dispatcher asked.

"We're on our way to the hospital," he said. "My girlfriend and I are both injured."

"What is your location?" she asked. "An ambulance can meet you."

He glanced at Bethany. She was weeping again. He had no idea about her physical injuries, but she was clearly traumatized. An assessment right away was probably smarter than waiting the hour drive to the emergency room in Junction. And both of his hands were beginning to throb with pain. He took stock of his location. "We're almost to the turnoff for search and rescue headquarters," he said. "We'll meet the ambulance in the parking lot."

Five minutes later, he pulled almost to the door of the search and rescue building. A light over the door flickered on.

Bethany had quieted. "I'm okay," she said when he turned to her. "How are your hands?"

He didn't want to look at his hands or think about the damage done to them. "The ambulance will meet us here," he said instead.

Lights flashed behind him, but instead of the ambulance, a Rayford County Sheriff's Department SUV pulled up. Bethany's brother stepped out and approached the Jeep.

Ian rolled down the window. "Hello, Aaron," he said.

"Hello, Ian." He looked past him and his mask of calm slipped. "Bethany? The dispatcher said an ambulance was meeting us here. Are you okay?"

"I'm okay," she said. "Just a little shook up. Ian is the one who's hurt. He burned his hands saving us."

Aaron looked at Ian again. "Let me see."

Reluctantly, Ian held up his hands. Aaron shone a flashlight on the blistered flesh and winced. Ian closed his eyes against a wave of nausea. "Oh, Ian," Bethany breathed.

Aaron swung the beam over to light up his sister. "You're bleeding. And what's that in your hair?"

She ran a hand through her hair, and bits of glass fell onto the seat beside her. "Ian broke a window to get out of the trailer. I think some of the glass cut me. The cuts aren't deep."

The wail of the arriving ambulance drowned out Aaron's next words. He pulled open the Jeep door as the ambulance came to a stop. "Stay there," he said as Ian started to get out. "Let them come to you."

They arrived soon after, Hannah Gwynn and a hefty man, his dark beard shot through with gray. "Hannah, I'm glad to see you," Bethany said as the woman leaned in to look at Ian.

"Hello, Bethany," Hannah said. "What's going on?"

"Ian's hands are burned," Bethany said before Ian could answer.

"I drove here no problem," Ian said. "And I can get out of the Jeep."

"If you're sure there's no other injuries," Hannah said. "Adrenaline can mask a lot of pain, at least initially."

"I'm okay." He started out of the Jeep. Hannah put a hand out to steady him as he stood. On the other side of the vehicle, Aaron and the male EMT were helping Bethany.

Hannah led him over to the ambulance and had him sit in the open doorway. Bright lights from inside illuminated the area around them. "What's your pain level on a scale of one to ten?" she asked.

"Um, five? Maybe six?" He was becoming more aware of the ache in his hands by the minute.

"Are you allergic to any medications?"

He assured her he wasn't, that he didn't have any underlying medical conditions and didn't take any medications.

"Your arms and face are a little burned, too." She carefully examined him. "First degree. They'll be uncomfortable, but nothing worse than a bad sunburn. You'll want to have a doctor look at those hands, though. I'm going to clean and bandage them, then we'll transport you to the hospital. Are you experiencing pain anywhere else?" She strapped a blood pressure cuff to his arm as she spoke.

"No." He looked over his shoulder toward Bethany. The male EMT was leading her to the ambulance.

"I'm going to dress some minor cuts and make sure we've got all the glass out of her," the EMT said.

"I'm fine." She flashed a smile at Ian. It was a wobbly smile, but it lifted his spirits. "How is Ian?" she asked Hannah.

"He's going to be okay," Hannah said. She removed the blood pressure cuff. "He'll need treatment for his hands and they won't feel that great for a while, but you'll both be okay."

Aaron moved over to Ian's side. "What happened?" he asked. "The 911 operator said you called in a fire and that you thought it was deliberately set."

"We were in the trailer when we heard the crackling and smelled smoke," Ian said. "Then the smoke alarms started going off, and we could see flames coming from the kitchen."

"Were you cooking earlier? Maybe you left a burner on," Aaron said.

"We weren't cooking. This wasn't a cooking fire. When we tried to go out the front door, the door was jammed. I tried breaking it down, but I couldn't."

Bethany joined them. "When I tried to call 911, our phones wouldn't work," she said.

"I have satellite internet," Ian said. "When it's working, we can use Wi-Fi to make calls. Otherwise there's no service in Humboldt Canyon."

"How did you get out?" Aaron asked.

"Ian hit the window with a chair," Bethany said. "He had to hit it a few times to get it to break, and as soon as it did, the fire really roared to life. It was terrifying. And then I had trouble climbing out of the window." Her eyes widened as she remembered that terror. "Ian had to pick me up and throw me out." She reached over and gripped his shoulder. "You saved my life."

He couldn't speak past the knot in his throat. All he could do was nod and blink back the stinging in his eyes.

"Did you see anyone suspicious in the area in the last day or two?" Aaron asked.

"Walt Spies was waiting for us when we pulled in tonight," Bethany said.

"Walt Spies?" Aaron looked surprised. "What was he doing there?"

"He came to tell me if I didn't stop the via ferrata project, bad things were going to happen," Ian said.

"Walt threatened you?" Hannah asked.

Aaron sent her a quelling look. "What did Walt say, exactly?"

"He showed us a note he had received that said if he didn't stop the via ferrata, he would be next."

"The note said, 'Stop the via ferrata, or you're next,'" Bethany said. "It was typed. He said someone left it in his home mailbox. I think he was making up the whole story to divert suspicion away from him. He's been the biggest opponent of the project all along, and now this fire starts not half an hour after he left us."

"He could have driven a short way up the canyon and walked back," Ian said.

"Did you see any other vehicles or any other people around when you left?" Aaron asked.

"No one until we were almost to town."

"I'll call this in," he said. "In the meantime, you should get those burns seen to. I'll take Bethany home."

"No. I'm staying with Ian." She glared at him, and Ian wondered if Aaron was going to make the mistake of ordering her to go home. Bethany was already furious, and that wasn't going to help matters.

But apparently the man did have some sense. "At least call and let Mom and Dad know you're okay," he said. "Half the town listens to the emergency scanner. This is going to be all over the area by morning."

"I'll call them," she said.

"I'm going to give you something for the pain," Hannah said to Ian. "Then I recommend you let us transport you to the hospital. You need to have your hands seen to as soon as possible."

He didn't protest, since the bulky bandages on both hands made doing much of anything impossible, and the pain medication they had administered was already making his vision fuzz at the edges. Bethany kissed his cheek and promised to follow him to the hospital.

"Be careful," he told her as he lay back on the gurney.

"Don't worry." Aaron spoke from behind her. "I'll follow your Jeep all the way to Junction."

"You don't have to do that," she said, anger sharpening her voice once more.

"Someone tried to kill you tonight," he said. "I'm not willing to take a chance at them trying to force your Jeep off the road or ambush you on some dark stretch of road."

"You should be doing something more useful than babysitting me—like trying to find the person who set the fire."

They appeared ready to square off for an argument, so Ian interrupted. "He's right," he said. "Don't take any chances. Let him follow you."

She leaned into the back of the ambulance and touched Ian's leg. "All right. I'll do it for you. But they have to find out who's doing these awful things. This can't go on."

Maybe it was time to give up, Ian thought, though he couldn't say the words out loud. Risking someone's life—Bethany's life—wasn't worth continuing.

But everything in him rebelled against quitting. Against letting his unseen enemy win.

BETHANY WAITED AT the hospital while the emergency room doctor treated Ian. Aaron had insisted on waiting with her. She ignored him, focused on her worry over Ian and her fury over whoever had done this to them. Remembering those frantic moments in the trailer when Ian had picked up that heavy chair and hurled it at the window, only to have it bounce off made her shaky inside. And then when he had finally broken the glass, the fire had roared to life. She had literally felt it licking at her back and smelled her own singed hair. She had been terrified and panicked as she'd tried to climb out through the broken glass.

Then Ian had grabbed hold of her and pushed her out. In those moments in his arms afterward, lying on the cool ground while the inferno had raged only a few feet away, she had never felt more cherished.

The doors from the outside hissed open, and Sheriff Travis Walker entered. Bethany sat up straighter. Everything about the sheriff, from his crisp, pressed uniform to his movie-star looks, made her want to be on her best behavior. He zeroed in on Aaron. "Deputy Ames," he said.

Aaron sat upright, almost dropping his phone. "Sir."

The sheriff turned to Bethany. "How are you doing, Miss Ames?"

"I'm okay," she said. "I mean, I'm pretty shook up, but physically, I'm fine. Ian was burned pretty badly when he pulled me out of the trailer, though."

"I wanted to hear from you what happened," he said. "And Ian, too, when the doctors agree it's okay to talk to him."

"Of course."

The sheriff took the seat across from her, which Aaron had vacated. Her brother stood to one side, arms folded, like a bodyguard. "Tell me, in your own words, what happened tonight," Travis said.

"Where do you want me to start?"

"Start with when you got to the trailer. Was that this evening?"

"Yes. We got there about seven o'clock. It was already pretty dark."

"Did you see any other vehicles on the way into the canyon?"

"Not after we turned onto the county road. But when we pulled up to the trailer, Walt Spies was waiting for us." She told them about Walt and his warning to Ian and the note he'd said someone had sent him.

"We talked to Walt," the sheriff said. "He says he was home by seven fifteen. His wife backs up that story."

"He still could have started the fire and it didn't burn enough for us to notice until half an hour later," she said.

"We'll be checking into all of that," the sheriff said. "What happened after Walt left?"

Bethany told the same story she had related to Aaron and Hannah. "Ian said someone had jammed the door so it wouldn't open. And our cell phones wouldn't work. You should check to see if anyone tampered with the satellite dish."

"We haven't had a chance to examine the door," Walker said. "But we found the satellite dish. Someone or something had smashed it."

The door to the emergency room opened, and Ian stepped out. Both hands were wrapped in bulky bandages, and the skin of his arms and face were bright red, glistening with some kind of ointment or cream.

Bethany leapt up and went to him, though she resisted the urge to throw her arms around him, out of fear of hurting him. "What did the doctor say?" she asked.

"I'll have some pain, not too much scarring. I have to come back tomorrow to have the burns cleaned and dressed, but I should regain full use of my hands."

The sheriff joined them. "Mr. Seabrook, I have some questions for you."

"He already talked to me," Bethany said to Ian.

"All right."

They returned to the grouping of chairs where she and the sheriff had been sitting. Ian took the chair beside Bethany, while Aaron resumed his place next to the sheriff. Travis went through the same questions he had asked Bethany. Ian confirmed their conversation with Walt. He hadn't seen anyone suspicious around the canyon, and he hadn't received any new threats.

"Walt gave us the note he received," the sheriff said. "We'll take a closer look, though I don't know if it's going to tell us anything else."

"Do you know if the firefighters are finished in the canyon?" Ian asked. "Is the fire out?"

"They're keeping someone there overnight to make sure it doesn't flare up again," Travis said. "The trailer is a total loss, but the fire didn't spread to any equipment or construction supplies."

"I'm sure the fire was deliberately set," Ian said. "The front door was definitely jammed, and the damage to the satellite dish points to someone not wanting us to be able to summon help quickly."

"We'll know more after the fire department completes their investigation," Travis said. "But the preliminary opinion is that this was arson."

"Not just arson," Ian said. "Attempted murder. Smashing the satellite dish made it impossible to call for help."

"Who hates you enough to try to kill you—and Bethany?"

The questions jolted her. Part of her had known she could have been killed in the fire, but hearing the words out loud, and the acknowledgment that someone could have wanted her to die, threw her world off-balance.

"I don't know," Ian said. He didn't look as afraid as she felt, but maybe that was the pain meds he had been given. Mostly he looked tired. Defeated.

"What about the protestors?" Travis asked. "Have any of them been particularly aggressive?"

"No. There hasn't been any picketing or even anonymous notes since the day the climber was injured."

"Do you have any security cameras?" Travis asked.

He grimaced. "I have a whole system of cameras ordered, but I'm on a waiting list to get the system installed."

"Is there anything else we need to know?"

Ian shook his head. "I can't think of anything."

"Where will you be staying, in case we need to contact you?"

"I've got a hotel room here in Junction. Tomorrow I'm going to arrange for a new trailer for the worksite."

"Is that safe?" Bethany asked.

"I'll be fine." His mouth tightened, and the defeated look receded. "I'm not going to let whoever this is put a stop to the project."

"The site of the fire and the immediate surroundings are still cordoned off as a crime scene," the sheriff said.

"I have contractors scheduled to work in the canyon," Ian said. "They're mostly cleaning up now."

"They can do their work, as long as they avoid the cordoned-off area." The sheriff turned to Bethany. "I'll need you and Ian to come into the office and read and sign your statements—tomorrow, if possible."

She nodded. "I'll be there," Ian said.

When the sheriff and Aaron were gone, she turned to him. "You didn't have to book a hotel room," she said. "You could come back to my place."

"I'm not sure your parents would like that. And before you remind me that you're a grown woman, they own the apartment."

"They couldn't expect me to kick you out on the street."

"I'll be fine in the hotel. It's only for a couple of days. And I don't want to do anything to come between you and your family."

There were times when she would have welcomed more distance between herself and her parents and siblings, but probably not the kind Ian meant—the serious, even permanent kind.

"They just need to get to know you," she said. Sure, Ian was reserved and a little intimidating. Maybe not the kind of man they had ever envisioned her with, if they had pictured her with anyone at all. But she had recognized the soft, vulnerable place inside him that very first day in the rental office, when he'd cooed at the infant she'd held. "I know they'd love you then."

Ian patted her shoulder with one bandaged hand. "It takes time to get to know someone. Let's give that to them instead of forcing the issue."

He was also sensible. Not the daredevil she had expected when she'd learned he was a mountain climber who drove a Porsche.

"You may have noticed—I'm not the most patient person in the world," she said.

"I've got more than enough patience for both of us, and you inspire me to be a little more impulsive."

"I wouldn't call you impulsive." But he hadn't hesitated when it had come to risking his life to save hers. She slipped her arm in his and leaned close. "I hate that your hands are injured. Do you hurt very much?"

"They'll heal," he said. "And you're okay. That's all that matters."

"I'm here because you saved me."

"You would have gotten out on your own."

She wasn't so sure about that. The flames had come close to overwhelming her. Would she have found the strength on her own to escape them?

The door to the waiting room opened again, and Aaron reappeared. "Time to go home, Bethany," he said.

"I have to take Ian to his hotel," she said.

"I've called an Uber." He stepped away from her. "Go with Aaron. The doctor said they'll reduce the bandages tomorrow, and I should be able to drive again. My Jeep will be fine in the garage here until then."

Bethany wanted to argue that he shouldn't be alone tonight. But maybe that was being too clingy. "Call me tomorrow," she said.

"I will." He hesitated, then bent and kissed her. A proper kiss, too, which left her feeling a little dreamy. Cherished—there was that word again. Loved, but not overwhelmed by anyone else's expectations. A feeling she could get used to.

*Chapter Seventeen*

Despite the pain medication that the doctor had assured him would knock him out, Ian slept fitfully that night. Dreams of Bethany, engulfed in flames, kept startling him awake. He finally fell into a fitful sleep and roused late the next morning, his hands aching and mind racing.

He ordered room service, then called Bethany. She answered on the second ring, her cheery "Good morning" making him smile. "I wanted to make sure you got home all right," he said.

"I was exhausted. I tried to talk Aaron into running his police lights on the way home so we could get there faster, but the old stick-in-the-mud refused. Then he insisted on coming into my apartment and checking out everything before he would leave me to go to sleep in peace."

"He's a good brother," Ian said.

She sighed dramatically. "He is. How are you feeling?"

"Not great, but the pain—and these awkward bandages— are more annoying than anything else. I'm going to talk the doctor into something less bulky and more manageable. After I'm done at the hospital, I'll see about getting a new trailer delivered to the canyon. Then I'm going to drive out there and see how construction is progressing. And I have to find time to put the final touches on my presentation to the county commissioners."

"When is the meeting about your permit?" she asked.

"Thursday evening. I just got word this morning."

"You're making me tired just listening to you. Is there anything I can do to help?"

"Stay safe."

"You stay safe. I don't like the idea of you moving back out to the canyon before the sheriff has figured out who's doing these things."

"I don't think it's a climber," he said.

"Why not?"

"The climbers I know can be protective of their routes and competitive with each other, but they aren't violent people. It's not a violent sport—the opposite, really."

"Maybe this is a climber who had a mental break or has anger issues," she said. "Or something that makes him not-so-typical."

"Maybe. But I can't shake the feeling there's something else behind this. If I could figure out what that something is, maybe that would point to whoever is responsible for this harassment."

"Then I hope you figure it out. And I have to go. A tour group is arriving."

Ian wanted to say something about how much she meant to him, but the words wouldn't come out before she said goodbye and ended the call. He tried to turn his attention to his presentation to the county commissioners, but his thoughts kept returning to the puzzle of who could be behind these attacks. Who could be so upset about the development in Humboldt Canyon that they would resort to violence? Was it really Walt Spies?

He searched through the contacts in his phone and found the number for the county offices. When the receptionist answered, he asked to speak to Walt. "This is Ian Seabrook," he said.

"I heard someone tried to burn down your place." Walt sounded almost cheerful, but maybe that was Ian misinterpreting his hearty tone.

"They did," he said. "Bethany and I came close to being killed."

"I'm sorry to hear that. But none of that would have happened if you had stopped the project at the first sign of trouble."

"Is that how you got to where you are today—stopping at the first sign of trouble?"

"I come from a different generation than you do, son. You don't know what a real obstacle is."

"You're probably about the same age Abby and Gerald Boston would be if they had lived," Ian said. "Did you know them?"

"That couple they found in that cave? I knew of them."

"So you wouldn't have any reason to be upset that their bodies were found in that cave?" Maybe they had been right when they'd speculated the attacks on him were linked to the Bostons.

"Are you accusing me of something?" Walt asked.

"I just thought the person who's been trying so hard to stop me from building the via ferrata might object to what else I might find in that canyon. Maybe there are more secrets hiding underground, waiting to be uncovered."

Walt snorted. "I don't know what you're talking about."

"I let the sheriff know you were hanging around my place in Humboldt Canyon right before the fire."

"I already spoke to him about that. It's an uncomfortable coincidence, but I didn't set that fire. I haven't had anything to do with the things that have happened in that canyon, and if I hear you're telling people anything to that effect, I will sue." *Click.*

Ian almost smiled. Walt had hung up on him. A sure sign that Ian had shaken him up.

JUST AFTER NOON, Bethany was wondering if she had time to run up to her apartment and make a sandwich for lunch when the door to the tour office opened and Craig Boston came in. He was still in a walking boot, using a cane. Bethany stood to greet him. "Mr. Boston. It's good to see you."

"I wanted to thank you again for all your help the day I busted my ankle," he said.

"I was happy to do it."

His expression sobered. "I heard about the fire up in Humboldt Canyon last night. Somebody said you were there."

"I think the whole town has heard," she said. "I haven't gotten this much attention from people since I fainted on stage during a Christmas concert when I was sixteen." She had fielded at least six phone calls this morning from people she barely knew, asking about the fire. And four others had stopped by to see her.

"Is it true you were trapped in that trailer?" Craig asked.

"Yes. But I'm all right. Ian saved me." She wanted people to know that about Ian—that he wasn't the rich guy trying to take advantage of the town that some people had portrayed him as. He was the kind of man who would save a woman from a burning building. "He was burned pretty badly on his hands and arms, but he's going to be okay."

"That's good."

"Can I help you with something?"

He shifted his cane to his other hand. "My niece and her husband and their two children are coming into town to visit, and they're looking for things to do. Are any of your tours suitable for kids?"

"What ages?"

"Boys, six and eight."

"We have a tour to the old ghost town of Millford that would be perfect. Lots of fun but safe ruins to explore, and the guides tell fun stories along the way." She selected a brochure from the rack to her right. "They talk about gold mines in the area and the mule trains that used to carry supplies up and down the mountains. It's one of our most popular tours."

"Great. I'll give this to them." He tucked the brochure into his pocket but showed no sign of leaving. "Did you ever find out any more about my late relatives, Gerald and Abby?"

"Not much. Ian and I visited the historical society and read through old newspapers. It seemed like Katherine was the only person who hated Gerald enough to kill him, but I don't see how she could have done it."

"Katherine would need help to pull it off. She could have never overpowered two people, even before the accident that made it difficult for her to walk."

"Do you have any idea who she was with the day she was injured? The man who was driving the car?"

"We never knew for sure."

She didn't miss the hesitation in his words. "Did you have your suspicions?"

"I shouldn't accuse anyone without proof."

"This isn't a court and I'm not a police officer," she said. "I just want to know for my own curiosity."

Craig looked pained. "I heard a rumor it might have been Walt Spies."

"Walt!" She almost choked on the word.

"He and Gerald were good friends. And Walt dated Katherine before she and Gerald married. I heard a rumor they continued seeing each other, even after the wedding. Gerald found out about it when she was hurt, and that finally led to him filing for divorce."

"Ian and I went to the cemetery to see Katherine's grave," Bethany said. "Someone has been leaving flowers there. Any idea who that might be?"

"Whatever you do, don't say anything to Walt. He always had a terrible temper, and I don't think that improved with age. In any case, Katherine was a very pretty woman. She probably had lots of admirers."

"Were you one of them?"

She had meant the words as gentle teasing, but his reaction startled her. His face flushed bright red, and he fumbled with his cane. "Gerald was my uncle and my friend," he said. "I never would have had anything to do with a woman he was involved with."

"I'm sorry. I didn't mean to offend you," she said. Why did she always say the first thing that came into her head?

Craig relaxed a little. "It's okay. I've talked enough, keeping you from your work. Thanks for the brochure."

He hobbled out of the building. Bethany picked up her phone to text Ian—she had to tell him about this new development. But the door opened again, and Dalton and Carter entered. They were scheduled to team up for a big group tour leaving at 1:00 p.m.

They stopped in front of her desk. "Are you okay?" Carter asked.

"Why does everyone keep asking that? I'm fine."

"Aaron said you were almost killed," he said.

"When did you talk to Aaron?"

They exchanged a look peculiar to them, as if they were communicating telepathically. "He called us last night," Dalton said.

"He said we needed to help him keep a better eye on you," Carter said.

"I'm not some child you have to babysit."

"Okay, okay." Carter held up both hands. "Don't get so upset. It's just…" He looked away, jaw clenched.

"You scared us, okay?" Dalton said.

Carter looked back at her. "You're the only sister we've got."

Her anger evaporated, and she blinked rapidly, her eyes stinging. "I love you, too," she said. "But I'm okay. Really. And Ian and I are both going to be careful."

"Do they have any idea who set the fire?" Dalton asked.

"I don't think so," she said. "Have either of you heard anything?"

They both shook their heads. "No."

"I don't think it's a climber," Carter added.

"Ian doesn't think so, either," she said.

"Then who was it?" Dalton asked.

"I don't know," she said. "But I'm going to be paying special attention Thursday night at the county commissioners' meeting. You two could do me a favor to help."

Carter looked wary. Maybe he was remembering other "favors" she had asked of him, from dating a friend of hers who'd been overly possessive to driving her and four preteen friends to a K-pop concert and serving as their parent-approved chaperone. "What do we have to do?" he asked.

"Attend the meeting and watch to see if anyone is acting unusual."

Dalton nudged his twin. "What do you think?"

"I think I'd rather eat dirt than sit through a county commissioners' meeting." Carter blew out a breath. "But I'll do it for you, sis."

## Chapter Eighteen

On Thursday evening, the county commissioners' meeting was standing-room only, with the overflow crowd spilling into the hallway on the top floor of the county government building, across the street from Eagle Mountain City Hall. Ian eased past groups of people he recognized as climbers, their faces familiar to him from past expeditions and gatherings at popular climbing hot spots, as well as some who had protested against the via ferrata. Some of them greeted him by name or even patted him on the back, while others glared silently. A few stared at his bandaged hands—less bulky than the wrapping applied at the hospital, but the layers of stark white gauze still reminded him of cartoon hands on animated characters.

A woman with a dark ponytail and a clipboard checked his name off a piece of paper and directed him to sit near the front of the room on the right side. As he made his way to his seat, he scanned the other occupants of the room and spotted Bethany. She smiled and waved, and he nodded in greeting, a little unnerved by how glad he was to see her. One friendly face in a sea of faces he already thought of as hostile. Wasn't that the people who attended this kind of thing—those who wanted to speak against the project?

He had just settled into his seat when a door on one side of the chamber opened and the five county commissioners filed in to sit along one side of a long table at the front of the room. Walt Spies took the middle seat. He was dressed as usual, in worn jeans and a checked shirt. Though Ian knew he was over seventy, he had the erect posture and broad shoulders of a younger man. Two men and two women flanked Walt at the table, all wearing casual clothing and sober expressions.

Walt banged his gavel once, and the crowd hushed. "I call to order this meeting of the Rayford County, Colorado, County Commissioners," he said.

They sang the national anthem, followed by a prayer, then reviewed the minutes of the last meeting. "The only item on tonight's agenda is the consideration of the application for an operating permit for the Eagle Mountain Via Ferrata, to be operated by Seabrook Enterprises, LLC." Walt shuffled through a stack of papers. "We have a number of people who wish to speak on this issue, so we'll begin now."

A climber who introduced himself as Jeremy Leslie spoke first. Baby-faced and wiry, Jeremy fidgeted as he read from a piece of notepaper clutched in his hand. "I think you should vote against letting this via ferrata operate in Humboldt Canyon," he said. "Climbers have used that canyon free of charge for decades now, establishing a precedent of public use. That precedent should be maintained."

When Jeremy had finished his short statement, he looked up and grinned. Cheers rose from the back of the room, and Walt had to bang his gavel to restore order.

Next up was the president of the local tourism bureau. "We think this could be a very good thing for the community," he said. "They've been huge draws in other locations throughout the mountain west. It would bring in tourists who would spend money on lodging, meals, gear and guides. We don't see a downside."

More cheers as he exited the podium, and Eldon Ramsey took his place. "I'm a local climber," Eldon introduced himself. "I also volunteer with search and rescue. I had a lot of objections to this project initially. I didn't climb a lot in Humboldt Canyon, but I liked knowing it was available—and free. As a SAR volunteer, I also worried about the potential for a via ferrata to attract unskilled daredevils who might get hurt and strain our resources.

"But after talking with Ian and seeing his plan for the canyon," he said, "I feel better about the project. He's got a lot of safety protocols built in. And he's designing a course I think would be fun for beginners and more experienced climbers like me. So I think you should vote to approve the project."

Next was a young woman who said she had heard a lot of talk against the via ferrata around town. "But what nobody ever talks about is that property was for sale," she said. "Anyone could have purchased it and put up apartment buildings or a waste dump or anything else. The canyon is outside city limits, and it isn't zoned. As much as we might all like to keep everything pristine and untouched, the truth is someone was going to buy that property and develop it in some way. I'm just glad it's something like this, which leaves most of the canyon intact. So I think you should vote to approve the via ferrata."

Half a dozen other people followed, speaking for or against the project. Animal lovers, outdoor enthusiasts, skeptics and all-around grouches had their turn at the podium. The commissioners listened and sometimes took notes. Then it was Ian's turn to speak.

Calm settled over him as he approached the podium. He had been here before, at the start of a difficult pitch, harnessed and ready. He had all the tools to make this moment a success—all he needed was grit and a little luck.

"For those of you who don't know me, I'm Ian Seabrook," he began. "I've been a professional mountain climber for ten years. I've met some of you at climbing venues and on expeditions over the years. I love the mountains and I love climbing. I want to share that love with other people—people who might not have the time or money or experience to climb on their own. They can come to the via ferrata and have an expert take them through the course. They'll finish with a new perspective on the landscape they've been traversing and a new understanding of what they're capable of. And some of them will go on to pursue the sport, as a hobby or even professionally."

Ian studied the faces of the men and women behind the table in front of him. Only Walt Spies betrayed impatience, his lips thinning as he pressed them together, the lines around his eyes deepening. The others were impossible to read, blank and pleasant—skilled poker players revealing nothing.

He glanced at his notes once more. "I've heard from a lot of you since I arrived in Eagle Mountain and announced my plans for Humboldt Canyon. Some of what I've heard isn't repeatable in public." Nervous laughter. "A lot of you have offered constructive criticism and valuable input. I've met with search and rescue volunteers, and they've given me good ideas for how to make the course safer. The climbers in the community have pointed out ways I could make the course fun for more advanced climbers while still making it doable for beginners," he continued. "Others have taught me about the history of the area, a history I'm trying to showcase both through design elements such as mimicking the old tramways and shaft houses used in historic mines in these mountains and in plaques that give visitors an insight into the history of the area. For those of you who have expressed concerns about the environmental impact of this project, I can assure you we're following green principles and doing everything we can to lessen our impact on wildlife.

"I want to close by acknowledging that change can be hard. But change can also be a positive thing. I'm not here to sweep into town, make a big fuss and leave. I came to these mountains because they're a special place. I want to stay and help make them even more special. Thank you."

Applause. A few whistles. He turned to see Bethany standing, smiling broadly. Eldon and Ryan and some of the search and rescue volunteers stood also—along with, he was surprised to see, all three of the Ames brothers. He nodded to them in appreciation, then sat as Walt banged the gavel once more.

"I make a motion that we take a vote on whether or not to approve a preliminary operating permit for the Eagle Mountain Via Ferrata," the blond-bobbed woman at the end of the table said.

"I motion that we table a vote until we can obtain more information," said the man next to her.

Groans rose from the crowd. Walt tapped his gavel. "Do I have a second for the motion to take a vote now?" he asked.

"I second," the other woman at the table said.

"All those in favor of granting the operating permit, signify by saying *aye*."

"Aye!" Ian couldn't be sure who had spoken.

"Opposed?" Walt asked.

"Nay."

Walt studied his fellow commissioners. "I show three in favor and two opposed."

A cheer rose from Ian's supporters—a larger crowd than he had expected. Walt's expression didn't change. "Mr. Seabrook, we are granting the operating permit for the Eagle Mountain Via Ferrata, but if any safety or traffic concern arise, you will be asked to address them or risk revocation of the permit."

Ian stood. "Yes, sir. And thank you."

"Do I have a motion to adjourn?" Walt asked.

There was a motion, then a second, and the meeting came to a close.

A crowd swarmed around Ian, some asking questions, some wanting to compliment his presentation. He fended off handshakes with a show of his bandaged hands and looked past them all in search of Bethany.

At last he spotted her at the back of the room with her brothers. He made his way to them. "Good job," Dalton said.

"You were wonderful!" Bethany threw her arms around him. Ian patted her back, aware of her brothers watching him with, if not outright hostility, a certain amount of wariness.

"Ian, before you leave, just a few questions for the paper." A curly-haired woman with wire-rimmed glasses approached, notebook in hand. "Tammy Patterson, *Eagle Mountain Examiner*," she introduced herself. "Now that the via ferrata has been approved by the county, do you think the vandalism you've experienced will end?"

"I hope so," he said. "I've also added twenty-four-hour security to the site. Anyone who sneaks onto the property to make trouble will be arrested and prosecuted."

"I'll make sure people know," Tammy said. "When will you open to the public?"

"I'm aiming for the middle of next month," he said. "I'll make an official announcement when I have a firm date. There are going to be lots of exciting things happening, for locals and visitors alike."

"Thanks," she said. "I'll look forward to hearing more about that."

Arm around Bethany, he turned away.

Carter laid a hand on his shoulder. "Did you mean it about staying in Eagle Mountain?" he asked.

"I want to make my home here, though I'll still need to travel—for work and to climb," Ian said.

"And you really hired security guards?" Dalton asked.

"I should have done it weeks ago," he said.

"Why didn't you?" Carter asked.

Because he hadn't wanted to believe things were that bad. Because he didn't want to add to his image of the rich guy wanting to keep everyone else out. Because he'd been too proud to believe he needed help. "I should have," he repeated. "No excuses."

"I guess I'll feel better about Bethany being out there with a security detail," Carter said.

"I'm so touched," she said and stuck her tongue out at her brother.

"Speaking of spending time in the canyon." Ian looked

down at Bethany. "No pressure, but are you ready to come work for me?" he asked.

"I am." The look in her eyes made his heart leap.

"We're going to figure this out," he added.

Not just the job, but the future—something he hadn't spent much time thinking about before. Bethany had changed that.

## Chapter Nineteen

*Three weeks later*

"I guess this is the kind of party a millionaire throws," Carter said. He surveyed the crowd gathered in Humboldt Canyon for the pre-opening bash for the via ferrata. Bar tents and canopied pavilions housing buffet tables were spread out around the canyon. A local band played soft rock and pop from a stage near the start of the via ferrata course, and the various platforms, bridges and ladders were festooned with lights that glittered against the canyon walls.

"I could get used to this," Dalton said as he helped himself to a glass of champagne from a passing server. "Maybe you should marry this dude, Beth."

"Hush!" Her cheeks burned as Ian hurried toward them. They hadn't really talked about his decision to stay in Eagle Mountain or what that meant for them as a couple. It was enough that he wasn't leaving. He had said before that he was patient, and she was trying to adopt that attitude, too.

Ian kissed Bethany, then shook Carter's and Dalton's hands. "Glad you could come."

"We weren't going to miss this," Carter said. He turned to greet Ryan, Eldon and their dates as they arrived.

"I think most of the search and rescue volunteers are here already," Ian said.

"I think everyone in town is here," Bethany said. She had spotted several sheriff's deputies, a group of local climbers and some volunteer firefighters. "Is that the mayor?" She gestured toward a silver-haired man in an aloha shirt who waved from one of the catwalks along the canyon walls.

"I've got some people giving him, the town councilors and the county commissioners a tour of the course," he said. "Not all of it, but the easier stuff."

"Is Walt Spies here?" She sipped champagne and tried to pick out the irascible commissioner.

"He is," Ian said. "Though he declined to try the course."

"Let's hope he's not looking for some way to sabotage everything," she said.

"Another reason I invited the sheriff and his deputies," he said. "In case of trouble, I'll have plenty of help on hand."

"And you have your own guards." Her gaze shifted to one of several beefy, uniformed men who were patrolling the party.

"It may be overkill, but I want people to know I won't stand for trouble," he said.

"Ian, this is awesome." A bearded young man wearing a T-shirt that proclaimed Eat, Sleep, Climb clapped him on the back. "I can't wait for tomorrow."

"I'm looking forward to it, too," Ian said.

"Tomorrow?" Dalton asked after the climber had moved on.

"I invited a bunch of local climbing guides to play around on the course tomorrow," Ian said. "I want them to get to know it so they can guide tourists on it."

"A person doesn't have to have a guide to climb, though, right?" Carter asked.

"They don't. But we're going to strongly recommend most people hire a guide."

"Ian! Over here." A photographer gestured to him, then motioned to the mayor and other gathered officials, who were grouped at the base of the cliffs. "We want to get some pictures."

"I'll be right back," he said.

Carter and Dalton drifted away with some of the search and rescue volunteers while Bethany headed toward the portable toilets arranged behind a screen next to the newly completed welcome center. As she was leaving, she almost collided with a man with a cane. "Mr. Boston!" She hurriedly stepped back. "I'm sorry. I wasn't watching where I was going."

"No harm done," Craig said.

She looked down at his leg. "You're out of your walking boot."

"Yeah. I still need the cane, but I'm doing good."

"I'm so glad you're here." She touched his arm. "There's something I want you to see."

Bethany slowed her pace to allow him to keep up with her and led him to the base of the cliffs below the caves. "Ian put this up in memory of Gerald and Abby," she said.

The plaque gave the years of Gerald's and Abigail Boston's births and estimated death and ended with the sentiment *Together Forever in Love*. Above this were headshots of each of them, taken from the photos Caleb had uncovered at the historical society, at Bethany's request.

Craig stared, clearly so moved he couldn't speak. His throat worked and his knuckles whitened on his cane. "Ian did this?" he asked at last.

"Yes. We wanted people to remember them."

"Where did you get those pictures?" he asked.

"You remember I said I found some photographs at the historical society? I missed these on my initial search, then a researcher there found these for me. But you need to see this one, too." She led the way to the image of him and Walt with Gerald and the three women. "I don't know for sure that this was taken in Humboldt Canyon, but it's a great shot of young people enjoying the outdoors. And I was able to confirm that Abby S. really is Gerald's Abby. Her photo here matches the one the researcher found that was definitely identified as her."

Craig remained silent, his mouth tight.

"I hope you don't mind," Bethany said. "We don't identify you by name."

He leaned closer to study the image on the plaque. "Has Walt seen this?" he asked.

"I don't know."

Craig shook his head. "He won't like it. He won't like people seeing that he knew Gerald."

"Why would he object to that?" she asked.

"There was bad blood between them. Over a woman, I think."

"Bethany! Come look at this!" She turned to see Carter gesturing for her to join him and the other search and rescue volunteers.

She wanted to stay and question Craig more. What woman had Walt and Gerald fallen out over? Did Craig mean Katherine? Was Walt angry enough to have murdered Gerald?

"I have to go," Craig said.

"Wait!"

But he was already hobbling away, moving faster than she would have thought possible with a cane.

Still pondering his words, she went to join the SAR volunteers. "Get a load of this photo of you from the last climbing clinic," Carter said.

She leaned in to view the image on Eldon's camera. There she was, in helmet and harness, dangling off a cliff, a big smile on her face. "I look like someone who knows what she's doing," she said.

"I never knew you were such a good actress," Carter said. "Let me see."

The others made room for Aaron, in his deputy's uniform, to crowd in beside her. "Is everything okay?" she asked him.

"No sign of trouble." He stepped back and pulled her with him. "Anything I need to know about?"

"No, it's going well. We open in a week, and we already have almost all the entry slots filled."

"Have you done the course yet?" he asked.

"Not yet. I'm waiting until Ian can take me."

"Until Ian can take you where?" The man in question returned to her side. "Hello, Aaron."

"You're going to take me on the via ferrata," she said.

"I want to do that," he said. "I want you to be able to tell people about the experience and answer any questions they might have."

"How's the new job working out?" Aaron asked.

"I'm really enjoying it," she said.

"Mom hired someone to take your place at Peak Jeep Tours."

"Ashlynn. I trained her. She's really nice."

"I don't think Mom is happy with someone she can't boss around as much."

"She still has Carter and Dalton."

Aaron grinned. "Why do you think I refused to work for her and Dad?"

They bumped fists in solidarity, and he moved on. Bethany turned to Ian. "This is a great party," she said. "I'm so proud of what you've done."

"Thanks. Everyone seems to be having a good time."

"Did you know Craig Boston is here?"

"I invited him. I didn't know he made it."

"I ran into him and showed him the memorial for Gerald and Abby. He was so moved he was speechless. I also showed him the group photo of him with Gerald and Walt and the three women."

"What did he think of that one?"

"He asked if Walt had seen it. Then he said Walt wouldn't like it because he wouldn't want people to know he had been friends with Gerald. Craig said the two had a falling out over a woman. But he left before I could ask him what woman." She leaned closer and lowered her voice. "Craig mentioned one day that he had heard Walt and Katherine dated before Gerald married her. I wanted to follow up on it, but I couldn't think where to begin. Then so much else was going on that it slipped my mind. But maybe Walt had a reason for wanting Gerald and Abby dead." A chill swept over her as she spoke.

"Don't let Walt hear you say that," Ian said.

"I won't. But I'm going to mention it to Aaron. Just so he can keep an eye on Walt." She looked around at the milling crowd. "Where is Walt?"

"I don't know," Ian said. "Maybe he left already." He put his arm around her. "Come on. It's almost time for the ribbon cutting."

IAN MADE A speech in which he thanked as many people as he could remember who'd helped make the via ferrata a reality. He introduced the mayor, the town council members and the county commissioners, along with the sheriff and the construction manager. The photographer from the paper took a lot of photos. Ian cut through a ribbon stretched across the front of the welcome center with a pair of giant scissors, then the band started up again and he invited people to enjoy the food, the music and the evening.

It was after ten when the last cars pulled out of the parking area. The catering crew cleaned up, the band packed its instruments, and Ian and Bethany were finally alone. They sat in two folding chairs in front of the welcome center, drinking the last of a bottle of champagne he had liberated from the caterers and admiring the lights strung across the canyon walls.

"It's so quiet with everyone gone," she said.

"There's still a security guard here somewhere," Ian said. Since the night of the fire, he had at least one guard on duty, twenty-four hours a day. No one had tried to enter the canyon illegally, but Ian wasn't going to take chances. More sabotage to the climbing route could injure or kill a tourist. A tragedy like that would ruin Ian's reputation—and be terrible for the town, beyond the impact it would have on an innocent family.

Bethany laced her fingers with his. "You've done a great job," she said. "A lot of people would have given up."

"I'm too stubborn to give up." He sipped champagne, the bubbles fizzing on his tongue. "Besides, I had to make this project work so I'd have an excuse to stay here with you."

When she didn't answer, he turned to look at her. "Is something wrong?"

"No, I—" She cleared her throat. "I was so relieved when you said at the county commissioners' meeting that you wanted to stay in Eagle Mountain," she said. "Before that, I was trying so hard not to be upset about you going away. I mean, the very first day we met, you said you were only going to stay in Eagle Mountain until the via ferrata was complete. And then later, you talked about moving on to other places, to start new projects and do more climbing. Then I found those notes you made about Argentina... I knew you were going to leave and I was going to be hurt and there wasn't anything I could do about it. I couldn't stay away because...because I've fallen in love with you."

"Oh, Bethany." Ian set down his glass and leaned toward her. He intended to put his arms around her, maybe even pull her into his lap.

She was crying now, dashing tears from her eyes with her fingers. "I'm just being silly."

"You're not being silly." He touched her under the chin, nudging her until she looked up at him. "I couldn't stay away from you, either," he said. "It's why I wanted to stay. Why I'm going to stay."

He kissed her and tried to put everything he was feeling into that kiss. He wasn't good with words, more at home alone on a mountainside than talking to anyone, even her. But he owed it to her—to them—to try to share his feelings, no matter how scary that felt.

She pulled away. "What was that?"

"What was what?"

"I heard something." She looked past him, searching the canyon walls. "What's that up on that platform?" She pointed midway through the climbing route. "Is that a person?"

Ian followed her gaze and saw a shadowy figure, like someone sitting on the platform. "Are they asleep?" Bethany asked.

"Or drunk," he said. *Or dead?* He pulled out his phone to call 911, then put it back. Drinking too much at a party wasn't a crime. He'd go up there, help them down and call them a ride home.

"It's not moving at all," Bethany said. "I'm not sure it's even a person. Maybe somebody put a stuffed dummy up there—as a joke."

"Who would make a joke like that?" he asked.

"My brothers," she said. "And half the volunteers with search and rescue. Maybe some of the local climbers." She shrugged. "You should take it as a compliment, that they consider you someone they can joke with."

He relaxed. A joke. That was nothing to get upset about. "I'll climb up there and check it out."

"You're going to climb up there in the dark?" Her voice rose in alarm.

"It's not that far," he said. "And there are lights. You can go into the trailer and wait for me."

"No way am I waiting down here by myself in the dark," she said. "I'm going with you."

BETHANY HAD BEEN prepared for Ian to argue with her, and she had been ready to point out that she was a trained search and rescue volunteer. If he got into trouble, he would want someone like her by his side. Which was a total bluff. Ian Seabrook needed her help on the via ferrata he had designed about as much as Miss America needed Bethany's beauty tips.

But she didn't get to try out her argument. Ian looked her

up and down—she was wearing tennis shoes with her sundress because she refused to stand around in a rocky canyon in heels, and she had bike shorts underneath the dress because even at a party, she had to be ready for a search and rescue call. "Let's get harnesses and helmets," he said.

She had never climbed a via ferrata. She had never climbed any significant distance. She had never climbed in the dark.

"This is going to be easy," he said as he showed her where to clip her safety line. "I'm going to tell you where to put your hands and feet. You just do as I say. Do you trust me?"

Bethany nodded. "I do." She trusted him more than anyone else in her life. She trusted him *with* her life.

He put her in front of him so he could direct her as she climbed. The first pitch was easy, moving up a series of iron rings. Then a sideways scramble, using the hand-and footholds he directed her to. As unsettling as it was to climb in semidarkness, it helped that if she looked down, she couldn't really see anything. She kept her eyes up and reminded herself that she was clipped onto the safety cable. She wasn't going to fall.

The platform where they had seen the shadowy figure was a third of the way through the one-and-a-half-mile route. The platform itself was strung with white party lights, and as she drew closer, she could see that it was the figure of a man, slumped against the canyon wall, a hat pulled down low over the face. Could it be a person, sleeping off too much alcohol?

"Hello!" she called just before she stepped onto the platform. "Wake up!"

She took two steps forward, feeling a little foolish for shouting at a dummy, though it was a very realistic dummy.

Ian moved onto the platform behind her. "What the—" But the words died as the figure lurched to its feet. A hand pushed back the hat and a familiar figure glared at them.

"Mr. Boston, what are you doing here?" Bethany asked, even as he raised a pistol and pointed it at them.

## Chapter Twenty

"How did you get up here?" Ian demanded. Though his gaze was drawn to the gun in Craig's hand, he forced himself to look at the man's face, though much of it was in shadow.

"My ankle has been healed for weeks," Craig said. "I only wore the boot and carried the cane so you'd believe I was hurt worse than I really was."

"What are you doing here?" Bethany asked.

"I'm trying to stop you from making a big mistake," he said.

"What mistake?" Ian took a step toward the man, but Craig waved the pistol.

"Back off, or I'll shoot," he said.

Ian froze, acutely aware that Bethany stood between him and the gunman. He needed to find a way to get in front of her. "What mistake are you trying to prevent?" he asked again.

"Nobody even remembered Gerald and Abby until you came along," Craig said. "If anyone did think of them, they believed they moved away. You had to go uncovering their bodies and letting everyone know they were murdered. And you won't let people forget, with your photographs and memorial plaques. As long as people remember, they're going to keep looking for the person who killed them."

Had Craig killed his uncle? But asking that might anger him enough to pull the trigger. Instead, Ian asked, "Were you the one who shot at me? Did you set the fire?"

"I had to silence you."

"We didn't mean to upset you," Bethany said.

Craig turned his head toward her, though the hand that held the gun remained steady. "That picture was the last straw," he said. "With me and Abby."

"Abby was with you?" she asked.

"She was mine before Gerald ever knew her. Katherine was mine first, too. Then Gerald decided he wanted them and took them from me. I was upset about Katherine at first. Who wouldn't be? But then I saw he had done me a favor, taking Katherine off my hands. I met Abby, and I knew what love truly was."

"I'm sorry that happened," Bethany said. She sounded so calm. Had her search and rescue training taught her to be so calm in a crisis, or did that come naturally?

"Abby was with *me* that day we rode horses," Craig continued. "You're right. It was here in this canyon. Gerald had never even seen her before that day. But as soon as he saw her, he decided he had to have her. He didn't stop until he had stolen her from me. He even tried to kill Katherine so she would be out of the picture."

"How did he try to kill Katherine?" Bethany asked.

If only she could keep Craig talking, maybe Ian could get to his phone. He slid one hand toward his pocket.

"Gerald was driving the car the day Katy was hurt," Craig said. "He ran over her and drove off. When she tried to tell people what had really happened, he told everyone she was a drunk, that she had been cheating on him with another man. She didn't deserve that. I went to see her in the hospital—because I was a true friend, even though I wasn't in love with her anymore. She told me the whole story. When Gerald divorced her and married Abby, it broke her heart. She really did start drinking then. He ruined her life."

"Who set fire to Gerald and Abby's house?" Bethany asked.

"That was me. I didn't want to hurt them, just frighten them." He chuckled, a sound more chilling than any of his previous anger. "He thought Walt set that fire. Gerald even accused him of it."

"Why would Gerald accuse Walt?"

"Because Walt was Katherine's friend, too. Walt believed her story about the accident. Told Gerald if he didn't set aside money to support Katherine, he would tell everyone what he had done. The two of them argued, but in the end, Gerald gave in. He wanted everyone—especially Abby—to think he was a good person. Abby had no idea." He jerked his head back toward Ian. "Stop fidgeting. Don't think I don't see you over there."

"What did you do, Craig?" Bethany asked. "To Gerald?"

"All I wanted was Abby to leave him and come back to me. I asked them to meet me here, in the canyon, where Gerald and Abby first met. I told them I had a present for them. They had no reason to suspect me. I was careful to not let Gerald see how much I hated him," he said. "All I wanted was to get him out of the picture. He didn't deserve to live—after the way he had treated Katherine. The way he treated me. We were like brothers growing up, yet he had betrayed me twice. I knew if I could make Abby see what he was really like, she would love me again."

He fell silent, head bowed. Ian tensed. They had to keep him talking. Talking and not shooting.

"They agreed to meet you?" Ian asked.

"Yes. I led them up to the caves. They had never been in there before. I told them it was incredibly beautiful, with a lot of crystals and stuff. I knew they would want to see it," he said. "But when we got in there, I confronted Gerald about stealing Abby from me. I told her what he had done to Katherine, what he had done to me. Gerald denied everything, then he tried to shoot me. I wrestled with him, and the gun went off. Then I heard a scream and realized the bullet had hit Abby. I tried to go to her, but Gerald pulled me away."

"Oh." One soft syllable from Bethany, so full of sympathy and horror.

"He cradled her in his arms and told her everything I said was lies," Craig said. "He told her I had never really loved her. I couldn't stand it, knowing she would go to her grave believing the lies he was telling her. I picked up the pistol and shot him. Then I left them.

"I told everyone I knew that I had seen them leaving town. A few days later I came back and set off dynamite to trigger a rock slide. I worked with explosives in the mines and knew just where to set the charges," he said. "I figured if anyone suspected it had been done on purpose, they would blame Walt because he lived next to the canyon, and I stole the dynamite he had left over from blasting out a foundation for a new house. But no one even suspected.

"And then you two came along and I was reading about the murders in the papers. Then you found out I lived here and brought me to the sheriff's attention. I tried everything I could think of to get you to go away. Let the dead stay buried."

"Did you put the wedding ring in the cave after we found their remains?" Bethany asked.

Craig nodded. "I bought that ring for Abby. I left it as a kind of memorial for her."

He was looking down, the barrel of the gun aimed down as well. Ian pulled his phone from his pocket. All he had to hit was one number—

Pain burned through his shoulder even as the crack of the shot reverberated around the canyon. Bethany screamed, and Ian staggered back, then dropped to his knees, sick and dizzy. He gripped his injured shoulder, blood seeping through his hands then watched, helpless, as Bethany grappled with Craig.

He braced himself for the sound of another gunshot, but instead Craig shoved Bethany off the catwalk. She fell, her scream cut off like a door had slammed.

BETHANY'S SHOULDER AND hip crashed into the jagged rock below the catwalk, and she clutched in the darkness for any kind of purchase. Then she was jerked up short, like a yo-yo on the end of a string. She clung to the rock, one foot on a narrow outcropping, the other dangling free. The safety cable had done its job and arrested her fall, but how long could she cling here?

She looked up and, through the mesh of the catwalk, saw Craig kneeling on the edge, looking down. At the other end of the platform, Ian lay still. She choked back a sob and sent up a silent prayer that Ian was still alive. She couldn't give into that fear, and she was afraid to make a sound. If

Craig realized she was still here and not dashed on the rocks below, he might unclip the safety cable.

The catwalk began to shake, and footsteps thundered across it. A figure launched itself at Craig. "No!" a man shouted. At first Bethany thought it was the security guard, then the wrestling pair rolled into the light and she recognized Walt Spies.

The two men shouted obscenities at each other, then something bounced on the catwalk and dropped over the edge. The pistol. Walt was on his back now, Craig on top of him. Bethany stared up at the tableau, her arms and legs straining to maintain their precarious hold on the rock.

Ian rose to his knees, staggering to his feet. He moved toward the two combatants, then kicked Craig in the head. Craig howled and raised up, and Walt pushed him off. "You're not going to kill me!" he shouted and punched Craig in the face.

Craig crumpled and lay curled on the catwalk. Walt pulled himself upright. "Make a move, and I'll shove you right over the side," he said. Then he turned to Ian. "The sheriff is on the way."

"Ian!" Bethany shouted.

He looked down between his feet. "Bethany?"

"I'm on the rock, right under the catwalk. The safety line caught me. But I don't think I can get up."

"Hang on," Ian said. "Help is coming."

"What are you doing here, Walt?" she called.

"I came back to check on you two," he said. "I saw the photo you posted, of the six of us riding horses. I'd forgotten about that day, but seeing it reminded me of all the bad blood between Craig and his uncle Gerald—things I hadn't thought about in decades. It worried me that maybe he was behind all the trouble you've been having. Call it instinct, I guess. I wanted to come back and tell you to keep an eye on him, even though you didn't appreciate my warning before."

"You told us you didn't know Gerald," Ian said.

"I didn't. Not really. I knew Craig. He knew our family rented out horses for rides in the canyons around here. He arranged that outing. That was probably the first time I ever met Gerald."

"Who was Susan?" Bethany asked, remembering the third woman in the photograph.

"A woman I was dating at the time."

"And Katherine was Gerald's wife, and Abby was Craig's girlfriend," Bethany said.

"Abby was his date. I don't know how serious things were between them."

"Was he telling the truth when he said Gerald stole Abby from him?" Ian asked.

"I heard all about that later. Gossip spreads in a small town, and Eagle Mountain was very small back then. I know the day I took them riding, Gerald was flirting with Abby. She was flirting back. His wife, Katy, was plenty steamed. Craig was more sullen by the minute. I cut the ride short, it was so unpleasant. Then later I heard Katy and Gerald were getting divorced. When he married Abby I kind of put two and two together."

"Craig said you knew the truth about Katherine's accident," Bethany said. "That Gerald was the one who hurt her."

"Katy and I got to be friends after that riding trip. Nothing romantic, just friends. She liked horses and came out to the ranch several times to ride. She had a quick temper and was jealous of Gerald, but I guess he gave her reason to be. I saw him and Katy in his car the afternoon she was hurt. So when I visited her in the hospital and she told me Gerald was the one who had hurt her, I believed her."

He turned to Ian, who was leaned back against the rock, clutching his shoulder. "When I got here, I found your security guard unconscious near the welcome center. It looked like someone hit him in the head with a rock. I called 911, then came looking for you."

"Thank God you did," he said and slid down to a sitting position.

Sirens wailed in the distance, and soon red-and-blue emergency lights strobed off the canyon walls. An ambulance, two sheriff's department SUVs and the search and rescue Jeep parked in the clearing below.

Walt stood at the edge of the catwalk and waved. "We're up here!"

Bethany winced in the sudden glare of a spotlight. "Bethany, is that you?" She recognized Aaron's voice, tight with alarm.

"I'm okay!" she shouted. "I just need a little help getting out of here."

"Ian Seabrook has a gunshot wound," Walt shouted. "Craig Boston shot him."

"No!" Craig staggered to his feet and lurched toward the catwalk railing. He started to climb over the railing, but Walt pulled him back.

"Somebody get up here and help me with this idiot!" Walt shouted.

Within minutes, the catwalk and approach to it were swarming with people. Aaron and another deputy placed Craig in handcuffs and led him away. Danny and Tony tended to Ian while Ryan and Sheri worked their way over to Bethany.

"Are you hurt?" Sheri asked.

"No. Just kind of stuck."

"It's going to be easier if you climb down from here," she said. "We'll help."

With their assistance, Bethany made it to the ground. Carter and Dalton met her there and crushed her between them.

"What were you doing up there?" Carter demanded.

"It's a long story," she said. "Right now, I need to see Ian."

Sheri helped her out of her harness. "The ambulance already left," she said. "Ian lost some blood, but the gunshot wound doesn't appear to have hit anything vital."

"They've got a surgeon waiting to see him in Junction," Danny said.

Aaron led Bethany over to the sheriff. "We need to know what happened," Sheriff Walker said.

She sat in the front seat of the sheriff's SUV and told him and Aaron everything that had happened on the catwalk, including Craig's story of what had happened to Abby and Gerald Boston.

"It sounds like he suppressed everything over the years and the discovery that Gerald and Abby were murdered brought it all back," the sheriff said.

Gage walked over to the SUV with Walt. "I've taken Walt's statement," the sergeant said. "He says he remembered there was bad blood between Gerald and Craig when they were younger and felt compelled to come back here and warn Ian to be careful of Craig."

"Walt saved us." Bethany slid out of the SUV and hugged the older man, who awkwardly patted her back.

She pulled away and looked him in the eye. "Why were you so against the via ferrata?"

"All the reasons I said in the meetings. I live right next door to this place. I worry about traffic, littering, even crime. But I was outvoted."

"Ian will do his best to see that you aren't bothered by any of that," she said.

"I'm going to hold him to it."

Aaron put his hand on her shoulder. "Let me take you home," he said.

"I need to go to the hospital."

He hesitated, then nodded. "All right. I'll take you to the hospital."

IAN WOKE TO the sharp tang of disinfectant and a monotonous beeping he couldn't place. As his vision cleared, he recognized the bright lights and pale green walls of a hospital room. Then Bethany's face loomed over him.

"How are you feeling?" she asked.

"Numb." His head felt wrapped in cotton wool and disconnected from the rest of his body.

"That's probably the anesthesia." This from a man, who turned out to be Bethany's brother, Aaron. The sight of the sheriff's deputy uniform brought the memory of how Ian had ended up here rushing back. "Craig Boston shot me," he said.

"Craig is in custody now," Aaron said. "You don't have to worry about him."

"They operated on your shoulder to remove some fragments of bone and repair some ligaments," Bethany said. "You're going to be sore and you'll need physical therapy, but you should regain full use of it."

"That's good." He studied her, trying to keep her features focused. "You got off the cliff okay?"

"I did. And under my own power, with a little help from Ryan and Sheri." She squeezed his uninjured arm. "When you're well again, we can do the whole via ferrata. Together."

Aaron cleared his throat. "I need to get your statement," he said. "But tomorrow will be soon enough. I'll give you two a few minutes alone, then I have to take Bethany home, or our parents will probably disown us both."

Ian nodded, then looked back to Bethany. "It's not doing anything for my image that you keep meeting me at hospitals," he said.

"We're both alive," she said. "That's all that matters."

He caught her hand in his. "I love you. I should have said it before. I've almost lost you twice now, and I'm not going to let another day pass without making sure you understand that."

"I know you love me, but it's nice to hear it." She kissed his cheek. "I love you, too."

"I'm not going to leave you," Ian said. "You know that, right?"

"I know." She kissed him again. "I'm going to leave you now, but just for a few hours. Then I promise you're never going to get rid of me."

"I like the sound of that. There's just one other thing."

"Oh?"

"You're fired."

"What?"

"You can't be my employee anymore. I want you to be my partner instead."

Her cheeks flushed. "Your business partner?"

"Business partner. And life partner."

"Are you proposing?"

Not the reaction he had expected. "Is this a bad time?"

She laughed. "I just want to make sure that's not the anesthesia talking."

"It's not." Ian kissed her knuckles—the only part of her he could reach. "I almost asked you last night, then I chickened out. Did I mention I'm a big coward when it comes to relationships?"

"I don't think anyone is an expert at these things." She stroked his cheek. "But I'm willing to figure it out together. I predict we've got years and years to find our way."

"That's what I want," he said. "Years and years of being together."

"It's what I want, too." Bethany bent and kissed him again. A kiss that told him everything he needed to know about how much she loved him—and how good they would be together.

\* \* \* \* \*

# COMING SOON!

We really hope you enjoyed reading this book. If you're looking for more romance be sure to head to the shops when new books are available on

## Thursday 19th June

To see which titles are coming soon, please visit
**millsandboon.co.uk/nextmonth**

---

# MILLS & BOON

# FOUR BRAND NEW BOOKS FROM
## MILLS & BOON MODERN

The same great stories you love, a stylish new look!

**Conveniently ARRANGED**
LYNNE GRAHAM — LORRAINE HALL
2 BOOKS IN ONE

**WANTED: HIS HEIR**
MAYA BLAKE — DANI COLLINS
2 BOOKS IN ONE

**DEFIANT Brides**
Tara Pammi — Michelle Smart
2 BOOKS IN ONE

**THE BILLIONAIRE'S LEGACY**
ABBY GREEN — NATALIE ANDERSON
2 BOOKS IN ONE

## OUT NOW

Eight Modern stories published every month, find them all at:

### millsandboon.co.uk

# OUT NOW!

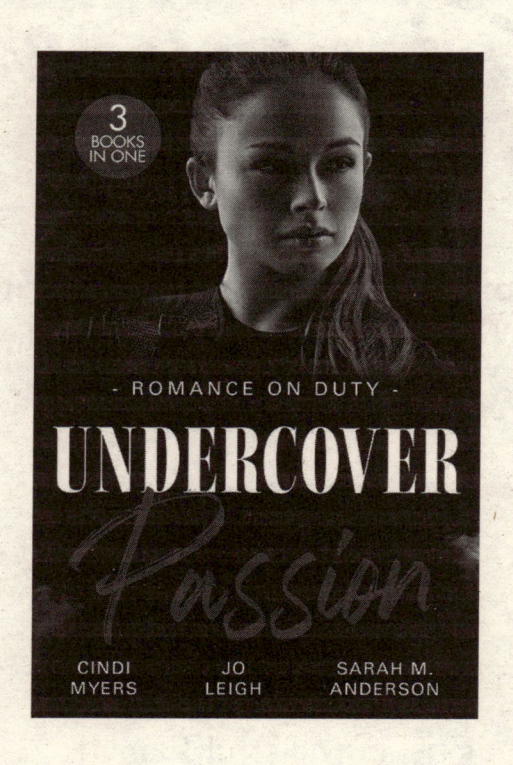

## ROMANCE ON DUTY
## UNDERCOVER *Passion*

3 BOOKS IN ONE

CINDI MYERS · JO LEIGH · SARAH M. ANDERSON

Available at millsandboon.co.uk

MILLS & BOON

# LET'S TALK
## *Romance*

For exclusive extracts, competitions and special offers, find us online:

- **f** MillsandBoon
- **X** @MillsandBoon
- **◎** @MillsandBoonUK
- **♪** @MillsandBoonUK

Get in touch on 01413 063 232

For all the latest titles coming soon, visit
millsandboon.co.uk/nextmonth